Praise for Mark Alpert's *Final Theory*

"*Final Theory* is a stupendous read! Real characters, real science, a deliciously explosive premise, and a breakneck plot combine to make this one of the finest science-based thrillers to appear in a long time. *Final Theory* rules."

—Douglas Preston, *New York Times* bestselling author of *Blasphemy* and *Tyrannosaur Canyon*

"Wow! Einstein would have loved this book. It's a great thriller, it has a sure feel for politics, and the science is both fun and solid. He always dreamed that he would discover a unified theory that explained all of nature's forces. Now this book makes the quest come alive."

—Walter Isaacson, *New York Times* bestselling author of *Einstein*

"*Final Theory* has everything I love in a novel: heart-pounding tension, astonishing plot twists, and fascinating science. Mark Alpert manages to make physics more thrilling than I ever imagined!"

—Tess Gerritsen, *New York Times* bestselling author of *The Bone Garden*

"An ingenious twist on Einstein's genius."

—Thomas Greanias, *New York Times* bestselling author of *Atlantis Rising*

"Alpert has a rare gift for combining cutting-edge science with an unrelenting pace and edge-of-the-seat action. An impressive debut."

—Kyle Mills, *New York Times* bestselling author of *Rising Phoenix*

"I have always been fascinated by the potential of science, the point where physics appears to defy its own laws and behave in uncertain ways. Thanks to this wonderful novel, I have reunited with an old passion and enjoyed a journey full of unexpected twists and drama."

—Javier Sierra, *New York Times* bestselling author of *The Secret Supper*

Final Theory

A NOVEL

Mark Alpert

A Touchstone Book
Published by Simon & Schuster
New York London Toronto Sydney

Touchstone
A Division of Simon & Schuster, Inc.
1230 Avenue of the Americas
New York, NY 10020

Copyright © 2008 by Mark Alpert

This Touchstone export edition June 2008

TOUCHSTONE and colophon are registered trademarks of Simon & Schuster, Inc.

For information about special discounts for bulk purchases, please contact Simon & Schuster Special Sales at 1-800-456-6798 or business@simonandschuster.com.

Designed by William Ruoto

Graphics by Bryan Christie Design

Manufactured in the United States of America

10   9   8   7   6   5   4   3   2   1

Library of Congress Cataloging-in-Publication Data

Alpert, Mark, 1961–
   Final theory : a novel / Mark Alpert.
      p.   cm.
   "A Touchstone Book."
   1. Physics teachers—Fiction.   2. Unified field theories—Fiction.   3. Einstein, Albert, 1879–1955—Influence—Fiction.   I. Title.
PS3601.L67F56   2008
813'.6—dc22   2007041831

ISBN-13: 978-1-4165-9050-7
ISBN-10:   1-4165-9050-1

For Lisa, who has filled my universe with wonders

The unleashed power of the atom has changed everything save our modes of thinking, and thus we drift toward unparalleled catastrophe.

—ALBERT EINSTEIN

Chapter One

HANS WALTHER KLEINMAN, ONE OF THE GREAT THEORETICAL physicists of our time, was drowning in his bathtub. A stranger with long, sinewy arms had pinned Hans's shoulders to the porcelain bottom.

Although the water was only thirty centimeters deep, the pinioning arms kept Hans from raising his face to the surface. He clawed at the stranger's hands, trying to loosen their grip, but the man was a *shtarker*, a young vicious brute, and Hans was a seventy-nine-year-old with arthritis and a weak heart. Flailing about, he kicked the sides of the tub, and the lukewarm water sloshed all around him. He couldn't get a good look at his attacker—the man's face was a shifting, watery blur. The *shtarker* must have slipped into the apartment through the open window by the fire escape, then rushed into the bathroom when he realized that Hans was inside.

As Hans struggled, he felt the pressure building in his chest. It started in the center, right under his sternum, and quickly filled his whole rib cage. A negative pressure, pushing inward from all sides, constricting his lungs. Within seconds it rose to his neck, a hot choking tightness, and Hans opened his mouth, gagging. Lukewarm water rushed down his throat, and now Hans devolved into a creature of pure panic, a twisting, squirming primitive animal going into its final convulsions. *No, no, no, no, no, no!* Then he lay still, and as his vision faded he saw only the wavelets at the surface, rippling just a few centimeters above him. A Fourier series, he thought. And so beautiful.

But it wasn't the end, not yet. When Hans regained consciousness he was lying facedown on the cold tiled floor, coughing up bathwater. His eyes ached and his stomach lurched and each breath was an excruciating gasp. Coming back to life was actually more painful than dying. Then he felt a sharp blow to his back, right between his shoulder blades, and heard someone say in a jaunty voice, "Time to wake up!"

The stranger grabbed him by the elbows and rolled him over. The back of Hans's head banged against the wet tiles. Still breathing hard, he looked up at his attacker, who was kneeling on the bathroom rug. A huge man, a hundred kilograms at the least. Shoulder muscles bulging under his black T-shirt, camouflage pants tucked into black leather boots. A bald head, disproportionately small compared with his body, with black stubble on his cheeks and a gray scar on his jaw. Most likely a junkie, Hans guessed. After he kills me, he'll tear the place apart, hunting for my valuables. Only then will the stupid *putz* realize I don't have a goddamn cent.

The *shtarker* stretched his thin lips into a smile. "Now we'll have a little talk, yes? You can call me Simon, if you like."

The man's voice had an unusual accent that Hans couldn't place. His eyes were small and brown, his nose was crooked, and his skin was the color of a weathered brick. His features were ugly but indistinct—he could be Spanish, Russian, Turkish, almost anything. Hans tried to say, "What do you want?" but when he opened his mouth he only retched again.

Simon looked amused. "Yes, yes, I'm so sorry about that. But I needed to show you that I'm serious. And better to do that right away, eh?"

Oddly enough, Hans wasn't afraid now. He'd already accepted the fact that this stranger was going to kill him. What disturbed him was the sheer impudence of the man, who kept smiling as Hans lay naked on the floor. It seemed clear what would happen next: Simon was going to order him to reveal the number of his ATM card. The same thing had happened to one of Hans's neighbors, an eighty-two-year-old woman who'd been attacked in her apartment and beaten until she gave up the number. No, Hans wasn't afraid—he was furious! He coughed the last drops of bathwater out of his throat and propped himself up on his elbows. "You made a mistake this time, you *ganef*. I have no money. I don't even have a bank card."

"I don't want your money, Dr. Kleinman. I'm interested in physics, not money. You're familiar with the subject, I assume?"

At first Hans simply grew more enraged. Was this *putz* making fun of him? Who did he think he was? After a moment, though, a more disturbing question occurred to him: How did this man find out my name? And how does he know I'm a physicist?

Simon seemed to guess what Hans was thinking. "Don't be so surprised, Professor. I'm not as ignorant as I look. I may not have any advanced degrees, but I'm a fast learner."

Hans had surmised by now that this man was no junkie. "Who are you? What are you doing here?"

"Think of it as a research project. On a very challenging and esoteric topic." His smile broadened. "I admit, some of the equations weren't easy to understand. But I have some friends, you see, and they explained it very well."

"Friends? What do you mean, friends?"

"Well, perhaps that's the wrong word. *Clients* would probably be better. I have some very knowledgeable and well-financed clients. And they hired me to get some information from you."

"What are you talking about? Are you some kind of spy?"

Simon chuckled. "No, no, nothing so grandiose. I'm an independent contractor. Let's just leave it at that."

Hans's mind was racing now. The *shtarker* was a spy, or maybe a terrorist. His exact affiliation was unclear—Iran? North Korea? Al-Qaeda?—but that didn't matter. They were all after the same thing. What Hans didn't understand was why the bastards had targeted him of all people. Like most nuclear physicists of his generation, Hans had done some classified work for the Defense Department in the fifties and sixties, but his specialty had been radioactivity studies. He'd never worked on bomb design or fabrication, and he'd spent most of his professional life doing theoretical research that was strictly nonmilitary. "I have some bad news for your clients, whoever they are," Hans said. "They picked the wrong physicist."

Simon shook his head. "No, I don't think so."

"What kind of information do you think I can give you? Uranium enrichment? I know nothing about that! And nothing about warhead design either. My field is particle physics, not nuclear engineering. All my research papers are available on the Internet, there's nothing secret about them!"

The stranger shrugged, unperturbed. "You've jumped to the wrong conclusion, I'm afraid. I don't care about warheads and I don't care about your papers. I'm interested in someone else's work, not yours."

"Why are you in my apartment, then? Did you get the wrong address?"

Simon's face hardened. He pushed Hans down on his back and placed one hand flat on his rib cage, leaning forward so he could put his whole weight on it. "This person happens to be someone you knew. Your professor at Princeton fifty-five years ago? The wandering Jew from Bavaria? The man who wrote *Zur Elektrodynamik bewegter Körper*? Surely you haven't forgotten him?"

Hans struggled to breathe. The *shtarker*'s hand felt impossibly heavy. *Mein Gott,* he thought. This can't be happening.

Simon leaned over some more, bringing his face so close that Hans could see the black hairs inside his nostrils. "He admired you, Dr. Kleinman. He thought you were one of his most promising assistants. You worked together quite closely in his last few years, didn't you?"

Hans couldn't have replied even if he'd wanted to. Simon was pushing down on him so hard he could feel his vertebrae grinding against the cold tiles.

"Yes, he admired you. But more than that, he trusted you. He conferred with you about everything he worked on during those years. Including his *Einheitliche Feldtheorie.*"

At just that moment one of Hans's ribs snapped. On his left

side, on the outer curve, where the tensile strain was greatest. The pain knifed through his chest and Hans opened his mouth to scream, but he couldn't even draw enough breath to cry out. *Oh Gott, Gott im Himmel!* All at once his rational mind disintegrated, and he was afraid, he was terrified! Because he saw what this stranger wanted from him, and he knew that in the end he would be unable to resist.

Simon finally eased off and removed his hand from Hans's chest. Hans took a deep breath, and as the air whooshed in he felt the knife of pain again on his left side. His pleural membrane was torn, which meant that his left lung would soon collapse. He was weeping from the pain and shuddering with each breath. Simon stood over him with his hands on his hips, smiling contentedly, quite satisfied with his work. "So do we understand each other? Do you see what I'm looking for?"

Hans nodded, then closed his eyes. I'm sorry, *Herr Doktor,* he thought. I'm going to betray you now. And in his mind's eye he saw the professor again, saw him as clearly as if the great man were standing right there in the bathroom. But it was nothing like the pictures that everyone knew, the photographs of the unkempt genius with the wild white hair. What Hans remembered was the professor in the last months of his life. The drawn cheeks, the sunken eyes, the defeated grimace. The man who'd glimpsed the truth but, for the sake of the world, couldn't speak it out loud.

Hans felt a kick in his side, just below his broken rib. The pain ripped through his torso, and his eyes sprang open. One of Simon's leather boots rested on Hans's bare hip. "No time for sleeping," he said. "We have work to do. I'm going to get some paper from your desk and you're going to write everything down." He turned around and walked out of the bathroom. "If there's something I don't understand, you'll explain it to me. Like a seminar, yes? Who knows, you might even enjoy it."

Simon headed down the hallway toward Hans's bedroom. A moment later Hans heard rummaging noises. With the stranger out of sight, some of Hans's fear lifted and he was able to think again, at least until the bastard came back. And what he thought about were the *shtarker*'s boots, his shiny black storm-trooper boots. Hans felt a wave of disgust. The man was trying to look like a Nazi. In essence, that's what he was, a Nazi, no different from the thugs in brown uniforms that Hans had seen marching down the streets of Frankfurt when he was seven years old. And the people Simon worked for, those nameless "clients"? Who were they if not Nazis?

Simon returned holding a ballpoint pen in one hand and a legal pad in the other. "All right, from the beginning," he said. "I want you to write the revised field equation."

He bent over, offering the pen and pad, but Hans didn't take them. His lung was collapsing and each breath was a torture, but he wasn't going to help this Nazi. "Go to hell," he rasped.

Simon gave him a mildly scolding look, the kind you'd give to a misbehaving five-year-old. "You know what I think, Dr. Kleinman? I think you need another bath."

In one swift motion he picked Hans up and plunged him into the water again. Once more Hans struggled to raise his face to the surface, bashing himself against the sides of the tub as he clawed at the *shtarker*'s arms. If anything, the second time was more terrifying than the first, because now Hans knew exactly what lay ahead—the tightening agony, the frantic twisting, the mindless descent into blackness.

Hans fell deeper into unconsciousness this time. It took a tremendous effort to emerge from the abyss, and even after Hans opened his eyes he felt like he hadn't fully awoken. His vision was fuzzy around the edges and he could take only shallow breaths.

"Are you there, Dr. Kleinman? Can you hear me?"

The voice sounded muffled now. When Hans looked up he saw the silhouette of the *shtarker*, but his body seemed to be surrounded by a penumbra of vibrating particles.

"I really wish you'd be more reasonable, Dr. Kleinman. If you look at the situation in a logical way, you'll realize that all this subterfuge is absurd. You can't hide something like this forever."

Hans looked a little closer at the penumbra surrounding the man and saw that the particles weren't actually vibrating—they were popping in and out of existence, pairs of particles and antiparticles appearing like magic from the quantum vacuum and then disappearing just as quickly. This is amazing, Hans thought. If only I had a camera!

"Even if you don't help us, my clients will get what they want. Perhaps you didn't know this, but your professor had other confidants. He thought it would be clever to parcel the information among them. We've already contacted a few of these old gentlemen, and they've been most helpful. One way or another, we'll get what we need. So why make this hard on yourself?"

The evanescent particles seemed to grow larger as Hans stared at them. Upon closer inspection it became clear that they weren't particles at all but infinitely thin strings stretching from one curtain of space to another. The strings shivered between the undulating curtains, which curled into tubes and cones and manifolds. And the whole elaborate dance was proceeding exactly as predicted, exactly as *Herr Doktor* had described!

"I'm sorry, Dr. Kleinman, but my patience is wearing thin. I don't enjoy doing this, but you leave me no choice."

The man kicked him three times in the left side of his chest, but Hans didn't even feel it. The diaphanous curtains of space had folded around him. Hans could see them so clearly, like curving sheets of blown glass, brilliant and impenetrable, yet soft to the touch. But the other man obviously couldn't see them. Who was this man, anyway? He looked so clownish standing there in his black leather boots. "Don't you see them?" Hans whispered. "They're right in front of your eyes!"

The man let out a sigh. "I guess this will require a more vigorous kind of persuasion." He retreated to the hallway and opened the door to the linen closet. "Let's see what we have here." After a moment he returned to the bathroom carrying a plastic bottle of rubbing alcohol and a steam iron. "Dr. Kleinman, could you tell me where the nearest electric outlet is?"

Hans forgot about the man. He saw nothing but the lacy folds of the universe, curving around him like an infinitely soft blanket.

Chapter Two

DAVID SWIFT WAS IN AN UNUSUALLY GOOD MOOD. HE AND Jonah, his seven-year-old son, had just spent a marvelous afternoon in Central Park. To cap off the day, David had bought ice-cream cones from a pushcart at Seventy-second Street, and now father and son were strolling through the sultry June twilight toward David's ex-wife's apartment. Jonah was in a good mood, too, because in his right hand—his left hand held the ice-cream cone—he brandished a brand-new, triple-shot Super Soaker. As Jonah walked down the sidewalk he idly pointed the high-tech water gun at various random targets—windows, mailboxes, a few clusters of pigeons—but David wasn't concerned. He'd emptied the gun's reservoir before they'd left the park.

Jonah somehow managed to lick his ice cream while sighting down the barrel of the Super Soaker. "So how does it work again? Why does the water come out so fast?"

David had explained the process twice before, but he didn't mind repeating it. He loved having this kind of conversation with his son. "When you move that red thing, the pump handle? That pushes the water from the big reservoir to the smaller one."

"Wait, where's the smaller one?"

David pointed at the back of the gun. "It's right here. The smaller reservoir has some air in it, and when you pump water into the tank there's less room for the air. The air molecules get squeezed together and start pushing on the water."

"I don't get it. Why do they push the water?"

"Because air molecules are always bouncing around, see? And when you squeeze them together, they bounce against the water more."

"Can I bring the gun to school for show-and-tell?"

"Uh, I don't know . . ."

"Why not? It's science, right?"

"I don't think they allow water guns in school. But you're right, there's definitely science in this thing. The guy who invented the Super Soaker was a scientist. A nuclear engineer who worked for NASA."

A bus lunged down Columbus Avenue and Jonah tracked it with his water gun. He seemed to be losing interest in the physics of Super Soakers. "Why didn't *you* become a scientist, Dad?"

David thought for a second before answering. "Well, not everyone can be a scientist. But I write books about the history of science and that's also fun. I get to learn about famous people like Isaac Newton and Albert Einstein and teach courses about them."

"I don't want to do that. I'm gonna be a real scientist. I'm gonna invent a spaceship that can fly to Pluto in five seconds."

It would've been amusing to talk about the Pluto spaceship, but now David was uncomfortable. He felt a strong need to improve his standing in his son's eyes. "A long time ago, when I was in graduate school, I did some real science. And it was all about space."

Jonah turned away from the street and stared at him. "You mean spaceships?" he asked hopefully. "Spaceships that can go a billion miles per second?"

"No, it was about the shape of space. What space would look like if there were only two dimensions instead of three."

"I don't get it. What's a dimension?"

"A universe with two dimensions has length and width, but no depth. Like a giant sheet." David held out his hands, palms down, as if he were smoothing an infinite sheet. "I had this teacher, Professor Kleinman? He's one of the smartest scientists in the whole world. And we wrote a paper together about two-dimensional universes."

"A paper?" The excitement seemed to drain from Jonah's face.

"Yeah, that's what scientists do, they write papers about their discoveries. So their colleagues can see what they've done."

Jonah turned back to watch the traffic. He was so bored, he didn't even bother to ask what the word *colleagues* meant. "I'm gonna ask Mom if I can take the Super Soaker to show-and-tell."

A minute later they walked into the apartment building where Jonah and his mother lived. David had lived there, too, until two years ago, when he and Karen had separated. Now he had a small apartment of his own farther uptown, closer to his job at Columbia University. Every weekday he picked up Jonah from school at three o'clock and delivered him to his mother four hours later. The arrangement allowed them to avoid the considerable expense of hiring a nanny. But David's heart always sank as he walked through the lobby of his old building and entered the sluggish elevator. He felt like an exile.

When they finally reached the fourteenth floor, David saw Karen standing in the apartment's doorway. She hadn't changed out of her work clothes yet; she wore black pumps and a gray business suit, the standard uniform of a corporate lawyer. With her arms folded across her chest, she scrutinized her ex-husband, glancing with evident disapproval at the stubble on David's face and his mud-caked jeans and the T-shirt emblazoned with the name of his softball team, the Hitless Historians. Then her eyes fixed on the Super Soaker. Sensing trouble, Jonah handed the gun to David and slipped past his mother into the apartment. "Gotta pee," he yelled as he ran to the bathroom.

Karen shook her head as she stared at the water gun. A stray lock of blond hair dangled beside her left cheek. She was still beautiful, David thought, but it was a cold beauty, cold and unyielding. She raised her hand to her face and whisked the blond lock to the side. "What the hell were you thinking?"

David had prepared himself for this. "Look, I already told Jonah the rules. No shooting at people. We went to the park and shot at the rocks and trees. It was fun."

"You think a machine gun is an appropriate toy for a seven-year-old?"

"It's not a machine gun, all right? And the box said, 'Ages seven and up.'"

Karen narrowed her eyes and pursed her lips. It was an expression she often made in the heat of an argument, and David had always hated it. "You know what kids do with those Super Soakers?" she said. "There was a story about it on the news last night. A bunch of kids in Staten Island put gasoline in the gun instead of water so they could turn it into a flamethrower. They nearly burned down their whole neighborhood."

David took a deep breath. He didn't want to fight with Karen anymore. That was why they'd split up—they were fighting all the time in front of Jonah. So it made no sense at all to continue this conversation. "Okay, okay, calm down. Just tell me what you want me to do."

"Take the gun home with you. You can let Jonah play with it when you're watching him, but I don't want that thing in my house."

Before David could respond, he heard the telephone ring inside the apartment. Then he heard Jonah call out, "I'll get it!" Karen's eyes swept sideways and for a moment it looked like she was going to make a dash for the phone, but instead she just cocked her ear to listen. David wondered if it was her new boyfriend. She'd started dating another lawyer, a hearty gray-haired gent with two former wives and a lot of money. David wasn't jealous in the usual sense—he'd lost his passion for Karen a long time ago. What he couldn't stand was the thought of that glad-handing coot getting chummy with Jonah.

Jonah came to the doorway with the cordless phone in his hand. He stopped in his tracks, probably puzzled by the anxious looks on both his parents' faces. Then he held the phone toward David. "It's for you, Dad."

Karen's face fell. She looked betrayed. "That's strange. Why would anyone call you here? Don't they have your new number?"

Jonah shrugged. "The man on the phone said he's with the police."

❈ ❈ ❈

DAVID SAT IN THE BACKSEAT of a taxi speeding north toward St. Luke's Hospital. It was getting dark now and all the eager Thursday-night couples were lining up outside the restaurants and bars on Amsterdam Avenue. As the taxi hurtled through the traffic, careening past the slow-moving buses and delivery trucks, David stared at the neon signs above the restaurants, the lurid orange letters flashing by.

Attacked, the police detective said. Professor Kleinman had been attacked in his apartment on 127th Street. Now he was in critical condition at the emergency room of St. Luke's. And he'd asked for David Swift. Whispered a phone number to the paramedics. You better hurry, the detective said. David asked, "Why? What's wrong?" and the detective said, "Just hurry."

David squirmed with guilt. He hadn't seen Professor Kleinman in over three years. The old man had become a recluse since he'd retired from Columbia's physics department. Lived in a tiny apartment on the edge of West Harlem, gave all his money to Israel. No wife, no kids. His whole life had been physics.

Twenty years earlier, when David was a grad student, Kleinman had been his adviser. David had liked him from the start. Neither aloof nor severe, he sprinkled Yiddish into his discourses on quantum theory. Once a week David went to Kleinman's office to hear him elucidate the mysteries of wave functions and virtual particles. Unfortunately, all the patient explanations weren't enough; after two years of frustration, David had to admit he was in over his head. He simply wasn't smart enough to be a physicist. So he quit the graduate program and switched to the next best thing: a Ph.D. in the history of science.

Kleinman was disappointed but understanding. Despite David's failings as a physics student, the old man had grown fond of him. They stayed in touch over the next ten years, and when David began research for his book—a study of Albert Einstein's collaborations with his various assistants—Kleinman offered his personal recollections of the man he called *Herr Doktor.* The book, *On the Shoulders of Giants,* was tremendously successful and made David's reputation. He was now a full professor in Columbia's History of Science program. But David knew it didn't mean much. Compared with a genius like Kleinman, he'd accomplished nothing.

The taxi screeched to a halt in front of the St. Luke's emergency room. After paying the driver, David rushed through the automatic glass doors and immediately spied a trio of New York City police officers standing next to the intake desk. Two of them were in uniform: a middle-aged sergeant with a bulging gut and a tall, thin rookie who looked like he was barely out of high school. The third was a plainclothes detective, a handsome Latino man in a neatly pressed suit. That's the man who called me, David thought. He remembered the detective's name: Rodriguez.

His heart pounding, David approached the officers. "Excuse me? I'm David Swift. Are you Detective Rodriguez?"

The detective nodded soberly. The two patrolmen, though, seemed amused. The paunchy sergeant smiled at David. "Hey, you got a permit for that thing?"

He pointed at the Super Soaker. David was so distracted he'd forgotten he was still holding Jonah's water gun.

Rodriguez frowned at the sergeant. He was all business. "Thank you for coming, Mr. Swift. Are you a relative of Mr. Kleinman?"

"No, no, I'm just a friend. A former student, actually."

The detective looked puzzled. "He was your teacher?"

"Yes, at Columbia. How is he? Is he badly hurt?"

Rodriguez placed a hand on David's shoulder. "Please, come with us. He's conscious but not answering our questions. He insists on talking to you."

The detective led David down a corridor while the two patrolmen walked behind. They passed a pair of nurses who looked at them gravely. This was not a good sign. "What happened?" David asked. "You said he was attacked?"

"We got a report of a burglary in progress," Rodriguez said

without emotion. "Someone across the street saw a man enter the apartment from the fire escape. When the officers arrived they found Mr. Kleinman in the bathroom, critically injured. That's all we know at this time."

"What do you mean, critically injured?"

The detective looked straight ahead. "Whoever did this was a very sick individual. Mr. Kleinman has third-degree burns on his face, chest, and genitals. He also has a collapsed lung and damage to his other organs. The doctors say his heart is failing now. I'm very sorry, Mr. Swift."

David's throat tightened. "Can't they operate?"

Rodriguez shook his head. "He wouldn't survive."

"Goddamn it," David muttered. He felt more anger than grief. He clenched his fists as he thought of Dr. Hans Walther Kleinman, that kind and brilliant old man, being pummeled by some sadistic street punk.

They came to a room marked TRAUMA CENTER. Through the doorway David saw two more nurses in green scrubs standing beside a bed that was surrounded by medical equipment—a cardiac monitor, a crash cart, a defibrillator, an IV pole. From the corridor David couldn't see who was lying on the bed. He was about to step into the room when Detective Rodriguez grabbed his arm.

"I know this will be difficult, Mr. Swift, but we need your help. I want you to ask Mr. Kleinman if he remembers anything from the attack. The paramedics said that while he was in the ambulance, he kept repeating a couple of names." Rodriguez looked over his shoulder at the rookie patrolman. "What were those names again?"

The boy cop flipped through the pages of his notebook. "Uh, hold on a second. They were German names, I remember that. Okay, here they are. Einhard Liggin and Feld Terry."

Rodriguez looked intently at David. "Do you know either of those people? Were they associates of Mr. Kleinman?"

David repeated the names silently: Einhard Liggin, Feld Terry. They were unusual, even for German. And then it hit him.

"They're not names," he said. "It's two words in German. *Einheitliche Feldtheorie.*"

"What does it mean?"

"Unified field theory."

Rodriguez just stared at him. "And what the hell is that?"

David decided to give the same explanation he would've given Jonah. "It's a theory that would explain all the forces of nature. Everything from gravity to electricity to the nuclear forces. It's the Holy Grail of physics. Researchers have been working on the problem for decades, but no one's come up with the theory yet."

The paunchy sergeant chuckled. "Well, there's our perp. The unified field theory. Should I put out an all-points?"

Rodriguez frowned at the sergeant again, then turned back to David. "Just ask Mr. Kleinman what he remembers. Anything at all would be helpful."

David said, "All right, I'll try," but he was perplexed now. Why would Kleinman repeat those particular words? Unified field theory was a somewhat old-fashioned term. Most physicists now referred to it as string theory or M-theory or quantum gravity, which were the names of the more recent approaches to the problem. What's more, Kleinman hadn't been enthusiastic about any of these approaches. His fellow physicists were going about it all wrong, he'd said. Instead of trying to understand how the universe works, they were building gaudy towers of mathematical formulas.

Rodriguez gave him an impatient look. He took the Super Soaker out of David's hands and nudged him toward the Trauma Center. "You better go in now. He may not have long."

David nodded, then stepped into the room. As he approached the bed, the two nurses tactfully backed off and focused on the cardiac monitor.

What he noticed first were the bandages, the thick gauze pad taped to the right side of Kleinman's face and the blood-soaked wrappings across his chest. The dressings covered most of Kleinman's body and yet they still didn't conceal all his injuries. David could see patches of dried blood under the old man's white hair and purple hand-shaped bruises on both of his shoulders. But the worst thing was the dark blue tinge to his skin. David was familiar enough with physiology to know what it meant: Kleinman's heart could no longer pump the oxygenated blood from his lungs to the rest of his body. The doctors had strapped an oxygen mask to his face and put him in a sitting position to drain the fluid from his lungs, but these interventions weren't having much effect. David felt a fullness in his own chest as he stared at Professor Kleinman. The old man already looked like a corpse.

After a few seconds, though, the corpse began to move. Kleinman opened his eyes and slowly raised his left hand to his face. With curled fingers he tapped the clear plastic mask that covered his mouth and nose. David leaned over the bed. "Dr. Kleinman? It's me, David. Can you hear me?"

Although the professor's eyes were watery and dull, they locked on David. Kleinman tapped his oxygen mask again and then grasped the vinyl air bag that hung below, filling and emptying like a third lung. After fumbling for a moment, he got a good grip on the thing and started tugging.

David grew alarmed. "Is something wrong? Is the air not getting through?"

Kleinman pulled harder at the bag, which twisted in his hand. His lips were moving behind the plastic mask. David leaned closer. "What is it? What's wrong?"

The old man shook his head. A drop of sweat ran down his brow. "Don't you see it?" he whispered from behind the mask. "Don't you see?"

"See what?"

Kleinman let go of the bag and held his hand up in the air, turning it around slowly as if he were displaying a prize. "So beautiful," he whispered.

David heard a moist rattle in Kleinman's chest. It was the fluid backing up into his lungs. "Do you know where you are, Professor? You're in the hospital."

Kleinman kept staring with wonder at his hand, or more specifically, at the empty space cupped in his palm. "Yes, yes," he rasped.

"Someone attacked you in your apartment. The police want to know if you remember anything."

The old man coughed, spraying pinkish spittle on the inside of his mask. But his eyes remained on the invisible prize in his hand. "He was right. *Mein Gott,* he was right!"

David bit his lip. He knew now beyond a doubt that Kleinman was dying, because he'd witnessed a similar struggle once before. Ten years earlier he'd stood by his father's hospital bed and watched him die of liver cancer. David's father, John Swift, was a bus driver and former boxer who'd abandoned his family and drunk himself to death. At the end he didn't even recognize his son. Instead he thrashed under the bedsheets and cursed the names of the once-famous welterweights who'd beaten him senseless thirty years before.

David grasped Kleinman's hand. It was soft and limp and very cold. "Professor, please listen. This is important."

The old man's eyes locked on him again. They were the only part of him that still seemed alive. "Everyone thought . . . that he failed. But he succeeded. He succeeded!" Kleinman spoke in short bursts, taking shallow breaths in between. "But he couldn't . . . publish it. *Herr Doktor* saw . . . the danger. Much worse . . . than a bomb. Destroyer . . . of worlds."

David stared at the old man. *Herr Doktor?* Destroyer of worlds? He clasped Kleinman's hand a bit tighter. "Try to stay with me, okay? You need to tell me about the man who hurt you. Do you remember what he looked like?"

The professor's face was shiny with sweat now. "That's why . . . the *shtarker* came. That's why . . . he tortured me."

"Tortured?" David felt a sickening jolt.

"Yes, yes. He wanted me . . . to write it down. But I didn't. I didn't!"

"Write what down? What did he want?"

Kleinman smiled behind the mask. *"Einheitliche Feldtheorie,"* he whispered. *"Herr Doktor's* . . . last gift."

David was bewildered. The easiest explanation was that the professor was hallucinating. The trauma of the attack had dredged up memories from half a century ago, when Hans Kleinman was a young physicist at Princeton's Institute for Advanced Study, hired to assist the legendary but ailing Albert Einstein. David had written about it in his book: the endless stream of calculations on the blackboard in Einstein's office, the long futile search for a field equation that would encompass both gravity and electromagnetism. It was not unreasonable that Kleinman, in his final delirium, would think back to those days. And yet the old man didn't seem delirious at that moment. His chest was wheezing and he was sweating profusely, but his face was calm.

"I'm sorry, David," he rasped. "Sorry I never . . . told you. *Herr Doktor* saw . . . the danger. But he couldn't . . . he couldn't . . ." Kleinman coughed again, and his whole body shuddered. "He couldn't burn . . . his notebooks. The theory was . . . too beautiful." He let out another violent cough and then he suddenly doubled over.

One of the nurses rushed to the other side of Kleinman's bed. Grabbing the professor by his bruised shoulders, she propped him back up to a sitting position. David, who was still holding Kleinman's hand, saw that his oxygen mask was filled with pink froth.

The nurse quickly removed the mask and cleaned out the sputum. But when she tried to put it back on, Kleinman shook his head. She grasped the back of his neck to hold him still, but he batted the mask away with his free hand. "No!" he croaked. "Stop it! Enough!"

The nurse glared at him, then turned to her partner, who was still staring at the cardiac monitor. "Go get the resident," she ordered. "We need to intubate."

Kleinman leaned against David, who put his arm around the old man to keep him from toppling. The gurgling in his chest seemed louder now and his eyes darted wildly. "I'm dying," he rasped. "There's not . . . much time."

David's eyes began to sting. "It's all right, Professor. You're going to be all—"

Kleinman raised his hand and gripped the collar of David's shirt. "Listen . . . David. You must . . . be careful. Your paper . . . remember? The one we worked on . . . together? Remember?"

It took David a moment to realize what the professor was referring to. "You mean back in grad school? 'General Relativity in a Two-Dimensional Spacetime'? That paper?"

He nodded. "Yes, yes . . . you were close . . . very close . . . to the truth. Once I'm gone . . . they might come after you."

David felt an uneasy prickle in his stomach. "Who are you talking about?"

Kleinman tightened his grip on David's collar. "I have . . . a key. *Herr Doktor* gave me . . . this gift. And now I give it . . . to you. Keep it . . . safe. Don't let . . . them get it. Understand? No one!"

"A key? What—"

"No time . . . no time! Just listen!" With surprising strength, Kleinman pulled David close. The old man's wet lips brushed his ear. "Remember . . . the numbers. Four, zero . . . two, six . . . three, six . . . seven, nine . . . five, six . . . four, four . . . seven, eight, zero, zero."

As soon as he spoke the last digit, the professor let go of David's collar and slumped against his chest. "Now repeat . . . the sequence."

Despite his confusion, David did as he was told. He put his lips near Kleinman's ear and repeated the sequence. Although David had never been able to master the equations of quantum physics, he had an aptitude for memorizing long strings of numbers. When he was done, the old man nodded.

"Good boy," he murmured against David's shirt. "Good boy."

The nurse stood beside the crash cart, preparing for the intubation. David watched her pick up a silver, scythe-shaped instrument and a long plastic tube with black tick marks along its length. They're going to slip that thing down the professor's throat, he thought. And then David felt something warm against his stomach. He looked down and saw a rivulet of viscous pink fluid spilling out of Kleinman's mouth and pouring down his chin. The old man's eyes were closed and his chest had stopped gurgling.

WHEN THE EMERGENCY-ROOM RESIDENT finally arrived, he kicked David out of the Trauma Center and called for reinforcements. Soon half a dozen doctors and nurses surrounded Kleinman's bed, trying to resuscitate the professor. But David knew it was hopeless. Hans Kleinman was gone.

Rodriguez and the two patrolmen intercepted him as he lurched down the corridor. The detective, still holding the Super Soaker, wore a sympathetic look. He handed the water gun back to David. "How did it go, Mr. Swift? Did he tell you anything?"

David shook his head. "I'm sorry. He was going in and out. It didn't make a lot of sense."

"Well, what did he say? Was it a robbery?"

"No. He said he was tortured."

"Tortured? Why?"

Before David could answer, someone down the hallway shouted, "Hey, you! Hold it right there!"

It was a tall, ruddy, thick-necked man with a crew cut and wearing a gray suit. He was flanked by two more ex-linebackers who looked much the same. The three of them marched down the corridor at a brisk clip. When they reached the cops, the guy in the middle took his ID out of his jacket and flashed the badge. "Agent Hawley, FBI," he announced. "Are you the officers working the Kleinman case?"

The fat sergeant and the rookie patrolman stepped forward so that they stood shoulder to shoulder with Rodriguez. They sneered in unison at the federal agents. "Yeah, that's our case," Rodriguez replied.

Agent Hawley gave a hand signal to one of his companions,

who headed for the Trauma Center. Then Hawley reached into the pocket of his jacket again and pulled out a folded letter. "We're taking over now," he said, passing the letter to Rodriguez. "Here's the authorization from the U.S. Attorney's Office."

Rodriguez unfolded the letter. He scowled as he read it. "This is bullshit. You don't have jurisdiction here."

Hawley's face was expressionless. "If you have a complaint, you can take it up with the U.S. attorney."

David studied Agent Hawley, who was turning his blank face from left to right, surveying the hallway. Judging by his accent, he definitely wasn't from New York. He sounded like an Oklahoma farm boy who'd picked up his conversational skills in the Marine Corps. David wondered why this no-nonsense FBI man was so interested in the murder of a retired physicist. He felt the prickle in his stomach again.

As if sensing David's discomfort, Agent Hawley pointed at him. "Who's this guy?" he asked Rodriguez. "What's he doing here?"

The detective shrugged. "Kleinman asked for him. His name's David Swift. They just finished talking and he—"

"Son of a bitch! You let this guy talk to Kleinman?"

David frowned. This agent was a real asshole. "I was trying to help," he said. "If you'd shut up for a minute, the detective would explain it to you."

Hawley abruptly turned away from Rodriguez. He narrowed his eyes and stepped toward David. "Are you a physicist, Mr. Swift?"

The agent loomed over him, but David kept his voice steady. "No, I'm a historian. And it's Dr. Swift, if you don't mind."

While Hawley tried to stare him down, the agent who'd gone to the Trauma Center returned. He sidled up to Hawley and whispered something in his ear. For a fraction of a second Hawley tightened his lips into a grimace. Then his face turned blank and hard again. "Kleinman's dead, Mr. Swift. That means you're coming with us."

David almost laughed. "Coming with you? I don't think so."

But before the last words were out of his mouth, the third FBI agent had slipped behind him, yanked back his arms, and snapped a pair of handcuffs around his wrists. The Super Soaker clattered to the floor.

"What the hell are you doing?" David yelled. "Am I under arrest?"

Hawley didn't bother to reply. He grabbed David's arm just above the elbow and turned him around. The agent who'd handcuffed him picked up the Super Soaker, holding it at arm's length as if it were a real weapon. Then all three FBI men escorted David down the corridor, moving swiftly past the dumbfounded doctors and nurses. David looked over his shoulder at Detective Rodriguez and the patrolmen, but the officers just stood there.

One of the agents marched ahead and opened the door to a stairway. David was too scared to protest. As they hurried down the stairs toward the emergency exit, he remembered something Professor Kleinman had said just a few minutes before. It was part of a famous quote from J. Robert Oppenheimer, another great physicist who'd worked with Einstein. The words had run through Oppenheimer's mind when he witnessed the first test of the atomic bomb.

Now I am become Death, the destroyer of worlds.

Chapter Three

SIMON WAS PLAYING TETRIS IN THE DRIVER'S SEAT OF HIS
Mercedes, keeping one eye on the electronic game that was running on his cell phone and the other on the entrance to St. Luke's
Hospital. Tetris was the perfect game for situations like this. It en-
tertained you without taking your mind off the job. Jabbing the cell
phone's buttons, Simon could easily maneuver the Tetris blocks into
place while observing the cars and taxis that pulled up to the emergency room. Relaxed yet watchful, he started looking at the vehicles
on Amsterdam Avenue as if they were oversized Tetris blocks—
squares and T-bars and zigzags and L-shapes—cruising down the
darkening street.

It's all about flexibility, Simon thought. No matter what game
you're playing, you have to be willing to adjust your strategy. Just
look at what happened with Hans Kleinman tonight. At first the job
had seemed simple enough, but Kleinman's mind went soft before
Simon could get anything useful out of him. Then, to make mat-
ters worse, a pair of patrol cars pulled up in front of the professor's
apartment building. Simon was surprised, but he didn't panic—he
simply adjusted his strategy. First he evaded the police by climbing
the fire escape to the roof and jumping to the warehouse next door.
Then he got into his Mercedes and followed the ambulance taking
Kleinman to St. Luke's. He had a new plan: Wait until the police
officers leave the emergency room, and then—if Kleinman was still
alive—take another crack at getting the *Einheitliche Feldtheorie* out
of him.

Simon admired the professor, actually. He was a tough little
bastard. He reminded Simon of his old commander in the Spetsnaz,
Colonel Alexi Latypov. Alexi had been an officer in the Russian

special forces for almost three decades. Quick, smart, and ruthless, he'd led Simon's unit through the worst years of the war in Chechnya, teaching his men how to outwit and outfight the insurgents. And then, during a raid on one of the Chechen camps, a sniper shot Alexi's brains out. A terrible thing, but not unexpected. Simon recalled something his commander had once said: Life is nothing but shit, and whatever comes afterward is probably worse.

The Tetris blocks piled up at the bottom of the cell phone's screen, forming a craggy mountain with a deep hole at the far left. Then a straight I-bar began to descend. Simon whipped it to the left and four rows of blocks vanished with a software-generated sigh. Very satisfying. Like slipping the knife in.

A moment later Simon saw a black Chevrolet Suburban with tinted windows come down Amsterdam Avenue. The car slowed as it approached the hospital, then parked by the loading dock. Three large men in identical gray suits jumped out of the car and marched in formation toward the hospital's service entrance, flashing their badges at the startled security guard. Even though they were almost thirty meters away, Simon recognized the men from their gait: ex-Marines and ex-Rangers assigned to headquarters duty, most likely with the FBI. American intelligence was apparently interested in Professor Kleinman, too. That explained why the police had arrived so quickly at his apartment. The federal agents must have planted a few listening devices in Kleinman's walls, which would've picked up Simon's conversation with the professor.

The agents went inside the hospital, presumably to interview Kleinman before the old man expired. Simon wasn't pleased by this development, but he wasn't overly perturbed either. Although he had a healthy respect for American agents—they had good training, good discipline—he knew he could eliminate all three of them without much trouble. Simon had an edge: because he worked on his own, his instincts were keener. That was one of the two great advantages of a freelance career.

The other advantage was the money. Since he'd left the

Spetsnaz, Simon could earn more cash in one day than a whole platoon of Russian paratroopers could earn in a year. The trick was to find clients who were wealthy but desperate. A surprising number of people, corporations, and governments fell into this category. Some were desperate for power, others for respect. Some wanted missiles, others plutonium. Whatever the assignment, Simon had no qualms. It was all the same to him.

As he waited for the FBI agents to return, Simon thought about contacting his current client. The mission had deviated quite a bit from the original plan, and his clients usually liked to be informed of such changes. But in the end he decided it wasn't necessary. This client was perhaps more desperate than any he'd ever dealt with. The first time the man called, Simon had thought it was a joke; it seemed ridiculous, paying good money for a scientific theory. But as Simon learned more about the mission, he began to see the potential applications of this theory, both military and otherwise. And it dawned on him that this particular job could give him something infinitely better than money.

Before he expected it to happen, the three agents emerged from one of the hospital's emergency exits. They had a prisoner in tow. He was a bit shorter than the FBI men but trim and athletic, dressed in sneakers and jeans and one of those baseball-team T-shirts that Americans are so fond of. His hands were cuffed behind his back and he turned his head this way and that, like a frightened bird, as two of the agents pushed him toward the Suburban. The third agent was carrying a brightly colored toy gun. Simon chuckled—was the FBI field-testing water guns now? The whole scene was quite odd, and for a moment Simon wondered whether this arrest was related to Kleinman at all. Perhaps the prisoner was merely some eccentric New Yorker who'd threatened the doctors with his Super Soaker. But just before the agents shoved the prisoner into the car, they slipped a black hood over his head and cinched it below his chin. Okay, Simon thought. The prisoner isn't a random madman. He's someone the agents want to interrogate.

The driver of the Suburban switched on his headlights and pulled away from the curb. Simon slunk low in his seat as the car passed by. He was going to let the FBI men get a couple of blocks ahead before following them. There was no point in sticking around the hospital any longer—the fact that the agents had left without Kleinman was a strong indication that the old man was dead. Luckily, though, the professor appeared to have shared some of his secrets with a younger colleague.

Simon pressed the off button on his cell phone, ending the game of Tetris, but before the device shut down, it flashed a photograph on the screen, a photo that was programmed to appear whenever he turned the phone on or off. It was a stupid thing to do, saving a personal photo on a phone he used for business, yet he did it anyway. He didn't want to forget their faces. Sergei with his corn-silk hair and bright blue eyes. Larissa in her blond curls, just a few weeks shy of her fourth birthday.

The screen went black. Simon put the phone back in his pocket and shifted the Mercedes into gear.

IT WAS A WOMAN'S VOICE with a thick southern accent. "All right, Hawley, you can take it off now."

David gasped for air as the hood came off. He felt nauseous from breathing for so long through the black cloth, which was damp with his own sweat. He squinted at first, his eyes painfully adjusting to the fluorescent light.

He was seated at a gray table in a bare, windowless room. Standing beside his chair was Agent Hawley, who rolled up the black hood and stuffed it into his pocket. Hawley's two partners were inspecting the Super Soaker, methodically opening the water gun's reservoirs and peering into each hole. And sitting across the table was someone new, a broad-shouldered, big-bosomed, sixtyish woman with an impressive helmet of platinum-blond hair. "You all right, Mr. Swift?" she asked. "You look a little ragged."

David was not all right. He was scared and disoriented and

still handcuffed. And now, to top things off, he was thoroughly confused. This woman didn't look like an FBI agent. In her bright red jacket and loose-fitting white blouse, she looked like a grandmother dressed up for a bingo game. "Who are you?" he asked.

"I'm Lucille, honey, Lucille Parker. But you can call me Lucy. Everyone does." She reached for a pitcher of water and a couple of Dixie cups that were sitting on the table. "Hawley, take them cuffs off Mr. Swift."

Agent Hawley grudgingly unlocked the handcuffs. David rubbed his sore wrists and studied Lucille, who was pouring water into the paper cups. Her lipstick was the exact same color as her jacket. Her face was pleasantly creased, with plenty of laughter lines around the eyes, and she had a pair of reading glasses hanging from a beaded chain around her neck. But she also had a coiled wire running behind her left ear, the same radio headset that all the government agents used. "Am I under arrest?" David asked. "Because if I am, I want to speak to a lawyer."

Lucille smiled. "No, you ain't under arrest. Sorry if we gave you that impression."

"Impression? Your agents handcuffed me and put a goddamn bag over my head!"

"Let me try to explain, honey. This building is what we call a secure facility. And we have a standard procedure for bringing people inside. We can't divulge the exact location, so we have to use the hood."

David stood up. "Well, if I'm not under arrest, I'm free to leave, right?"

Agent Hawley gripped David's shoulder. Still smiling, Lucille shook her head. "I'm afraid it's a little more complicated than that." She slid one of the Dixie cups toward him. "Sit down, Mr. Swift. Have a drink of water."

The hand on David's shoulder grew heavier. He took the hint and sat down. "It's Dr. Swift," he said. "And I'm not thirsty."

"You want something stronger, maybe?" She winked at him

in a disturbingly flirtatious way, then reached into her jacket and pulled a silver flask out of the inside pocket. "This here is genuine Texas white lightning, a hundred and eighty proof. A friend of mine down in Lubbock has a still. He got a special license from the ATF so he can do it legally. Care for a snort?"

"No, thank you."

"That's right, I forgot." She put the flask back in her jacket. "You never touch the stuff, do you? Because of your daddy, right?"

David stiffened in his chair. Some of his friends and colleagues knew that he'd sworn off drinking long ago, but only his ex-wife and a few of his oldest buddies knew why. And now Lucille had casually tossed it out. "What's going on?" he demanded.

"Calm down, honey. It's in your file." She reached into a bulky purse hanging from the back of her chair and pulled out two folders, one thick and one thin. She put on her reading glasses and opened the thin folder. "Let's see, family history. Father's name, John Swift. Professional boxer, 1968 to 1974. Nickname, the Two-fisted Terror. Hey, that's a good one."

David didn't respond. His father had never lived up to his nickname in the ring. The only people he'd ever successfully terrorized were the members of his own family.

Lucille skimmed to the bottom of the page. "Overall record, four wins, sixteen losses. Hired as a bus driver for the Metropolitan Transit Authority, 1975. Terminated after arrest for driving while intoxicated, 1979. Sentenced to three years at Ossining after conviction for assault, 1981." She closed the folder and looked David in the eye. "I'm sorry. It must've been awful."

Clever, he thought. It was probably a standard technique that the FBI taught at its academy. First show the subject that you already know his secrets. Then move in for the kill. "You have quite a research department here," David observed. "Did you dig up all this stuff in the past half hour?"

"No, we started your file a few days ago. We collected material on everyone who worked with Kleinman, and you were listed as a coauthor on one of his papers." She picked up the thick folder. "This is the file for the late professor himself." She opened the folder, shaking her head as she leafed through it. "Let me tell you, some of this physics is rough going. I mean, what the hell is the Kleinman-Gupta effect anyway? It's mentioned half a dozen times in here but I can't make heads or tails of it."

David examined her closely. He couldn't tell whether she was sincerely ignorant or just playing dumb to get him to talk. "It's a phenomenon that happens when certain unstable atoms decay. Dr. Kleinman discovered it with his colleague Amil Gupta in 1965."

"That's where the radiation comes from, right? When the atoms decay?"

He frowned. "Look, I'd be happy to tell you all about it, but I'm not going to do it here. Take me to my office and we can talk."

Lucille took off her reading glasses. "I can see you're getting impatient, Mr. Swift, but you'll have to bear with me. You see, Professor Kleinman had access to classified information, and we suspect there may have been a breach."

David looked askance. "What are you talking about? It's been forty years since he worked for the government. He stopped doing military work after he finished his radiation studies."

"This ain't the kind of thing he would've advertised. After Kleinman retired from Columbia, he participated in a Defense Department project."

"And you think that's why he was attacked?"

"All I can say is that Kleinman possessed some highly sensitive material and now we have to track it down. If he told you anything when you were in his hospital room, you need to let us know."

Lucille leaned toward him, her elbows on the table. She wasn't smiling or calling him honey anymore; her face had turned dead serious. David had no trouble believing she was an FBI agent now. He just didn't believe her story. "I'm sorry, but this doesn't sound right. It doesn't sound like Dr. Kleinman. He regretted the military work he did. He said it was immoral."

"Maybe you didn't know him as well as you thought."

David shook his head. "No, it doesn't make sense. He organized protests at Columbia. He persuaded every physicist there to sign a statement against nuclear weapons."

"I never said he was working on weapons. He approached the Defense Department after 9/11. He offered to help the counterterrorism effort."

David considered the possibility. It was far-fetched but not inconceivable. Kleinman was an expert on radioactive decay, particularly the decay of the uranium atoms used in nuclear warheads. That kind of knowledge could certainly be applied to counterterrorism. "So what was he working on?" David asked. "A new kind of radiation detector?"

"I'm not at liberty to say. But I can show you something." She picked up Kleinman's folder again and riffled through its contents. After some searching, she pulled out a reprint of an old research paper and handed it to David. It was about ten pages long and slightly yellowed with age. "You can look at this. It's one of the few things in his file that ain't classified."

The paper had been published in *Physical Review* in 1975. The title was "Measurements of the Flux of Rho Mesons" and the author was H. W. Kleinman. David had never seen this paper before; the topic was fairly obscure, and he hadn't studied it in graduate school. Worse, the article was loaded with fantastically complex equations.

"This is why we brought you here, Mr. Swift. The first priority of a counterterrorism operation is to make sure the terrorists don't know our defenses. So we have to find out what Kleinman might've told them about our work."

David scrutinized the article, trying his best to understand. Kleinman had apparently discovered that focusing a beam of radiation on uranium atoms could generate intense showers of particles called rho mesons. Although the article said nothing about the practical uses of the research, the implications seemed clear: this technology could detect the enriched uranium in a nuclear warhead, even if the bomb was enclosed in lead shielding. David thought again of his last conversation with Kleinman and began to wonder if he'd misinterpreted the professor's final words. When Kleinman had warned about the "destroyer of worlds," could he have been thinking of a nuclear weapon smuggled into the United States?

"Was he working on an active scanning system?" David asked. "Something that could detect a warhead hidden in a truck or a shipping container?"

"I can neither confirm nor deny," Lucille answered. "But I think you see now why we're taking this so seriously."

David was just about to look up from the paper when he noticed something on the last page. There was a table comparing the properties of the rho meson with those of its close cousins, the omega and phi mesons. The thing that caught David's eye was the last column of the table, which listed the lifetimes of the particles. He stared at the numbers for several seconds.

"So what did Kleinman say, Mr. Swift? What did he tell you?" Lucille gazed at him earnestly, acting like a doting grandmother again. But now David saw through it.

"You're lying," he said. "Dr. Kleinman wasn't working on a detector. He wasn't working for the government at all."

Lucille put on a hurt, uncomprehending look, opening her mouth wide. "What? Are you . . ."

David tapped his finger on the last page of Kleinman's paper. "The lifetime of a rho meson is less than 10^{-23} second."

"So? What does that mean?"

"It means your research department screwed up when they concocted this cover story. Even if a rho meson were moving at the speed of light, it would go less than a trillionth of an inch before it decayed. You couldn't detect those particles coming from a nuclear warhead, so it would be impossible to build a scanning system based on this paper."

The hurt look remained on Lucille's face, and for a moment David thought she was going to play innocent. After a couple of seconds, though, she closed her mouth, firmly pressing her lips together. The lines around her eyes deepened, but these weren't laughter lines. Lucille was pissed.

"Okay, let's start over," David said. "Why don't you tell me the real reason why you're so interested in Dr. Kleinman? It's some kind of weapon, isn't it? Some classified weapon that you won't breathe a word about, but you're spending billions of dollars on it anyway?"

She didn't reply. Instead she took off her jacket and draped it over the back of her chair. A shoulder holster rode against the side of her blouse, and in the holster was a sleek black pistol.

As David stared at the gun, Lucille turned to the two agents who were still inspecting the Super Soaker. "You boys finished with that damn thing yet?"

One of the agents came over and placed the water gun on the table. "It's clean, ma'am," he reported.

"What a relief. Now contact logistics and tell 'em we're gonna need transportation to the airport in ten minutes."

The agent retreated to the far end of the room and began muttering into the microphone hidden in his sleeve. Meanwhile, Lucille twisted around in her chair and reached into the pocket of her jacket again. This time she pulled out a pack of Marlboros and a Zippo lighter emblazoned with the Lone Star of Texas. She glared at David as she shook a cigarette out of the pack. "You're a real pain in the ass, you know that?" She turned to Hawley, who was still standing beside David's chair. "Ain't this guy a pain in the ass, Hawley?"

"Big-time," he replied.

Lucille stuck the cigarette in the corner of her mouth. "Just look at him. He probably don't approve of smoking either. Probably thinks we should go outside if we want to light up." With a flick of her wrist she opened the Zippo and lit her cigarette, blowing the first plume of smoke into David's face. "Well, I got some news for you, Swift. We can do whatever the fuck we want." She closed the Zippo and slipped it back in her jacket. "You understand?"

While David wondered how to respond, Lucille gave Agent Hawley a nod. A moment later he smacked the side of David's head. "You got a hearing problem?" he shouted. "Agent Parker asked you a question."

David gritted his teeth. It was a hard smack and it stung like hell, but in this case the insult was worse than the injury. His stomach churned with outrage as he looked up at Hawley. Only the presence of the semiautomatics in the agents' holsters kept him in his seat.

Lucille smiled. "I got another piece of news for you. Remember the nurse who was in Kleinman's hospital room? Well, one of our agents talked to her." She took a deep drag on her cigarette and blew out another plume of smoke. "She said the professor whispered some numbers in your ear."

Shit, David thought. The nurse.

"A long string of numbers, she said. She don't remember them, of course. But I bet you do."

He did. He saw the sequence of numbers in his mind's eye, almost as if they were floating in the air in front of him. That was the way David's memory worked. The digits crossed his field of view in the same order that Dr. Kleinman had gasped them.

"You're gonna tell us those numbers now," Lucille said. She rolled up the left sleeve of her blouse, exposing an antique watch on a silver band. "I'm gonna give you thirty seconds."

While Lucille leaned back in her chair, Agent Hawley removed the black hood from his pocket. David's throat tightened as he stared at the thing. Jesus, he thought, how the hell did this happen? These agents seemed to think it was perfectly within their rights to put a hood over his head and beat him to a pulp. And now the only sensible choice was to forget Dr. Kleinman's warnings and tell them the numbers. For all David knew, the sequence could be meaningless anyway. And even if the numbers weren't random, even if they were the key to something horrendous, why should he be responsible for keeping the secret? He hadn't asked for this. All he'd done was write a research paper on relativity.

He gripped the edge of the table to steady himself. He had five, maybe ten seconds left. Lucille's eyes were fixed on her watch and Hawley was straightening out the black hood, and as David stared at them he realized that even if he revealed the numbers, the agents wouldn't let him go. As long as the digits remained in his head, he was a security risk. His only hope was to make a deal, preferably with someone higher in the chain of command than Agents Parker and Hawley. "I need some assurances before I tell you anything," he said. "I want to speak with someone higher up."

Lucille frowned. "What do you think this is, a department store? You think you can complain to the manager if you don't like the service?"

"I need to get some idea why you want the numbers. If you can't tell me the reason, take me to someone who can."

Lucille let out a long sigh. She took the cigarette out of her mouth and drowned it in one of the Dixie cups. Then she pushed her chair back and stood up, wincing a bit as she straightened her knees. "All right, Mr. Swift, you're gonna get your wish. We're gonna take you to a place where you'll have plenty of folks to chat with."

"Where? Washington?"

She chuckled. "No, this place is a bit farther south. A lovely little spot called Guantánamo Bay."

Adrenaline flooded David's body. "Wait a second! I'm a citizen! You can't—"

"Under the authorization of the Patriot Act, I'm declaring you an enemy combatant." She turned to Hawley. "Put the cuffs back on him. We'll do the shackles after we get in the car."

Hawley grabbed his arm and shouted, "Get up!" but David remained frozen in his seat, his heart pumping fast and his legs quivering. Hawley raised his voice still louder: "I said GET UP!" and he was just about to yank David to his feet when one of the other agents tapped him on the shoulder. It was the guy who was supposed to call logistics on the radio. He looked a little pale.

"Uh, sir?" he whispered. "I think we have a problem."

Lucille overheard him. She butted between Hawley and his partner. "What is it? What's the problem?"

The pale agent was so flustered it took him a couple of seconds to find his voice. "I can't raise logistics. I tried every frequency but there's no response. There's nothing but static on every channel."

Lucille gave him a skeptical look. "There's something wrong with your radio." She reached for the microphone that was clipped to the collar of her blouse and pressed the push-to-talk button. "Black One to logistics. Logistics, do you read?"

But before she could get an answer, a deep percussive boom shook the walls.

AS SIMON WALKED TOWARD THE garage where the black Suburban was parked, it occurred to him that if he ever wanted to switch careers he could always find work as a security consultant. After all, who could offer better advice on how to defend a government or corporate facility than someone who had some experience breaking into them?

He could certainly give the FBI a few tips. Inside the guardhouse booth at the entrance to the garage there was only one agent, a stocky young grunt in an orange windbreaker and a New York Yankees cap, which was his not-so-convincing attempt to look like an ordinary parking attendant. Stationing one agent in the guardhouse instead of two was a mistake, Simon thought. You should never cut corners on perimeter defense, and most especially not on the night shift.

Simon had changed into a stylish business suit and carried a leather briefcase now. When he knocked on the booth's bulletproof glass, the agent looked him over, then opened the door a crack. "What is it?" he asked.

"Sorry to bother you," Simon said, "but I was wondering about the monthly rates for parking here."

"We don't—"

Simon wrenched the door open and slammed his shoulder

into the agent's gut, knocking him down on his back. There was only one surveillance camera in the booth and it was pointed so high it couldn't view the floor. Another mistake. Lying on top of the agent, Simon thrust his combat knife into the man's heart and kept him pinned to the floor until he stopped moving. It wasn't really his fault, Simon thought. It was an institutional failure.

When Simon stood up he was wearing the windbreaker and the Yankees cap. He'd also removed the Uzi and the field munitions from his briefcase. Hiding the submachine gun under the windbreaker, he exited the booth and walked down the long ramp to the garage.

There were plenty of video cameras trained on him now, so he kept his head down. He turned a corner and saw half a dozen Suburbans parked near an unmarked steel door. When he was about ten meters away the door opened and an agitated man in a gray suit peered out. "Anderson!" he shouted. "What the hell are you—"

Simon lifted his head and fired his Uzi at the same time. Conveniently, the agent fell facedown and his prostrate body kept the door from closing. Simon raced to the doorway, arriving just in time to cut down a third agent who'd rushed to his partner's aid. This is atrocious, Simon thought. They're making it too easy.

Just past the doorway was the command-and-control room where the unfortunate agents had been stationed. Simon first disabled the radio transceiver, then scanned the bank of video monitors. He found his target on the screen marked SUB-3A, which showed one of the interrogation rooms on the sub-basement level. Simon was already familiar with the layout of the complex; over the years he'd developed several sources in American intelligence who'd revealed, for a small fee, a great deal about the workings of their agencies.

Only one more barrier remained, a second steel door at the far end of the room. This door had an alphanumeric keypad controlling the lock. For a moment Simon regretted killing the agents so quickly—he should've kept at least one of them alive long enough to surrender the entry code. Luckily for him, the FBI had committed yet another foolish error, installing a single dead bolt on the door instead of a stronger locking mechanism.

Simon removed half a kilogram of C-4 from his munitions bag. It took him eighty-three seconds to mold the explosive around the bolt, insert the blasting caps, and run the detonator cord across the control room. Crouched behind a pillar, Simon called out, *"Na zdorovya!"*—a traditional drinking toast, the Russian equivalent of "Cheers!" Then he detonated the charge.

AS SOON AS THEY HEARD the blast, Lucille and Hawley and the two other agents pulled out their Glocks. There was no enemy in sight, but they took out their semiautomatics anyway and pointed them at the closed door of the interrogation room. For the first time in his life, David wished he had a gun, too.

"Son of a bitch!" Hawley cried. "What the hell was that?"

Lucille seemed a bit calmer. She gave her agents a hand signal, holding up her index and middle fingers. The three men slowly approached the door. Then Hawley grasped the knob and flung the door open, and his two partners dashed into the corridor. After an anxious second they both yelled, "Clear!"

Lucille breathed a whoosh of relief. "All right, listen up. Hawley stays here to secure our detainee. The others come with me to identify the threat and reestablish communications." She gathered the folders that were lying on the table and scooped them under her arm. Then she turned to David. "You're gonna sit in that chair, Mr. Swift, and you ain't gonna make a sound. Agent Hawley's gonna be standing just outside that door. If you make so much as a peep, he's gonna come back in here and shoot your sorry ass. Understand?"

She didn't wait for an answer, which was just as well—David was too terrified to speak. Instead she barreled into the corridor, brushing past Hawley, who still had his hand on the doorknob. "Uh, ma'am?" he asked. "What's the fallback? What if I can't hold the position?"

"If it comes to that, you're authorized to take the necessary steps."

Hawley went into the corridor and closed the door behind him. David heard the lock slide into place. Then the room became so quiet he could hear the hum of the fluorescent lights overhead.

Necessary steps. The meaning of the phrase became apparent as David sat there. He had information that the FBI, for whatever reasons, considered valuable. So valuable, in fact, that the Bureau would go to great lengths to make sure it didn't fall into the wrong hands. In all likelihood, they'd destroy the information before letting anyone else take it. Even if it meant destroying him. In his mind's eye he saw Agent Hawley reenter the room, pointing his gun.

David jumped to his feet. He couldn't stay here, he had to get out! He looked around the room, searching wildly for some escape route, maybe a ceiling panel he could pry loose, an air duct he could crawl through. But the ceiling and walls were solid concrete, blank and white. There was nothing in the room except the chairs and the gray table, which held the pitcher of water, the Dixie cups, and the thoroughly inspected Super Soaker.

Then he noticed something else. In her haste, Lucille had left her bright red jacket on the back of her chair. Tucked in its pockets were a Zippo lighter and a flask of alcohol. And David remembered what his ex-wife had said about the dangers of Super Soakers.

SIMON HAD ONE GOOD THING to say about the security at the FBI complex: at least they hadn't put the circuit breakers in an obvious place like the command-and-control room. He had to follow the twists and turns of the exposed cables before he found the utility closet. But his opinion of the agency plummeted once again when he saw that the closet was unlocked. He shook his head as he entered the small room and located the electrical panel. Incredible, he thought. If I were a taxpayer, I'd be outraged.

With the flip of a switch, the complex went dark. Then Simon reached into his pocket and took out his new toy, a pair of thermal infrared goggles. He turned on the device and adjusted the head strap so the binocular scope fit snugly over his eyes. It was a much better technology than the U.S. Army's night-vision scopes, which worked by intensifying faint visible light; the thermal goggles showed heat, not light, so they could operate in total darkness. On his display screen, the still-warm computers and monitors in the room glowed brightly while the cold steel door was jet-black. He could easily find his way to the staircase by following the cooling fluorescent lights that had just been shut off. Simon smiled in the darkness—he loved new technologies. Now he was ready to hunt down his quarry, the trim, athletic prisoner who'd reminded Simon of a frightened bird.

He descended two flights of stairs before he heard footsteps. Very quietly, he backtracked up the steps to the landing and pointed his Uzi at the entrance to the stairway. After a few seconds he saw three separate flashlight beams lancing down the corridor. This was not exactly a mistake on the agents' part; under the circumstances, they had little choice but to use their flashlights. Still, the result was the same. On the infrared display Simon saw a warm hand gripping a bright cylinder and a ghastly face that looked like it had been dipped in glow paint. Before the agent could aim the flashlight at him, Simon fired two rounds into his shining head.

A gruff voice yelled, "Cut the lights!" and the two other flashlight beams disappeared. Without making a sound, Simon came down the stairs, stepped over the body of the dead agent, and peered around the corner. Two figures crouched in the corridor, one about ten meters away and the other a little farther behind. The closer agent was in a shooting stance, holding his pistol with both hands and rapidly sweeping it back and forth, looking for a target in the darkness. The infrared image was so precise that Simon could see gray trails of cooler sweat dripping down his white face. Simon picked off the poor bastard with one shot to the forehead, but before he could take out the third agent, a bullet whizzed by his right ear.

Simon ducked around the corner as another bullet streaked past. The third agent was firing blindly in his direction. Not bad, he thought. At least this one has some spirit. He waited a few seconds, then peered down the corridor again to get a fix on his adversary. The agent had turned sideways to present a smaller target, and on the infrared screen Simon saw a thick, sturdy figure with trunk-like legs and a pair of massive breasts. He hesitated before raising his Uzi—the agent was a babushka! She could be Simon's grand-mother! And in that moment of hesitation she fired three more shots at him.

He flattened himself against the wall. Jesus, that was close! He raised his gun and prepared to return fire, but the babushka turned tail and vanished around a corner.

Simon was angry now. The old woman had humiliated him! He started to go after her, moving silently down the corridor. Before he got very far, though, he heard a muffled shout coming from somewhere behind him. He stopped in his tracks and spun around. He heard another shout, a distant but very loud male voice, so loud that it could be heard through the walls and across the complex: "Your heard me, Hawley! Open the goddamn door!"

With great reluctance Simon abandoned his pursuit of the ba-bushka. He'd take care of her later. Right now he had a job to do.

THE LIGHTS WENT OUT JUST as David slipped his hand into Lucille's jacket. He froze like a pickpocket caught in the act. Agent Hawley, standing guard outside the locked door, was equally surprised by the sudden blackout; David heard him cry, "Son of a—" before he stopped himself and went silent.

David took a deep breath. Okay, he thought. This doesn't change a thing. Whether the lights are on or off, I still have to get out of here. He pulled the silver flask out of the inside pocket of Lucille's jacket and set it gently on the table, being careful not to make a sound. Then he dug a little deeper and removed Lucille's Zippo. For a moment he considered lighting it so he could see what he was doing, but he knew that Hawley might notice the glow coming through the gap under the door. No, David had to do this blind. He put the lighter on the table, carefully memorizing its position. Then he reached for the Super Soaker.

Luckily, he'd become fairly expert at handling the water gun. He'd filled and refilled the gun's reservoir at least a dozen times when he was playing with Jonah just a few hours before, and now he could easily find the opening to the tank and take off the lid by touch. The memory of his afternoon with Jonah stopped him for a second, and his stomach clenched as he wondered if he'd ever see his son again. No, he told himself, don't think about it. Just keep going.

He grabbed the silver flask and unscrewed the cap. It held maybe seven or eight ounces of liquor, and as Lucille had promised, it was nearly pure alcohol—the fumes stung David's eyes as he poured the stuff into the Super Soaker. But was it enough? He needed at least a pint or so to generate the shooting pressure in the gun's second reservoir. Shit!

Even though the room was pitch-black, he closed his eyes so he could think. Water. There were two Dixie cups of water somewhere on that table. And you could dilute alcohol up to 50 percent and it would still burn. After some careful groping, he found one of the Dixie cups, fished out the dead cigarette and poured about three ounces of water into the tank. Then he located the other cup and poured in three more ounces. That was as much as he could risk. He hoped to hell it was enough.

David closed the gun's tank and quietly pumped the handle. In the darkness he pictured the alcohol/water mix streaming into the second reservoir and putting pressure on the air molecules inside. When he'd pumped as much as he could, he rotated the gun's nozzle until it was set on *Wide Blast*. The alcohol would burn more easily if it were scattered in droplets. Then he reached for the Zippo in its remembered spot, but just as he was about to grasp it he heard two sharp cracks echoing down the corridors of the complex. It was gunfire. Startled, he knocked the lighter off the table and it skittered into the darkness.

The room seemed to tilt. David felt like he was drowning at the bottom of a black ocean. He stared helplessly at the abyss into which the Zippo had fallen, and then he got down on his hands and knees and began groping for it. He methodically covered the whole area from the table to the walls, sweeping his arms in wide arcs across the cold linoleum, but he couldn't find the damn thing.

More gunshots echoed down the corridor, closer this time. David frantically scoured the floor, jamming his fingers into every corner. Jesus God Christ! Where the hell is it? Then he banged his head against one of the chairs, and as he reached under the table he felt the Zippo.

Trembling, he opened the lighter and spun the flint wheel. The flame arose like an angel, a small miracle from heaven. David leaped to his feet, grabbed the Super Soaker, and pointed it at the door. He heard a third burst of gunfire as he positioned the flame in front of the plastic nozzle, but he didn't flinch this time. "Hawley!" he shouted. "Open the door! You gotta let me out!"

A low voice hissed from the other side of the door. "Shut up, asshole!"

Hawley obviously didn't want to draw the attention of whoever was shooting nearby. But David had a feeling they were coming anyway. "You heard me, Hawley!" he bellowed. "Open the goddamn door!"

Several seconds passed. He's preparing himself, David thought. His position has become untenable and now he has to take the necessary steps. His only option is to kill me.

Then the door opened and David pulled the trigger.

SIMON CAME TO AN INTERSECTING corridor and saw yet another federal agent on the infrared screen. This one stood in front of a door, clutching the knob with one warm hand and holding a pistol in the other. Curious, Simon crept a little closer, keeping his Uzi trained on the man. The agent stood there for several seconds like a nervous suitor, muttering, "Son of a bitch, son of a bitch," as if to calm himself. Then he opened the door wide and reached into his pocket for a flashlight. All at once, a brilliant white plume erupted from the doorway.

Simon was blinded. The scorching plume expanded until it filled every corner of his screen, turning the display into a blank white rectangle. He tore off the useless goggles and ducked into a protective crouch, crossing his arms over his head. It was some sort of incendiary device, but it didn't smell like gasoline or white phosphorus. Oddly, it smelled more like homemade vodka. The fireball dissipated after a couple of seconds, leaving a few small, bluish flames rising from a puddle on the floor. The FBI agent staggered backward, then began rolling on the floor like a log, trying to extinguish the fringe of blue fire on his jacket.

Then Simon heard a quick series of rubbery squeaks. The noise was already moving past him by the time he realized what it was: the sneakers of the prisoner. Simon automatically raised his Uzi and pointed it in the direction of the rapid footsteps, but he didn't dare take a shot. He wanted the man alive. So he scrambled to his feet and started chasing him down the pitch-black corridor. Simon was just a few strides from tackling the man when he heard something clatter to the floor, something plastic and hollow, and in the next instant he stepped on the thing and lost his balance. It's that damn water gun, he realized as he tumbled backward. The base of his skull smacked against a door frame.

He lay there in the dark, stunned, for maybe ten or fifteen seconds. When he opened his eyes, he saw the still-smoldering FBI agent run right past him, rushing after the escaped prisoner. A true American idiot, Simon thought. Dedicated but oblivious. After taking a deep breath to clear his head, Simon stood up and put the thermal goggles back on. The display system had reset itself and the screen was working normally again. Then he picked up his Uzi and sprinted down the corridor.

✳   ✳   ✳

DAVID PLUNGED INTO THE DARKNESS, thinking of nothing but escape. He heard a loud thud behind him after he dropped the Super Soaker, but he didn't turn around, he just kept running. Without slowing down, he lit the Zippo again, and the flame illuminated a small circle around him. At first he saw nothing but blank walls on either side of the corridor, but then he spotted a gleaming red exit sign above a door to a stairway. He headed straight for it and rammed his shoulder against the door. To his dismay, it didn't budge. He tried the knob, but it didn't turn. Unbelievable! How could they lock an exit door? And as he stood there, fruitlessly jiggling the knob, he heard a distant roar—"Son of a bitch!"—and then the echoing footfalls of Agent Hawley.

David started running again. He made a left and raced down a different corridor, desperately searching for another stairway, another exit. He was scanning both sides of the hall and running as fast as he could when he tripped over something that felt like a sack of laundry. David relit his Zippo and saw that he was sprawled on top of a corpse. It was one of Hawley's gray-suited partners, with a pair of bloody holes in his forehead. Choking with horror, David leaped to his feet. Then he noticed that the body lay at the foot of a staircase.

A moment later Hawley rounded the corner and appeared at the end of the corridor. He went into a shooting stance as soon as he saw the Zippo, so David doused the light and dashed up the stairway. He climbed in the darkness, madly grabbing the railing and barking his shins on the steps, with Hawley just a few seconds behind him. After ascending three flights, he spied a faint yellow glow coming through a jagged doorway. He ran through a room full of smashed video monitors, then hurtled over two more corpses without a second thought. He was in a parking garage now and he could smell the sweetly polluted New York air. He bolted up the ramp toward the glorious streetlight.

But it was at least a hundred feet to the top of the ramp and there was nowhere to take cover, so he knew he was doomed when he looked over his shoulder and saw Hawley at the bottom of the slope. The agent had a big smile on his burned and blackened face. He slowly raised his Glock, taking careful aim. Then a shot rang out and Hawley crumpled to the ground.

David stared at the agent's body, which had collapsed into a fetal position. For a moment he thought someone was playing a joke on him. He was too confused to feel any relief and too scared to stop running. His legs carried him up the ramp and within seconds he stood on a deserted street overhung by office buildings. He read the sign on the corner: Liberty and Nassau streets. He was in Lower Manhattan, just three blocks north of the Stock Exchange. But he heard police sirens now, so he kept on moving, jogging west toward Broadway and the Hudson River.

BY THE TIME SIMON FINISHED off the charred FBI agent and reached the top of the ramp, half a dozen patrol cars were coming down Liberty Street. The babushka, he thought. She must have radioed the NYPD for backup. He ducked behind a shuttered newsstand as the cars screeched to a halt and the cops rushed into the parking garage. The prisoner was just a block ahead, at the corner of Broadway and Liberty, but Simon couldn't risk walking past all those police officers, not when he had an Uzi hidden under his windbreaker. So he slipped down Nassau Street instead and dashed one block north to Maiden Lane, hoping to intercept his quarry. When he reached Broadway, though, he saw no sign of the prisoner. Simon raced along the avenue, glancing down each of the side streets, but the man was nowhere in sight. *"Yobany v'rot!"* he cursed, smacking his thigh in frustration.

But his fury lasted only a moment. It's all about flexibility, he reminded himself. He just needed to adjust his strategy again.

Standing on the street corner, panting like a dog, Simon thought about the prisoner. There were only so many places he could go, and they were all fairly predictable. The first step was to identify the man and determine his connection to Professor Kleinman. Then it was just a matter of tracking down his contacts. Sooner or later, Simon knew, this fellow in sneakers would lead him to the *Einheitliche Feldtheorie*.

Simon caught his breath as he walked back to where he'd parked his Mercedes. He felt a grim satisfaction as he looked up at the skyscrapers on Broadway, the dark towers looming over the street. Very soon, he thought, all this will be gone.

Chapter Four

Lucille sat in a conference room at the FBI's office on Federal Plaza, speaking on a secure phone line with the Bureau's director. She'd evacuated the complex on Liberty Street and set up a temporary command post at the New York regional headquarters. All the off-duty agents in the area had been rousted from their beds and given new orders. And now, at fifteen minutes after midnight, Lucille handled the difficult task of delivering the bad news to her boss.

"They surprised us," she admitted. "First they eliminated logistics and disabled our communications. Then they cut off the power and went after the detainee. We lost six agents." Lucille was amazed she could report this so calmly. Six agents. What a fucking nightmare. "I take full responsibility, sir."

"Shit, who the hell did this? Did you get any video?"

"No, sir, unfortunately the surveillance systems were destroyed. But we have some idea who we're dealing with. They carried Uzis and used C-4. Probably had infrared scopes, too."

"Are you thinking Al-Qaeda?"

"No, it was too sophisticated for them. Maybe the Russians. Or maybe the Chinese or the North Koreans. Hell, it might even be the Israelis. It was a pretty slick operation."

"What about the detainee? You think he's in league with them?"

Lucille hesitated before answering. To be honest, she didn't know what to make of David Swift. "At first I would've said no. I mean, the guy's a history professor. No criminal record, no military service, no unusual travel or international phone calls. But he admitted that Kleinman gave him a numeric key, probably an encryption code for a computer file. Maybe they were trying to sell the information, but the deal went sour."

"What are the chances of getting him back? The secretary of defense is going nuts over this. He's calling me every half hour for an update."

She felt a twinge of distaste. The goddamn SecDef. He'd forced the Bureau to do the dirty work on this case, and yet he wouldn't reveal what it was all about. "Tell him it's under control," she said. "We got the New York police running checkpoints at the bridges and tunnels, with bomb-sniffing dogs to check for traces of C-4. We also have agents stationed at all the train and bus stations."

"Do you have a photo of the detainee? For identification purposes?"

"We got a driver's license photo from New York DMV and a photo from the jacket of some book he wrote. *On the Shoulders of Giants,* it's called. We're printing flyers now and we should be able to distribute them to our agents in the next hour or so. Don't worry, he ain't going nowhere."

DAVID RAN UPTOWN ALONG THE Hudson River. After his escape from the FBI agents, he had one overriding impulse: to get as far away as possible from the complex on Liberty Street. But he was too anxious to hail a cab or hop on a subway, too worried about being pulled over by a patrol car or stopped by a transit cop. So he ran up the bike path that paralleled the river, blending in with the late-night exercise fanatics, the joggers and cyclists and Rollerbladers adorned with gleaming reflective strips.

He made it all the way to Thirty-fourth Street, more than three miles away, before he slowed to a halt. Breathing hard, he leaned against a lamppost and closed his eyes for a moment. Christ, he whispered. Christ Almighty. This can't be happening. He'd spent five minutes listening to the dying words of a physics professor and now he was running for his life. And what had Kleinman said that was so goddamn important? *Einheitliche Feldtheorie.* Destroyer of worlds. David shook his head. What the hell was going on?

One thing was clear: The FBI agents weren't the only ones who wanted Kleinman's secret. Someone else had tortured the professor, someone else had attacked the complex on Liberty Street. And David had no idea who they were.

Alarmed by this thought, he opened his eyes and scanned the bike path. He couldn't stay here. He had to make a plan. He knew it would be unwise to go to his or Karen's apartment; the FBI probably had both places under surveillance by now. For the same reason, he couldn't risk going to any of his friends or colleagues either. No, he needed to get out of New York City. Get some cash, get on the road, maybe figure out a way to cross the Canadian border. He couldn't rent a car—the federal agents would quickly see the transaction on his credit card, then broadcast his license-plate number to every state trooper in the Northeast—but maybe, if he was lucky, he could get on a train or a bus without being noticed.

David found an ATM and withdrew as much cash as he could from his checking and credit-card accounts. The FBI would discover these transactions, too, but there was no avoiding it. Then he made a beeline for Penn Station.

As soon as he walked through the station's Eighth Avenue entrance, though, he knew he was too late. The area in front of the ticket windows was swarming with police officers and National Guardsmen. At the entrances to the tracks the cops were asking every passenger for identification, and bomb-sniffing German shepherds were inspecting every purse, briefcase, and pant leg. Cursing himself, David headed for the other side of the station. He should've gotten on a train an hour ago at the PATH station downtown.

As David approached the Seventh Avenue exit, a fresh wave of police officers suddenly poured into the concourse and formed a solid line blocking the stairways and escalators. Oh shit, David whispered. One of the cops pulled out a bullhorn. "Okay, people," he boomed. "Line up in front of the stairway and take out your drivers' licenses. We need to see some ID before you can leave the station."

Trying his best to look casual, David turned around and retraced his steps, but there were cops at the Eighth Avenue exits now, too. Exposed and panicky, he started looked for a hiding place, some newsstand or fast-food joint where he could duck in for a few minutes and gather his wits, but most of the shops on the concourse were closed for the night. The only places still open were a Dunkin' Donuts crowded with police officers and a dismal little bar called the Station Break. David hadn't seen the inside of a bar in years, and just the thought of entering the Station Break made his gorge rise. But this was no time to be picky.

Inside the bar, a dozen beefy, bearded guys in their twenties were cavorting around a table loaded with Budweiser cans. All the men wore identical custom-made T-shirts with the words PETE'S BACHELOR PARTY printed above a buxom silhouette. They were noisy as hell and had apparently driven everyone else out of the place except for the bartender, who stood behind the cash register with a disgusted frown. David took a seat at the bar, smiling, pretending nothing was wrong. "I'll have a Coke, please."

Without a word, the bartender reached for a cloudy glass and filled it with ice. David saw a pair of restroom doors at the far end of the bar but no emergency exit. There was a television on the wall, but the sound was turned off; a young blond anchorwoman stared soberly into the camera next to the words TERROR ALERT.

"Hey, she's fucking hot!" one of the bachelor partiers yelled. He staggered to his feet so he could get a better look at the anchorwoman. "Oh yeah! Read me the news, baby! Come on, read it to Larry! Larry wants the whole story, baby!"

While his friends laughed uproariously, Larry approached the bar. He had a gut the size of a beach ball hanging over his belt. His eyes were bloodshot and manic, his beard was sprinkled with bits of popcorn, and he smelled so strongly of Budweiser that David had to hold his breath. "Hey, bartender!" Larry yelled. "How much is a shot of Jagermeister?"

The bartender's frown deepened. "Ten dollars."

"Jesus H. Christ!" Larry thumped a fat fist on the bar. "That's why I never come into the fucking city anymore!"

Ignoring him, the bartender gave David his Coke. "That's six dollars."

Larry turned to David. "See what I mean? It's a fucking rip-off! It's three times more expensive than Jersey!"

David said nothing. He didn't want to encourage the guy. He had enough to worry about already. He handed the bartender a twenty.

"It's the same with the titty bars," Larry continued. "We just came from a place called the Cat Club? On Twenty-first street? The girls there wanted fifty bucks for a lap dance. Can you believe that? Fifty fucking bucks! So I said, Fuck this shit, let's go back to Metuchen. There's a club on Route 9, the Lucky Lounge? The girls there are just as good, and a lap dance is only ten bucks."

David wanted to strangle the guy. The police officers and Guardsmen were closing in, patrolling just outside the Station Break with their German shepherds and M-16s, but instead of planning a way out of this mess, David had to listen to this jerk from New Jersey. He shook his head in frustration. "Excuse me, but right now I'm—"

"Hey, what's your name, pal?" Larry stuck out his right hand.

David gritted his teeth. "It's Phil. Listen, I'm a little—"

"Good to meetya, Phil! I'm Larry Nelson." He found David's hand and pumped it vigorously. Then he pointed at his friends. "These are my buddies from Metuchen. See Pete over there? He's getting married on Sunday."

The bridegroom was slumped over the table, his head nearly hidden by the Budweiser cans. His eyes were closed and one side of his face was pressed flat against the tabletop, as if he were trying to hear the rumble of the trains pulling into the station. David grimaced. That was me twenty years ago, he thought. A stupid kid getting soused with his friends. The only difference was that David hadn't needed an excuse like a bachelor party to get hammered. During his last few months in graduate school, he drank himself into a stupor every night of the week.

"We were gonna take the twelve-thirty train back to Jersey," Larry added, "but then the cops started checking ID and the fucking line stretched all the way across the station and we missed the train. Now we gotta wait an hour for the next one."

"What if you don't have any ID?" David asked. "They won't let you on the train?"

"Nah, not tonight. We saw one guy, he said he left his wallet at home? The cops pulled him out of the line and took him away. It's one of those fucking terror alerts. Yellow alert, orange alert, I can't remember which."

David's stomach twisted. Jesus, he thought, I'll never make it out of here. The whole damn country is looking for me.

"The one good thing about all this," Larry added, "is that I don't have to work tomorrow morning. I got the evening shift this week, so I don't have to show up at the police station till four in the afternoon."

David stared at him for a moment, the unkempt beard, the beer belly. "You're a cop?"

He nodded proudly. "A dispatcher for the Metuchen PD. Just started two weeks ago."

Amazing, David thought. He'd found the one cop in the tristate area who wasn't searching for him. At first he saw only the oddness of this chance meeting, but after a few seconds he also saw the opportunity. He tried to remember what little he knew about New Jersey geography. "I live pretty close to Metuchen, you know. In New Brunswick."

"No shit!" Larry turned to his friends. "Hey, dudes, listen up! This guy's from New Brunswick!"

Several of them halfheartedly raised their beer cans in salute.

Their spirits were running down, David thought. They needed a pick-me-up. "Look, Larry, I'd like to do something for your friend Pete. In honor of his wedding and all. How about if I buy everyone a shot of Jagermeister?"

Larry's eyes widened. "Hey, that would be great!"

David got off his stool and held his hands straight up in the air as if he were a football referee calling a touchdown. "Jager shots for everybody!"

Suddenly revived, the bachelor partiers let out a whoop. When David turned to the bartender, though, the man didn't look too pleased. "Let's see the money first," he said. "It's gonna be a hundred thirty."

David pulled a thick roll of twenties out of his pocket and laid it on the bar. "Just keep 'em coming."

KAREN LAY IN BED NEXT to Amory Van Cleve, the managing partner of Morton McIntyre & Van Cleve, listening to the odd whistle that came from the sleeping lawyer's nostrils. This was the first time she'd noticed it, even though she'd been dating Amory for several weeks now. The whistle had three separate notes—F above middle C as he drew in a breath, dropping first to D and then to B flat as he exhaled. (Karen had studied music before going to law school.) After a while she realized why it sounded so familiar: they were the first three notes of "The Star-Spangled Banner." Karen suppressed a laugh. Her new boyfriend was just an old-fashioned patriot at heart.

He lay on his back with his manicured hands clasped over his chest. Karen slid closer to him, eyeing his full head of gray hair, his patrician nose and chin. He looked pretty damn good for a sixty-year-old, she decided. And even though he had some flaws besides the nocturnal whistle, even though his hearing was a bit weak and he wasn't the world's most vigorous lover, his good points made all these flaws seem trivial. Amory was dignified, mannerly, and cheerful. And best of all, he knew what Karen wanted. He knew what mattered to her. This was something that David had never seemed to grasp, despite three years of courtship and nine of marriage.

A siren moaned down Columbus Avenue. There seemed to be a lot of them tonight. Probably heading for a fire somewhere, or maybe a water-main break. She'd check the papers in the morning.

Of course she couldn't blame it all on David. Karen herself hadn't realized what she wanted until halfway through their marriage. When they'd met, she was a naive twenty-three-year-old, a piano student at the Juilliard School waging a losing battle against more talented contenders. David was five years older and already a successful professor in Columbia's History of Science program. Karen fell in love with him because he was funny and handsome and smart, and she began to imagine the future they would build together. After their wedding she abandoned Juilliard and enrolled in law school. Jonah's birth interrupted her studies for a year, but within a decade she was a senior associate at Morton McIntyre & Van Cleve, earning more than twice as much as her husband. Moreover, she knew exactly what she wanted now: a comfortable home for her family, a private school for her son, and a more prominent place in the city's social circles.

Karen could forgive David for not sharing these interests—he was a scientist at heart, so he didn't care about appearances. What she couldn't forgive was his complete disregard for her desires. He seemed to take a perverse pleasure in looking as disheveled as possible, wearing jeans and sneakers to his classes and letting days go by without shaving. Part of it was his chaotic upbringing, no doubt. He'd grown up with an abusive father and a beaten, cowering mother, and although he'd fought hard to overcome that trauma, his victory was only partial. David became a wonderful father to his own son, but a very poor husband. Whenever Karen brought up an idea, he squashed it. He wouldn't even consider moving to a bigger apartment or applying to private schools for Jonah. The breaking point came when he refused an offer to become chairman of the history department. The position would've given them an extra $30,000 a year, enough to renovate their kitchen or make the payments on a country home, but David turned it down because he said it would "interfere with his research." Karen gave up on him after that. She couldn't live with a man who wouldn't budge an inch for her.

Oh, stop thinking about David, she told herself. What was the point? She had Amory now. They'd already talked about buying an apartment. A place on the East Side would be a nice change. Maybe a three-bedroom in one of those Park Avenue buildings. Or a town house with a roof garden. It would cost a bundle, but Amory could afford it.

Karen was so busy envisioning the perfect apartment that she didn't hear the doorbell ring the first time. She heard the second ring, though, because it was accompanied by someone pounding on the door. "Mrs. Swift?" an urgent bass voice called. "Are you there, Mrs. Swift?"

She sat up in bed, her heart racing. Who on earth would come knocking at her door at this hour? And why were they using the married name she'd given up two years ago? Alarmed, she grabbed Amory's shoulder and gave him a shake. "Amory! Wake up! Someone's at the door!"

Amory rolled his head and mumbled something. He was a heavy sleeper.

"Open up, Mrs. Swift," another deep voice called. "This is the FBI. We need to speak to you."

The FBI? What was this, a practical joke? Then she remembered the phone call from a few hours ago, the call from the police detective asking for David. Was that it? Did David get himself into some kind of trouble?

She gave Amory another shake, a real solid one, and he opened his eyes. "What?" he croaked. "What is it? What's going on?"

"Get up! There's some men at the door! They say they're with the FBI!"

"What? What time is it?"

"Just get up and see who it is!"

Amory sighed, then reached for his glasses and got out of bed. He put a maroon bathrobe over his yellow pajamas and tightened the belt. Karen threw on an old T-shirt and stepped into a pair of sweatpants.

"This is your last chance!" a third voice bellowed. "If you don't open the door, we're knocking it down! Do you hear, Mrs. Swift?"

"Now, now, hold on!" Amory replied. "I'll be there in a moment."

Karen followed him out of the bedroom but hung back a few feet. While Amory went to the foyer, she instinctively positioned herself in front of the door to Jonah's bedroom. Her son, thank God, was a heavy sleeper, too.

Amory bent over a bit so he could peer through the peephole. "Who are you gentlemen?" he asked through the front door. "And what are you doing here so late?"

"We told you, this is the FBI. Open up."

"I'm sorry, but I need to see your badges first."

Karen stared at the back of Amory's head as he squinted into the peephole. After a few seconds, he looked over his shoulder at her. "They're FBI agents, all right," he said. "I'll see what they want."

Karen started to shout, "Wait, don't—" but she was too late. Amory unlocked the dead bolt and turned the knob. The next instant, the front door swung open and two enormous men in gray suits tackled Amory, throwing him down on his back and pinning him to the floor. Two more agents leaped over him and rushed into the apartment, a tall, broad-shouldered blond man and a thick-necked black man. It took Karen a second to realize that they were both pointing guns at her.

"Don't move!" the blond one shouted. His face was tense, pale, monstrous. Without taking his eyes off her, he gave his partner a hand signal. "Go check the bedrooms."

Karen took a step back. She felt the door of Jonah's bedroom against her spine. "Please, don't! I have a child! He's—"

"I said DON'T MOVE!" The blond man came toward her. The gun shook in his hand as if it had a life of its own.

Through the bedroom door she heard footsteps, then a weak, frightened "Mommy?" But the agents didn't seem to hear. Both of them were moving toward her now, their guns raised high and their eyes fixed on the door as if they were trying to see behind it. "STEP ASIDE!" the blond one ordered.

Karen stood there, paralyzed, not even breathing. Oh Jesus oh Jesus they're going to shoot him! Then she heard Jonah's footsteps right behind her and heard the brassy jiggling of the doorknob and in one swift motion she spun around and pushed the door open and threw herself on top of her son. "NO, NO!" she screamed. "DON'T HURT HIM!"

The agents stood over her, their massive frames filling the doorway, their guns pointed straight down, but it was all right, it was all right. She was covering every inch of Jonah's body with her own. The top of his head was nestled under her chin and his shoulders were pinioned beneath her breasts. She could feel him shaking in fear and confusion, crying "Mommy, Mommy!" against the wood floor. But he was safe.

While the blond agent stood guard above her, the black one went inside the bedroom and opened the closet door. "Clear!" he yelled. Then he proceeded to inspect the other rooms. In the background, beneath the sound of Jonah's crying and the agents' shouts, Karen could hear Amory's outraged voice. "What do you think you're doing?" he yelled. "You can't search the place without a warrant! This is a clear violation!"

After a few seconds, the black agent returned to give his report to the blond one, who seemed to be in charge. "No one else is here," he said. "And the old man doesn't fit the description."

The blond agent stepped away from her, moving into the foyer to confer with his partners. He put his gun back in its holster. Karen sat up, clutching Jonah to her chest, and shuddered with relief. Amory lay on his stomach a few feet away, his hands tied behind his back with some kind of plastic cord. "You're going to be sorry about this, gentlemen!" he yelled. "I'm on close terms with the U.S. attorney!"

The blond agent scowled at him. "Shut up, Grandpa," he said. Then he turned to Karen. "Where's your ex-husband, Mrs. Swift?"

Amazingly, Karen wasn't afraid anymore. Now that the agent had put his gun away, she felt nothing but contempt for him. "Is that why you burst in here? To look for David?"

"Just answer the—"

"You fucking bastard! You pulled a gun on a seven-year-old boy!"

While Karen glared at the FBI man, Jonah tugged the front of her shirt. His face was damp and splotchy. "Where's Daddy?" he cried. "I want Daddy!"

For a moment the agent seemed to falter. His Adam's apple bobbed as he gazed at Karen and Jonah huddled in the doorway. But soon his features hardened again. "David Swift is wanted for murder. We had to take the necessary precautions."

Karen raised her hand to her mouth. No, she thought. It's impossible. David had plenty of faults, but violence wasn't one of them. The most violent thing she'd ever seen him do was punch the inside of his softball glove after his team lost a game. He never let his feelings get out of control. He'd learned from his father what could happen otherwise. "That's a lie!" she said. "Who told you that?"

The agent narrowed his eyes. "I knew some of the men he killed, Mrs. Swift. Two of them were my friends." He stared at her for another second, cold and unflinching. Then he spoke into the microphone hidden inside the sleeve of his jacket. "This is Agent Brock. We got three to bring in. Contact headquarters and tell 'em we have a woman and a minor."

Karen tightened her hold on Jonah. "No! You can't do this!"

The agent shook his head. "It's for your own safety. Till we find your ex-husband." He reached into the pocket of his jacket and removed a couple of strips of plastic cord.

"HERE'S TO PHIL! You the man, Phil! You the fucking MAN!"

Around the table at the Station Break, the members of Pete's bachelor party raised their glasses of Jagermeister to toast David's alter ego, the generous Phil from New Brunswick. This was the third round of drinks that David had bought, and their spirits were now fully revived. Larry held a glass in each hand and chanted, "Phil! Phil! Phil!" before downing the two shots in quick succession. Even Pete, the drunken bridegroom, briefly lifted his head from the table to mutter, "You the man!" David responded in kind, throwing his arm around Pete and shouting, "No, YOU the man! You the MAN, you crazy fuck!" But though David bellowed and guffawed with the rest of them, he never let a drop of alcohol touch his lips. He surreptitiously slid his shot glasses toward Larry, who was only too happy to empty them.

After the chorus of You-the-Man's had died down, Larry staggered to his feet. "And don't forget Vinnie!" he yelled. "Here's to Vinnie, that pussy-whipped fuck, who couldn't be here tonight because his girlfriend thinks we're a bad fucking influence!"

Everyone shouted variations on "Fuck that bitch!" Meanwhile, Larry opened a plastic bag that lay on the table and took out a neatly folded blue shirt. It was one of the custom-made T-shirts that everyone else was wearing, with the words PETE'S BACHELOR PARTY printed on the front. "Look at this!" Larry boomed. "Because Vinnie couldn't make it, I got this extra fucking T-shirt on my hands!" He shook his head in disgust. "You know what I'm gonna do? I'm gonna make his fucking girlfriend pay for it!"

The partiers shouted, "Yeah, make the bitch pay!" and similar sentiments, but David just stared at the T-shirt. After some thought, he slammed his fist on the table to get everyone's attention. "I'll buy the T-shirt from you, Larry!" he announced. "How much is it?"

Larry seemed taken aback. "Aw, Phil, you don't have to. I mean, you already bought all these drinks and—"

"No, no, I insist! I want to buy it! I want to be an official member of Pete's fucking bachelor party!" He stood up and shoved a twenty-dollar bill into Larry's open hand. Then he grabbed the T-shirt and put it on, slipping it over his softball-team shirt.

Everyone cheered, of course. "Phil! Phil! Phil! Phil!" Then

someone yelled, "Hey, it's almost one-thirty, we're gonna miss the fucking train again!" and the bachelor partiers stumbled out of their seats. "Let's go!" Larry ordered. "We gotta get to the Lucky Lounge before it closes! Someone help Pete!"

While two of the partiers grabbed Pete by the elbows, David saw his chance. He shouted, "Wait for me!" in a slurred voice and then toppled to the floor, carefully breaking his fall with his outstretched palms.

Larry bent over him, stinking of Jagermeister. "Hey, Phil, you all right?"

"I'm a little . . . fucked up," David replied, trying to sound as drunk as possible. "Could you . . . gimme a hand?"

"Sure, buddy, no problem!" Larry grasped David's arm, picked him up, and steered him toward the door of the Station Break. David leaned against the big man's shoulder as they lurched out of the bar. Although David hadn't gotten drunk in nearly twenty years, he could easily imitate the swaying gait, the stooped posture. The memory of it was in his bones.

The station's concourse was nearly empty of commuters now but still teemed with police officers. Half a dozen cops stood in front of the entrance to Track 10, which was where the bachelor partiers were converging. Larry pumped his fist in the air as they approached the officers. "All right, NYPD!" he boomed. "We're behind you, man! Go get those fucking terrorists!"

"Yeah, go get the fuckers!" someone else shouted. "KILL 'EM ALL!"

A gaunt police sergeant held out his hands as if stopping traffic. "Okay, fellas, settle down," he said. "Just take out your driver's licenses."

David's stomach churned as the others pulled out their wallets. Okay, he thought. Here goes. He made a big show of patting his jeans pockets, first the front, then the back. "Shit!" he yelled. "Oh shit!" He fell to his hands and knees and began a dim-witted, drunken search of the floor.

Larry bent over him again. "What's wrong, Phil?"

"My wallet," David gasped, clutching Larry's shoulder. "Can't find . . . my fucking wallet."

"Did you leave it in the bar?"

David shook his head. "Shit . . . don't know . . . it could be . . . anywhere."

The police sergeant noticed the commotion and came over. "What's the matter here?"

"Phil lost his wallet," Larry told him.

With his mouth hanging open and his head lolling to the side, David looked up at the sergeant. "I don't . . . understand . . . it was . . . right here . . . a second ago."

The cop furrowed his brow. His mouth was a tight, grim line. Uh-oh, David thought. This one is a hard-ass. "You don't have any ID on you?"

"He's Phil," Larry explained. "From New Brunswick." He pointed at the "Pete's Bachelor Party" T-shirt. "He's with us."

The sergeant frowned. "You need ID to get on the train."

As if on cue, a high-pitched chime sounded from the station's speaker system. "Attention," a prerecorded voice announced. "Last call for the Northeast Corridor Line train boarding on Track Ten, with service to Newark, Elizabeth, Rahway, Metuchen, New Brunswick, and Princeton Junction. All aboard on Track Ten."

"We gotta get on that train!" Larry shouted. He frantically dug into the pocket of his pants and pulled out his own wallet, opening it for the police sergeant. "Look, I'm with the Metuchen PD. My badge is right here. I'm telling you, Phil's with us. He's my bud."

The sergeant looked at the badge, still frowning, still reluctant to give them a break. And at that moment David heard a dog barking. He turned his head and saw a National Guardsman and his German shepherd passing under the arrivals/departures board, about fifty feet away. The dog was heading straight toward them, pulling at his leash with such enthusiasm that the Guardsman had to lean backward to keep his balance. Oh Christ, David thought. The fucking animal can smell something on me.

He closed his eyes and a wave of nausea hit him. It's hopeless, he thought. They're going to arrest me and hand me over to the FBI and take me back to one of their interrogation rooms. He could see it in his mind's eye, the bare windowless room with the fluorescent lights overhead and the gray-suited FBI agents standing around the metal table. Another wave of nausea surged through him, and this one was so strong that David suddenly bent over double and let out a dry heave. A thin rope of saliva spilled from his mouth to the linoleum floor.

"Watch out!" Larry warned. "Phil's gonna hurl!"

The police sergeant quickly stepped back. "Ah, shit!" he cried. "Get him away from me!"

David lifted his head and looked up at the sergeant. The man was curling his lip, visibly repelled. On impulse, David stumbled closer to the officer and made a gagging noise, a wet guttural "Uhhhhhhhh!"

The sergeant pushed David away, shoving him toward Larry. "Fuck, get this guy out of here!" he yelled. "Go on, get him on the train!"

"Yes, sir!" Larry replied, grabbing David under the armpits. And together they rushed down the staircase to Track 10 and onto the one-thirty train to Metuchen.

SIMON SAT AT AN ANTIQUE desk in one of the preposterously over-priced suites at the Waldorf-Astoria. The hotel charged $2,000 a night for a stuffy parlor facing Park Avenue and a bedroom decorated like a czarist bordello. Simon was successful enough to afford the rate, but out of principle he refused to pay it; instead, he'd filched a credit-card number from one of the Internet's leaky conduits. An unsuspecting Oregonian named Neil Davison was paying for Simon's stay at the Waldorf, as well as for the rack of lamb and the half liter of Stolichnaya he'd ordered from room service.

As Simon knocked back another glass of vodka he stared at his laptop's screen, which displayed the Web page of Columbia University's physics department. Conveniently, the list of the department's faculty members included a color photograph of each professor, lecturer, and postdoctoral fellow. Simon slowly scrolled down the page, studying each face. It seemed logical to assume that Kleinman's accomplice would be a physics professor. The *Einheitliche Feldtheorie* would surely be too intricate for a layman to understand; one probably needed a thorough grounding in relativity theory and quantum mechanics just to recognize the mathematical terms in the revised field equations. And yet Simon didn't see the man in sneakers anywhere on the physics department's Web page. He proceeded to check the faculty listings of twenty other universities with prominent physics departments—Harvard, Princeton, MIT, Stanford, and so on—but still found no sign of his quarry among the photo galleries of smiling scientists. After an hour he slammed the laptop shut and tossed the empty bottle of Stoli into the trash. It was infuriating. All he needed was the man's name.

To calm himself, Simon went to the window and stared at the lights of Park Avenue. Even at two o'clock in the morning, the taxis were still streaming down the street. As he watched the cabs jockey for position, Simon wondered whether he'd missed something, some crucial biographical detail from Professor Kleinman's life that would reveal the identity of his associate. Perhaps the man was Kleinman's nephew or godson, or maybe the bastard child from some long-ago affair. Simon went to the closet, opened his duffel bag, and removed the book he'd used to track down Kleinman. It was a long book, more than five hundred pages, packed with useful information about all the physicists who'd assisted Albert Einstein in the last years of his life. *On the Shoulders of Giants,* it was called.

As Simon opened the book he caught a glimpse of something familiar. He turned to the inside flap of the back cover. There, just below a lavish blurb from *Library Journal,* was a photograph of the author.

Simon smiled. "Hello, David Swift," he said out loud. "It's a pleasure to meet you."

Chapter Five

DESPITE THE PLEADING OF LARRY, PETE, AND THE OTHER bachelor partiers, David declined to get off the train at the Metuchen stop. He said his wife would kill him if he didn't go straight home to New Brunswick, but he promised to join his new friends at the Lucky Lounge some other night. The whole drunken crew gave him high fives as they exited the train and chanted, "Phil! Phil! Phil! Phil!" as they stood on the platform. David acknowledged their cheers with a thumbs-up, then slumped back in his seat, exhausted.

As the train pulled away from the station, David began to shiver. The air-conditioning seemed unbearably cold. He folded his arms across his chest and rubbed his shoulders to warm himself, but he couldn't stop trembling. He recognized what was happening: it was a post-traumatic stress reaction, his body's delayed response to all the terrifying events of the past four hours. He closed his eyes and took several deep breaths. It's all right, he told himself. You're speeding away from New York now. You're leaving them all behind.

He opened his eyes when the train pulled into the New Brunswick station. He'd stopped shivering by now and he could think a little more clearly. He decided to stay on the train until it reached Trenton. Then he'd get on a Greyhound bus heading for Toronto. But as the doors closed and the train continued westward, David began to see the flaws in this plan. What if they were checking ID at the bus stations, too? He couldn't exactly count on finding another bachelor party. And by the time the bus reached the Canadian border, the police would probably be looking for him there as well. No, taking a bus was too risky, unless he could get his hands on a fake driver's license. And how the hell was he going to manage that?

Too agitated to sit, David started pacing the aisle of the nearly empty train car. There were only three other passengers: a pair of teenage girls in short skirts and an elderly man in an argyle sweater, speaking quietly into his cell phone. For a moment David considered calling Karen and Jonah on his own phone, but he knew that as soon as he turned on the device, it would send a signal to the closest cellular tower and the FBI would know where he was. What made it so frustrating was that David was getting worried about his ex-wife. He had a feeling that the men in gray suits might try to question her.

Soon the conductor announced, "Now arriving at Princeton Junction. Service here to Princeton via the Princeton Branch Line." It was the repetition that did it, the three *Princeton*s in a row. David immediately thought of someone who could help him. He hadn't seen this person in almost twenty years but he knew she still lived in Princeton. There was little chance that the FBI would be waiting for him at her house; although the Bureau had obviously done a thorough investigation of his past, he doubted that they'd uncovered anything about her. Best of all, she was a physicist, one of the pioneers of string theory. David suspected that only a physicist could make any sense of the story he had to tell.

The train came to a stop and the doors opened. David stepped onto the platform and walked toward the branch-line track that led to Princeton University.

BACK IN 1989, WHILE DAVID was still a graduate student in physics, he attended a conference at Princeton on string theory. At the time, the scientific community was abuzz with the new idea because it promised to resolve a long-standing problem. Although Einstein's theory of relativity explained gravity to perfection, and quantum mechanics could account for every nuance of the subatomic world, the two theories were mathematically incompatible. For thirty years

Einstein had tried to unify the two sets of physical laws, with the aim of creating a single overarching theory that could explain all the forces in nature. But all of Einstein's published solutions turned out to be flawed, and after his death many physicists concluded that his quest had been misguided. The universe, they said, was just too complex to be described by a single set of equations.

Starting in the 1970s, though, some physicists revived the idea of a unified theory by hypothesizing that all the fundamental particles were actually minuscule strings of energy, each less than a trillionth of a trillionth of a millimeter long. By the 1980s, the string theorists had refined their model by claiming that the strings vibrated in ten dimensions, six of which were curled into manifolds too small to see. The theory was indefinite, incomplete, and incredibly unwieldy, and yet it fired the imaginations of researchers all over the world. One of them was Monique Reynolds, a twenty-four-year-old grad student in Princeton's physics department.

David saw her for the first time at the closing session of the conference, which was held in a large auditorium in Jadwin Hall. Monique stood on the stage, getting ready to deliver a presentation on multidimensional manifolds. What he noticed first was how tall she was, a full head taller than the wizened chairman of the physics department, who introduced Monique as "the brightest young student I've ever had the pleasure of working with." David wondered if perhaps the old man had grown overly fond of her, because in addition to being tall, this woman was beautiful. Her face was like one of the ancient portraits of Athena, the Greek goddess of wisdom, but instead of a helmet she wore a crown of intricately woven cornrows, and her skin was the color of a Kahlúa and cream. A long dress made from yellow-and-red Kente cloth draped her shoulders, and several gold bracelets hung from each of her brown arms. In the drabness of Jadwin Hall she blazed like a particle shower.

Women physicists were uncommon enough in the 1980s, but a black female string theorist was a rare phenomenon indeed. The scientists in the auditorium regarded her as they would any other rare phenomenon, with a mixture of awe and skepticism. As soon as she began her presentation, though, they accepted her as one of their own, because she spoke their language, the abstruse tongue of mathematics. Moving to the blackboard, she scribbled a long sequence of equations, each crowded with the symbols representing the fundamental parameters of the universe: the speed of light, the gravitational constant, the mass of the electron, the strength of the nuclear force. Then, with an ease that David could only envy, she manipulated and transformed the dense thickets of symbols until they condensed into a single, elegant equation that described the shape of space around a vibrating string.

David couldn't follow every step of her argument; by this point in his graduate career he'd realized the limits of his own mathematical abilities, and usually he felt an overwhelming frustration and jealousy when he witnessed the skills of a genius like Monique. But as she worked her magic on the blackboard and calmly answered the questions of her colleagues, David felt no bitterness whatsoever. Without a struggle, he surrendered to her powers. After she finished her presentation, he jumped out of his seat and made his way to the stage so he could introduce himself.

Monique raised her eyebrows when David mentioned his name. A look of surprise and pleasure crossed her face. "Sure, I know you!" she exclaimed. "I just read the paper you did with Hans Kleinman. Relativity in a two-dimensional spacetime, right? That was a nice piece of work."

She clasped his hand and gave it a squeeze. David was dumbfounded—he couldn't believe she'd actually read his paper. "Well, it's nothing, really," he replied. "Not compared with your work, I mean. Your presentation was absolutely amazing." He tried to think of a more intelligent comment, but he came up blank. "I was blown away. I really was."

"Oh Lord, stop!" She let out a laugh, a wonderful high-pitched swoop. "You're making me feel like a movie star!" Then she moved a step closer to him and lightly rested her hand on his forearm, as if they were old friends. "So you're at Columbia, right? How's the department over there?"

Their conversation continued for the next several hours, moving first to the faculty lounge, where David met some of the other grad students in Princeton's department, and then to a local restaurant called the Rusty Scupper, where the small group of budding physicists ordered margaritas and debated the relative merits of chiral and nonchiral string theories. After a few drinks David admitted to Monique that he hadn't understood some parts of her presentation, and she was happy to fill the gaps in his comprehension, patiently explaining each mathematical procedure. After a few more drinks he asked her how she got interested in physics, and she told him it was all because of her father, a man who never got past ninth grade himself but was always devising interesting theories about the world. By midnight David and Monique were the last customers left in the restaurant, and by 1 A.M. they were groping each other on the couch in Monique's tiny apartment.

For David, this sequence of events was fairly typical. He was in the middle of the six-month drinking binge that had clouded his second year in graduate school, and when he was drinking with a woman he usually tried to go to bed with her. And though Monique was more intelligent and beautiful than most of the women he'd slept with, she was typical in other ways—she was impulsive, lonely, and seemed to be hiding some unhappiness. So everything was progressing along the usual lines, but as Monique got up from the couch and unzipped her Kente dress, letting it fall to her ankles in a colorful heap, something went wrong. As soon as David saw her naked body, he started crying. It was so sudden and unaccountable that at first David thought it was happening to Monique, not him. He thought, Why is she crying? Did I do something wrong? But no, she wasn't crying. The sobs were coming from his own throat, and the tears were running down his own cheeks. He quickly got to his feet and turned away from her, humiliated. Christ, he thought, what the hell is happening to me?

After a few seconds he felt Monique's hand on his shoulder. "David?" she whispered. "Are you all right?"

He shook his head, trying desperately to hide his face. "I'm sorry," he muttered, stepping away from her. "I better go."

But Monique held on to him. She wrapped her arms around his waist and pulled him closer. "What's wrong, baby? You can tell me."

Her skin was soft and cool. He felt something give inside him, and all at once he knew why he was crying. Compared with Monique Reynolds, he was worthless. The week before, he'd failed his comprehensive exams, which meant that Columbia's physics department would soon ask him to leave the graduate program. The drinking had certainly contributed to his failure—it's pretty much impossible to understand quantum field theory when you're chronically hungover—but even if he'd been stone-cold sober for the whole semester, he doubted that the result would have been any different. What was worse, his father had predicted this would happen. When he'd visited the old man two years before, in the seedy hotel room that John Swift had occupied since his release from prison, he'd laughed when David told him about his plans to become a physicist. "You'll never be a scientist," his father had warned. "You'll just fuck it up."

But David couldn't reveal any of this to Monique. Instead he unclasped her hands from his waist. "I'm sorry," he said again. "But I have to go."

He kept crying as he walked away from Monique's apartment and across the darkened Princeton campus. You idiot, he muttered, you fucking idiot. It's the booze, all the goddamn booze. You can't think straight anymore. He stopped near one of the college's under-graduate dorms and leaned against the Gothic stone building for a minute to clear his head. No more drinking, he told himself. You've had your last drink.

But when he got back to New York the next day, the first thing he did was go to the West End Tavern on Broadway and order a shot of Jack Daniel's. He hadn't bottomed out yet. It wasn't until two months later, after he'd been officially kicked out of Columbia's physics program, that he descended to a level of degradation that was awful enough to make him quit drinking forever.

In the following years, as David straightened out his life and pursued his doctorate in history, he occasionally thought about getting in touch with Monique to explain what had happened. But he never did. In 2001, he came across an article about her in *Scientific American.* She was still at Princeton and still pursuing string theory, which had advanced considerably since the 1980s but remained just as indefinite, incomplete, and unwieldy as ever. Monique was now exploring the possibility that the extra dimensions predicted by string theory were not curled into infinitesimal manifolds but lay behind a cosmic barrier that prevented us from seeing them. David was less interested in the physics, though, than in the biographical details revealed in the last few paragraphs of the article. Monique, as it turned out, had grown up in Anacostia, the poorest neighborhood in Washington, D.C. Her mother had been a heroin addict and her father had been shot to death in a robbery when she was just two months old. David felt an ache in the center of his chest as he read this. She'd told him that her father had inspired her to become a physicist, but she'd never actually known the man.

David thought about Monique again after his marriage fell apart, and a few times he came close to calling her. But each time he put down the phone and Googled her instead, typing her name into the search engine and checking out the Web sites that popped up. He'd learned this way that she was now a full professor of physics, that she'd participated in a Web chat about African history, and that she'd run the New York Marathon in three hours and fifty-two minutes, a very respectable time for a forty-three-year-old woman. His best discovery, though, was a photograph of Monique in the online version of the *Princeton Packet,* which showed her standing in front of a modest two-story house with a large front porch. David recognized the place immediately: it was 112 Mercer Street, the house where Albert Einstein had lived for the last twenty years of his life. In his will, Einstein had insisted that the house not be turned into a museum, so it remained a private residence for professors associated with Princeton's Institute for Advanced Study. The caption below the photo noted that Professor Reynolds had recently moved into the home, replacing a faculty member who'd retired.

That's where David headed as he got off the train at the Princeton station. He crossed the darkened campus again, clean and sober now but still desperate, and he doubted that Monique would be happy to see him.

LUCILLE WAS ON THE PHONE with her agents in Trenton when the secretary of defense barged into the conference room. She was so surprised she nearly dropped the receiver. She'd met the SecDef just once before, at a White House ceremony announcing a new counterterrorism initiative, and they'd exchanged only a handshake and a few pleasantries. But now the man loomed right in front of her, his square head cocked at a belligerent angle, his small eyes squinting disapproval behind his rimless glasses. Although it was three o'clock in the morning, his thin gray hair was neatly combed and his tie hung ramrod straight from an impeccable Windsor knot. A two-star air-force general trailed behind him, carrying the secretary's briefcase.

"Uh, I'll call you back," Lucille said into the phone. She hung up and dutifully rose to her feet. "Mr. Secretary, I—"

"Sit down, Lucy, sit down." He waved her back to her seat. "No need for formalities. I just wanted to see for myself how the operation was going. The air force was kind enough to fly me to New York."

Great, Lucille thought. It would've been nice if someone had warned me. "Well, sir, we think we have a fix on the detainee. We have information that he's in New Jersey now and we're—"

"What?" The secretary leaned forward and turned his head to the side, as if he were trying to compensate for a bit of deafness in one ear. "I thought you had the guy pinned down in Manhattan. What about all the checkpoints at the bridges and tunnels?"

Lucille shifted uncomfortably in her seat. "Unfortunately, there was a delay in getting David Swift's photo to the police. Once we distributed the flyers, an officer assigned to Penn Station recognized the suspect. He said Swift boarded a New Jersey Transit train at about one-thirty."

"How did he get on the train? Did he have false papers?"

"No, the suspect apparently joined a group of men who were rushing aboard. A bunch of drunk yahoos, basically. In the confusion, the officer failed to check for ID."

The secretary frowned. The left corner of his mouth turned down like a fishhook. "That's inexcusable. If this were a real army, that officer would be shot. He'd be executed at dawn by the members of his own unit."

Lucille was unsure how to respond. She decided to ignore the bizarre comment entirely. "I just spoke with our agents in New Jersey. They boarded the train at the Trenton station but didn't find the suspect. Now we're looking into the possibility that Swift got off the train with the drunk guys. The officer at Penn Station said they were from Metuchen."

"That doesn't sound very promising. What other leads do you have?"

"We've positioned surveillance teams at the residences of Swift's colleagues in Columbia's history department. Several of them live in New Jersey, so there's a good chance he may go to one of them for help. And we brought in Swift's ex-wife for questioning. She's downstairs with her son and her boyfriend, an older fellow named Amory Van Cleve. We're going to—"

"Wait, what did you say his name was?"

"Amory Van Cleve. He's a lawyer, the managing partner of Morton McIntyre and—"

"Jesus!" The secretary raised his hand to his forehead. "Don't you know who that is? Van Cleve was one of the biggest contributors in the last election, for Christ's sake! He raised twenty million dollars for the president's campaign!"

Lucille stiffened. She didn't like the sound of this. "Sir, I'm just following the orders of the Bureau's director. He told me to pursue this case with all due vigor, and that's what I'm doing."

Grimacing, the secretary took off his glasses and pinched the bridge of his nose. "Believe me, Lucy, I want you to be aggressive. I want you to throw everything you have at this case. This project is one of the Pentagon's top priorities. If the information should fall into the hands of the Iranians or the North Koreans, the consequences would be catastrophic." He put his glasses back on and squinted at her, his eyes like a pair of snipers. "But you can't use the standard interrogation techniques on someone like Amory Van Cleve. He's one of the top Republican fund-raisers in the country. When the president was up here last spring, they played golf together!"

"Well, what do you suggest, sir?"

He looked over his shoulder at the air-force general. Without a word, the man opened the briefcase, pulled out a folder, and handed it to the secretary, who began leafing through its contents. "Okay, it says here that this guy Swift has a history of substance abuse."

"He had a drinking problem when he was in his twenties," Lucille clarified.

The SecDef shrugged. "Once a drunk, always a drunk. We can say that the guy moved on to cocaine, and he's been dealing the stuff to the rich brats at Columbia. The Bureau was about to arrest him at his crack house in Harlem, but he and his friends managed to surprise the agents and kill half a dozen of them. How's that for a cover story?"

Lucille tried to think of a diplomatic answer. "There's a few problems. First of all, the Bureau wouldn't ordinarily—"

"I don't need to know the details. Just fix up the story and give it to Van Cleve and the ex-wife. Maybe they'll lose enough sympathy for Swift that they'll tell us where he might be hiding. And give the same story to the press, too. That way we can get a nationwide manhunt going."

Lucille shook her head. Christ on a crutch. Keeping the SecDef informed was one thing, but taking orders from him was another. What made this bozo think he could run a law enforcement operation? "I don't know if that's the right approach," she said. "Maybe we should contact the director of the Bureau and—"

"Don't worry, the director will go along with it. I'm gonna talk to him as soon as I get back to Washington." He closed the folder and handed it back to the air-force general. Then he turned on his heel and headed out of the conference room, with the general following close behind.

Lucille stood up, indignant. "Hold on a minute, Mr. Secretary! I think you should reconsider!"

He didn't even turn around. He just raised his arm in farewell as he marched out the door. "No time for second-guessing, Lucy. You go to war with the army you have."

DAVID HAD VISITED EINSTEIN'S HOME on Mercer Street once before, when he was writing *On the Shoulders of Giants*. Because it was a faculty residence, the house wasn't open to the public, but after David made a special request explaining his purposes, the Institute for Advanced Study had granted him permission for a half-hour visit. It turned out to be invaluable to his research. He spent most of his allotted time in the study on the second floor, which was where Einstein did nearly all his work in his final years. Three of the room's walls were lined with floor-to-ceiling bookshelves and the fourth had a picture window overlooking the backyard. David had felt a strange giddiness as he gazed at the desk by the window. His mind stretched back half a century and he could practically see Einstein hunched over that desk, scratching away with his fountain pen for hours on end, filling page after page with spacetime metrics and Ricci tensors.

Approaching the house in darkness now, David saw that the

grounds had been spruced up sometime in the past decade. Someone had put flowerpots on the front porch and pruned the unruly
vine that had once spiraled around the drainpipe. Very quietly, David walked up the porch steps to the front door. He pressed the
doorbell, which was surprisingly loud, and waited. To his dismay, no
lights came on. After half a minute, he rang the bell again, listening
carefully for signs of life inside the house. Shit, he thought, maybe
no one's home. Maybe Monique went away for the weekend.

Growing desperate, he was about to press the bell a third time
when he noticed something odd: the door frame had recently been
rebuilt. The new jambs were still unpainted and a new lock had been
installed in the door, its brass keyhole gleaming. The workmanship
seemed hasty and slipshod, very different from the tidy appearance
of the rest of the house. But before he could ponder this any further,
he heard someone yell, "Hey, asshole!" just a few feet behind him.

David spun around and saw a barefoot, bare-chested young
man coming up the porch steps. Dressed only in a pair of jeans,
he had long blond hair and impressive pectoral muscles, but the
thing that really caught David's attention was the baseball bat in
his hands. "Yeah, I'm talking to you," the man said, unnecessarily.
"What the hell are you doing? Making sure no one's home?"

David stepped away from the door, holding his hands out to show
they were empty. "I'm sorry to bother you so late. I'm David—"

"Sorry? You say you're sorry? You're gonna be a hell of a lot
sorrier in a minute, dickface."

As soon as the man reached the top step, he swung the bat at
David. It sliced the air just inches from his head, coming so close he
could hear it whistle. "Jesus!" he cried, backing away. "Stop it! I'm a
friend!"

The man kept coming. "You're not my friend. You're a fucking
Nazi." He drew back the bat and prepared to swing again.

There was no time to think, so David's instincts took over. He
knew how to fight. His father had taught him the fundamental rule:
Don't be afraid to fight dirty. He stayed out of range until the blond

guy swung the bat, then rushed forward and kicked him in the nuts. As the guy doubled over, David slammed a forearm into his chest, knocking him over. His bare back hit the porch with a resounding slap, and as he struggled to catch his breath David wrenched the bat out of his hands. Within three seconds, it was all over.

David leaned over the now-prostrate man. "Okay, let's try it again," he said. "I'm sorry to bother you so late. My name is—"

"Freeze, motherfucker!"

David looked up and saw Monique in the doorway, pointing a gun at him. Her gorgeous eyes glowered as she held the snub-nosed revolver in both hands. A bright yellow nightshirt hung down to her thighs and swayed gently in the night breeze. "Drop the bat and step away from him," she ordered.

David did as he was told. He let the bat clatter to the porch and took three steps backward. "Monique," he said. "It's me, David. I'm—"

"Shut the fuck up!" She kept the gun pointed at his head, obviously not recognizing him. "Keith, are you all right?"

The bare-chested man propped himself up on his elbows. "Yeah, I'm okay," he said, but he sounded a bit woozy.

"Monique, it's me," David repeated. "David Swift. We met at Strings '89, when you delivered your paper on Calabi-Yau manifolds."

"I told you to shut up!" she yelled, but David could tell he'd gotten her attention. Her brow furrowed.

"David Swift," he said again. "I was a grad student at Columbia. Relativity in a two-dimensional spacetime. Remember?"

Her mouth opened in recognition, but as David had predicted, she wasn't pleased. If anything, she seemed angrier now. She frowned as she lowered the revolver and flipped the safety switch. "What the hell's going on? Why did you come here in the middle of the night like this? I almost blasted your head off."

"You know this guy, Mo?" Keith asked. He managed to rise to his feet.

She nodded. "I knew him in graduate school. Barely." With a flick of her wrist she opened the gun's cylinder and dumped the bullets into her palm.

A light came on in the house next door. Shit, David thought. If we don't quiet down, someone's going to call the cops. He gave Monique a beseeching look. "Listen, I need your help. I wouldn't have bothered you if it wasn't important. Can we go inside and talk?"

Monique kept frowning. After a few seconds, though, she let out a sigh. "Ah hell. Come in. I won't be able to get back to sleep anyway."

She held the door open for him. Keith picked up the bat and for a moment David thought he was going to take another swing at him, but instead he shook his hand. "Hey, man, I'm sorry," he said. "I thought you were one of those Nazi assholes. They've been giving Mo some trouble."

"Nazis? What are you talking about?"

"You'll see when we get inside."

David stepped through the doorway into a small living room with a brick fireplace on one side and a bay window on the other. He remembered from his previous visit that a handsome wood mantelpiece hung above the fireplace, but now it looked like someone had taken an ax to it. The varnished shelf was scored with deep gouges along its whole length. The fireplace itself had been vandalized, too; at least a dozen bricks had been dug out or chipped off. The living room's walls were pocked with gaping holes that must have been made with a sledgehammer, and the floorboards had been ripped up in several places, creating dark, jagged craters underfoot. Worst of all, there were swastikas everywhere: carved into the mantelpiece, chiseled into the remaining floorboards, spray-painted on the walls. A pair of large red swastikas had been painted on the ceiling somehow, and between them were the words NIGGA GO HOME.

"Oh no," David whispered. He turned to Monique, who'd put the gun and bullets on the mantelpiece and was now staring at the ceiling.

"Skinhead punks, probably high school kids," she said. "I've seen them hanging out at the bus stop, in their leather jackets and Doc Martens. They probably saw the picture of me in the newspaper and thought, oh boy, here's our big chance. A nigger bitch living in the house of the world's most famous Jew. What could be better?"

David winced. "When did this happen?"

"Last weekend, when I was visiting some friends in Boston. The fuckers were clever about it. They waited till no one was home, then they pried open the front door. They didn't spray-paint the outside walls because they knew someone might spot them from the street."

David thought of the study on the second floor. "Did they vandalize the upstairs rooms, too?"

"Yeah, they hit almost every part of the house. They even tore up the lawn in the backyard. Luckily, they left the kitchen alone and they didn't do too much damage to the furniture." She pointed at a black leather sofa, a chrome coffee table, and a bright red Barcelona chair, all items that had obviously never belonged to Einstein.

Keith stepped over one of the holes in the floor, his thumbs hooked in the front pockets of his jeans. David noticed now that he had a tattoo of a rattlesnake on his left shoulder and the fresh, earnest face of a twenty-one-year-old. "When we heard you ring the bell, we thought it was one of the punks again, checking to make sure the house was empty. We figured the kids would just run away if we turned on the lights, so I went out the backdoor to surprise 'em."

Monique slipped her arm around Keith's waist and leaned her head against his tattooed shoulder. "Keith's a sweetheart," she said. "He's stayed with me every night this week."

Keith responded by grasping Monique's hip and kissing the top of her head. "What else could I do? You're my best customer." He turned to David, a big smile on his youthful face. "See, I work on Mo's car. At the Princeton Auto Shop. She's got a bitchin' Corvette, but it's temperamental."

David stared at them for a moment, confused. Monique, a re-nowned string theorist, was dating her car mechanic? It seemed so unlikely. But he quickly dispelled the thought from his head. He had bigger things to worry about. "Monique, could we sit down somewhere? I know this is a bad time for you, but I'm in a lot of trouble right now, and I need to figure out what's going on."

She raised an eyebrow and looked at him carefully, as if sensing for the first time how desperate he was. "We can go in the kitchen," she said. "It's a mess but at least there's no swastikas."

The kitchen was large and modern; it had been added to the house a few years before to replace the cramped galley kitchen where Einstein's second wife, Elsa, had once cooked. A wide marble-topped counter ran under a bank of cabinets, and a round table sat in a breakfast nook. But though the kitchen was big even by subur-ban standards, every available space was filled to overflowing with boxes, books, lamps, and knickknacks that had been displaced from other parts of the house. Monique led David to the breakfast table and removed a stack of books from one of the chairs. "Sorry about this," she said. "I had to move some stuff down here because the study is such a disaster area."

David helped her clear the table and chairs. As he carried a stack of books to the windowsill, he recognized one of the volumes near the top. It was *On the Shoulders of Giants*.

Monique let out an exhausted groan as they sat down. Then she turned to Keith, gently placing her hand on his knee. "Baby, could you make some coffee? I'm dying for a cup."

He patted her hand. "Sure thing. Colombian Supremo, right?"

She nodded, then watched him walk to the coffee machine on the other side of the kitchen. Once he was out of earshot, she leaned across the table toward David. "All right. What's the problem?"

WHEN SIMON WAS IN THE Spetsnaz, fighting the Chechen insurgents, he'd learned a useful technique for locating the enemy. It could be summed up in ten words: to find someone, you have to know what he wants. A Chechen rebel, for example, wants to kill Russian soldiers, so you should look for him in the mountains near military bases. Very simple. But with David Swift, there was a complicating factor: the Americans were looking for him, too. Assuming this history professor had any sense at all, he'd steer clear of his apartment and his office at Columbia and any other place where the FBI might be waiting. So Simon had to improvise again. With the help of the Internet, he began an investigation into David Swift's secret desires.

At 3 A.M. he was still staring at his laptop in the overpriced suite at the Waldorf-Astoria. He'd managed to hack into Columbia's internal network and soon made a fortunate discovery: the network administrator was monitoring the Internet activity of the faculty members, probably to make sure they weren't watching porn during office hours. Simon chuckled—the Soviets would've loved this. And better yet, the activity records weren't even encrypted. With a few keystrokes he was able to download the URLs of every Web site David Swift had visited in the past nine months.

A long list of Web addresses ran down the laptop's screen, 4,755 in all. Too many to examine individually. But there was a way to shorten the list: look at the Google searches only. What you search for reveals what you desire, Simon thought. Google was the new window on the human soul.

Simon found 1,126 searches. Still too many, but now he could focus on the search terms. He had a program on his laptop that could identify the Christian names in any sample of text. An analysis of the remaining URLs showed that David Swift had typed a name in 147 of his searches. Now the list of Web addresses was short enough that Simon could inspect each one, but Swift had made the job much easier for him. There was only one name that appeared more than once. On three separate dates since September, David Swift had searched for someone named Monique Reynolds. And when Simon did the search himself, he quickly saw why.

He called the hotel's reception desk and told the concierge to have his Mercedes ready in five minutes. He was going to New Jersey to visit the last home of the wandering Jew from Bavaria.

DAVID TOOK A DEEP BREATH. "Hans Kleinman's dead," he started. "He was murdered tonight."

Monique jerked backward in her chair as if she'd been struck. Her lips parted, forming a bewildered *O*. "Murdered? How? Who did it?"

"I don't know. The police said it was a burglary gone bad, but I think it was something else." He paused. His theory about the professor's murder was sketchy at best, and he was even less sure how to explain it to Monique. "I talked to Kleinman in the hospital just before he died. That's how this whole nightmare started." He was about to tell her what had happened at the FBI complex on Liberty Street, but he stopped himself. Better take it slow. No need to frighten her just yet.

She shook her head, staring blankly at the polished surface of the kitchen table. "Lord," she whispered. "This is awful. First Bouchet and now Kleinman."

The first name gave David a jolt. "Bouchet?"

"Yeah, Jacques Bouchet of the University of Paris. You know him, don't you?"

David knew him well. Bouchet was one of the grand old men of French physics, a brilliant scientist who'd helped design some of Europe's most powerful particle accelerators. He was also one of Einstein's assistants in the early fifties. "What happened to him?"

"His wife called the director of the Institute today. She said Bouchet died last week and she wanted to set up an endowment in his honor. The director was surprised because he hadn't seen Bouchet's obituary anywhere. His wife said the family had kept it quiet because it was a suicide. Apparently he slit his wrists in the bathtub."

David had interviewed Bouchet as part of his research for *On the Shoulders of Giants*. They'd shared a magnificent dinner at the physicist's country home in Provence and played cards until three in the morning. He was a wise, funny, carefree man. "Was he sick? Is that why he did it?"

"The director didn't say anything about that. But he did mention that the wife sounded very distraught. Like she still couldn't believe it."

David's mind began to race. First Bouchet and now Kleinman. Two of Einstein's assistants dying within a week of each other. Of course they were all quite old now, in their late seventies and early eighties. One would expect them to start dying off. But not this way.

"Do you have a computer I can borrow?" he asked. "I need to check something on the Web."

Looking confused, Monique pointed at a black laptop sitting beside a box on the kitchen counter. "You can use my MacBook, it's got a wireless connection. What are you looking for?"

David moved the laptop to the table, turned it on, and called up Google's home page. "Amil Gupta," he said as he typed the name into the search engine. "He also worked with Einstein in the fifties."

In less than a second the search results appeared on the screen. David quickly scrolled down the list. Most of the entries were about Gupta's work at the Robotics Institute at Carnegie Mellon University. In the 1980s, after he'd spent thirty years as a scientist, Gupta abruptly left the world of physics and started a software company. Within a decade he was worth several hundred million dollars. He became a philanthropist, donating his money to various quirky research projects, but his main interest was artificial intelligence. He gave $50 million to the Robotics Institute and a few years later became its director. When David had interviewed Gupta, it had been a real struggle to keep him on the subject of Einstein. All he wanted to talk about was robots.

David scanned at least a hundred search results before he satisfied himself that there was no terrible news about Gupta. But it wasn't much comfort. He could be dead already but no one had discovered the body yet.

As he stared at the laptop's screen, Keith came to the table holding a mug of coffee in each hand. He gave one to David. "Here you go," he said. "You want milk or sugar with that?"

David took the mug gratefully. His mind was crying out for caffeine. "No, no, black is fine. Thanks."

Keith handed the other mug to Monique. "Listen, Mo, I'm gonna head upstairs. I gotta be at the shop at eight tomorrow." He put his hand on her shoulder and leaned over a bit, bringing his face close to hers. "You gonna be all right?"

She squeezed his hand and smiled. "Yeah, I'll be fine. Go get some rest, baby." She kissed his cheek and then patted him on the butt as he walked off.

David studied her face as he gulped down his coffee. Easy to see how she felt. She was obviously fond of the hunk. And even though Monique was twenty years older than her boyfriend, she seemed just as young at that moment. Her face had hardly changed since the last time David had seen her, on the couch in her tiny grad school apartment.

After a few seconds, Monique noticed he was staring at her. Embarrassed, David brought the coffee mug to his lips and drank half of it in great scalding swallows. Then he set it down on the table and turned back to the laptop. He had one more name to check. He typed *Alastair MacDonald* into the search engine.

MacDonald was the unluckiest of Einstein's assistants. In 1958, he suffered a nervous breakdown and had to leave the Institute for Advanced Study. He went home to his family in Scotland, but he never recovered; he started behaving erratically, shouting at passersby on the streets of Glasgow. A few years later he attacked a policeman, and his family had him committed to an asylum. David visited him there in 1995, and although MacDonald shook his hand and sat down for an interview, he said nothing in response to

David's questions about his work with Einstein. He just sat there and stared straight ahead.

A long list of results came up on the screen, but on close inspection they turned out to be different people—Alastair Mac-Donald the Scottish folksinger, Alastair MacDonald the Australian politician, and so on. No sign of Alastair MacDonald the physicist.

Monique stood up and looked over his shoulder. "Alastair MacDonald? Who's he?"

"Another of Einstein's assistants. This guy sort of fell off the map, so it's hard to find any information about him."

She nodded. "Oh yeah, you mentioned him in your book. The one who went crazy, right?"

David felt a flush of pleasure. She'd read *On the Shoulders of Giants* pretty carefully. He went to the windowsill, picked up Monique's copy of his book, and opened it to the chapter about MacDonald. He found the name of the asylum, Holyrood Mental Institution, then bent over the laptop and typed the words into the search engine, right next to *Alastair MacDonald*.

Only one result came up, but it was recent. David clicked on the Web address and an instant later a page from the online version of the *Glasgow Herald* appeared on the screen. It was a brief news item dated June 3, just nine days ago.

INQUIRY AT HOLYROOD

The Scottish Executive Health Department announced today that it would conduct an inquiry into a fatal accident at the Holyrood Mental Institution. One of the residents, 81-year-old Alastair MacDonald, was found dead in the facility's hydrotherapy room early Monday morning. Department officials said MacDonald drowned in one of the therapy pools after leaving his room sometime during the night. The department is seeking to determine if lapses in supervision by the night-shift staff contributed to the accident.

David shivered as he stared at the screen. MacDonald drowned in a therapy pool, Bouchet slit his wrists in a bathtub. And he remembered now what Detective Rodriguez had told him at St. Luke's Hospital: the police had found Kleinman in his bathroom. The three old physicists were linked not only by their history with Einstein, but by a horrible modus operandi. The same bastards who'd tortured Kleinman to death had also killed MacDonald and Bouchet, disguising their murders as an accident and a suicide. But the motive, what was the motive? The only clues were Kleinman's last words: *Einheitliche Feldtheorie.* Destroyer of worlds.

Monique leaned against David so she could read the news brief over his shoulder. Her breath quickened as she took it all in. "Shit," she whispered. "This is very strange."

David turned around and looked her in the eye. Ready or not, it was time to present his hypothesis. "What do you know about Einstein's papers on unified field theory?"

"What?" She took a step backward. "Einstein's papers? What does that—"

"Just bear with me for a second. I'm talking about his attempts to derive a field equation that incorporated gravity and electromagnetism. You know, his work on five-dimensional manifolds, post-Riemannian geometry. How familiar are you with those papers?"

She shrugged. "Not very. That stuff is only of historical interest. It doesn't have any relevance to string theory."

David frowned. He'd hoped, perhaps unrealistically, that Monique would know the subject backward and forward, so she could help him examine the possibilities. "How can you say that? There's definitely a connection with string theory. What about Einstein's work with Kaluza? They were the first to postulate the existence of a fifth dimension. And you've spent your whole career studying extra dimensions!"

She shook her head. The expression on her face was that of a long-suffering professor explaining the basics to an ignorant fresh-man. "Einstein was trying to come up with a classical theory. A the-ory with strict cause and effect and no weird quantum uncertainties. But string theory derives from quantum mechanics. It's a quantum theory that includes gravity, and that's completely different from what Einstein was working on."

"But in his later papers, he took a new approach," David ar-gued. "He was trying to integrate quantum mechanics into a more general theory. Quantum theory would be a special case in a larger classical framework."

Monique waved her hand dismissively. "I know, I know. But in the end, what came of it? None of his solutions held up. His last papers were total nonsense."

David's face warmed. He hated her tone. Maybe he wasn't a mathematical genius like Monique, but this time he knew he was right. "Einstein discovered a working solution. He just didn't pub-lish it."

She cocked her head and gave him a quizzical look. The cor-ners of her lips turned up ever so slightly. "Oh, really? Did someone send you a long-lost manuscript?"

"No, that's what Kleinman told me before he died. He said, '*Herr Doktor* succeeded,' those were his exact words. And that's why he was killed tonight, that's why all of them were killed."

Monique heard the urgency in his voice and her face turned se-rious. "Look, David, I understand you're upset, but what you're sug-gesting is impossible. There's no way Einstein could've formulated a unified theory. All he knew about was gravity and electromagne-tism. Physicists didn't understand the weak nuclear force until the sixties and they didn't figure out the strong force until ten years later. So how could Einstein come up with a Theory of Everything if he didn't understand two of the four fundamental forces? It's like building a jigsaw puzzle without half the pieces."

David thought about it for a moment. "But he wouldn't have to know all the details to construct a general theory. It's more like a crossword puzzle than a jigsaw. As long as you have enough clues, you can figure out the pattern, and then you can fill in the blank spaces later."

Monique was unconvinced. David could see from the look on her face that she thought the idea was absurd. "Well, if he came up with a valid theory, why didn't he publish it? Wasn't that his lifelong dream?"

He nodded. "Yes, it was. But all this was happening just a few years after Hiroshima. And even though Einstein had nothing to do with actually building the atom bomb, he knew that his equations had pointed the way. $E = mc^2$, huge amounts of energy from tiny bits of uranium. It was agonizing for him. He once said, 'If I knew they were going to do this, I would have become a shoemaker.'"

"Yes, yes, I've heard all this before."

"Well, think about it for a minute. If Einstein did find a unified theory, wouldn't he worry that the same thing might happen again? He knew he had to figure out the implications of the discovery, all the possible consequences. And I think he foresaw that the theory could be used for military purposes. Maybe to create something even worse than a nuclear bomb."

"What do you mean? What could be worse?"

David shook his head. This was the weakest link in his argument. He had no idea what the *Einheitliche Feldtheorie* was, let alone what it could unleash. "I don't know, but it must've been something terrible. Bad enough that Einstein decided he couldn't publish the theory. But he couldn't abandon it either. He believed physics was a revelation of God's handiwork. He couldn't just erase the theory and pretend it never existed. So he entrusted it to his assistants. He probably gave each one a little piece of the theory and told them to keep it safe."

"What good would that do? If the theory was so terrible, his assistants couldn't publish it either."

"He was thinking of the future. Einstein was a hopeless optimist. He really thought that in a few years the Americans and

Russians would lay down their arms and form a world government. Then war would be outlawed and everyone would be at peace. And his assistants just had to wait until that day before revealing the theory." Unexpectedly, David's eyes began to sting. "They waited their whole lives."

Monique gave him a sympathetic look, but she clearly didn't believe a word of what he said. "It's an extraordinary hypothesis, David. And extraordinary claims require extraordinary proof."

David steeled himself. "Kleinman told me a series of numbers when I saw him in the hospital tonight. He said it was a key that Einstein had given him, and now he was giving it to me."

"Well, that's hardly—"

"No, that's not the proof. The proof is what happened afterward."

Then he told her about his interrogation at the FBI complex and the massacre that followed. At first she just stared at him, incredulous, but as he described how the lights went out and the gunfire echoed down the corridors, she unconsciously gripped the hem of her nightshirt and bunched it in her fist. By the time he finished, Monique seemed just as shell-shocked as he'd been when he emerged from the parking garage on Liberty Street. She grabbed his shoulder. "My God," she whispered. "Who attacked the place? Were they terrorists?"

"I don't know, I never saw them. I just saw the dead FBI agents. But I bet they're the same people who killed Kleinman and Bouchet and MacDonald."

"How do you know? Maybe the FBI killed them. It sounds like the government and the terrorists are after the same thing."

He shook his head. "No, the FBI would've taken them in for questioning. What I think happened is that the terrorists found out about the unified theory first. Maybe Kleinman or Bouchet or MacDonald let something slip. So the terrorists went after them, torturing each one for information. But after they started turning up dead, the American intelligence agencies must've figured out that something was going on. That's why the FBI agents showed up so quickly at the hospital. They probably had Kleinman under surveillance."

David's voice had risen as he outlined the scenario, and his last words rang against the walls of the kitchen. Catching himself, he looked at Monique to see her reaction. Her face was no longer quite so skeptical, but she still wasn't convinced. She let go of his shoulder and stared again at her laptop, which had by now reverted to its screen saver, an animation of a rotating Calabi-Yau manifold. "It doesn't make sense," she said. "I mean, maybe you're right about the killings, maybe the terrorists were going after Kleinman and the others because of some secret project they were all working on. But I can't believe the project was a unified field theory that Einstein's assistants had been hiding for fifty years. It's just too implausible."

He nodded again. He could understand her disbelief. It wasn't simply a preference for quantum over classical theories. Her whole life's work was at stake here. David was suggesting that all the accomplishments that she and her fellow string theorists had achieved over the past two decades, all the painstaking advances and hard-won insights and brilliant reformulations, were irrelevant. A scientist who'd died before most of them were born had already captured their ultimate prize, the Theory of Everything. And this possibility was, to put it mildly, a little hard to accept.

He turned away from Monique, wondering how to convince her. He had an extraordinary claim but no extraordinary proof. He didn't even have much in the way of ordinary proof. As he stared at the blank walls of the kitchen, though, a new thought occurred to him. It wasn't a pleasant thought; in fact, it was so abhorrent that his heart started knocking against his breastbone. But it was evidence.

"Look around," he said, turning back to Monique and pointing at the walls and cabinets. "Look at this kitchen. There's no damage here, no graffiti. Not a single swastika."

She gazed at him, uncomprehending. "Yeah? So?"

"Why would a bunch of New Jersey skinheads trash every room in this house except the kitchen? Doesn't that seem a little odd?"

"What does this have to do with—"

"There weren't any skinheads, Monique. Somebody tore this place apart to look for Einstein's notebooks. They searched under the floorboards and dug holes in the backyard and poked through the plaster to check the spaces between the walls. And they put swastikas everywhere to make it look like vandalism. They didn't touch the kitchen because it was added to the house long after Einstein died, so he couldn't have hidden anything there. And they didn't touch your furniture for the same reason."

Monique raised her hand to her mouth. Her long slender fingers touched her lips.

"If I had to guess," David continued, "I'd say it was the FBI that did the search. The terrorists wouldn't have bothered to wait until you'd left the house for the weekend. They would've just killed you in your sleep. And I'd also guess that the agents didn't find any notebooks. Einstein was too clever for that. He wouldn't have left anything in writing."

Although Monique's hand covered the lower half of her face, David could still observe the change in her expression. First her eyes widened in fear and surprise, but within seconds they narrowed and a deep vertical crease appeared between her eyebrows. She was livid, absolutely furious. Neo-Nazi skinheads were bad enough, but federal agents who would spray-paint swastikas on the wall to cover up a clandestine operation? That was another class of evil entirely.

She finally lowered her hand and grabbed David's shoulder again. "What were the numbers Kleinman gave you?"

SIMON HAD NO TROUBLE GETTING across the Hudson River. There was a checkpoint at the entrance to the Lincoln Tunnel, where a pair of police officers ordered him to roll down his window and a bomb-sniffing dog poked its snout into the car, but Simon had changed his clothes at the Waldorf and showered every trace of C-4 off his skin, so the German shepherd just gazed dumbly at the steering wheel. Simon showed the officers his ID—an expertly forged New York State driver's license—and they waved him through.

Five minutes later he was on the New Jersey Turnpike, racing along the causeway that spanned the dark, dank Meadowlands. He could drive as fast as he liked because the highway was nearly empty at four o'clock in the morning and all the state troopers were assisting the New York police at the bridges and tunnels. So he tore past Newark Airport at ninety miles per hour, then banked west toward the sprawling Exxon refinery.

It was the deadest part of night, the very bottom. Up ahead, the distillation towers of the refinery rose from the blackness. A gas fire streamed from one of the flare stacks, but the flames were thin and flickering, as weak as a pilot light. The road seemed to darken as Simon sped by the maze of pipes and petroleum tanks, and for a few seconds he felt like he was traveling underwater. On the blank screen of his mind he saw two faces, the faces of his children, but it wasn't the comforting image he'd saved on his cell phone. In this picture, Sergei and Larissa weren't smiling. Sergei's eyes were closed as he lay in a muddy ditch, his arms streaked with long black burns and his hair caked with blood. But Larissa's eyes were wide open as if she were still alive, as if she were still staring in horror at the fireball that had engulfed her.

Simon hit the accelerator and the Mercedes leaped forward. He soon reached Exit 9 and barreled onto Route 1 South. He'd be in Princeton in fifteen minutes.

40 26 36 79 56 44 7800

DAVID WROTE THE NUMBERS IN PENCIL on a sheet of notebook paper. He passed it to Monique and immediately felt a powerful urge to snatch the paper back and tear it to shreds. He was afraid of those sixteen digits. He wanted to destroy them, bury them, erase them forever. But he knew he couldn't. He had nothing else.

Monique held the paper in both hands and scrutinized the numbers. Her eyes darted from left to right, looking for patterns, progressions, geometric sequences. On her face was the same focused stare that David had seen when she delivered her paper on Calabi-Yau manifolds at the string theory conference. Like the face of the goddess Athena preparing for battle.

"The distribution looks nonrandom," she noted. "There are three zeroes, three fours and three sixes, but only a single pair, the pair of sevens. In a numeric sequence of this size, it's improbable to have more triplets than pairs."

"Could it be a key for decrypting a computer file? Kleinman used the word *key*, so that would be logical."

She kept her eyes on the numbers. "The size is about right. Sixteen digits, and each can be transformed to four bits of digital code. That would make sixty-four bits in all, which is the standard length for an encryption cipher. But the sequence has to be random for the technique to work." She shook her head. "With a nonrandom sequence, you could break the code too easily. Why would Kleinman choose an imperfect key like that?"

"Well, maybe it's a different kind of key. Maybe it's more like an identifying label. Something to help us find the file instead of decrypt it."

Monique didn't respond. Instead she brought the paper a little closer to her face, as if she were having some difficulty reading the numbers. "You wrote this sequence in an odd way."

"What do you mean?"

She turned the sheet of paper around so he could see it. "The numbers are bunched up a bit. Slightly wider spaces after every second digit. Except at the end, where the spacing is even."

He took the paper from her. She was right, the first twelve digits were arranged in two-digit blocks. He hadn't consciously written it that way, but there it was. "Huh," he grunted. "That *is* odd."

"Did Kleinman specify this grouping when he gave you the sequence?"

"No, not exactly." He closed his eyes for a moment and saw Professor Kleinman again, sitting up in his hospital bed as he choked out his last words. "His lungs were failing, so the numbers came out in gasps, two at a time. And that's the way I see the sequence in my memory now. A half-dozen two-digit numbers and a four-digit number at the end."

"But is it possible that the grouping was intentional? That Kleinman wanted you to organize the numbers that way?"

"Yeah, I suppose. But how does that change things?"

Monique grabbed the paper and placed it on the kitchen table. Then she found a pencil and drew lines between the two-digit blocks.

40/26/36/79/56/44/7800

"If you order the sequence this way, it looks even less random," she said. "Forget about the four-digit number for now and just look at the two-digit numbers. Five of the six are between twenty-five and sixty. Only the seventy-nine falls outside that range. That's a fairly tight grouping."

David stared at the numbers. They still looked pretty random to him. "I don't know. It looks like you're doing some picking and choosing to make a pattern."

She frowned. "I know what I'm doing, David. I've spent a lot of time studying data points from particle-physics experiments, and I know a pattern when I see one. For some reason the numbers are clustered in a narrow band."

He stared at the sequence again and tried to see it from Monique's point of view. Okay, he thought, the numbers seem to be clustered below sixty. But couldn't this simply be a chance arrangement? To David's eye, the sequence looked just as random as the winning numbers for the New York Lotto, which he played from time to time despite the pitifully bad odds. The lottery numbers also tended to cluster below sixty, but that was only because the highest number you could pick was fifty-nine.

And then he saw it, clear as day. "Minutes and seconds," he said.

Monique didn't seem to hear. She stayed bent over the kitchen table, studying the sequence.

"You're looking at minutes and seconds," he said, a little louder this time. "That's why the numbers are below sixty."

She looked up at him. "What? You're saying this is some kind of time measurement?"

"No, not time. These are spatial dimensions." David gazed at the sequence once more and now its meaning opened up like a flower, with all six of its petals perfectly arranged. "They're geographic coordinates, latitude and longitude. The first two-digit number is angular degrees, the second is arc minutes, and the third is arc seconds."

Monique stared at him for a moment, then turned to look at the numbers. Her face broke into a smile, one of the loveliest smiles David had ever seen. "All right, Dr. Swift," she said. "It's worth a shot."

She went to her laptop and started tapping the keyboard. "I'll punch in the coordinates on Google Earth. Then we can get a look at the place." She found the program and typed in the numbers. "I'm assuming the latitude is forty degrees north, not south. Otherwise you'd be somewhere in the Pacific Ocean. And for longitude, I'm assuming it's seventy-nine degrees west, not east."

David stood beside her so he could see the laptop's screen. The first image that came up was a grainy satellite photo. At the top was a large building shaped like an *H* and at the bottom was a row of smaller buildings shaped like *L*s and plus signs. The structures were too big to be houses but not tall enough to be office towers. And they weren't arrayed in a street grid or located next to a highway; instead, most of the buildings were situated at the periphery of a long rectangular courtyard crisscrossed by walkways. A campus, David thought. It was a college campus. "Where is this place?"

"Hold on, I'll call up the street map." Monique clicked on

an icon that put labels on each of the buildings and streets. "It's in Pittsburgh. The coordinates are centered on this building right here." She tapped a point on the screen and squinted to read the label. "The address is 5000 Forbes Avenue. Newell-Simon Hall."

David recognized the name. He'd visited the building once before. "That's at Carnegie Mellon. The Robotics Institute. Where Amil Gupta is."

Monique tapped a few more keys and found the institute's Web site. She clicked on the page that contained the list of faculty members. "Check out the phone numbers," she said, looking over her shoulder at David. "Everyone has a four-digit extension beginning with seventy-eight."

"What's Gupta's extension?"

"His personal line is 7832. But he's the director of the institute, right?"

"Yeah, for the past ten years."

"Look at this. The extension for the director's office is 7800." She beamed in triumph. "Those are the last four digits in Kleinman's sequence."

She was so exhilarated by their success that she pumped her fist in the air. But David just stared at the faculty list on the laptop's screen. "Something's wrong," he said. "This can't be the right message."

"What are you talking about? It makes perfect sense. If Einstein really did come up with a unified theory, he probably told Gupta about it, too. Kleinman was telling you to go to Gupta to safeguard the theory. It's obvious!"

"That's the problem. The message is too obvious. Everyone knows that Gupta worked with Einstein. The FBI knows it, the terrorists know it, there's a whole goddamn chapter about it in my book. So why did Kleinman go to all the trouble of devising this complicated code if that's the only thing he wanted to say?"

She shrugged. "Shit, you're asking the wrong person. I have no idea what was going through Kleinman's head. Maybe this was the best plan he could think of."

"No, I don't believe it. Kleinman wasn't stupid." He grabbed the sheet of paper with the sixteen numbers. "There's got to be something else hidden in this sequence. Something we're missing."

"Well, there's only one way to find out. We have to talk to Gupta."

"We can't call him. I'm sure the feds have tapped his phone by now."

Monique turned off her laptop and closed the screen. "Then we have to go to Pittsburgh."

She took the laptop to the kitchen counter and zipped it into a leather carrying case. Then she found a small overnight bag and began filling it with various items from the kitchen cabinets and drawers: a battery charger, a Totes umbrella, an iPod, a box of SnackWell's. David watched her in alarm. "Are you crazy? We can't just show up at Gupta's house! The FBI probably has the place under surveillance. Unless they've already shipped him off to Guantánamo." Or unless the terrorists have already tortured him to death, he thought. "Either way, we won't get anywhere near him."

Monique zipped up the overnight bag. "We're two smart people, David. We'll figure out a way." Holding the bag in one hand and the laptop case in the other, she headed out of the kitchen.

David followed her into the living room. "Wait a second! We can't do this! The police are already hunting for me! It was a miracle that I even got out of New York!"

She stopped in front of the vandalized fireplace and rested her bags on the floor. Then she picked up the revolver from the mantelpiece and flicked open the cylinder. The vertical crease had reappeared between her eyebrows, and her mouth was a tight grim line. "Look up there," she said, pointing her gun at the two red swastikas on the ceiling and the words NIGGA GO HOME. "Those assholes broke into my house—*my house!*—and wrote this shit on my walls. You think I'm gonna let them get away with that?" She scooped up the bullets from the mantelpiece and began dropping them, one by one, into the cylinder's chambers. "No, I'm gonna get to the bottom of this. I'm gonna figure out what's going on here and then I'm gonna make those motherfuckers pay."

David focused on the revolver in Monique's hands. He didn't like the looks of this. "That gun's not going to do you any good. They've got hundreds of agents and thousands of cops. You can't just shoot your way through."

"Don't worry, I'm not planning to start any gunfights. We're going to be sneaky, not stupid. No one knows you're with me, so the FBI won't be looking for my car. You just keep your face hidden and we'll be all right." She inserted the last bullet into its chamber and closed the cylinder. "Now I'm going upstairs to get some clothes. You want me to get you a razor from Keith's shaving kit?"

He nodded. He couldn't argue with her anymore. She was like a force of nature, unyielding and unstoppable, bending the whole fabric of spacetime around her. "What are you going to tell Keith?"

Monique picked up both bags with one hand and carried the gun in the other. "I'll just leave him a note. I'll tell him we had to go to a conference or something." She went to the foyer and started climbing the staircase. "He won't get too upset about it. Keith's got three other girlfriends he can spend time with. The boy has amazing stamina."

He nodded again. So her relationship with Keith wasn't that serious. David found, to his surprise, that he was quite pleased by this fact.

SIMON WAS TEARING DOWN ALEXANDER ROAD, just half a mile from Einstein's house, when he saw the flashing lights in his rearview mirror. It was a blue-and-white patrol car from the Princeton Borough Police Department. *"Yob tovyu mat!"* he cursed, slamming his fist against the steering wheel. If this had happened just a minute earlier, when he was on Route 1, he would've simply stepped on the gas—his Mercedes was an SLK 32 AMG, which could easily outrun any American-made car—but now he was on the local streets and there was too great a chance of getting trapped. He had no choice but to pull over.

He stopped on the shoulder of a deserted stretch of road, about fifty meters from the entrance to a county park. No houses or stores nearby and no traffic on the street. The patrol car stopped about ten meters behind him, leaving its headlights on, and just sat there for several infuriating seconds. The officer inside was probably radioing a description of Simon's vehicle to his dispatcher. Finally, after half a minute, a brawny man in a blue uniform stepped out of the police car. Simon tilted his side-view mirror so he could examine the officer. A young fellow, twenty-five years old at the most. Muscular arms and shoulders, but a bit pudgy around the waist. Probably spends most of his shift sitting in his car, waiting for drunk undergraduates to speed by.

Simon rolled down his window as the officer approached the Mercedes. The young man rested his hands on the driver's-side door and leaned in to the car. "Mister, do you have any idea how fast you were going?"

"One hundred forty-three kilometers per hour," Simon replied. "More or less."

The officer frowned. "This isn't a joke. You could've killed somebody. Give me your license and registration."

"Certainly." Simon reached into his jacket. He had a forged driver's license but no registration for the Mercedes, which he'd stolen from a dealership in Connecticut two days before. So instead of grasping his wallet, he pulled out his Uzi and shot the officer in the forehead.

The man tumbled backward. Simon started the Mercedes and peeled off. In a few minutes some passing motorist would notice the body and within half an hour the Princeton police would be searching for his vehicle. But that was all right. He didn't plan to stay in town very long.

KEITH WAS DREAMING ABOUT MONIQUE'S CORVETTE. She'd brought the car into the shop and told him it was running hot, but when he lifted the hood he saw the engine was missing. That guy David Swift was curled up where the engine block should have been. Keith turned to Monique to ask her what was going on, but she playfully darted behind him.

He felt a hand on his shoulder. This was real, not a dream. A hand gripped his shoulder and gently rolled him onto his back. Must be Monique coming back to bed, he thought. Probably wants a little loving. She was a good lay but needy as hell. "Ah, Mo," he groaned, keeping his eyes closed. "I told you, I gotta wake up early."

"You're not David Swift."

The unfamiliar voice jolted him awake. He opened his eyes and saw the silhouette of a bald head and a thick neck. The man's hand had shifted to Keith's throat and was now pressing down hard, pinning him to the bed. "Where are they?" he asked. "Where did they go?"

The fingers curled around Keith's windpipe. He lay there, immobile, too terrified to resist. "Downstairs!" he rasped. "They're downstairs!"

"No, they're not."

Keith heard a rustling in the darkness and saw a quick flash. It was a long straight blade reflecting the bluish light of dawn that was coming through the bedroom window.

"All right, my friend," the man said. "We're going to have a little talk."

Chapter Six

KAREN PACED INSIDE AN INTERROGATION ROOM AT THE FBI offices in Federal Plaza. First she walked past the steel door, locked from the outside. Then she passed a mirror that ran almost the whole length of the wall, most likely a one-way mirror allowing agents on the other side to view the interrogations. Finally she marched by a blue-and-gold sign with a picture of an eagle and the words FEDERAL BUREAU OF INVESTIGATION—PROTECTING AMERICA. Several chairs surrounded a metal table in the center of the room, but Karen was too agitated to sit. Instead she circled the room at least fifty times, dizzy with fear and outrage and fatigue. The agents had taken Jonah away from her.

At 5 A.M. she heard footsteps in the corridor outside the locked door. A key turned in the lock, and a moment later the agent who'd arrested her stepped into the room. Tall, blond, and muscle-bound, he still wore that ugly gray jacket with the shoulder holster bulging underneath. Karen remembered his name as she charged toward him: Agent Brock. The bastard had handcuffed a seven-year-old boy. "Where's my son?" she demanded. "I want to see my son!"

Brock stretched out his hands as if to catch her. He had cold blue eyes. "Whoa, slow down! Your son's all right. He's asleep in one of the rooms down the hall."

Karen didn't believe it. Jonah had screamed like a banshee when the agents pulled him out of her arms. "Take me there! I need to see him right now!"

She tried to move around Brock to get to the door, but the agent sidestepped in front of her. "Hey, I said slow down! You can see your son in a minute. I have to ask you a few questions first."

"Look, I'm a lawyer, all right? I may not practice criminal law, but I know this is illegal. You can't hold us here without charges."

Brock grimaced. He obviously didn't care for lawyers. "We can file charges if that's what you want. How about criminal child neglect? Does that sound legal enough for you?"

"What? What are you talking about?"

"I'm talking about your ex-husband's drug habit. And how he financed it by selling cocaine to his students at Columbia. He did most of his dealing in Central Park just after he picked up your son from school."

Karen just stared at him. It was the most ludicrous thing she'd ever heard. "That's insane! The worst thing they do in the park is play with Super Soakers!"

"We have surveillance videos showing the transactions. According to our sources, Swift has been running this business for years."

"Jesus Christ! I would've known if David was dealing dope in the park!"

Brock shrugged. "Maybe, maybe not. One thing's for sure, though: the Family Court will want to find out whether you were involved, too. They may decide to take custody of your son until they investigate the matter."

Karen shook her head. Brock was lying. As a corporate lawyer, she earned her keep by negotiating merger agreements, and she could usually tell when the other side was bluffing. "Okay, prove it. Show me those surveillance videos."

Brock moved a step closer. "Don't worry, you'll see them on the news tonight. You see, your ex-husband wanted to expand his business, so he started working with the Latin Kings. I assume you've heard of them?"

She looked askance. "You're saying that David made friends with a bunch of gangsters?"

"The Latin Kings control the drug trade in Upper Manhattan. They're also the fuckers who killed our agents last night. They shot three agents who were doing an undercover buy from Swift and another three who were part of the surveillance team."

Karen let out a disgusted snort. The story was absurd. Anyone who knew David would recognize that immediately. But why was the FBI concocting this bullshit? What were they trying to hide? Stepping away from Brock, she moved toward the metal table and sat down in one of the chairs. "All right, Agent Brock, for the moment I'll take your word for it. What do you want from me?"

He pulled a notebook and pencil out of his jacket. "We need information on your ex-husband's contacts. Particularly anyone who lives in New Jersey."

"New Jersey? Is that where you think David is?"

Brock scowled. "Let me ask the questions, okay? We've already got the names of his colleagues at Columbia. Now we're working on a list of friends, acquaintances, that kind of thing."

"I'm not the best person to ask. David and I have been divorced for two years."

"No, you're definitely the best person. You see, Swift is a fugitive now and he's probably looking for a friend to help him out. A very close friend, if you know what I mean." He cocked his head and gave her a knowing look. "Does he have any friends like that in New Jersey?"

Karen shook her head again. How pathetic, she thought. Brock was trying to play on her jealousies. "I have no idea."

"Come on. You don't know anything about his love life?"

"Why should I care? We're not married anymore."

"Well, what about before your divorce? Did David ever fool around? Take any late-night trips across the George Washington Bridge?"

She looked him in the eye. "No."

Brock stood in front of Karen's chair. He rested one hand on the edge of the table and leaned over, bringing his face within inches of hers. "You're not being very cooperative, Karen. Don't you want to see your son?"

Her stomach clenched. "Are you threatening me?"

"No, not at all. I just wanted to remind you about the Family Court. Unless we give them a favorable report, they may assign your son to foster care. You don't want to lose him, do you?"

Brock's face was so close that Karen could smell his mouthwash, a sickly spearmint odor. For a second she thought she was going to vomit. But instead she pushed her chair back and got to her feet. She brushed past Brock and headed straight for the one-way mirror at the other end of the room. She tried to peer through the glass but all she could see was her own reflection. "Okay, assholes," she said, addressing the mirror. "Have you figured out yet who you're fucking with?"

In the mirror she saw Brock coming toward her. "No one's there, Karen. It's just you and me."

She pointed her index finger at the glass. "Amory Van Cleve. Does the name ring a bell? He knows half the lawyers in the Justice Department, and he's not going to be pleased when I tell him what you've been doing to me."

Brock was just a few feet behind her now. "All right, enough of this. You better—"

"Get this asshole out of my sight!" Karen shouted, pointing at Brock but keeping her eyes on the mirror. "If he's still here by the time I count to ten, Amory's gonna lower the boom. You hear me? He's gonna talk to his friends at Justice and make sure all of you go to jail!"

For about five seconds the room was silent. Even Brock shut his mouth as he waited to see what would happen. Then Karen heard footsteps in the corridor again. The door opened and an older woman in a white blouse and reading glasses stepped into the room. "Are you all right, honey?" she drawled. "I heard some shouting and I thought—"

Karen spun around. "Don't even start!" she yelled. "Just take me to my son!"

DAVID AWOKE IN THE LOW-SLUNG passenger seat of Monique's Corvette. Groggy and disoriented, he gazed out the windshield. The car was traveling on an interstate through a lush, hilly landscape, vivid green in the morning light. A herd of brown cows stood in a wide sloping meadow next to a big red barn and a newly plowed field. It was a lovely thing to see, and for a long moment David just stared at the calm, motionless cattle. Then he felt a dull ache in his lower back, no doubt caused by all the running he'd done the night before, and he remembered why he was speeding across the country.

He shifted in the uncomfortable bucket seat. Monique was looking at the road ahead, one hand on the steering wheel and the other rummaging inside a box of vanilla crème SnackWell's. Before she'd left her house, she'd changed into a white peasant blouse and khaki shorts, and now she also wore a pair of earphones for her iPod, which rested in her lap. Her head bounced ever so slightly in time with the music. At first she didn't notice that David was awake, and for a few seconds he watched her from the corner of his eye, staring at her gorgeous neck and long, cocoa-colored thighs. After a while, though, he began to feel like a voyeur, so he yawned to get her attention. He stretched his arms as far as he could in the Corvette's cramped interior.

Monique turned to him. "Finally!" she said. "You've been out for three hours." She pulled off her earphones and David heard a raucous snatch of rap music before she shut down the iPod. Then she offered him the box of SnackWell's. "Want some breakfast?"

"Yeah, sure, thanks." As soon as David took the box, he realized he was ravenous. He stuffed two of the cookies into his mouth, then grabbed three more. "Where are we?"

"Beautiful western Pennsylvania. We're less than an hour from Pittsburgh."

He saw the readout on the dashboard clock: 8:47. "You're making good time."

"Are you crazy?" she scoffed. "If I were driving like usual we'd be there already. I'm staying below seventy just in case there's any state troopers around."

David nodded. "Good idea. They probably have my picture by now." He pulled two more cookies out of the SnackWell's box. Then he looked at Monique again and belatedly noticed the bags under her eyes. "Hey, you must be exhausted. You want me to drive for a while?"

"No, I'm fine," she said quickly. "I'm not tired."

She gripped the steering wheel with both hands now, as if to solidify her claim on it. She clearly didn't like the idea of him driving her car. Well, it was understandable, he thought. Her Corvette was a real beauty. "Are you sure?"

"Yeah, I'm okay. I like long drives. I do some of my best thinking when I'm on the road. You know my latest paper in *Physical Review*? 'Gravitational Effects of Noncompact Extra Dimensions'? I came up with the idea while I was driving down to D.C. one weekend."

That's where she's from, he remembered, the Anacostia section of Washington, D.C. Where her father was murdered and her mother became a heroin addict. David wanted to ask Monique whether she still had family there, but he didn't. "So what were you thinking about just now?" he asked instead. "Before I woke up, I mean?"

"Hidden variables. Something you're probably familiar with."

David stopped eating and put down the SnackWell's box. Hidden variables were an important part of Einstein's quest to find a unified theory. In the 1930s, he became convinced that there was an underlying order to the strange quantum behavior of subatomic particles. The microscopic world looked chaotic, but that was only because no one could see the hidden variables, the detailed blueprints of the universe. "So you're trying to figure out how Einstein did it?"

She frowned. "I still can't picture it. Quantum theory just won't fit into a classical framework. It's like trying to shove a square peg into a round hole. The mathematics of the two systems are totally different."

David tried to recall what he'd written about hidden variables in *On the Shoulders of Giants*. "Well, I can't help you with the mathematics. But Einstein felt strongly that quantum mechanics was incomplete. In all his letters and lectures, he always compared it to a game of dice. The theory couldn't tell you exactly when a radioactive atom would decay, or exactly where the ejected particles would end up. Quantum mechanics could only give you probabilities, and Einstein found that unacceptable."

"Yeah, yeah, I know. 'God doesn't play dice with the universe.'" She rolled her eyes. "It's a pretty arrogant statement, if you ask me. What made Einstein think he could tell God what to do?"

"But the analogy goes deeper than that." David had just remembered a paragraph from his book. "When you throw a pair of dice, the numbers look random, but they really aren't. If you had perfect control over all the hidden variables—how hard you throw the dice, the angle of their trajectory, the air pressure in the room— you could throw sevens every single time. There are no surprises if you understand the system perfectly. And Einstein thought the same was true of elementary particles. You could understand them perfectly if you found the hidden variables connecting quantum mechanics to a classical theory."

Monique shook her head. "It sounds good in principle, but believe me, it's not so simple." She took one hand off the steering wheel and pointed at the countryside in front of them. "You see all this nice scenery here? That's a good picture of a classical field theory like relativity. Beautifully smooth hills and valleys outlining the curvature of spacetime. If you spot a cow walking across the field, you can calculate precisely where he'll be in half an hour. But quantum theory? That's like the nastiest, funkiest part of the South Bronx. All kinds of weird, unpredictable things are popping out of thin air and tunneling through the walls." She moved her hand in rapid zigzags to convey a sense of quantum craziness. "That's the problem in a nutshell. You can't make the South Bronx magically appear out of a cornfield."

Monique reached for the box of SnackWell's and pulled out another cookie. She stared at the road ahead as she bit into the thing, and even though she'd just declared that the whole endeavor was futile, David could tell she was still thinking over the problem. It occurred to him that she might have more than one reason for going to Pittsburgh. Until that moment he'd assumed that her chief motivation was anger, her visceral hatred of the FBI agents who'd invaded her home, but now he began to suspect that something else was driving her. She wanted to know the Theory of Everything. Even if she couldn't publish it, even if she couldn't tell another living soul about the theory, she wanted to know.

And David wanted to know it, too. A memory from the night before came back to him. "Professor Kleinman mentioned something else last night. The relativity paper I did in graduate school."

"The one you cowrote with Kleinman?"

"Yeah. 'General Relativity in a Two-Dimensional Spacetime.' He brought it up just before he gave me the sequence of numbers. He said I'd come close to the truth."

Monique raised an eyebrow. "But that paper didn't present any realistic models of the universe, did it?"

"No, we were looking at Flatland, a universe with just two spatial dimensions. The mathematics is a lot easier when you don't have to deal with three of them."

"What were your results? It's been so long since I read the thing."

"We found that two-dimensional masses don't exert a gravitational pull on each other, but they do change the shape of the space around themselves. And we formulated a model for a two-dimensional black hole."

She gave him a puzzled look. "How the hell did you manage that?"

David understood her confusion. In three dimensions, black holes were born when giant stars collapsed under their own weight. But in two dimensions there would be no gravitational attraction to trigger the collapse. "We created a scenario where two particles collided with each other to form the hole. It was pretty complicated, so I don't remember all the details. But there's a copy of the paper on the Web."

Monique thought about it for a moment, tapping one of her fingernails on the steering wheel. "Interesting. You know what I said before about classical theory being so beautiful and smooth? Well, black holes are the big exception. Their physics is funky as hell."

She lapsed into silence as they barreled down the Pennsylvania Turnpike. David saw a sign on the side of the road: PITTSBURGH, 37 MILES. He felt a spike of anxiety as he realized how close they were. Instead of pondering the possible outlines of Einstein's unified theory, they should be figuring out a way to reach Amil Gupta. The FBI agents probably had the Robotics Institute under surveillance, watching everyone who approached Newell-Simon Hall. And even if David and Monique managed to slip through the cordon, what could they do next? Warn Gupta of the danger and persuade him to leave the country? Somehow sneak him across the border to Canada or Mexico, someplace where he'd be safe from both the FBI and the terrorists? The task was so enormous that David could hardly begin to contemplate it.

After a while Monique paused her mental calculations and turned to him. David thought she was going to ask another question about his Flatland paper, but instead she said, "So you're married now, right?"

She'd aimed at a matter-of-fact tone but hadn't quite pulled it off. David heard a slight hesitation in her voice. "What gave you that idea?"

She shrugged. "When I read your book I saw it was dedicated to someone named Karen. I figured that must be your wife."

Her face was blank, determinedly uninterested, but David saw through it. It was pretty damn unusual to remember the name on a dedication page. Monique had obviously retained a healthy curiosity about him since the night they'd spent together twenty years ago. She'd probably Googled him just as many times as he'd Googled her. "We're not married anymore. Karen and I got divorced two years ago."

She nodded, still expressionless. "Does she know anything about this? About what happened to you last night, I mean?"

"No, I haven't talked to her since I saw Kleinman at the hospital. And I can't call her now because the FBI will trace it." His anxiety spiked again as he thought of Karen and Jonah. "I just hope those goddamn agents don't start harassing them."

"Them?"

"We have a seven-year-old son. His name is Jonah."

Monique smiled. Seemingly against her will, the smile broke through her studied indifference, and once again David was struck by how lovely it was. "That's wonderful," she said. "What's he like?"

"Well, he loves science, that's no surprise. He's already working on a spaceship that can go faster than the speed of light. But he also loves baseball and Pokémon and generally raising hell. You should've seen him in the park yesterday with that Super—" David stopped himself as he recalled what had happened to the Super Soaker.

Monique waited a few seconds, looking at the road ahead, obviously expecting to hear more. Then she glanced at him and the smile died on her face. "What's wrong?"

He took a deep breath. His chest felt as tight as a drum. "Jesus," he whispered. "How the hell are we gonna get through this?"

She bit her lower lip. Keeping one eye on the traffic, she reached over to his seat and rested her hand on his knee. "It's all right, David. Let's take it one step at a time. The first thing we need to do is talk to Gupta. Then we can work out a plan."

Her long fingers patted his kneecap. She gave him a reassuring squeeze, then turned her attention back to the highway. And even though her gesture hadn't eased David's fears one bit, he was still grateful.

A minute later Monique pointed at another road sign. This one said NEW STANTON SERVICE AREA, TWO MILES AHEAD.

"We better stop here," she said. "We're almost out of gas."

David kept his eye out for state troopers as they coasted into the service area. No patrol cars in front of the Shell station, thank God. Monique pulled up in front of the self-service pumps and filled the Corvette's tank with Shell Ultra Premium while David slunk low in the passenger seat. Then she got back in the car and drove toward the service area's parking lot. They passed a large concrete building containing a Burger King, a Nathan's, and a Starbucks.

"I hate to make things difficult, but I need to pee," she said. "What about you?"

David scanned the parking lot and saw no police cars. But what if a trooper was stationed inside the building, standing just outside the men's room? The chances were remote, but it was still a risk. "I'll stay in the car. I can pee into a cup or something."

She gave him a warning look. "Just watch what you're doing. You better not get pee on the car seat."

She parked in a vacant corner of the lot, about thirty feet away from the nearest vehicle. David handed her a couple of twenty-dollar bills. "Could you pick up a few things while you're in there? Maybe some sandwiches, some water, some chips?"

"You mean you're getting tired of SnackWell's?" She smiled again as she opened the driver's-side door and headed for the rest-rooms.

Once she was gone, David realized that he did need to urinate pretty badly. He searched the Corvette for a container of some sort, groping under the seats for an empty water bottle or a discarded coffee cup, but he had no luck—the car was immaculate. No junk anywhere, not even in the glove compartment. He supposed he could wait for Monique to return with the newly purchased water bottles and empty one of those, but he didn't like the idea of peeing into the thing while she stood nearby. At a loss, he gazed across the parking lot and noticed a grassy picnic area under a stand of trees about fifty feet away. A family was eating Burger King breakfast sandwiches at one of the picnic tables, but it looked like they were about to leave. The young mother was screaming at the kids to pick up their trash while the father stood by impatiently, the car keys already in his hand.

After a few minutes the family departed for their minivan and David stepped out of the Corvette. He walked toward the picnic area, looking first over one shoulder, then the other. The only person in sight was an old man walking his dachshund along the edge of the parking lot. David strode past the picnic tables, positioned himself behind the biggest tree, and unzipped his fly. When he was finished he headed back to the Corvette, much relieved. But as he stepped from the grass to the asphalt, the elderly dog walker came rushing toward him. "Hey you!" he shouted.

David froze. For a second he imagined it was an undercover cop in disguise. But as the man came closer, David saw that he was genuinely ancient. His lips were flecked with spittle and his pink face was as wrinkled as a raisin. He thrust a rolled-up newspaper at David's chest. "I saw what you did!" he scolded. "Don't you know they have bathrooms here?"

Amused, David gave the old gent a smile. "Look, I'm sorry. It was an emergency."

"It's disgusting, that's what it is! You should be—"

The old man abruptly stopped berating him. He stared at David, squinting, then glanced at the newspaper in his hand. Some of the color drained out of his face. He stood there for a second with his mouth hanging open, exposing a row of skewed, yellow teeth. Then he spun around and started running away, pulling frantically on the dachshund's leash.

At that same moment David heard Monique yell, "Get back here!" She stood beside the Corvette, holding a bulky plastic bag. As he jogged toward her, she tossed the bag into the car, got in the driver's seat, and started the engine. "Come on, come on, get in!"

As soon as David slipped into the passenger seat, the Corvette took off. Monique gunned the engine and within seconds they were out of the service area and on the entrance ramp to the turnpike. "Jesus Christ!" she yelled. "Why'd you have to start talking to that geezer?"

David was shaking. The old man had recognized him.

The needle on the speedometer rose toward ninety. Monique floored the gas pedal and the Corvette rocketed down the highway. "The next exit better be close," she said. "We have to get off this road before your friend calls the cops."

In his mind's eye David saw the dog walker again. The rolled-up newspaper, he thought. That's how he recognized me.

As if sensing his thoughts, Monique reached into the plastic bag that sat between them and pulled out a copy of the *Pittsburgh Post-Gazette.* "I saw this in the newsstand next to Starbucks." She handed him the paper.

David found the story at the top of the front page. The headline read SIX AGENTS KILLED IN NEW YORK DRUG RAID and below, in smaller type, *Police Seeking Columbia Professor.* And next to the headline was the black-and-white photograph of David that had appeared on the back flap of *On the Shoulders of Giants.*

SIMON GAZED AT THE TRANQUIL Delaware River from Washington Crossing State Park in New Jersey. He stood in a deserted parking lot overlooking the river, leaning against the side of a bright yellow Ferrari.

He'd taken the car—a 575 Maranello coupé—from the garage of the Princeton Auto Shop. Keith, the car mechanic he'd found in Monique Reynolds's house, had told him where to find the keys. This was a very helpful development, considering that Simon had been forced to abandon his Mercedes after his run-in with the officer from the Princeton Borough Police. It would've been even more helpful if Keith had revealed where David Swift and Monique Reynolds had gone, but the young mechanic insisted he didn't know, even after Simon had cut off three of his fingers and sliced his bowels open.

Simon shook his head. All he had to go on now was the hand-written note that Monique had left on the kitchen counter. He pulled the folded sheet of paper out of his pocket and studied it again, but it offered no clues.

Keith: I'm so sorry about this, but David and I had to rush off. He has some important results that we need to evaluate. I'll call you when I get back.

P.S.: There's orange juice in the fridge and bagels in the breadbasket. Don't forget to lock the door.

The final lines were partly obscured by a bloody thumbprint that Simon had made when he'd picked up the note. Before he left the house, he took the bagels with him. Keith had already eaten his last meal.

Simon put the note back into his pocket and checked his watch: 9:25. Nearly time for his daily chat with his client. Every morning at exactly nine-thirty Henry Cobb called him to get an update on the mission. "Henry Cobb" was almost certainly an alias. Simon had never met the man in person—they'd hammered out their contract over the phone, using various codes that Henry had devised—but judging from his accent, his real name was more likely Abdul or Muhammad. Although Simon hadn't figured out the man's nation-ality yet, his hometown was definitely somewhere between Cairo and Karachi. Given that Simon had spent so many years killing Muslim insurgents in Chechnya, he found it a bit surprising that an Islamic group would choose to hire him. But perhaps he wasn't giving the jihadis enough credit. If they were truly committed to their cause, they wouldn't care about anything except getting the best man for the job. And Simon, as the Chechens could attest, had an excellent track record.

Whatever the nature and nationality of Henry's organization, one thing was clear: they had significant resources. To prepare Si-mon for the mission, Henry had sent him a whole crate of textbooks on particle physics and general relativity, as well as several dozen issues of *Physical Review* and the *Astrophysical Journal.* More important, Henry had wired $200,000 to cover Simon's expenses and promised to pay another million when the job was finished.

The ironic thing, though, was that Simon would've gladly done the work for free if he'd known from the start what it was all about. He hadn't perceived the full extent of Henry's ambitions until a week ago, when he'd visited the Provençal country home of Jacques Bouchet. Simon had confronted the French physicist while he was in the bathtub, and after a brief, watery struggle the old man started talking. Unfortunately, he knew only a few pieces of the *Einheitliche Feldtheorie,* but he told Simon quite a lot about the possible consequences of misusing the equations. Bouchet had obviously expected Simon to be horrified by this information, perhaps horrified enough to abandon the mission altogether, but instead Simon was exultant. As luck would have it, his client's desires neatly dovetailed with his own. Feeling a surge of triumph, he kept interrogating Bouchet until the old man sat shivering in the tub. Then he slit the physicist's wrists and watched the clouds of blood billow in the bathwater.

At 9:29, Simon reached for his cell phone and opened it in anticipation of Henry's call. Sergei and Larissa appeared on the screen, smiling expectantly. Be patient, Simon whispered. It won't be long now.

At precisely nine-thirty, the phone rang. Simon raised the device to his ear. "Hello, this is George Osmond," he said. His own alias.

"Good morning, George. So good to speak with you again." The slow, careful voice with the Middle Eastern accent. "Tell me, how was the game last night?"

For some reason, Henry relied on baseball metaphors in most of his codes. Although their veiled conversations sometimes verged on the ridiculous, Simon had to admit that the precautions made sense. Since 9/11, no phone call was safe. You had to assume that the government was listening to everything. "The game was a little disappointing," he said. "Scoreless, actually."

A long pause. Henry was clearly not pleased. "What about the pitcher?" That was their code word for Kleinman.

"Never got a chance to play. He's out for the season, I'm afraid."

An even longer pause. "How did this happen?"

"It was interference from the Yankees. You can read about it in today's newspapers. Of course, the reporters didn't get all the details straight. They tried to turn it into another drug scandal."

This time the silence stretched for nearly half a minute. Simon pictured his client in a white dishdasha robe, strangling a strand of worry beads. "I'm not happy about this," he finally said. "I was counting on this pitcher. How are we going to win without him?"

"Don't worry, I have another prospect. A younger man, a very promising player. He worked closely with the pitcher, I believe."

"Have I heard of this player before?"

"He's mentioned in the newspapers, too. A college player. I think he has what we need."

"Do you know where he is?"

"Not just yet. I came close to contacting him last night but he left town suddenly."

Henry let out a dissatisfied grunt. Not a patient man, obviously. But his type seldom was. "This is unacceptable," he said. "I'm paying you a good salary and I expect better results than this."

Simon felt a twinge of irritation. He prided himself on his professionalism. "Calm down. You'll get your money's worth. I know someone who can help me find this player."

"Who?"

"An agent in the Yankee organization."

Another long silence followed, but this one was different. It was a wondering, dumbfounded silence. "With the Yankees?" his client muttered. "You have a friend there?"

"Strictly a business relationship. You see, the Yankees are sure to track down this player sooner or later. As soon as they know where he is, the agent will pass the information to me."

"For a fee, I assume?"

"Naturally. And I'm going to need a substantial increase in my budget to cover it."

"I've told you before, money isn't a problem. I'm willing to pay all necessary expenses." His voice was conciliatory now, almost deferential. "But are you sure you can trust this man?"

"I've scheduled a meeting with the agent to assess his intentions. He's due to arrive in a few minutes, actually."

"Well, I'll let you go, then. Please keep me informed."

"Certainly."

Simon frowned as he closed the phone and put it back in his pocket. He hated dealing with clients. It was by far the most disagreeable part of his job. But he wouldn't have to do it much longer. If everything went according to plan, this mission would be his last.

He turned back to the Delaware River and the line of oak trees on the other side. According to a sign at the water's edge, this was the place where General Washington ferried his troops across the river. On the night of December 25, 1776, he led 2,400 insurgents from Pennsylvania to New Jersey so he could surprise the British army in its barracks in Trenton. The river was so peaceful now, it was hard to believe that anyone had ever died here. But Simon knew better. Death ran just below the rippling surface of the water. It was in all rivers, all countries. The entire universe was saturated with it.

The whine of an SUV interrupted his thoughts. Simon looked over his shoulder and saw a black Suburban turn in to the parking lot. No other vehicles were in sight, which was a good sign. If the FBI were planning an ambush, they would've sent a whole convoy.

The Suburban parked at the other end of the lot and after a few seconds a man in a gray suit stepped out of the car. Although he wore sunglasses and stood nearly fifty meters away, Simon immediately knew it was his contact. The man had a distinctive slouch, standing with his shoulders hunched and his hands in his pockets. The breeze tousled his hair as he started walking across the asphalt. There was probably a semiautomatic in the shoulder holster under his jacket, but that was all right—Simon was armed, too. He was willing to take his chances if it came to a shoot-out.

The agent stopped a few meters from the Ferrari. He pointed at the car, grinning. "Nice ride," he said. "Must've cost you a bundle."

Simon shrugged. "It's nothing. Just a tool of the trade."

"Just a tool, huh?" He walked around the Ferrari, admiring its lines. "I wouldn't mind getting a tool like that for myself."

"That may be possible. My offer still stands."

The agent ran his fingers along the Ferrari's spoiler. "Sixty thousand, right? That was the deal?"

Simon nodded. "Thirty payable now. The other thirty if your information leads to the suspect's capture."

"Well, I guess this is my lucky day. I just got a transmission from headquarters while I was driving down here." He folded his arms across his chest. "You got the money on you?"

Keeping his eyes on the agent, Simon reached with one hand into the Ferrari. He picked up the black briefcase that had been resting on the driver's seat. "The first payment's in here. In twenty-dollar bills."

The agent stopped looking at the car. All his attention was on the briefcase now. The man's greed was overpowering, which is why Simon had cultivated this particular contact. "We got a report that a citizen spotted Swift an hour ago. At a rest stop on the Pennsylvania Turnpike."

Simon glanced at the Pennsylvania side of the river. "Where? Which rest stop?"

"New Stanton Service Area. About thirty miles east of Pittsburgh. The state police put up roadblocks, but they haven't found him yet. He probably got off the highway already."

Without any hesitation, Simon handed the briefcase to the

agent. He was anxious to get going. "I'll be in touch with you about the second payment. Expect a call within twelve hours."

The agent clutched the briefcase with both hands. He seemed stunned by his good fortune. "I'm looking forward to it. It's a pleasure doing business with you."

Simon got into the Ferrari and started the engine. "No, the pleasure is mine, Mr. Brock."

FROM HIS VANTAGE POINT A hundred yards away, David gazed at Newell-Simon Hall, trying to remember the exact location of Amil Gupta's office. He and Monique were crouched inside an empty classroom in the Purnell Arts Center, a neighboring building on the Carnegie Mellon campus. The classroom was apparently used for a course in theatrical set design; scattered among the desks were several flat wooden boards painted to look like trees, houses, cars, and storefronts. A large panel showing the front of a barbershop, with the words SWEENEY TODD running across the top, stood next to the window that David and Monique were peering through. All the two-dimensional facsimiles gave the room a disorienting feel, like the interior of a fun house. David thought of his paper on Flatland, a universe without depth.

It was almost noon. After the fiasco at the New Stanton Service Area, they'd spent more than an hour navigating the backstreets of the Pittsburgh suburbs, staying off the main roads so they could get to Carnegie Mellon without encountering any patrol cars. Once they arrived, Monique hid her Corvette among the hundreds of sports cars parked in the university's main lot, and then they made their way across campus on foot. They chose the Purnell Arts Center for their reconnaissance because it sat on a rise above Newell-Simon Hall, offering an excellent view of the parking lot between the two buildings.

The first thing David noticed was the Highlander robotic vehicle, a custom-designed Hummer with a big silver orb mounted on its roof. He'd read about the car in *Scientific American*. One of

Gupta's pet projects, the Highlander could travel hundreds of miles without a driver. A couple of students from the Robotics Institute were testing the vehicle, watching it autonomously navigate the parking lot. The orb on the car's roof contained a laser scanner that detected the obstacles in its path. One of the students held a radio control box that would immediately shut off the engine if the robot car went haywire.

The second thing David noticed was the Suburbans. Two black SUVs were parked near the entrance to Newell-Simon and another two were positioned at the back of the lot. He pointed them out to Monique. "You see all those SUVs? Those are government cars."

"How do you know?"

"I saw a bunch of them in the FBI's garage in New York." Next he pointed at a pair of men in T-shirts and shorts who were tossing a football back and forth. "Check out those guys with the football. Why are they playing catch in the middle of a parking lot?"

"They look a little too old to be students," Monique noted.

"Exactly. And look at the bare-chested guy lying on the grass over there. That has to be the palest sunbather I've ever seen."

"There's two more sitting in the grass on the other side of the building."

David shook his head. "It's my own damn fault. They probably beefed up the surveillance here once they found out we were on the turnpike. They know we're trying to get to Gupta."

He turned away from the window and slumped against the wall. It was a trap. The undercover agents were just waiting for him to show up. But oddly enough, David wasn't panicked. His fears had subsided, at least for the moment, and now all he felt was outrage. He thought of the front-page article in the *Pittsburgh Post-Gazette*, the elaborate cover story that portrayed him as a drug dealer and a murderer. Jesus Christ, he muttered. These assholes think they can get away with anything.

Monique leaned against the wall next to him. "Well, the next step is obvious. You stay here and I'll go in."

"What?"

"They're not looking for me. Those agents have no idea I'm with you. All they know is that some old man saw you at the rest stop."

"What if the guy also saw the license plate on your car?"

She looked askance. "That geezer? He was running for his life after he recognized you. He didn't see a thing."

David frowned. He didn't like Monique's plan at all. "It's too risky. Those agents are eyeballing everyone who comes near that building. For all we know, they've got pictures of every theoretical physicist in the country, and if they figure out who you are, they're sure to get suspicious. They've already been to your house, remember?"

She took a deep breath. "I know it's risky. But what else are we going to do? You have a better idea?"

Unfortunately, he was out of ideas. He turned away from her and looked around the room, hoping for some inspiration. "What about a costume?" he ventured. "This is a theater department, so there's probably some costumes around here. Maybe you can wear a wig or something."

"Please, David. Anything we find here is only going to make me look ridiculous. And that'll just draw more attention."

"That's not necessarily true. What if you—"

Before David could finish, he heard a loud rumbling in the hallway outside the classroom. Monique cried, "Shit!" and reached for the revolver tucked into her shorts, but David grabbed her wrist. That was the last thing they needed. He pulled her behind the large wooden panel depicting Sweeney Todd's barbershop. Soon the rumbling stopped and they heard the jangling of keys. David was certain that a team of FBI agents stood on the other side of the door, ready to storm into the classroom. But when the door opened he saw only the building's cleaning lady, a young woman in a pale blue smock pushing a large canvas Dumpster.

Monique clutched David's shoulder in relief, but neither of

them stirred from their hiding place. Peeking around the edge of the *Sweeney Todd* scenery, David watched the cleaning woman wheel the Dumpster across the classroom. When she got to the far end, she picked up a trash can full of discarded art supplies—the sawed-off edges of wooden boards, a huge wad of paint-soaked rags—and poured its contents into the Dumpster. She was a tall, thin black woman wearing a T-shirt and denim shorts under her smock. Probably not more than twenty-three years old, but already her face was careworn, exhausted. She scowled as she shook the trash can over the Dumpster and in that moment David realized that the cleaning woman and Monique, despite the difference in their ages, looked very much alike. They had the same long legs, the same defiant tilt of the head. David continued staring at her as she lowered the empty trash can to the floor and began pushing the Dumpster out of the classroom. Just as she reached the door, he came out of hiding. Monique tried to stop him but she was too slow.

"Excuse me?" David said to the cleaning woman's back.

She whirled around. "Jesus! What the . . . ?"

"Sorry to startle you. My colleague and I were putting the final touches on the set for tonight's show." He motioned for Monique to come forward. Gritting her teeth, she stepped into the open. David placed his hand on the small of her back and nudged her forward. "This is Professor Gladwell," he said, "and I'm Professor Hodges. Of the drama department."

The cleaning woman pressed her hand to her chest, still recovering from her surprise. She regarded David and Monique angrily. "You scared the shit out of me! I thought this room was empty till one o'clock."

David smiled to put her at ease. "Usually it is, but we're doing some last-minute work for the show tonight. It's a very big opening, very exciting."

The woman didn't seem impressed. "Well, what do you want? You got something you want to throw out?"

"Actually, I was wondering about that smock you're wearing. Is there any chance we can borrow it for a few hours?"

Her lips formed an incredulous oval. She glanced down at her smock, which had a patch saying CARNEGIE MELLON BUILDING SERVICES just above her left breast. "This thing? What do you want it for?"

"One of the characters in our show is a cleaning lady, but I'm not happy with the costume we have now. I want something more like your uniform. I just need to show it to our costume designer so she can copy it."

The woman narrowed her eyes. She wasn't buying it. "Look, I gotta wear this uniform while I'm working," she said. "If I let you borrow it, I gotta get another one from janitorial supplies and that's a long walk back."

"I'm willing to compensate you for the inconvenience." David reached into his pocket and pulled out a roll of twenties. He peeled off ten of them.

She stared at the $200 in his hand. She wasn't any less suspicious than before, but now she had reason to ignore her suspicions. "You're gonna pay me for the uniform?"

He nodded. "The drama department has a budget for emergencies like this."

"And you're gonna give it back when you're done?"

"Definitely. You can pick it up this afternoon."

Still looking at him warily, she began to take off the smock. "Just don't tell anyone else in Building Services about this, all right?"

"Don't worry, I won't say a word." Another thought occurred to him. "And we're also going to need your Dumpster. As a prop for the show."

She gave the smock to David. "I don't care about the Dumpster. There's another one in the basement I can use." She whisked the $200 out of his hand and quickly left the room, as if she were afraid he'd change his mind.

David waited a few seconds, then locked the door to the classroom. With the blue smock draped over his arm, he turned to Monique. "All right, I've got your costume."

She stared grimly at the uniform. "A cleaning woman. How original." Her voice was bitter.

"Hey, I'm sorry. I just thought . . ."

"Yeah, I know what you thought." She shook her head. "Black women clean offices, right? So if those FBI agents see me pushing a Dumpster into that building, they won't give me a second look."

"If you don't want to—"

"No, no, you're right. That's the saddest thing about it, you're absolutely right." She grabbed the smock from David's arm and shook out the wrinkles. The blue fabric whipped through the air. "It doesn't matter how many degrees you earn or how many papers you publish or how many prizes you win. In their eyes, I'm just a cleaning woman."

She put her arms through the uniform's sleeves and started buttoning it up. For a moment it looked like she was going to cry, but she bit her lip and fought it off. David felt a knot of guilt in his stomach. Whatever his intentions, he'd hurt her badly. "Monique," he started. "It's my fault. I didn't—"

"You're damn right it's your fault. Now get in there."

She pointed at the load of trash inside the canvas Dumpster. Confused, David looked at her. "In there?"

"That's right. You can lie on the bottom and I'll pile the garbage on top of you. Then both of us can get inside the building to see Gupta."

Shit, he thought. And it was his own idea.

LUCILLE PARKER SAT IN ONE of the passenger seats of the C-21, the air force's version of the Learjet, as it streaked over western Pennsylvania. She looked out the window and saw the turnpike stretched like a rope across the green hills and valleys. Somewhere along its length was the service area where David Swift had been spotted, but Lucille couldn't find it. Most likely they'd passed it already. Up ahead she could see the city of Pittsburgh, a gray blot straddling the Monongahela River.

The call from the Bureau's director came in just as the plane began its descent. Lucille picked up the handset of the ARC-190, the air-force radio that enabled secure communications with the ground. "Black One here."

"Hello, Lucy," the director said. "What's going on?"

"I'm about ten minutes from Pittsburgh International. There's a vehicle waiting for me at the airport."

"What about the stakeout?"

"No sign of the suspect, but it's early yet. We have ten agents surrounding Gupta's building and another ten inside. Video cameras in the lobby and all the entrances, and listening devices on all the floors."

"Are you sure this is the right way to play it? Maybe we should just grab Gupta now and see what he knows."

"No, if we detain Gupta now, the word will get out pretty quick. Swift won't come anywhere near the place. But if we keep our heads low, we can nab both of them."

"All right, I'm counting on you, Lucy. The sooner we finish this job, the better. I'm getting tired of fielding calls from the SecDef." The director let out a long sigh. "Is there anything else you need? More agents, more support?"

Lucille hesitated. This was going to be tricky. "I need the personnel files for every agent in the New York region."

"Why?"

"The more I think about what happened at Liberty Street last night, the more I'm convinced there's been a breach. The attackers knew too much about our operations. I think they had help from inside."

The director sighed again. "Jesus. Just what we need."

IT WAS DARK AND UNCOMFORTABLE and smelled a lot worse than David had expected. Most of the garbage piled on top of him was inoffensive stuff—papers, rags, bits of cloth, and so on—but someone had thrown the remains of a breakfast burrito into the trash and now the sulfurous aroma of rotten eggs permeated the bottom of the Dumpster. Adding injury to insult, the jagged edge of a wooden board lay across his back and dug into his shoulder blades whenever the wheels of the Dumpster hit a bump. David winced as Monique pushed him out of the Purnell Arts Center and down the path toward Newell-Simon Hall.

After a minute or so his eyes adjusted to the dark and he noticed a small vertical tear in the Dumpster's canvas lining. Wriggling on his elbows and knees, he inched forward until he could peer through the opening. They were in the parking lot now; just ahead was the Highlander robot car, which was moving briskly toward the service entrance of Newell-Simon. Monique was following the vehicle and the pair of graduate students who were tracking its progress. The plan seemed to be working. In a few more seconds they'd be inside the building. Then David heard someone yell, "Heads up!" and a second later there was a crash in the layers of junk above him. A blunt object struck the back of his head, mashing his nose against the bottom of the Dumpster. The pain was intense but he didn't make a sound. He soon heard footsteps, the slap of sneakers against asphalt. Through the tear in the canvas he saw a pair of pale, hairy legs, then another. Oh fuck, he thought. It's the football-tossing agents. They'd thrown their pigskin right into the Dumpster. Worse, the impact had jostled the garbage above him, exposing his shoulders and the top of his head.

The agents came closer. One of them was less than five feet away. David lay still, just waiting for the man to lean over the side of the Dumpster and spot him. Then he saw a third pair of legs, smooth and brown, step in front of the agent's. "Goddamn it!" Monique yelled. "You almost hit me with that thing!"

"Sorry, ma'am," the agent replied. "We didn't—"

"This ain't a playground! You boys should watch what you're doing!"

The man took a step back. With just a few words and a little attitude, Monique had thoroughly intimidated him. David had to admire her strategy. The best defense is a good offense.

The toes of Monique's sandals turned toward the Dumpster and she bent over its edge. David felt her hands on his back as she picked up the football and rearranged the trash to cover him. Then she turned back to the agents. "Here's your ball. Now go play somewhere else."

The pale legs retreated. The brown legs stood guard for a few seconds longer, and then they disappeared from view and the Dumpster began moving again.

Soon they passed through Newell-Simon's service entrance, a loading dock that also served as a garage for the Highlander. Monique steered toward the freight elevator and pressed the button. David held his breath until the elevator door opened and Monique pushed the Dumpster inside. As soon as the doors closed, she coughed twice in quick succession. Because they assumed the FBI had laced the building with listening devices, they'd agreed on a signaling system—when Monique coughed twice, it meant, "Are you all right?" David coughed once to answer in the affirmative, and then they arrived on the fourth floor.

After rolling down an immaculately clean corridor, they came to the reception area for Amil Gupta's office, which David recognized from his last visit to the Robotics Institute. A sleek black desk crowded with computer monitors stood in the center of the room, just as David remembered, but the receptionist was no longer the tall buxom blonde who'd made eyes at him as he'd waited for his interview with Gupta. It was a young man now, very young, eighteen years old at the most. David tilted his head a bit so he could get a better view of the teenager through the hole in the canvas. The kid was staring at a computer screen and madly manipulating a joystick beside the keyboard. He was most likely an undergraduate, a computer geek who'd finished high school a few years early and was now working his way through college by doing secretarial work for the

Robotics Institute. He had a somewhat pudgy face, with olive skin and thick black eyebrows.

Monique left the Dumpster behind and approached the boy's desk. "Excuse me?" she said. "I'm here to clean Dr. Gupta's office."

He didn't look up. His eyes stayed on the screen, darting back and forth to follow the convulsions of whatever computer game he was playing.

"Excuse me?" Monique repeated, a little louder this time. "I'm going into his office to empty the trash cans, all right?"

Still no response. The boy's mouth hung open as he stared at the screen, and the tip of his tongue rested on his lower lip. There was no emotion at all on his face, just a steady, machinelike concentration. The overall effect was a bit disconcerting. Maybe he wasn't a college student, David thought. It occurred to him that there might be something wrong with the boy.

Monique finally gave up on him and headed for the door behind the reception desk. She grasped the knob but it didn't turn. Frowning, she turned back to the teenager. "The door's locked," she said. "You gotta unlock it so I can do my job."

The boy didn't answer, but David heard a loud whirring start up somewhere nearby. It was the whine of an electric motor and it seemed to be moving toward the Dumpster. A bewildered look appeared on Monique's face as she gazed across the room. Then David saw what had caught her attention: a boxy silver machine, about the size of a suitcase, rolling toward her on caterpillar treads. It stopped at her feet, extended a robotic arm and pointed a bulb-shaped sensor at her.

The machine looked a bit like a tortoise with a very long neck. Monique and the robot regarded each other warily for a couple of seconds, and then a synthesized voice came out of the machine's speakers: "Good morning! I'm the AR-21 Autonomous Receptionist, developed by the students at the Robotics Institute. Can I help you?"

Monique gawked at the thing. She glanced at the human receptionist, probably wondering if he was playing a joke on her, but the teenager was still engrossed in his computer game.

The machine reoriented its sensor so that it tracked her face. "Perhaps I can be of service," it intoned. "Please tell me what you want and I will attempt to help you."

With obvious reluctance, she turned back to the machine and looked into its bulbous sensor. "I'm the cleaning woman. Unlock the door."

"I'm sorry," the AR-21 replied. "I didn't understand what you said. Could you please repeat?"

Monique's frown deepened. "The . . . cleaning . . . woman," she said, loudly and slowly. "Unlock . . . the . . . door."

"Did you say, 'Curriculum brochure'? Please answer yes or no."

She took a step toward the machine and for a moment David thought she was going to kick the thing. "I need . . . to get into . . . Dr. Gupta's . . . office. Understand? Dr. Gupta's . . . office."

"Did you say, 'Gupta'? Please answer yes or no."

"Yes! Yes! Dr. Gupta!"

"Professor Amil Gupta is the director of the Robotics Institute. Would you like to schedule an appointment with him?"

"Yes! I mean, no! I just need to clean his office!"

"Professor Gupta has office hours on Mondays and Wednesdays. His earliest available appointment is next Monday at three o'clock. Would that time work for you? Please answer yes or no."

Monique had reached her limit. Raising her hands in surrender, she stomped back to the Dumpster. David felt a jolt as she gripped the edge of the canvas lining, and then she began pushing the thing backward, out of the reception room. They moved rapidly down the corridor, the Dumpster's wheels rattling over the tile floor. Instead of returning to the freight elevator, though, Monique opened the door to a supply room and maneuvered the Dumpster inside.

As soon as the door closed, she reached into the load of trash and swept aside the crumpled papers and dirty rags that covered

David's head and shoulders. Propping himself on his elbows, he looked up and saw Monique's exasperated face leaning over the side of the Dumpster. The message was clear: she needed some help.

David cautiously raised his head and surveyed the room. The walls were lined with metal shelves holding an assortment of janitorial and office supplies—jugs of floor cleaner, packs of toilet paper, boxes of printer cartridges. In the corner was a large stainless-steel sink. No sign of any surveillance cameras. Of course the FBI could've hidden one somewhere, but David doubted that the federal agents would install an elaborate video system in a room that was so small and seldom occupied. Listening devices were a different matter, though; it would be no trouble at all to put one in every room in the building. Without saying a word, he clambered out of the Dumpster, went to the sink, and turned on the water full force. He'd seen this trick in a movie but had no idea whether it would really protect them from eavesdropping. To be safe, he pulled Monique close and whispered in her ear. "You have to go back to the reception room."

She shook her head. "No way," she whispered. "That damn robot is useless. Shitty communication software, that's the problem."

"Then go back there and get the kid's attention. Tap him on the shoulder if you have to."

"It's not gonna work. The boy looks like he's handicapped or something. And the FBI agents are probably listening to everything I say in there. If I make too much of a fuss, they're gonna get suspicious."

"Well, what are we going to do? Wait here until Gupta runs out of toilet paper?"

"Is there another way into Gupta's office?"

"I don't know! I haven't been here in years! I can't remember what—"

Something suddenly bumped into David's heel. It was just a light tap on the back of his sneaker, but it scared the shit out of him. He looked down and saw a blue disk, about the size of a Frisbee, slowly moving across the floor of the supply room and leaving a wet, zigzagging trail on the linoleum.

A second later Monique saw it, too, and let out a startled cry. David clapped his hand over her mouth.

"Don't worry," he whispered. "It's just a floor-cleaning robot. Another of Gupta's projects. It spreads cleaning fluid in a programmed pattern, then sucks up the dirty water."

She scowled. "Someone should step on that thing and put it out of its misery."

David nodded, staring at the device as it crawled away. It did look a bit like an oversize insect, with a spindly black antenna rising from the rim of the disk. Gupta outfitted all his robots with radio transmitters because he was obsessed with monitoring their progress. When David had interviewed Gupta ten years ago, the old man had proudly shown him a computer screen detailing the locations of all the autonomous machines wandering the corridors and laboratories of Newell-Simon Hall. The memory of that screen, with its flashing blips and three-dimensional floor plans, now gave David an idea.

"If we can't get to Gupta, we'll get him to come to us," he said, stepping toward the floor-cleaning robot. He leaned over to grasp the machine's antenna. "This'll get his attention." With a flick of the wrist he snapped off the spindly wire.

The robot immediately let out a deafening, high-pitched alarm. David jumped back. This wasn't the response he'd anticipated; he'd expected an alert that would appear only on Gupta's computer, not this ear-piercing shriek.

"Shit!" Monique cried. "What did you do?"

"I don't know!"

"Shut it off! Shut the thing off!"

David picked up the device and turned it over, frantically looking for a power switch, but there was nothing on the machine's underside but dripping holes and spinning brushes, and the whole thing was vibrating in his hands from the force of the alarm. Giving up, he ran to the sink and smashed the robot as hard as he could against the stainless-steel edge. The machine's plastic shell broke in two, spilling cleaning fluid and cracked circuit boards. The noise abruptly cut off.

David leaned over the sink, breathing hard. He turned to Monique and saw a queasy look on her face. She didn't say a word but it was clear what she was thinking. The FBI agents must've heard the alarm. Soon one of them would come into the supply room to investigate. Monique seemed paralyzed by the thought, and for several seconds she just stood there in the center of the room, her eyes fixed on the door. Looking at her, David felt something lurch inside him. They were trapped. They were helpless. Their plan had collapsed before it could even be conceived. They couldn't save themselves, much less the world.

Then the door opened and Amil Gupta stepped inside.

"OKAY, TALK TO ME. WHAT'S our status?"

Lucille stood in a mobile command post that the Bureau had towed to the Carnegie Mellon campus early that morning. From the outside it looked like an ordinary office trailer, a long beige box with aluminum siding, the kind of thing you'd typically see at a construction site, but on the inside it held more electronics than a nuclear sub. At one end was a bank of video screens displaying live images of the various offices, stairways, elevators, and corridors under surveillance in Newell-Simon Hall. A pair of technicians sat at a station facing the screens; in addition to scrutinizing the video displays, they wore headphones to monitor the conversations picked up by the listening devices. At the other end of the trailer, two more technicians examined the digital traffic on the Robotics Institute's Internet connections and monitored the building's radiation levels, which were always a concern in any counterterrorism operation. And in the trailer's midsection, Lucille was grilling Agent Crawford, her dutiful and ambitious second-in-command.

"Gupta's been alone in his office since ten o'clock," Crawford reported. He read his notes off the screen of a BlackBerry cradled in his hand. "At ten-fifteen, he went to the men's room, returned at ten-twenty. At eleven-oh-five, he went to the break room for a cup of coffee, returned at eleven-oh-nine. You can see him now on screen number one, right over there."

The screen showed Gupta at his desk, leaning back in his swivel chair and staring intently at his computer monitor. The man was small but spry, a five-foot-tall seventy-six-year-old with thin gray hair and a doll-like brown face. According to the file Lucille had read while en route to Pittsburgh, Gupta's small stature was the result of the malnutrition he'd suffered as a child in Bombay in the 1930s. But he certainly wasn't starving now; thanks to the sale of the software company he'd founded and the various investments he'd made in the robotics industry, he was worth about $300 million. Although the guy was scrawnier than a plucked hen, he wore a beautiful olive-green Italian suit that no government employee could ever afford. "What's on his computer?" Lucille asked.

"Software code, mostly," Crawford replied. "Our tap on his ISP cable shows that he downloaded a monster-size program, more than five million lines of code, as soon as he got into the office. In all likelihood, it's one of his artificial-intelligence programs. He's been making small changes to it for the past two hours."

"What about e-mail and phone calls?"

"He's gotten a dozen e-mails but nothing unusual, and all his incoming calls are going to voice mail. He obviously doesn't want to be disturbed."

"Any visitors come to his office?"

Agent Crawford glanced at his BlackBerry again. "One of his students, an Asian male who identified himself as Jacob Sun, came into the reception room and made an appointment to see him next week. No other visitors except a FedEx deliveryman. And a cleaning woman, she just left the reception room a minute ago."

"Did you run them through the biometric database?"

"No, we didn't see the need. None of the visitors fit the profile."

Lucille frowned. "What do you mean, 'fit the profile'?"

Crawford blinked twice in quick succession, his cocksure demeanor faltering a bit. "Uh, the profile of our targets, David Swift and his co-conspirators. The individuals we observed were clearly not—"

"Look, I don't care if it's a student or a cleaning woman or a ninety-nine-year-old biddy in a wheelchair. Anyone comes near Gupta's office, I want you to check 'em out. Get their images off the video and run 'em through the face-recognition system, you hear?"

He nodded rapidly. "Yes, ma'am, we'll do that right away. I'm sorry if—"

Before he could finish, one of the technicians let out a yelp and tore off his headphones. Crawford, who was very eager by this point to end his conversation with Lucille, moved toward the man. "What's wrong?" he asked. "Feedback?"

The technician shook his head. "Some kind of alarm just went off. On the fourth floor, I think."

Lucille's scalp began to tingle. "That's Gupta's floor, right?" At the same moment she turned to screen number one and saw the tiny old man rise from his chair and step away from the desk. "Look, he's on the move! He's heading out of the office!"

Crawford leaned over the technician's shoulder and pointed at an array of buttons below the video screens. "Switch to the camera in the reception room. Let's see where he's going."

The technician pushed a button. Screen number one now showed a homely teenage boy sitting at a reception desk and a strange mechanical contraption that looked like a miniature tank. No Gupta, though. They waited several seconds but saw no sign of him.

"Where did he go?" Lucille asked. "Is there another way out of his office?"

Crawford started blinking wildly. "Uh, I have to check the floor plan. Let me—"

"Shit, there's no time for that! Get some agents up there right now!"

DAVID GRABBED PROFESSOR GUPTA AND covered his mouth while Monique locked the door behind him. The old man was surprisingly light, hardly more than a hundred pounds, so it was relatively easy to carry him to the far corner of the supply room. As gently as he could, David rested Gupta against the wall and crouched beside him. The professor was nearly twice David's age and yet his delicate frame and small hands and unlined face gave him a remarkably childlike appearance. For a moment David imagined that he was holding Jonah, putting an arm around his son's shoulders to keep him warm and lightly touching his lips to quiet his crying.

"Dr. Gupta?" he whispered. "Do you remember me? I'm David Swift. I came here once before to interview you about your work with Dr. Einstein, remember?"

His eyes, jittery white marbles with dark brown centers, regarded David uncertainly for a second, then widened in recognition. His lips moved under David's hand. "What are you—"

"Please!" David hissed. "Don't speak above a whisper."

"It's for your own safety," Monique added, bending over David's shoulder. "Your offices are under surveillance. There may be listening devices in this room."

Gupta's eyes darted back and forth between David and Monique. He was obviously terrified, but he seemed to be trying to make sense of the situation. After a few seconds he nodded, acquiescing, and David removed his hand from the old man's mouth. Gupta nervously licked his lips. "Listening devices?" he whispered. "Who's listening?"

"The FBI, for certain," David replied. "And maybe others as well. Some very dangerous people are looking for you, Professor. We have to get you out of here."

He shook his head, bewildered. His unruly gray hair fell across his forehead. "Is this some kind of joke? David, I haven't seen you in years, and now you come in here with—" He stopped himself and pointed at Monique's uniform. "Who are you? You work for Carnegie Mellon Building Services?"

"No, I'm Monique Reynolds," she whispered. "Of the Institute for Advanced Study."

He looked at her carefully, as if trying to place her. "Monique Reynolds? The string theorist?"

She nodded. "That's right. I'm sorry if we've—"

"Yes, yes, I know you." He gave her a weak smile. "My foundation funds some particle-physics experiments at Fermilab, so I'm familiar with your work. But why are you dressed like that?"

David was getting impatient. It was just a matter of time before the FBI agents came to the supply room to find out what had tripped the alarm. "We have to get going. Professor, I'm going to help you into the Dumpster and then—"

"The Dumpster?"

"Please, just come with us. There's no time to explain."

David gripped Gupta's arm above the elbow and started to help him to his feet. But the old man refused to budge. With surprising strength he jerked his arm out of David's grasp. "I'm afraid you'll have to take the time. I'm not going anywhere until you tell me what's going on."

"Look, the agents are gonna be here any—"

"Then I recommend that you be quick about it."

Shit, David thought. That was the problem with these brilliant scientists, they were too damn rational. He gazed at the ceiling for a moment, trying to tamp his fears and clear his head. Then he looked Gupta in the eye. *"Einheitliche Feldtheorie,"* he whispered. "That's what they want."

The German words had a delayed effect on Gupta. At first he simply lifted his eyebrows in mild surprise and puzzlement, but after a few seconds his face went slack. He fell back against the wall, staring blankly at the shelves of janitorial supplies.

David leaned over him so he could continue whispering in the old man's ear. "Someone's trying to piece the theory together. Maybe they're terrorists, maybe they're spies, I don't know. First they went after MacDonald, then Bouchet and Kleinman." He paused, dreading what he had to say next. Gupta had worked with the other physicists for many years. He and Kleinman had been particularly close. "I'm sorry, Professor. All three of them are dead. You're the only one left."

Gupta looked up at him. The brown skin below his right eye twitched. "Kleinman? He's dead?"

David nodded. "I saw him in the hospital last night. He'd been tortured."

"No, no, no . . ." Gupta clutched his stomach and groaned. His eyes closed and his mouth opened. It looked like he was going to vomit.

Monique knelt on the floor and put her arm around the professor. "Shhh-shhh-shhh," she whispered, patting his back. "It's all right, it's all right."

David waited several seconds while Monique comforted the old man. But he couldn't wait too long. He imagined the FBI agents racing up the stairways of Newell-Simon Hall. "The government figured out what was going on," he said. "And now they want the theory, too. That's why the FBI put you under surveillance and why they've been chasing me for the past sixteen hours."

Gupta opened his eyes, wincing. His face was shiny with sweat. "How do you know all this?"

"Before Kleinman died, he gave me a code, a sequence of numbers. It turned out to be the geographic coordinates of your office. I think Kleinman wanted me to safeguard the theory somehow. Keep it away from both the government and the terrorists."

The professor stared at the floor and slowly shook his head. "His worst nightmare," he muttered. "This was *Herr Doktor*'s worst nightmare."

David felt a jolt of adrenaline. Blood jumped in his neck. "What was he afraid of? Was it a weapon?"

He kept shaking his head. "He never told me. He told the others, but not me."

"What? What do you mean?"

Gupta took a deep breath. With visible effort, he sat up and removed a handkerchief from his pocket. "Einstein was a man of conscience, David. He thought very carefully before selecting the people who would carry this burden." He raised the handkerchief and wiped the sweat from his brow. "In 1954, I was a married man, and my wife was pregnant with our first child. The last thing *Herr Doktor* wanted to do was put me in danger. So he parceled out the equations and gave them to the others instead—Kleinman, Bouchet, and MacDonald. None of them were married, you see."

Monique, who was still kneeling beside Gupta, shot David a worried look. Equally alarmed, David leaned a bit closer to the old man. "Wait a second," he whispered. "You're saying you don't know the unified theory? Not even part of it?"

He shook his head again. "I know that Einstein succeeded in formulating the theory and that he'd resolved to keep it secret. But I don't know any of the equations or the underlying principles. My colleagues had sworn to *Herr Doktor* that they wouldn't tell a soul, and they were very diligent about keeping their oath."

David's dismay was so strong it made him dizzy. He had to lean against the wall to keep his balance. "Hold on, hold on," he sputtered. "This doesn't make any sense. Kleinman's code pointed to you. Why did he send me here if you don't know the theory?"

"Perhaps you misinterpreted the code." Gupta had regained some of his composure and now he regarded David as if he were a student. "You said it was a numerical sequence?"

"Yes, yes, sixteen digits. The first twelve are the latitude and longitude of Newell-Simon Hall. The last four are the numbers in your phone—"

David stopped in midsentence. He'd heard something. A quick metallic rattle, quiet but unmistakable, coming from the door to the supply room. Someone was trying the knob.

❀ ❀ ❀

AGENT CRAWFORD HOVERED OVER THE video console, his anxious face less than ten inches from the screen. Through his radio headset he murmured instructions to the two-man team that was heading for Amil Gupta's office. Lucille stood behind him, scrutinizing all the activity in the command post. They'd secured the perimeter of Newell-Simon Hall, so there was no chance that Gupta could escape from the building. Still, Lucille couldn't relax until they'd located the guy.

On the video monitor she saw Agents Walsh and Miller march into Gupta's reception room. They were dressed like students, in shorts and T-shirts and sneakers, and each carried a large blue backpack. Not the cleverest disguise in the world, but it would have to do. The homely teenage boy was still sitting at the reception desk, but the strange miniature tank was gone now. One of the agents— Walsh, the taller one—approached the teenager.

"You have to get Professor Gupta!" he shouted. "There's a fire in the computer lab!"

The boy didn't even look up. He just stared at the large flat-panel screen that took up most of the space on his desk. Because the surveillance camera in the reception room was embedded in the wall behind him, Lucille got a glimpse of what was on his screen: an animated soldier in a khaki uniform running past a yellow block-house. Some kind of damn computer game.

Agent Walsh leaned across the desk and got in the boy's face. "Hey, are you deaf? This is an emergency! Where's Professor Gupta?"

The teenager simply tilted his head and continued playing his game. Meanwhile, Agent Miller went to the door to Gupta's office. "It's locked," he said. "See if there's a buzzer on the desk that opens the door."

Walsh maneuvered around the desk and shoved the boy's chair aside. As he bent over to examine the desktop, his hand hit the keyboard and the computer screen went blank. In that same instant the teenager leaped out of his chair and began to scream. It was a terrible, desperate, maniacal shriek, long and unwavering. The boy flapped his hands as he screamed, waving them wildly as if they were burning.

"Jesus!" Walsh cried, spinning around to face him. "Shut the fuck up!"

The teenager went rigid and screamed even louder. Oh shit, Lucille thought as she stared at the monitor. She'd seen this kind of behavior before. One of her sister's grandchildren down in Houston had the same problem. The boy was autistic.

She stepped forward and grabbed the radio headset from Agent Crawford. "Forget about the boy!" she yelled into the microphone. "Just get the door open!"

Walsh and Miller obediently opened their backpacks and removed the breaching equipment. Walsh positioned the forked end of the Halligan bar between the door and the jamb, and Miller swung the sledgehammer to pound the tool inside. After just three swings, they pried the door open and rushed into Gupta's office. Lucille saw the agents appear on another video monitor, striding past the professor's desk as they searched the room.

"He's not here," Walsh reported over the radio. "But there's another door in the back, sort of hidden behind the bookshelves. Should we proceed in that direction?"

"Hell, yes!" Lucille bellowed.

Beside her, Agent Crawford flipped through the floor maps of Newell-Simon Hall. "That door isn't in the plans," he said. "It must be a recent renovation."

Lucille looked at him with disgust. He was useless. "I want six more agents to get their asses to the fourth floor, you hear? Every room has to be searched, every goddamn room!"

While Crawford fumbled for his radio, one of the technicians came up to Lucille with a printout in his hand. "Uh, Agent Parker?" he said. "Can I interrupt for a second?"

"Christ! What now?"

"I've got, uh, the results of the database search you asked for? Running the surveillance images through the face-recognition system?"

"Well, spit it out already! Did you find anything?"

"Uh, yeah, I think I found something you might want to see."

"HEY, ANYONE IN THERE?"

All three of them froze when they heard the booming voice on the other side of the door. David, Monique, and Professor Gupta held their breath at the same time, and the only sound in the supply room came from the column of water still running in the sink.

Then there was an urgent pounding on the door, so violent it made the walls shiver. "This is the fire department! If anyone's in there, open up!"

Gupta clutched David's arm, his delicate fingers digging into the biceps. Again David thought of his son, remembering how Jonah clung to him when the boy was frightened. Gupta pointed at the door and gave him a questioning look. David shook his head. It definitely wasn't the fire department.

Now a clanking noise came from the corridor. Something heavy scraped against the door frame. A second later a thunderous slam shook the room. In the narrow gap between the door and the jamb, David saw the forked end of a metal bar poking through.

Monique pulled her revolver from the waistband of her shorts and this time David didn't stop her. He knew that they didn't have a chance in hell, that the FBI agents would cut them to pieces if they started shooting, but at that moment he wasn't thinking too clearly. In fact, he felt like he was drunk, drunk on fear and rage. It was stupid and suicidal, but he was too pissed off to care. Fuck it all, he thought. I'm not going down without a fight.

Luckily, Professor Gupta took control. He let go of David and grasped Monique's arm, forcing her to lower the gun. "You don't need that," he whispered. "I have a better idea."

Gupta reached into the inside pocket of his jacket and pulled out a handheld gadget that looked a bit like a BlackBerry but was obviously custom-designed. With his quick little thumbs he began stabbing the gadget's keyboard. On the miniature screen was a three-dimensional architectural layout, a map of Newell-Simon Hall with flashing icons scattered among the floors. David had seen this map before, on his previous visit to Gupta's office. The old man used it for tracking his robots.

Another tremendous slam pummeled the door. The noise made David jump, but Gupta stayed bent over his tiny screen, his thumbs working furiously. Jesus, David thought, what the hell is he doing? Then came the third slam, the loudest of all, and it was accompanied by a deep metallic groan, the sound of the steel door frame buckling under the pressure of the Halligan bar. The forked end now protruded several inches into the room, glinting silver gray under the fluorescent lights. One more tap and the door would burst open.

Then David heard a familiar whirring in the corridor outside the room. It was the whine of an electric motor, coming steadily closer. And then the synthesized voice of the AR-21 Autonomous Receptionist: "WARNING! Hazardous levels of radiation have been detected. Evacuate the area immediately . . . WARNING! Hazardous levels of radiation have been detected. Evacuate the area immediately . . ."

As if to confirm the robot's warning, a buildingwide alarm sounded from the public-address speakers and emergency strobe lights on the ceiling began to flash. Gupta had obviously rewired the building's electrical systems so he could control them with his handheld device. Beneath the noise of the alarm, David heard shouting in the corridor, the voices of the FBI agents yelling orders at one another. Then they dropped their breaching tools—David heard them clatter to the floor—and raced for the exit. Soon he could no longer hear their footsteps.

Grinning, Monique put her gun away and squeezed Professor

Gupta's shoulder. The old man smiled sheepishly and pointed at his handheld controller. "The warning was already in the program," he explained. "We originally developed this class of robots for the Defense Department. Reconnaissance in battlefield environments. The military version is called the Dragon Runner."

David helped Gupta to his feet. "We better get going. The agents will be back in a few minutes with their Geiger counters." He led the professor to the Dumpster and prepared to heave him inside. "It's not the most comfortable ride, but it got me into the building. You just have to lie still, okay?"

"Are you sure this is a good idea?" Gupta asked. "The FBI is looking for me now and the building is probably surrounded. Don't you think they'll search the Dumpster?"

Monique, who had already unlocked the door, stopped in her tracks. "Shit, he's right. We can't get out that way."

David shook his head. "We don't have a choice. We'll take the Dumpster as far as we can, until we get past the surveillance cameras, and then we'll just have to take our chances with the—"

"Those surveillance cameras?" Gupta interjected. "They transmit their signals wirelessly, correct?"

"Uh, yeah, I suppose," David answered. "I mean, it's a covert operation, so the FBI wouldn't want to string wires all over the place."

Gupta smiled again. "Then we can do something about it. Take me to room 407. The jamming equipment is in there. After that, we won't need the Dumpster."

"But how are we gonna get out of the building?" Monique asked. "Even if the cameras are down, they still have enough agents to cover the exits."

"Don't worry, I know a place we can go," Gupta replied. "My students will help us. But we have to get Michael first."

"Michael?"

"Yes, he sits at the desk in my reception area. He likes to play his computer games there."

The handicapped boy, David thought. The one who stared at the computer screen instead of answering Monique. "I'm sorry, Professor, but why do you—"

"We can't leave him behind, David. He's my grandson."

LUCILLE STUDIED THE PRINTOUT IN her hands. On the left side was an image from one of the surveillance cameras, a picture of a cleaning woman pushing a canvas Dumpster into Amil Gupta's reception room. On the right was a page from the FBI's dossier on Monique Reynolds, professor of physics at Princeton's Institute for Advanced Study. The Bureau had collected quite a bit of information about Professor Reynolds in advance of the undercover operation at her home on 112 Mercer Street. The agents in New Jersey reported that she had no criminal record, although her mother had a long list of drug arrests and her sister was a prostitute working in Washington, D.C. More to the point, Professor Reynolds had no apparent connections to any of Einstein's assistants; the Institute had granted her the honor of living at 112 Mercer Street simply because she was one of their most highly regarded physicists. The agents concluded that Reynolds was an innocent bystander and recommended that the Bureau disguise the search of her home, making it look like an act of vandalism. But now it seemed that this conclusion had been premature.

She's pretty, Lucille thought. Full lips, high cheekbones, swooping eyebrows. And about the same age as David Swift. Both of them had been graduate students in physics in the late 1980s. And Princeton, of course, was one of the stops on the New Jersey Transit train that Swift had boarded last night. Although Lucille couldn't possibly have guessed any of this beforehand, she nevertheless felt a twinge of humiliation as she stared at Monique's picture. Skinny bitch, she muttered. You and Swift almost fooled me. But I've got you now.

A commotion at the other end of the command post interrupted her thoughts. Agent Crawford stood in front of the video monitors, shouting into his headset. "Affirmative, retreat to the ground floor and hold your positions there. Repeat, hold your positions on the ground floor. We need to maintain the perimeter."

Lucille put down the printout and looked at Crawford. "What's going on?"

"We got a report of radiation on the fourth floor. I'm withdrawing everyone until we can get the hazmat team up there."

Lucille tensed. Radiation? Why didn't they detect it before? "Who reported it? And how many rems are we talking about?"

She waited impatiently while Crawford shouted the questions into his headset. After several endless seconds he got an answer. "It was an alarm that went off. From a surveillance drone, a Dragon Runner."

"What? We haven't deployed any surveillance drones!"

"But Agent Walsh said he was certain it was a Dragon Runner."

"Look, I don't care . . ." Lucille paused. She remembered something she'd seen on one of the video monitors just a few minutes ago. The odd contraption that looked like a miniature tank, rolling across the floor of Gupta's reception room. "Shit, that's one of Gupta's robots! It's a trick!"

Crawford stood there, looking confused. "A trick? What do you—"

She didn't have time to explain. Instead she ripped the headset off Crawford's bewildered face and spoke into the microphone. "Everyone return to their previous positions! There's no radiation danger in the building. Repeat, no radiation danger in—"

"Agent Parker!" one of the technicians called out. "Check out Monitor Five!"

Lucille looked at the screen just in time to see Monique Reynolds pushing her Dumpster down a corridor. She was straining against the thing, both hands gripping the edge of the cart and her torso bent almost horizontally. And jogging along beside her was the autistic teenager from Gupta's reception room.

Monique quickly passed out of the surveillance camera's range, but Lucille noted the device's location. She spoke into the microphone again. "All teams head for the southwestern corner of the fourth floor. The target has been observed in this area. Repeat, the southwestern corner of the fourth floor."

Lucille let out a long whoosh of breath and returned the radio headset to Crawford. All right, she thought, now it's just a matter of time. She gazed at the bank of video monitors and saw her agents dashing up the stairways of Newell-Simon Hall. In less than a minute they would converge on Monique Reynolds's position and pull Amil Gupta out of her Dumpster. And maybe David Swift, too, if he'd been stupid enough to enter the building with her. And then Lucille could forget about this whole lousy assignment and go back to her office at headquarters, where she wouldn't have to worry about theoretical physics or fugitive historians or the SecDef's nutty Buck Rogers ideas.

But while she was contemplating this happy prospect, every screen in the bank of video monitors suddenly went black.

AFTER DRIVING THE FERRARI AS fast as he dared for four and a half hours, Simon reached Carnegie Mellon and headed straight for the Robotics Institute. As soon as he turned off Forbes Avenue, though, he feared he was too late. A dozen burly men in shorts and T-shirts guarded the building's entrance; half of them were searching the backpacks and purses of the students trying to exit the lobby and half were warily surveying the crowd, their semiautomatics resting in barely concealed holsters.

Simon quickly parked the Ferrari and found a reconnaissance position behind a neighboring building. His intuition had been correct. David Swift and Monique Reynolds had traveled west to rendezvous with Amil Gupta. Simon was quite familiar with Gupta and his work with Dr. Einstein; in fact, when he'd first received his current assignment, he'd naturally assumed that Gupta would be one of his targets, along with Bouchet, MacDonald, and Kleinman.

But his client, Henry Cobb, had told him early on that Gupta wasn't worth pursuing. Although he'd been one of Einstein's assistants in the fifties, Gupta had no knowledge of the unified theory. Cobb didn't reveal how he'd discovered this intriguing fact, but he stated it with unequivocal certainty. So it was a bit amusing now to see the platoon of FBI agents surrounding the Robotics Institute, ready to pounce on a man who could unfortunately tell them nothing.

The problem, however, was that David Swift had also assumed that Gupta knew the theory, and now it looked like the federal agents had trapped him and his physicist girlfriend. Extracting them from the FBI's custody wouldn't be easy. The Bureau had beefed up the security of the operation; in addition to the agents in front of Newell-Simon Hall, there was another dozen at the service entrance and probably several more in the trailer that was serving as their command post. (He identified it right away from the profusion of antennas on its roof.) But Simon was undaunted. He knew that if he waited for the right moment, he could create a diversion. It was helpful that there were so many students in the area, gawking at the agents. He might need a human shield when he confronted the FBI men.

Simon pulled out a pair of tactical binoculars so he could observe the operation more closely. Outside the service entrance, a tall agent holding an M-16 stood next to a line of handcuffed women in pale blue smocks. Simon zoomed in on their faces: all five were black, but Monique Reynolds wasn't among them. A few yards away, two more agents were rooting through a canvas Dumpster, madly tossing newspapers and crumpled bags and scraps of wood into the air. Within twenty seconds all the garbage was strewn across the parking lot, and the agents stared dejectedly at the bottom of the cart. Then a heavyset woman in a white blouse and a red skirt trotted over to the agents and began shouting. Simon focused on her face, which was creased around the eyes and contorted with frustration. He felt a shock of recognition: it was the babushka! The big-bosomed woman who'd nearly killed him the night before! She was in charge of the operation here as well, and from the look on her face Simon could see that something had gone wrong. At least one of their targets had slipped away.

Then Simon spotted another swarm of agents surrounding a very peculiar-looking car. The vehicle's passenger compartment had been ripped off its chassis and in its place was a massive block of machinery topped by a large silver orb. Simon stared at the thing in wonder—he'd seen this vehicle before, in a magazine article about robotic cars. He remembered it clearly because the technology had fascinated him. The orb contained a rotating laser scanner designed to detect obstacles in the vehicle's path. The FBI men were giving the car a thorough inspection, shining their flashlights into every nook and cranny. One agent interrogated the pair of Robotics Institute students who were testing the car, while another got down on all fours and peered beneath the vehicle, looking for stowaways clinging to the undercarriage. Finally, the agents allowed the test to continue, and the students walked behind the robotic car as it navigated its way out of the parking lot.

But as the vehicle made a right onto Forbes Avenue and slowly cruised away, Simon noticed something odd: the silver orb didn't rotate as the vehicle made the turn. The laser scanner wasn't functioning, and yet the car didn't jump the curb or crash into the oncoming traffic. It executed a flawless turn, staying within its lane at all times. Simon knew this could mean only one of two things: either the vehicle was employing a different kind of obstacle-avoidance technology, or a driver was hidden somewhere inside the car.

Grinning, Simon put his binoculars away and rushed back to his Ferrari.

Chapter Seven

IN A DARK COMPARTMENT HIDDEN WITHIN THE HIGHLANDER vehicle, Amil Gupta hunched over the controls of the drive-by-wire panel. Four people were crammed inside the narrow space: David squeezed between Gupta and Monique, while Michael crouched at the other end of the compartment, playing with a Game Boy perched on his knees. Gupta had warned that his grandson would scream if he were touched, so David and Monique entwined in an uncomfortable embrace to keep a few inches between themselves and the teenager. Monique's butt pinned David's thigh to the floor and her elbows dug into his ribs. At one point, the back of her head smacked into David's chin, slamming his teeth shut on the tip of his tongue, but he didn't make a sound. He knew the FBI agents were right outside the vehicle. He could see them on the screen at the center of the drive-by-wire panel, which showed a live video feed from one of the Highlander's cameras.

The panel looked a bit like an aircraft's steering wheel, with black handgrips to the left and right of the central screen. Gupta twisted the right grip to accelerate the vehicle and squeezed the left one to brake it. In fits and starts, he maneuvered the Highlander out of the parking lot and away from the federal agents. As he turned onto Forbes Avenue he let out a whistle of relief. "I think we're safe now," he said. "None of the agents seem to be following us."

Gupta stayed in the right lane of the busy street, driving at a snail's pace so his students could keep up with the Highlander on foot. David noticed that the compass reading above the screen said EAST. "Where are we going?" he asked.

"No particular direction," Gupta replied. "I'm just trying to put some distance between us and those gentlemen from the FBI."

"Head for the East Campus Lot," Monique grunted. "That's where my car's parked. I can't stay cooped up like this much longer."

Gupta nodded. "All right, but it's going to take a few minutes to get there. I can drive the Highlander faster than this, but it would look very suspicious if I left my students behind."

The old man seemed quite adept at the drive-by-wire controls. He'd obviously done this before. "I don't understand something, Professor," David said. "Why did you put a driver-control system in a robotic vehicle?"

"The Highlander is an army contract," Gupta explained, "and the army wanted a robotic vehicle that could also be driven by soldiers if necessary. The Pentagon doesn't really trust the technology, you see. I argued against the idea, but they were insistent. So we designed the drive-by-wire system and the two-man cockpit. We put the cockpit in the dead center of the vehicle to maximize the amount of armor that could be layered around it."

"But why didn't the FBI agents realize there could be people inside? Don't they know about the army's projects?"

The professor chuckled. "Obviously you've never done any work for the government. All these research-and-development contracts are classified. The army won't tell the navy what it's doing, and the navy won't tell the Marines. Perfectly ridiculous, the whole thing."

David's right foot was growing numb from Monique's weight on his thigh. He tried to shift his leg a bit, being careful not to brush against Michael. The teenager's fingers were dancing over the buttons of the Game Boy but the rest of his body was motionless, locked in a rigid fetal curl. On the Game Boy's screen, a cartoon soldier fired his rifle at a squat yellow building. David watched the action for a few seconds, then leaned toward Gupta. "Your grandson seems a lot calmer now," he whispered. "The computer game has quite an effect on him."

"That's one of the symptoms of autism," Gupta said. "A preoccupation with certain activities to the exclusion of all else. It's his way of shutting out the world."

Gupta's tone was matter-of-fact. He spoke as if he were the boy's doctor, without a hint of regret or despair. To David, this seemed an amazing feat of emotional control. He could've never done the same if Jonah had been born with autism. "Where are his parents?"

The professor shook his head. "My daughter is a drug addict, and she's never told me who Michael's father is. The boy's lived with me for the past five years."

Gupta kept his eyes on the drive-by-wire screen, but his hands seemed to tighten around the panel. So much for emotional control, David thought. Even the most rational men have their weak spots. Rather than torment him further, David pointed at Michael's Game Boy. "Is that the same game that was running on the computer in your reception room?"

The professor nodded vigorously, eager to change the subject. "Yes, it's a program called Warfighter. The army uses it for combat training. The Robotics Institute had a contract to develop a new interface for the program, and Michael came into the computer lab one day while we were working on it. He took one look at the screen and he's been hooked ever since. I've tried to interest him in other computer games—Major League Baseball, that kind of thing—but all he wants to play is Warfighter."

Now Monique shifted her weight, moving her butt off David's thigh but mashing his kneecap. Her ass was firm and muscular. Despite the pain in his leg, David felt a surge of arousal. He hadn't been this close to a woman in a while. He wanted to lock his arms around her waist and drink in her clean scent, but this was obviously not the right moment. He turned back to Gupta. "Your institute does a lot of military work, doesn't it? The Dragon Runner, the Highlander, the Warfighter?"

Gupta shrugged. "That's where the money is. My foundation has substantial resources, but only the Pentagon has enough to fund these long-term research projects. But I've never worked on weaponry, mind you. Reconnaissance, yes, combat simulation, yes. But weaponry, never."

"Why do you think the military is so interested in the unified field theory? What kind of weapon could possibly come out of it?"

"I told you, I don't know the details of the *Einheitliche Feldtheorie*. But any unification theory must describe what happens to particles and forces at very high energies. Energies comparable to those in a black hole, for example. And it's conceivable that unexpected phenomena can occur in that realm."

Monique squirmed on top of David again. Her body felt tense, agitated. "But how could you build a weapon around those phenomena?" she asked. "There's no practical way to generate such high energies. You'd need a particle accelerator the size of the Milky Way galaxy."

"Maybe, maybe not," Gupta responded. "It's impossible to predict the consequences of a new discovery in physics. Look at *Herr Doctor*'s special theory of relativity. After he wrote the paper in 1905, it took him several months to realize that his equations led to the $E = mc^2$ formula. And forty more years passed before physicists learned how to use the formula to make an atomic bomb."

David nodded. "At a press conference in the thirties, someone asked Einstein if it was possible to release energy by splitting atoms. And he completely dismissed the idea. His quote was, 'It would be like shooting at birds in the dark in a country where there are few birds.'"

"Exactly so. *Herr Doktor* couldn't have been more wrong. And he certainly didn't want to repeat that error." The professor shook his head. "Thankfully I never had to carry the burden of the unified theory, but I knew what was at stake. It's not a physics problem, it's a problem of human behavior. Humans are simply not intelligent enough to stop killing each other. They will use any tools at their disposal to annihilate their enemies."

He fell silent just as the screen on the drive-by-wire panel showed the entrance to the vast East Campus Lot, which was several times larger than the parking lot they'd left five minutes ago. The professor guided the Highlander through the entrance and squeezed the left handgrip to bring the vehicle to a stop. Then he pressed a button that changed the image on the screen to a panoramic view of the whole lot. "I want to show you something," he said. "Dr. Reynolds, could you please locate your car on the screen?"

Monique craned her neck to get a closer look. After a few seconds she pointed at a red Corvette in the background, about a hundred yards away. "That's it. I remember I parked near that tour bus in the corner."

Gupta touched the screen at that spot and a white *X* began flashing over the Corvette. Then he pressed another button and folded his arms across his chest. "Now I've switched the Highlander to autonomous operation. Watch the screen."

Without Gupta touching the controls, the robotic vehicle began cruising across the parking lot. It took the shortest navigable path toward the Corvette, moving at about fifteen miles per hour and expertly weaving between the parked cars. About halfway there, a minivan suddenly backed out of its parking space, only ten feet in front of them. The screen showed the Highlander heading straight for the van's sliding door. David automatically extended his right foot, blindly hunting for a nonexistent brake pedal, but Gupta kept his arms folded across his chest. No intervention was needed, because the Highlander was already slowing. Working on its own, the vehicle glided to a stop.

"Remarkable, isn't it?" Gupta said, pointing at the screen. "Autonomous navigation is much more than a simple algorithm. It involves analyzing the landscape and identifying the hazards. It's an extremely complex decision-making process, and decision making is the key to intelligence and consciousness." He turned back to David and Monique. "This was the reason why I switched from physics to robotics. I saw that the world wasn't getting any closer to *Herr Doktor*'s dream, the dream of universal peace. And I recognized that his dream would never become a reality until there was a fundamental change in human consciousness."

The driver of the minivan shifted gears and moved out of the Highlander's path. After a moment the robotic vehicle resumed its trek toward the Corvette. Meanwhile, Gupta leaned against the wall of the compartment. "I thought artificial intelligence could serve as a bridge to this new consciousness," he said. "If we could teach machines how to think, we just might learn something about ourselves. I know this approach must sound utterly utopian, but for twenty years I had high hopes for it." He bowed his head and sighed. In the dim light from the navigation screen he looked exhausted. "But we've run out of time. Our machines have intelligence, but only the intelligence of a termite. Enough to navigate a parking lot, but no more."

The Highlander finally arrived at its programmed destination. The navigation screen showed the rear end of Monique's Corvette, just a few feet away; the letters on her vanity license plate read STRINGS. David turned to Gupta, hoping to hash out their next step, but the old man was still staring at the floor. "Such a waste, such a waste," he muttered, shaking his head. "Poor Alastair, the secret drove him mad. He went back to Scotland to forget the equations *Herr Doktor* had given him, but he couldn't erase them from his mind. Jacques and Hans, they were stronger men, but the theory tormented them, too."

Monique glanced over her shoulder and exchanged a look with David. They didn't have time for a long conference in the parking lot. The FBI agents were less than a mile away, and once they'd inspected every inch of Newell-Simon Hall, they were sure to expand the perimeter of their search. They might even decide to take a second look at the Highlander. Filled with renewed anxiety, David leaned toward Gupta and touched the old man's arm. "Professor, we have to go. How do you open the hatch?"

Gupta looked up but his eyes were unfocused. "You know what Hans told me the last time I saw him? He said it might be better for everyone if he and Jacques and Alastair let the unified theory die with them. I was shocked to hear him say that, because Hans loved the theory more than anyone. Whenever there was a major breakthrough in physics, like the discovery of the top quark or charge-parity violation, he'd call me up and say, 'See? *Herr Doktor* predicted it!'"

Despite his anxiety, David paused at the mention of his old mentor, Hans Kleinman. The poor lonely man, shuffling across the streets of West Harlem with the secrets of the universe locked inside his weary head. No wonder he'd never married, never had a family. And yet he hadn't been entirely friendless. He'd stayed in touch with Amil Gupta. "When was the last time you saw Dr. Kleinman?" David asked.

Gupta thought for a moment. "About four years ago, I believe. Yes, yes, four years. Hans had just retired from Columbia and he seemed a bit depressed, so I invited him to Carnegie's Retreat. We spent two weeks there."

"Carnegie's Retreat? What's that?"

"The name makes it sound grander than it really is. It's just an old hunting cabin down in West Virginia owned by Carnegie Mellon. The university makes it available to faculty members during the summer, but hardly anyone goes on vacation there. It's too remote."

A cabin in the woods. Kleinman and Gupta had spent some time there four years ago, but that was their only connection to the place, so neither the FBI nor the terrorists would know about it. "Are there any computers in this cabin?"

Gupta seemed taken aback by the question. He raised his hand to his chin and tapped his lips with his index finger. "Yes, we installed a computer system so Michael could play his games. He was thirteen then, yes."

Monique twisted around so she could look David in the eye. "What are you thinking? That Kleinman hid the equations there?"

He nodded. "It's a possibility. Kleinman's code said Professor Gupta had the theory, right? Amil doesn't know the equations, but maybe Kleinman secretly placed them on one of the professor's computers. Kleinman knew he couldn't use the computers at the Robotics Institute or Amil's home—those are the first places the government would look if it were hunting for the theory. This cabin in West Virginia would be a much better hiding place. Nobody except for Amil knows that Kleinman was ever there."

Gupta was still tapping his lips. He looked unconvinced. "I never saw Hans at the computer in Carnegie's Retreat. And if he was going to hide the theory there, why didn't he tell me?"

"Maybe he was afraid that someone would interrogate you. Or torture you."

Before Gupta could respond, Monique pointed at the Highlander's navigation screen. The two students who'd followed the vehicle from Newell-Simon Hall to the parking lot were waving at the camera, trying to get their attention. One of the young men was short and fat, while the other was tall and pimply, but they had identical looks of concern on their faces. "Shit!" Monique yelled. "Something's happening outside!"

Gupta saw the screen, too. He pushed another button on the control panel and the concealed hatch at the very top of the Highlander opened with a hiss. Monique and David scrambled out first, and then Gupta helped his grandson out of the vehicle. As soon as David's sneakers touched the asphalt, he heard the whine of the sirens. Half a dozen black-and-white patrol cars from the Pittsburgh Police Department raced down Forbes Avenue, heading for Newell-Simon Hall. The FBI had called in reinforcements.

Monique rushed to the Corvette and unlocked its doors. "Quick! Get in the car! Before they close the street!"

David was leading Professor Gupta and Michael to the passenger-side door when he stopped in his tracks. "Wait a second! We can't take this car!" He turned to Monique, pointing at her vanity license plate. "The FBI is probably reviewing its surveillance videos right now. Once they figure out who you are, every cop in Pennsylvania will be looking for a red Corvette with that plate number!"

"What else can we do?" Monique yelled back. "We can't take the Highlander, they'll be looking for that, too!"

The tall, pimply student timidly raised his hand. "Uh, Professor Gupta? You can borrow my car if you want. It's parked right over there." He pointed at a beat-up gray Hyundai Accent with a big dent in the rear fender.

Monique stared at the thing, her mouth open. "A Hyundai? You want me to leave my Corvette here and drive a Hyundai?"

Gupta went over to the pimply student, who'd already taken his car keys out of his pocket, and patted the young man on the back. "That's very generous of you, Jeremy. We'll return your car as soon as we can. And in the meantime, I think you and Gary should leave town for a few days. Take a bus to the Finger Lakes, do some hiking in the gorges. All right, boys?"

The students nodded rapidly, obviously delighted to do a favor for their adored professor. Jeremy gave the keys to Gupta, who passed them to David. But Monique still stood by the Corvette's open door, gazing mournfully at the car as if she'd never see it again.

As David came toward her, she shot him a reproachful look. "It took me seven years to save up for this car. Seven years!"

He reached past her to grab the overnight bag, the laptop case, and the bag of sandwiches Monique had bought that morning at the New Stanton Service Area. Then he dropped the keys to the Hyundai into her palm. "Come on, give the Accent a spin," he said. "I hear it's got a nifty little engine."

PEERING THROUGH HIS BINOCULARS, SIMON saw four figures emerge from the robotic car. He recognized David Swift, Monique Reynolds, and Amil Gupta right away. The fourth figure was a mystery—a gangly teenager with black hair and dusky skin. Gupta hovered over the boy, leading him out of the vehicle without touching him.

Yes, very mysterious. Simon's first impulse was a surprise assault, but this parking lot wasn't an ideal field of operations. Too open, too visible. More important, the small army of FBI agents was too close, and squadrons of patrol cars from the local police department were converging on the campus. Better to wait for a more advantageous opportunity.

The four figures headed first for Monique's Corvette (Simon had gotten a complete description of the car from Keith, the deceased mechanic), but after conferring briefly with the pair of Robotics Institute students, the quartet squeezed into a battered gray subcompact. The car zipped out of the parking lot and made a right on Forbes Avenue. Simon let them get a hundred meters ahead before following in his Ferrari. He planned to hold his fire until they reached a sufficiently secluded stretch of highway. After traveling for about a kilometer, the subcompact turned right again on Murray Avenue. They were heading south.

KAREN HAD ASSUMED THAT JONAH was still asleep. She'd put him to bed as soon as they'd come home from the FBI offices that morning, and when she went into his room to check on him a few hours later, he was still lying prostrate under his Spider-Man blanket, his face pressed into the red-and-blue pillow. But as she turned to leave the room he rolled over and looked at her. "Where's Daddy?" he asked.

She sat on the edge of his bed and brushed the blond hair out of his eyes. "Hey, sweetie pie," she murmured. "Feel better now?"

Jonah frowned and batted her hand away. "Why are the police looking for him? Did Daddy do something bad?"

Okay, Karen thought. Don't give him too much information. First find out what he knows already. "What did the agents tell you last night? After they took you away from me, I mean?"

"They said Daddy was in trouble. And they asked me if he had any girlfriends." He sat up in bed, kicking the blanket off his legs. "Are they angry at Daddy? Because he has girlfriends now?"

Karen shook her head. "No, honey, no one's angry. What happened last night was just a mistake, all right? Those agents came to the wrong apartment."

"They had guns. I saw them." Jonah's eyes widened as the memory came back to him. He gripped Karen's sleeve and bunched the fabric in his fist. "Are they gonna shoot Daddy when they find him?"

She wrapped her arms around her son and held him tight, resting her chin on his left shoulder. He started crying then, his small chest heaving against hers, and in a moment Karen was crying, too. They shared the same fear. The men with guns were looking for David, and sooner or later they'd find him. Her tears slipped down her cheeks and fell on Jonah's back. She could see the blots of moisture on his pajama top.

As she rocked Jonah in her lap, she stared at the picture hanging on the wall beside his bed. It was a drawing of the solar system that David had made for Jonah about two years ago, just before he moved out of their apartment. On a large yellow poster he'd sketched the sun and all its planets, as well as the asteroid belt and a few roving comets. David had worked on the thing for hours, carefully delineating the rings of Saturn and the Great Red Spot of Jupiter. At the time, Karen remembered, she'd been a little resentful of all the effort he'd put into it; he was willing to spend the whole day drawing a picture for Jonah, but he couldn't take five minutes to talk with his wife, even as their marriage was collapsing around them. Now, though, she recognized that David hadn't been so heartless. He'd simply retreated from the inevitable. Rather than engage in another fruitless argument, he bent over the yellow poster and did something he loved.

After a minute or so Karen wiped the tears from her face. All right, she thought, enough crying. It's time to do something. Grasping Jonah's shoulders, she held her son at arm's length and looked him in the eye. "Okay, listen to me. I want you to get dressed as quickly as you can."

He gave her a confused look, his cheeks puffy and flushed. "Why? Where are we going?"

"We're going to see a friend of mine. She can help us fix this mistake, so Daddy won't be in trouble anymore. Okay?"

"How can she fix it? Does she know the police?"

Karen placed her hand on his back, nudging him off the bed. "Just get dressed. We'll talk about it on the way down there."

While Jonah slipped out of his pajamas, she headed for her own bedroom to change into one of her business suits. Maybe her gray Donna Karan, the one she usually wore during contract negotiations. To carry out what she was planning, she needed to look respectable.

Before she could get very far, though, the doorbell rang. She froze for a moment, remembering how the FBI agents had stormed into the apartment the night before. Cautiously, she approached the front door and squinted through the peephole.

It was Amory. He stood on the doormat in his own gray business suit, looking anxious and tired. A gauze pad on his forehead covered the gash he'd gotten when the federal agents had tackled him. He held a cell phone to his ear and nodded several times, apparently finishing up a conversation.

Karen opened the door. Amory quickly closed the cell phone, then stepped inside the apartment. "Karen, you have to come downtown with me to the U.S. Attorney's Office. He wants to speak with you immediately."

She scowled. "What? Are you crazy? I'm not going back there!"

"It's not the FBI, it's the U.S. attorney. He wants to apologize for the conduct of the agents last night." He pointed to the gauze pad above his eyebrow. "He already apologized to me for the rough handling."

"Apologize?" Karen shook her head, dumbfounded. "If he wants to apologize, he should come up here and do it! He should get down on his knees and beg my son for forgiveness! And then he should bend over so I can kick him in the ass!"

Amory waited for her to finish. "He also has some new information about your ex-husband's case. They've identified one of David's co-conspirators in the drug business. She's a professor at Princeton named Monique Reynolds."

"Never heard of her. And there's no drug business, Amory. I told you, that's a cover story they fabricated."

"I'm afraid you may be wrong about that. This Reynolds is a black woman from Washington, and she has definite connections to the drug trade. Her mother's a junkie and her sister's a prostitute."

Karen waved her hand. "So what? That doesn't prove a damn thing. They're making up stories again."

"They've seen this woman with him, Karen. Are you sure David never mentioned her?"

Amory stared at her intently, studying her eyes. After a few seconds she grew suspicious. She could see the FBI's motive for putting out this story: they were still playing the girlfriend angle, still trying to inflame her jealousies so she would betray her ex-husband. But why was Amory studying her so carefully? "What's going on?" she asked. "Are you interrogating me?"

He chuckled at her question, but it sounded forced. "No, no, I'm just trying to establish the facts. That's what we lawyers do, we—"

"Jesus Christ! I thought you were on my side!"

He stepped toward her and placed his hand on her shoulder. Tilting his head, he gave her a fatherly smile, the kind he usually reserved for the junior associates at his law firm. "Please, calm down. Of course I'm on your side. I'm just trying to make things a little easier for you. I have some friends who are willing to help."

He stroked her arm, but the caress made her skin crawl. The old bastard was working with the FBI. Somehow they'd enlisted him to their cause. She shrugged his hand off. "I don't need your help, all right? I can take care of this myself."

His smile disappeared. "Karen, please listen. This is a very serious case and some very powerful people are involved. You don't want to make enemies of these people. It won't be good for you and it won't be good for your son."

She stepped around him and opened the front door again. She couldn't believe she'd ever slept with this asshole. "Get out of here, Amory. And you can tell your friends to go fuck themselves."

He grimaced, curling his patrician upper lip. With as much dignity as he could muster, he stepped out of the apartment. "I'd be careful if I were you," he said coldly. "I wouldn't do anything rash."

Karen slammed the door shut. She was planning to do something very rash indeed.

SITTING AT HIS DESK IN his West Wing office, the vice president poked unhappily at his dinner, a small, dry piece of chicken breast surrounded by steamed carrots. Ever since the veep's fourth heart attack, the chefs in the White House kitchen had been serving him bland, low-fat meals like this one. For the first year or so, he'd stoically accepted the new diet; his memory of the crushing chest pains was vivid enough to keep him on the straight and narrow. But as time went on, he became increasingly resentful. He yearned for a Porterhouse steak swimming in its juices or a fist-size lobster tail drenched in melted butter. The daily culinary deprivation put him in a foul mood, making him snap at his aides and Secret Service escorts. Nevertheless, he soldiered onward. The American people were counting on him. The president was a boob, a brainless figurehead who had a talent for winning elections but little else. Without the vice president's counsel and guidance, the whole administration would go straight to hell.

As he chewed his tasteless chicken he heard a knock on the door. Swallowing with difficulty, he answered, "Yes?" and a moment later his chief of staff stepped into the office. But before the man could say a word, the secretary of defense charged past him, rushing into the room with his square head lowered like a battering ram. "We need to talk," he declared.

The veep signaled his chief of staff to leave the office and close

the door behind him. The SecDef strode past the cluster of up-
holstered chairs in the center of the room, nearly knocking over a
Tiffany lamp on the end table. The man was brash, irascible, and
supremely overconfident, but he was one of the few people in the
administration whom the vice president could trust. They'd worked
together since the Nixon days. "What is it this time?" the veep
asked. "Another blast in Baghdad?"

He shook his head. "We have a problem with Operation
Shortcut."

The vice president pushed his dinner plate aside. He felt a
twinge in the center of his chest. "I thought you said everything was
under control."

"It's the goddamn FBI's fault. They've screwed up twice now."
The secretary removed his rimless glasses and jabbed the air with
them. "First they lost a detainee because they brought him to a
poorly defended installation, and then they let another target slip
away because they botched the surveillance. Now both of them are
on the run and the Bureau has no idea where they are!"

The twinge in the Vice President's chest sharpened. It felt like
a thumbtack under his breastbone. "Who are these targets?"

"They're professors, probably ultraliberal Looney Tunes. I
wouldn't be surprised if they're working with Al Qaeda. Or maybe
the Iranians are paying them off. Of course the Bureau doesn't have
a clue. The director put a woman in charge of the operation, that's
part of the problem."

"What's her name?"

"Parker, Lucille Parker. I don't know much about her except
that she's from Texas. But that explains everything. She's probably
got some connection with the Cowboy-in-Chief." He jerked his
head to the left, in the direction of the Oval Office.

The vice president took a sip from his glass of water, hoping it
would tamp the ache in his chest. Operation Shortcut had started
about two weeks ago after the National Security Agency picked up
something odd during its surveillance of the Internet. It was an e-

mail full of cryptic language and strange equations, traced to a computer at a mental institution in Glasgow, Scotland. At first the NSA dismissed it as the work of an inventive lunatic, but out of curiosity one of the agency's analysts began studying the thing. It turned out that the author of the message was a former physicist who'd once worked with Albert Einstein. The equations were just a fragment of a larger theory, but enough was there to convince the NSA to set up a task force to find the rest. The word from the experts was that this theory could give the United States a powerful new weapon in the war on terrorism.

But if there was one thing the vice president had learned during his forty years in government, it was that civil servants are incapable of doing anything quickly. By the time the NSA task force got its act together, three of its four intelligence targets were dead. Some foreign government or terrorist group was also pursuing the theory, and now the counterterrorism experts were saying that if it fell into the wrong hands the results could be disastrous. According to the memo from the NSA director, it could make 9/11 look like a skirmish. "So what's your plan?" the veep asked. "I assume you had a reason for coming to my office?"

The secretary nodded. "I need an executive order. I want to deploy the Delta Force in the Homeland sector. I want them patrolling the borders and actively pursuing the targets. It's time for the Pentagon to take over."

The vice president thought about it for a moment. Technically, the Posse Comitatus Act barred army units from taking part in law enforcement operations on U.S. soil. But exceptions could be made in national emergencies. "Consider it done," he said. "How fast can you get the troops to the States?"

"The force is in western Iraq now. I can have them airlifted Stateside in less than twelve hours."

AT EXACTLY 6 P.M., WHILE they were driving down Route 19 through the corrugated hills of West Virginia, the sound of simulated gunfire coming from Michael's Game Boy abruptly ceased. The device emitted a high-pitched *ping* and then a synthesized voice announced, "It's time for dinner." David looked over his shoulder at the backseat and saw Michael raise his head and turn to Professor Gupta, who was dozing next to his grandson. "It's time for dinner, Grandpa," the boy said.

These were the first words David had heard him say. His voice was as crisp and emotionless as the Game Boy's. Although David could clearly see the resemblance between Michael and his grandfather—they had the same thick eyebrows, the same unruly hair—the teenager's eyes were glassy and his face was blank. "It's time for dinner, Grandpa," he repeated.

Gupta blinked a few times and scratched his head. He leaned forward, looking first at Monique, who was driving the Hyundai, and then at David. "Excuse me," he said. "You don't happen to have any food in the car, do you?"

David nodded. "We bought some stuff this morning." He picked up the plastic bag of supplies Monique had purchased at the rest stop on the Pennsylvania Turnpike. "Let me see what's left."

While he rummaged through the bag, Monique took her eyes off the road for a moment and glanced at the rearview mirror. She'd been nervously scanning the highway for patrol cars for the past three hours, but now she focused on Gupta and his grandson. "The computer game tells him when to eat?" she asked.

"Yes, yes," Gupta replied, "we programmed Warfighter to automatically stop play for half an hour at mealtimes. And it shuts down overnight, of course. Otherwise, Michael would keep playing until he collapsed."

David found a prepackaged turkey sandwich at the bottom of the bag. "Does your grandson like turkey?"

Gupta shook his head. "No, I'm afraid not. Do you have anything else?"

"Not much. Just a bag of potato chips and a few Snack-Well's."

"Oh, he likes potato chips! But only with ketchup. He won't eat a potato chip unless it has exactly two dabs of ketchup on it."

Looking under the turkey sandwich, David found a few ketchup packets that Monique had luckily thrown into the bag. He passed them to Professor Gupta along with the potato chips.

"Yes, this is perfect," the professor said. "You see, Michael is very particular about what he eats. It's another symptom of autism."

While Gupta opened the bag of chips, Monique glanced again at the rearview mirror. Her lips were pressed into a thin line of disapproval. Potato chips and ketchup wasn't much of a dinner. "Do you and Michael live alone, Professor?" she asked.

Gupta took a chip out of the bag and squeezed a drop of ketchup onto it. "Oh yes, it's just the two of us. My wife died twenty-six years ago, unfortunately."

"Do you have anyone to help you care for your grandson? Like a babysitter, a nurse's aide?"

"No, we manage by ourselves. He really isn't much trouble. You just have to get used to his routines." Gupta squeezed another drop of ketchup onto the chip and handed it to his grandson. "Of course things would've been easier if my wife were still alive. Hannah had a wonderful way with children. She would've loved Michael with all her heart."

David felt a pang of sympathy for the old man. During his interview for *On the Shoulders of Giants*, Gupta had told David about the long string of personal tragedies that had befallen him in the years after he worked with Einstein. His first child, a son, died of leukemia when he was twelve years old. A few years later Hannah Gupta gave birth to a daughter, but the girl was badly injured in a car accident. And in 1982, just after the professor abandoned physics and started the software company that would make him rich, a stroke killed his wife at the age of forty-nine. At one point in the interview, Amil had shown David her picture, and now he remembered it clearly—a dark-haired Eastern European beauty, slender and unsmiling.

Gupta had mentioned something else about his wife during that interview, something vaguely disquieting, but David couldn't recall the details. He turned to the professor, twisting around in his seat. "Your wife, she was also a student at Princeton, wasn't she?"

The old man looked up from squeezing ketchup onto another potato chip. "No, not exactly. She attended some of the graduate seminars in the physics department but she never actually enrolled. Although she had a brilliant mind for science, the war interrupted her education, so she lacked the proper academic credentials."

Now David remembered. Hannah Gupta was a Holocaust survivor. She was one of the Jewish refugees that Einstein had helped to bring to Princeton after World War II. Einstein had tried to save as many European Jews as he could, sponsoring their immigration to the United States and finding them jobs at the university's laboratories. This was the connection that had brought Amil and Hannah together.

"Yes, I have some very fond memories of those seminars," Gupta continued. "Hannah sat in the back and every man in the room was sneaking looks at her. There was quite a competition among us to get her attention. Both Jacques and Hans were interested, too."

"Really?" David was intrigued. Gupta hadn't said anything in their previous interview about a romantic rivalry among Einstein's assistants. "How heated did it get?"

"Oh, not very. I was engaged to Hannah before Jacques or Hans could get up the nerve to speak to her." The professor smiled wistfully. "We all remained friends, thank goodness. Hans became the godfather to both my children. He was especially kind to my daughter after Hannah died."

Fascinating, David thought. He wished he'd known about this story earlier, so he could've included it in his book. As soon as the thought occurred to him, though, he realized how foolish it was. Einstein's discovery of the unified field theory was a much more glaring omission in *On the Shoulder of Giants* and every other biography of the physicist.

After a few more miles they turned west at County Highway 33, a one-lane road that snaked through the hills. Although there was still more than an hour of daylight left, the steep wooded hill-sides kept the road in shadow. Occasionally they passed a weathered trailer home or an abandoned car rusting under the trees, but those were the only signs of civilization. The road was empty now except for the Hyundai and a yellow sports car about a quarter mile behind them.

Monique glanced yet again at the rearview mirror. In the back-seat Professor Gupta was giving Michael another ketchup-spotted potato chip, slipping it right into the teenager's mouth as if he were feeding a baby bird. David thought it was an oddly touching sight, but Monique shook her head as she stared at them. "Where's your daughter now, Professor?" she asked.

He grimaced. "In Columbus, Georgia. It's a good town for drug addicts because Fort Benning is nearby. Plenty of metham-phetamine available for the soldiers."

"Have you tried sending her to a treatment program?"

"Oh yes, I've tried. Many times." He lowered his head and frowned at the ketchup packet in his hand, wrinkling his noise as if he'd just smelled something rotten. "Elizabeth is a very stubborn woman. She was just as brilliant as her mother but she never fin-ished high school. She ran away from home at fifteen and she's been living in squalor ever since. I won't even tell you what she does for a living, it's too abhorrent. Even if Michael weren't autistic, I would've taken custody of him."

Monique's eyebrows tilted downward and a vertical crease ap-peared between them. Over the past twenty-four hours David had learned what this meant. Her anger was a little surprising, actually—her own mother was a heroin addict, and he would've thought this experience would make her more sympathetic to Professor Gupta's troubles. But this wasn't the case at all. It looked like she wanted to reach into the backseat and grab the professor by his collar. "Your daughter won't go into treatment if you're the one who's suggesting it," she said. "There's too much bitterness between you. You need someone else to do the intervention."

Gupta leaned forward and narrowed his eyes. Now he looked angry, too. "I already tried that. I asked Hans to go down to Georgia and talk some sense into her. He went to the hovel where Elizabeth was living and threw away all her drugs and got her enrolled in an outpatient treatment center. He even found a decent job for her, doing secretarial work for one of the generals at Fort Benning." He pointed a finger at Monique's reflection in the rearview mirror. "And do you know how long that lasted? Two and a half months. She went on a binge and lost her job and stopped going to the treatment clinic. That's when Michael came to live with me for good."

Breathing hard, the old man slumped back in his seat. Michael sat next to him, oblivious, patiently waiting for his next potato chip. The professor pulled one out of the bag, but his hands were trembling so much now that he couldn't squeeze the ketchup packet. David was just about to ask him if he needed any help when the yellow sports car he'd seen a minute ago zoomed ahead of them. It raced at least eighty miles an hour down the curving road, veering into the opposite lane even though they were in a no-passing zone.

"Jesus!" he yelled, startled. "What the hell was that?"

Monique leaned forward to get a better look. "It's not a patrol car. Not unless the cops in West Virginia are driving Ferraris now."

"A Ferrari?"

She nodded. "A nice one, too: 575 Maranello coupé. There's only fifty of them in the whole country. Costs about three times as much as my Corvette."

"How do you know about it?"

"The dean of the engineering school at Princeton has one. I see him all the time at Keith's auto shop. It's an amazing car but it breaks down pretty regularly."

The Ferrari crossed the double yellow line, moving back into its proper lane. But instead of racing off, the car began to slow. Its speed dropped to seventy, then sixty, then fifty miles an hour. Within a few seconds it was creeping along at thirty miles per hour just a dozen yards ahead of them, and Monique couldn't pass because of all the blind curves in the road.

"What's with this guy?" David said. "First he blows by us and now he's sightseeing."

Monique didn't respond. She craned her neck over the steering wheel and squinted at the Ferrari as it crawled downhill. After a few seconds her cheek twitched. "It's got New Jersey plates," she said, her voice barely above a whisper.

At the bottom of the hill the Ferrari leaped forward, racing about a hundred yards ahead. Then the driver hit the brakes and the car stopped in front of a single-lane bridge, blocking their way.

IT WAS A TRICKY SITUATION. Simon needed to capture four targets in a moving vehicle without seriously injuring them or drawing any unwanted attention. First he considered ramming the subcompact off the road, but there were thick woods on both sides of the highway and he knew that their car would crumple like an accordion if it hit one of the trees. He'd have a hard time extracting his targets from the wreck, much less interrogating them. No, he needed to slow them down first.

Simon saw his opportunity when he came upon a one-lane bridge over a shallow stream. He swiftly positioned the Ferrari across the road, picked up his Uzi, and jumped out of the car. Resting the barrel of the gun on the Ferrari's hood, he aimed at the approaching subcompact. As soon as the car slowed enough to turn around, he would shoot its tires, and the rest would be simple. The vehicle was already so close that he could make out all four figures inside, including the gangly teenager in the backseat. It was a lucky thing, he thought, that they'd brought the youngster along. To make his targets more cooperative, he planned to start with the boy.

DAVID SPOTTED SOME MOVEMENT ON the far side of the Ferrari. A big, bald man in a black T-shirt and camouflage pants crouched behind the car. His head was cocked to the side with one eye open, gazing down the barrel of a stubby black machine gun. A cold wash of terror flooded David's chest. It was as if he could already feel the bullet entering his heart. His back went rigid against the bucket seat and his right hand squeezed the armrest on the door. But his eyes stayed fixed on the gunman behind the Ferrari, and in that fraction of a second he noticed that the muzzle of the man's weapon wasn't pointed directly at them. It was aimed a little lower, at the Hyundai's tires.

Monique saw the man, too. "Shit!" she yelled. "I'm turning around!"

Her foot came off the gas pedal, but before she could step on the brake, David reached over and grabbed her knee. "No, don't slow down! He's gonna shoot the tires!"

"What are you doing? Let go of me!"

"Head over there!" He pointed at a gap in the trees on the left side of the road, a rocky, overgrown path leading down to the stream. "Just hit the gas! Punch it!"

"Are you crazy? We can't—"

Three loud metallic clanks shook the Hyundai as a burst from the machine gun hit the front fender. Without any more argument, Monique stepped on the gas and jerked the car toward the side of the road.

Another round of bullets struck the back end of the Hyundai as it careened over a hummock and down the narrow path. Monique clung to the steering wheel and shouted, "Holy shit!" while David and Amil and Michael bounced in their seats and the whole car rattled like a suitcase full of silverware. Much too fast, they thudded over the clumps of weeds and loose stones and within a second they were sliding across the shallow stream, their momentum alone carrying them over the rocky streambed. The Hyundai's wheels churned up great rooster tails of water and then they were on the opposite bank and Monique floored it. The engine roared in protest, but the car climbed up the bank like a billy goat and found the path leading back to the highway. David looked in the side-view mirror as their tires hit the asphalt and saw the bald man standing on the bridge with the stock of the Uzi still braced against his shoulder. But he didn't fire at them. Instead he rushed back to the Ferrari and got in the driver's seat.

"Better gun it!" David shouted. "He's coming after us!"

A PATH FOR CANOEISTS, THAT'S what it was. So the privileged American pleasure seekers could bring their pickup trucks to the edge of the stream and slip their boats into the water. Simon cursed himself for not noticing it earlier.

As he returned to the Ferrari and shifted into first gear, he decided to adjust his strategy. No more clever attempts to capture the targets unharmed. As long as one of them survived, he could get what he needed.

MONIQUE STOMPED THE ACCELERATOR BUT they were ascending a high mountain ridge and the Hyundai struggled to reach seventy miles an hour. She slammed her fist on the steering wheel while the engine whined and knocked. "I told you we should've taken my Corvette!" she yelled, glaring at the speedometer.

David looked over his shoulder at the rear window. No sign of the Ferrari yet on the twisting road behind them, but he thought he could hear the car's throaty snarl in the distance. In the backseat Michael was staring at his Game Boy again, silently waiting for the screen to come back to life. It looked like he hadn't even noticed that anything was amiss. But Professor Gupta was thoroughly alarmed. He'd raised both hands to his chest and splayed them across the front of his shirt as if were trying to quiet his pounding heart. His eyes were unnaturally wide. "What's going on?" he gasped.

"It's all right, Professor," David lied. "We're going to be all right."

He shook his head fiercely. "I have to get out! Let me out of the car!"

A panic attack, David thought. He held his hands out, palms down, in a gesture he hoped would be calming. "Just take a deep breath, okay? A deep, deep breath."

"No, I have to get out!"

He unbuckled his seat belt and reached for the door handle. Luckily the door was locked, and before Gupta could unlock it, David scrambled into the backseat and restrained him, lying on top of the old man and holding his wrists. "I told you, we're going to be all right!" he repeated. But as the words left his mouth he looked out the rear window again and saw the yellow Ferrari about fifty yards behind them.

David quickly faced forward to warn Monique, but she'd already seen it. Her furious brown eyes were in the rearview mirror. "That's the dean's car!" she hissed. "That bald motherfucker took the dean's car!"

"He's gaining," David said. "Can't you go any faster?"

"No, I can't! He's in a Ferrari and I'm driving a fucking Hyundai!" She shook her head. "He must've gone to my house, looking for us! But he found Keith instead. That's how he got the car!"

The Ferrari drew steadily closer as they approached the top of the ridge. When the car was about twenty feet behind, David saw the bald man roll down the driver's-side window. Keeping his right hand on the steering wheel, the man leaned halfway out the window and pointed his Uzi at the Hyundai. David immediately grabbed Michael and Professor Gupta and shoved them to the floor behind the bucket seats. The teenager let out an ear-piercing scream as David covered the two of them with his body. "Get down!" he shouted at Monique. "He's gonna shoot!"

The first blast shattered the rear window, showering bits of safety glass on their backs. The second went right over their heads, the bullets streaking through the vehicle and punching holes in the windshield. Certain that Monique had been hit, David clambered to the front of the car to take control, but he found her still clutching the steering wheel, apparently unharmed. She wasn't bleeding anywhere but her cheeks were wet. She was weeping. "Keith's dead, isn't he?" she cried.

They both knew the answer, so there was no need to respond. David simply put his hand on her shoulder. "Let's just get the fuck out of here, okay?"

The Hyundai crested the ridge and started to pick up speed as they barreled downhill. The bald man fired his Uzi at them again but the bullets missed the car this time because the road turned sharply to the right. The Hyundai's tires squealed as they rounded the curve and David had to grab the dashboard to stop himself from lurching into Monique. "Jesus Christ!" he yelled. "Watch what you're doing!"

She didn't seem to hear him. She stared at the road ahead, her eyes trained on the double yellow line. Her right calf bulged from the effort of pressing the gas pedal and her hands gripped the steering wheel so tightly that the veins popped up between her knuckles. Her whole body was a tense arc of nerves and muscle, and on her face was a look of ferocious concentration. The mind that had plumbed the intricacies of string theory, the complex equations and topologies of extra-dimensional manifolds, was now calculating centrifugal forces.

Halfway down the slope the road straightened out, becoming a steep chute that sliced through the woods. The Hyundai was going faster than a hundred miles an hour now, but the Ferrari was still close behind. On both sides of the highway the trees whipped past, an unbroken blur of leaves and trunks and branches. And then David saw a break, about a hundred yards ahead. A narrow strip of asphalt branched off to the left, making a forty-five-degree angle with the highway. He glanced at Monique; she was looking at it, too.

Turning around, David stared at the Ferrari. The bald man was leaning out the car's window and leveling his machine gun at them, taking careful aim now. David had just enough time for a short, silent prayer. Not yet, he pleaded. Wait one more second before firing. Just one more second.

Then Monique swerved the Hyundai to the left, throwing David violently against the passenger-side door. The car tilted on its right wheels, on the verge of rolling over, but after an instant the left wheels bounced back to the pavement and the Hyundai leveled out and sped down the narrow road. Surprised, the bald man looked up from the Uzi's gun sight and belatedly tried to follow them by turning his steering wheel with one hand. He turned it too far. The rear end of the Ferrari swung forward, sending the car into a vicious counterclockwise spin. It glided across the road like a bright yellow pinwheel, almost beautiful in its velocity and strangeness and shine. Then it slid off the asphalt and smacked into one of the trees with a sickening crunch.

Monique eased up on the gas but continued down the road. Gazing through the Hyundai's shattered rear window, David saw the Ferrari wrapped around the gnarled trunk of an oak tree. Then the road went into an S-curve and the wreck passed out of sight.

KAREN AND JONAH STOOD IN the lobby of the New York Times building. A sullen, hawk-nosed man in a blue blazer sat behind the security desk, looking them over. "Can I help you?" he asked.

Karen gave him a big smile. "Yes, I'm here to see Ms. Gloria Mitchell. She's a reporter at the newspaper."

"Do you have an appointment?"

She shook her head. She hadn't tried calling Gloria because she suspected that the FBI had tapped her phone. "No, we're old friends. I just wanted to stop by her office and say hello."

The security guard reached for the telephone on his desk. "What's your name?"

"Karen Atwood." Her maiden name. "We were classmates at Forest Hills High School. We haven't talked in a while but she'll remember me."

The guard took his time dialing the number. Karen anxiously surveyed the lobby, looking for any FBI agents who might be tailing her. She was worried they might arrest her again before she could get to the newsroom. To calm her nerves, she squeezed Jonah's hand.

The guard finally got Gloria on the line. "Karen Atwood is here to see you," he said into the phone. There was a pause. "Yes, Karen Atwood." Another pause. Then he cupped his hand over the mouthpiece and turned to Karen. "She says she doesn't know anyone by that name."

Karen's chest tightened. How could Gloria have forgotten her? They'd taken gym class together for three years! "Tell her it's Karen Atwood from Forest Hills High. From Mr. Sharkey's gym class."

With an impatient sigh, the guard repeated the information over the phone. There was yet another pause, a long one this time, and then the guard said, "Okay, I'll send her up." He hung up the receiver and began writing Karen's name on a visitor's pass.

She breathed a sigh of relief. "Thank you."

Still sullen, the guard handed her the pass. "Ms. Mitchell's on the sixteenth floor. Go to the elevators on the left."

As Karen headed toward the elevator bank she kept expecting the men in gray suits to descend on her, but she and Jonah boarded the elevator without incident. She found it odd that the FBI agents would let her contact the newspaper. Maybe they assumed no reporter would believe her story. In truth, she didn't have much of a story to tell; although she knew the drug charges against David were bogus, she had no idea why the government would invent such lies. More to the point, it was her word against the U.S. attorney's. In the eyes of the world, she was just the wife of a drug-dealing professor, and no newspaper would take her accusations seriously.

Unless she had evidence, of course. And Karen wasn't going to the newsroom completely empty-handed. She remembered the name of the police detective who'd called her apartment the night before, the man who could tell the *New York Times* why David had been summoned to St. Luke's Hospital. It was Hector Rodriguez.

LUCILLE SAT BEHIND THE DESK in Amil Gupta's office, speaking on her cell phone with the director of the Bureau while her agents dissected the professor's computer. In the four hours since Gupta, Swift, and Reynolds had escaped from the Robotics Institute, her team had investigated every corner of the Carnegie Mellon campus, searching for clues to where the suspects had gone. Agent Walsh had interrogated a janitor with Carnegie Mellon Building Services who'd admitted selling her uniform to Reynolds and Swift, and Agent Miller had found Reynolds's Corvette in one of the campus parking lots. Although there was no denying that the Bureau had fucked up big-time, Lucille felt sure that with a little legwork her team would locate the suspects and take them into custody. And that's why she got so furious when the director informed her that the Pentagon was taking over.

"What the hell are they thinking?" she shouted into the phone. "The army can't do law enforcement! It's illegal for them to partici-pate in a domestic operation!"

"I know, I know," the director replied. "But they say they have an executive order. And the Delta Force has experience with man-hunts. In Iraq and Afghanistan, at least."

"But where are they gonna go? We don't have any leads yet on the suspects' whereabouts. They could be anywhere from Michigan to Virginia by now."

"According to the deployment plan, the troops are flying into Andrews Air Force Base and they'll spread out from there. They have helicopters and Stryker vehicles, so they'll be able to move pretty quickly."

Lucille shook her head. This was pure stupidity. Deploying a brigade of commandos wasn't going to help them find the fugitives. More likely the soldiers would end up shooting some drunk Bubba for speeding through one of their checkpoints. "Sir, just give me a little more time," she said. "I know I can find these bastards."

"It's too late, Lucy. The troops are already loading into their C-17s. You have control of the operation until midnight. Then we'll do the handoff to the Defense Department."

She said nothing. A silent protest. The director waited a moment, then said, "I've got to go to another meeting now. Call me in two hours with your plans for transferring control." Then he hung up.

For several seconds she just stared at the cell phone in her hand. The screen said CALL ENDED 19:29 and then it went back to displaying the familiar FBI seal. But she wasn't really looking at the screen; she was looking at the end of her career in the Bureau. For thirty-four years she'd struggled through the ranks, the only woman in an army of bullheaded men, and she'd succeeded by being tougher and smarter than any of them. She'd tackled bank robbers, infiltrated motorcycle gangs, foiled kidnappings, and wiretapped mobsters. A month ago the director had promised to make her the head of the Bureau's Dallas office, a plum job to cap off her decades of service. But now she saw that it wasn't going to happen. Instead of getting a promotion, she was going to be pushed into retirement.

Agent Crawford, her second-in-command, edged toward her warily, like a whipped dog approaching its master. "Uh, Agent Parker? We've finished the analysis of Gupta's computer system."

She pocketed the phone and turned to him. She was in charge for four more hours, so she might as well make the best of it. "Did you find any physics documents?"

"No, it's all robotics. Big files full of software code and hardware designs. We also found the program that allowed him to communicate with his robots. That's how he got the Dragon Runner to sound the radiation alert."

Lucille winced. She didn't like to be reminded of this screwup, but she couldn't ignore it either. She needed to see the source of her undoing. "Show me the program."

Crawford leaned over the desk and used the mouse to click on a triangular icon on the computer screen. A window appeared showing a three-dimensional layout of Newell-Simon Hall with a dozen flashing yellow dots scattered among the floors. "This screen shows the location and status of each robot," Crawford said. "Gupta was able to send them commands using a wireless device."

"Wireless?" She felt a flutter of hope in her chest. Because cell phones and other wireless devices periodically send signals to their networks, the Bureau could determine their approximate positions as long as they were turned on. "Can we track it down?"

"No, Gupta's device uses short-range radio only. To control robots at other locations, he sends the commands by landline to a local transmitting node, which then broadcasts the signal to the machines."

Shit, Lucille thought. She just couldn't catch a break. But then another idea occurred to her. "What other locations? Where else does he have robots?"

Crawford clicked on another icon and the screen changed to a map of the Carnegie Mellon campus. "There are some in the computer science department and a few at the engineering hall." He pointed to a cluster of flashing dots at the map's edge. "Also a few here at Gupta's house."

"Anywhere outside Pittsburgh?"

With another click of the mouse, a map of the United States unfolded across the screen. There were four flashing dots in California, one in Tennessee, one in West Virginia, two in Georgia, and half a dozen near Washington, D.C. "The Defense Department is testing Gupta's surveillance robots at several locations," Crawford explained. "And NASA is preparing one of his machines for a mission to Mars."

"What about this location?" Lucille pointed at the flashing dot in West Virginia. It was the closest one to Pittsburgh.

Agent Crawford clicked on the dot and a label appeared beside it: "Carnegie's Retreat, Jolo, West Virginia."

"That doesn't sound like a military base or a NASA center," Lucille noted. The flutter of hope in her chest became a steady pounding. She knew it was just a hunch, but over the years she'd learned to trust her hunches.

Crawford squinted at the label on the computer screen. "I haven't seen this name in any of Gupta's records. It could be the location of a private contractor, I suppose. Maybe one of the defense companies that do robotics work."

She shook her head. The dot was flashing in the southernmost part of the state, the heart of Hatfield-and-McCoy country. There were no defense contractors anywhere near the place. "Do we have any agents operating in that part of West Virginia?"

Crawford reached into his pocket for the BlackBerry he used to track the agents assigned to the operation. "Uh, let's see. Agents Brock and Santullo are on I-77, helping the state police run a roadblock. They're about fifty miles from Jolo."

"Tell Brock and Santullo to head over there as fast as they can. They're gonna need some backup, so round up a dozen agents and get the Learjet ready."

Crawford raised an eyebrow. "Are you sure about this? All we know at this point is—"

"Just do it!"

Chapter Eight

IT WAS FULLY DARK BY THE TIME THEY REACHED CARN-
egie's Retreat, but in the glare of the Hyundai's headlights David could see enough of the place to know that Andrew Carnegie
would've never spent a single night there. It was no more than a
shack, a one-story cabin constructed from railroad ties in a small
clearing in the woods. Fallen branches littered the front yard and
a clumpy carpet of wet leaves covered the porch. Carnegie Mellon
University had let the place fall into disrepair. It was clear that no
faculty members had visited the cabin since the previous summer,
if then.

David opened the passenger-side door and helped Professor
Gupta out of the backseat. The old man had recovered from his
panic attack but his legs were still wobbly. David had to hold him
by the elbow as they stepped over the dead branches. Monique and
Michael got out of the car, too, leaving the headlights on so they
could see where they were going. When they reached the front door,
Gupta pointed at a flowerpot that contained nothing but dirt. "The
key's under that pot," he said.

As David bent over to grasp the thing, he heard a distant,
muffled boom that echoed against the hills. He instantly straightened up, his muscles tensing. "Jesus!" he hissed. "What the hell was
that?"

Gupta chuckled and patted him on the back. "Don't worry,
it's just the locals. In the evenings they like to ramble through the
woods with their shotguns and hunt down their supper."

David took a couple of deep breaths. "I'm beginning to see why
none of the professors at your school come here."

"Oh, it's not so bad. The people in this area are quite interesting, actually. They have a church where they do snake handling on Sundays. They dance around the pulpit holding rattlesnakes over their heads. Amazingly, they hardly ever get bitten."

"Come on, let's get inside," Monique urged. She was peering nervously at the dark canopy of leaves overhead.

David bent over again, lifted the flowerpot, and picked up a rusty key. He inserted it into the lock, and after a couple of tries the key turned and the door opened. He ran his hand along the wall until he found the light switch.

Inside, the cabin looked a little more inviting. There was a stone fireplace against the far wall and a brown shag rug on the floor. A tiny kitchen with an ancient refrigerator was on the left and two small bedrooms on the right. In the center of the room was a massive oak table holding a computer, a monitor, and several peripheral devices.

Professor Gupta led them inside. "Come in, come in. I'm afraid there's nothing to eat, the cabin's been empty for so long." He went straight to the oak table to turn on the power for the computer system, but as he hunted for the power strip under the table, he saw something else. "Oh, look at this, Michael! I forgot that we left this thing here! And the batteries are still charged!"

Kneeling on the floor, Gupta flipped a few switches. David heard the whine of an electric motor and then saw a four-legged robot emerge from under the table. About two feet high and three feet long, the machine was designed to look like a miniature brontosaurus. Its body was made of shiny black plastic and its neck and tail were segmented, allowing them to undulate in a creepily realistic way as the robot lumbered across the floor. On its fist-size head were two red LEDs that looked like eyes, and on its back was a spindly black antenna. The mechanical creature halted in front of them and turned its head from side to side as if surveying the room. "Would you like to play ball, Michael?" asked a synthesized voice. The robot's plastic jaw flapped up and down as the words came out.

The teenager stopped playing Warfighter on his Game Boy. For the first time David saw him smile, and at that moment his joyful face looked a lot like Jonah's. Michael ran to the shag rug, picked up a bright pink ball that was lying there, and rolled it toward the dinosaur robot. The machine turned its head, following the ball with its sensors, then lumbered after it.

"It's programmed to go after anything pink," Gupta explained. "It has a CMOS sensor that can recognize the color."

The professor watched his grandson with evident pleasure. Monique, though, was getting impatient. She glanced at the computer on the oak table, then at David. He could tell what she was thinking: somewhere inside that hard drive might be the Theory of Everything. She was itching to see it. "Uh, Professor?" David said. "Could we look through the files now?"

The old man snapped out of his reverie. "Yes, yes, of course! I'm sorry, David, I got distracted." He pulled a chair up to the table and turned on the computer. David and Monique stood behind him, looking over his shoulder.

First Gupta opened the computer's documents folder. In the window appeared an inventory of all the files created by the various professors who'd visited Carnegie's Retreat since the computer system was installed. Gupta scrolled down to a folder labeled MICHAEL'S BOX. The contents were protected by a password, which Gupta typed in—REDPIRATE79—to open the folder. "These are the documents we made when we were here four years ago," he said, pointing at a list of seven Microsoft Word files. "If Hans hid the theory on the computer, it has to be somewhere in this folder, because all the other files on the hard drive were created afterward."

The seven documents were arranged in order of when they were last modified; the dates ranged from *July 27, 2004* at the top to *August 9, 2004* at the bottom. The first file was labeled VISUAL. The names of the next six files were all three-digit numbers: 322, 512, 845, 641, 870, and 733.

Gupta opened Visual. "I remember this one," he said. "On our first night here, I downloaded a research paper that one of my students had written about visual-recognition programs. But I never got a chance to read it. Maybe Hans opened the file and slipped some equations into it."

The title of the paper was "Probabilistic Subspaces in Visual Representation" and it was a typical grad-student effort: long, plodding, impenetrable. As Gupta scrolled through the pages, David kept expecting to see a sudden break in the text, a chunk of white space followed by an orderly sequence of equations that had nothing to do with visual recognition. But instead the paper went on and on, slogging through nine chapters, twenty-three figures, and seventy-two references.

"All right, that's one down," Gupta said when he reached the end. "Six more to go."

He clicked on the file labeled 322. The document was very large and took some time to open. After five or six seconds a long list of names appeared on the screen, each accompanied by a telephone number. The first name was Paul Aalami and the second was Tanya Aalto. Then came at least thirty Aarons and nearly as many Aaronsons. Professor Gupta scrolled downward and the window showed a seemingly endless parade of Abbotts, Abernathys, Ackermans, and Adamses. He scrolled faster and thousands of alphabetical entries rose from the bottom of the screen in a digital blur.

Monique shook her head, confused. "Why did you download a telephone directory?"

"Michael did it." Gupta jerked his head toward his grandson, who was still playing catch with the robot brontosaurus. "Autistic children often have odd obsessions. Some memorize train or bus schedules. A few years ago Michael went through a phase when he was obsessed with phone numbers. He'd read telephone directories, memorize them, transcribe them. Each of these files is a directory for a different area code."

David stared at the jumpy blur on the computer screen, which was moving much too fast to be readable. "Is there any way to tell whether Dr. Kleinman altered the files?"

"Unfortunately, the 'Track Changes' feature of the word-processing software was turned off, so I can't locate the changes automatically. I may have to eyeball the pages to see if Hans added anything."

Monique whistled. "Shit. If the other files are as long as this one, you're gonna be staring at that screen for hours."

Professor Gupta abruptly stopped scrolling down the directory. He gazed at the computer so intently that for a moment David thought the old man had miraculously stumbled upon *Herr Doktor*'s equations, shining like bright needles in the enormous haystack of data. But the screen showed nothing but a long chain of Cabots. "I have an idea," he said, moving the cursor to the top of the screen. "Any equation has to have an equals sign, correct? So I'll just search each file for that symbol." He clicked on the edit menu and opened the find window. "The search may take a couple of minutes, though. The files are so large."

David nodded. It was worth a shot.

THE ARGUN GORGE IS ONE of the most battle-scarred places in Chechnya, but in Simon's dreams the canyon was always pristine. He glided like a hawk above the narrow Argun River, which was flanked on both sides by the granite slopes of the Caucasus Mountains. He could see a road along the river's eastern bank, a highway built to transport Russian tanks and armored troop carriers, but now there was just a single vehicle on the road and it wasn't military. Simon swooped down into the canyon to get a closer look. After a couple of seconds he recognized the vehicle: it was his own car, his old gray Lada sedan. In the driver's seat was his wife, Olenka Ivanovna, her long blond hair streaming behind her, and in the backseat were his children, Sergei and Larissa. They were coming to visit Simon, who was stationed in the town of Baskhoi, about twenty kilometers farther south. The highway was safe—all the Chechen rebels in the

area had either been killed or driven deeper into the mountains—
but in his dreams Simon hovered over the car anyway, protectively
following it along the twisting road. And then the Lada rounded
a bend and Simon saw the black helicopter loaded with Hellfire
missiles.

In reality Simon never saw the attack. He didn't hear about it
until an hour afterward, when his commander informed him that
the American special forces had crossed into Chechnya again. After 9/11, the Delta Force had started operating just south of the
border, hunting down Al-Qaeda fighters who'd retreated with the
Chechens into the Republic of Georgia. At first the Russian army
had tolerated the presence of the Americans, but the alliance was
already showing signs of strain. The Delta Force's Apache helicopters kept straying into Russian territory, and they had a bad habit
of firing their missiles at noncombatants. As Simon drove his troop
carrier to the site of the reported American attack, he fully expected
to see another peasant massacre, another burning oxcart surrounded
by dead babushkas. Instead he saw the blackened shell of his Lada,
with his wife's charred skeleton still behind the wheel. The explosion had blown Sergei and Larissa out of the backseat and into a
muddy ditch between the road and the river.

Simon never learned the reason for the error, never discovered
how a team of specially trained commandos could have mistaken
his family for a band of terrorists. Because the Delta Force operation was classified, the American and Russian generals covered up
the incident. When Simon filed a protest, his commander gave him
a canvas bag filled with hundred-dollar bills. A condolence payment, they called it. Simon hurled the bag at his commander and
quit the Spetsnaz. He came to America, hoping to somehow locate
the pilot and gunner of the Apache, but it was an impossible task.
He didn't know their names or the call sign of their helicopter. He'd
have to slaughter every soldier in the special forces to be sure he got
the right ones.

In Simon's dreams, though, he saw the men's faces. He saw

the pilot holding the controls steady while the gunner launched the Hellfire. He saw the flames spurt from the back of the rocket as it lunged toward the gray Lada. Then Simon was suddenly in the backseat of the car with his children, gazing through the windshield at the approaching missile. He felt a tug on the collar of his shirt, the tug of a small hand holding him fast.

Simon opened his eyes. It was dark. He was firmly lodged between the driver's seat of the Ferrari and the air bag that had inflated from the steering wheel. The car had struck the tree on the passenger side, mangling the right half of the vehicle but leaving the left half unscathed. And someone was indeed tugging at his collar, but it wasn't Sergei or Larissa. It was a wizened old hillbilly, a gap-toothed sunken-cheeked native of Appalachia wearing a threadbare flannel shirt and a suspicious frown. He'd reached into the wrecked Ferrari and placed his hand on Simon's neck to check for a pulse. The man's pickup truck idled alongside the road, its headlight beams lancing into the woods.

Wrenching his left hand free of the air bag, Simon grasped the hillbilly by the wrist. The man jumped back. "Holy Jesus!" he yelped. "Yer alive!"

Simon kept his grip on the man's stringy forearm. "Help me out of here," he ordered.

The Ferrari's door wouldn't open, so the hillbilly pulled him out the window. Simon winced as his right foot touched the ground— the ankle was sprained. The Appalachian helped him toward the pickup. "I thought you were dead for sure," he marveled. "Come on, we gotta git you to the hospital."

The old man stank of sweat and tobacco and wood smoke. Filled with revulsion, Simon grabbed the hillbilly's shoulders and threw him against the side of the truck. Keeping his weight on his left foot, he clasped both hands around the fool's neck. "Did you see a gray Hyundai?" he demanded. "With a large dent in its rear fender?"

The man opened his mouth in astonishment. He raised his

hands to his throat and tried to loosen Simon's grip, but his small, trembling fingers couldn't gain purchase.

"ANSWER ME!" Simon shouted in his face. "DID YOU SEE THE CAR?"

He couldn't answer in words because Simon was crushing his windpipe, but he shook his head in a quick, spastic jitter.

"Then you're useless." Simon tightened his hold and felt the man's larynx crumple under his palm. The hillbilly kicked and squirmed against the side of the pickup, but Simon felt no sympathy whatsoever. This man was just a piece of writhing filth. Why should he be allowed to live and breathe while Sergei and Larissa rotted in their graves? It was intolerable. It was unforgivable.

Once the man was dead, Simon let him drop to the dirt. Then he limped back to the Ferrari and retrieved his Uzi and sidearms, which fortunately were undamaged. He transferred the guns to the pickup truck, then took out his cell phone and dialed a number from memory. He wasn't sure he'd get a signal because he was in such a remote area, but after a few seconds the line began to ring and a voice answered, "Brock here."

WHILE PROFESSOR GUPTA SEARCHED THE voluminous files on his computer, David wandered over to a window at the back of the cabin. He was too agitated to watch the screen as Gupta combed through the gigabytes of data. He needed a minute to catch his breath.

He couldn't see anything out the window at first, it was too dark. But by pressing his forehead to the glass and cupping his hands around his eyes, he could make out the silhouettes of the trees around the cabin and a gorgeous swath of night sky above them. Like all New Yorkers, David was always astounded by the multitude of stars he could see once he left the city. He spotted the Big Dipper first, hanging vertically like a question mark. He saw the Summer Triangle—Deneb, Altair, and Vega—and the zigzag of Cassiopeia. Then he looked straight up and gazed at the Milky Way, the unimaginably huge spiral arm of the galaxy.

It was sky-watching that had sparked David's interest in science nearly forty years before. At his grandmother's home in Bellows Falls, Vermont, he'd learned to identify the planets and the brightest stars. While his mother washed the supper dishes and his father drove into town to get drunk, he sat in the backyard and traced the constellations with his finger. By immersing his mind in the laws of physics—the theories of Kepler and Newton, Faraday and Maxwell—David found that he could distance himself from his father's drunken rages and his mother's mute despair. He spent his entire youth preparing to become a scientist, doggedly studying geometry and calculus in high school and going on to learn thermodynamics and relativity in college. So when his demons finally caught up to him at the age of twenty-three, pushing him out of the world of physics and into the dim barroom of the West End Tavern, it was much more than just a professional setback. He lost the great source of joy in his life. And though he later managed to crawl out of the abyss and make a successful career at the fringes of science, writing books about Newton and Maxwell and Einstein, he still felt like a failure. He knew he'd never get a chance to stand on the shoulders of those giants.

But as David stared at the sky above Carnegie's Retreat, he felt some of the old joy return to his heart. He saw the whole array of planets and stars as a tiny drop in a cosmic wave. Nearly 14 billion years ago a quantum cauldron had exploded to the size of the universe, leaving immense trails of matter and energy in its wake. No scientist in the world knew why this Big Bang happened, or what preceded it, or how it would all end. But the answers to those questions might finally be at hand, lurking somewhere in the circuit boards of Professor Gupta's computer. And David would be one of the first to see them.

He was so keyed up that when he felt a tap on his shoulder he nearly lost his balance. He spun around, expecting to see Gupta behind him, but the professor was still hunched over the oak table, squinting at the computer screen. Instead, it was Monique. She looked just as anxious as he was. "I want to ask you another question about the Flatland paper," she said. "About your model of a two-dimensional black hole."

Her request seemed to come out of nowhere, but after a moment David understood. Monique wanted to take one last guess at the Theory of Everything before Professor Gupta unveiled the equations. "What do you want to know?"

"Did your black hole contain CTCs?"

David hadn't heard the term in almost twenty years, but he remembered it. A CTC was a closed timelike curve. Essentially, it was a path that allowed a particle to travel back and forth in time, arriving at the same exact point where it started. "Yeah, we found CTCs in the model, but it wasn't so surprising to see them in a two-dimensional spacetime. Flatland has all kinds of weird, nonsensical things that you wouldn't necessarily see in a three-dimensional universe."

"And did the spacetime have a wormhole structure?"

David nodded. A wormhole was a tunnel through the hills and valleys of spacetime, a cosmic shortcut allowing objects to travel instantaneously from one region of the universe to another. In the two-dimensional world he and Dr. Kleinman had proposed, particles diving into the black hole would emerge in a separate universe on the other side. "Yeah, that's right. I'm surprised you know all this. I thought you said you didn't remember the paper that well?"

"I don't. But while we were driving down here, I started thinking about why Kleinman said your paper was close to the truth. And now I'm wondering if there might be a connection with geons."

This was a term he wasn't familiar with. Either he'd never learned it or he'd forgotten it completely. "Geons?"

"It stands for 'gravitational electromagnetic entity.' It's an old idea, going back to the fifties. The premise is that the elementary particles aren't objects sitting in spacetime—they're knots in the fabric of spacetime itself. Like tiny wormholes."

A vague recollection came to David. He'd heard the idea before, probably in a grad school class two decades ago. "Yeah, I think Kleinman might have mentioned that theory in a lecture once. But I got the impression that physicists abandoned the effort."

"That's because no one could formulate a stable geon. According to the equations, the energy would either implode or leak out. But a few years ago some researchers resurrected the idea as a possible unification theory. Their work is still pretty sketchy, but what they've come up with so far is a particle that looks like a microscopic wormhole with CTCs."

David shook his head. "And people are taking this seriously?"

"It's a fringe idea, I admit. Only a few people are working on it. But this is a classical field theory, something that Einstein could've come up with. And it has the potential for explaining the uncertainties of quantum mechanics."

"How?"

"The CTCs are the key. On the smallest scales of spacetime, causation becomes skewed. The particle is influenced by events in the future as well as the past. But an outside observer can't measure events that haven't happened yet, so he can never fully know the state of the particle. The best he can do is calculate probabilities."

David tried to picture it, a particle that somehow knew its own future. It sounded absurd, but he began to see the benefits of the idea. "So the future events are Einstein's hidden variables, right? A complete description of the universe exists, but it's unreachable at any one moment in time?"

She nodded. "God doesn't play dice with the universe after all. But humans have to, because we can't see the future."

What struck David the most was how excited Monique seemed. She shifted her weight from foot to foot as she talked about the theory, practically bouncing with enthusiasm. Theoretical physicists are an inherently conservative bunch; although their job is to build new models of reality with arcane equations and sometimes fanciful geometries, they also subject those models to intense scrutiny. David suspected that Monique had already analyzed possible objections to the geon theory and seen no fatal flaws. "What about particle interactions?" he asked. "What would they look like in this model?"

"Any interaction would have to involve a change in the topology of the local spacetime. Imagine two loops coming together and forming—"

She was interrupted by the sound of Gupta's hand smacking the table. The professor shouted, "Damn!" and glared at the computer screen.

Monique rushed over to him. "What is it? What did you find?"

Gupta clenched his fists in frustration. "First I searched the files for the equals sign. No results. Then I searched for the integral sign. Again, no results. Then it occurred to me that maybe Hans inserted the information into the computer's operating system instead of the documents folder. But I just ran a line-by-line comparison and found no alterations to the software." He turned to David, frowning. "I'm afraid you were mistaken. We've come all this way for nothing."

He sounded almost sick with disappointment. It was clear that the old man also yearned for a glimpse of the unified theory, maybe even more strongly than David or Monique did. But Gupta was giving up too easily, David thought. The answer was near. He was sure of it. "Maybe it's hidden somewhere else in the cabin," David suggested. "Maybe Dr. Kleinman put the theory on paper and hid it in a drawer or a cabinet. We should start looking."

Monique immediately began to survey the room, her eyes fixing on potential hiding places. But Gupta stayed in his chair and shook his head. "Hans wouldn't have done that. He knew that other professors from Carnegie Mellon came here for their vacations. He wouldn't have wanted one of them to stumble on the theory while searching the cabinets for some sugar."

"Maybe he hid the papers very carefully," David countered. "In a chink in the walls maybe. Or under the floorboards."

The professor kept shaking his head. "If that's the case, then the theory is gone. This cabin is infested with mice. They would've chewed up the entire *Einheitliche Feldtheorie* by now. *Herr Doktor*'s equations would be scattered among their droppings."

"Well, maybe Kleinman put the papers in a strongbox before hiding them. Or a biscuit tin, a Tupperware container. My point is, it couldn't hurt to look."

Gupta tilted his head back and sighed. His eyes were glassy with fatigue. "It might be wiser to rethink our assumptions. Why are you so convinced that Hans hid the theory here?"

"We went over this already. Kleinman wouldn't have hidden anything in your office or home, those places are too obvious. The theory would've fallen right into the government's hands if they came—"

"Slow down, please. We have to reexamine each step in your argument." He turned his chair around so that he was facing David. "Let's start with the code Kleinman gave you. Twelve of the numbers were the geographic coordinates of the Robotics Institute, correct?"

"Yes, latitude and longitude." David closed his eyes for a moment and saw the numbers again, floating across the backs of his eyelids. The sequence was permanently imprinted in his cortex. He'd probably remember it until the day he died. "And the last four digits were your phone extension."

"So we know that Hans wanted you to contact me. But that doesn't necessarily mean he hid the theory on one of my computers, or under the floorboards of some cabin where we went on vacation four years ago."

Gupta leaned back in his chair, stroking his chin. He'd reverted to his professorial role, grilling David as if this were a seminar in Boolean logic. Monique was listening intently, her eyes locked on the old physicist, but David was still thinking about the sixteen numbers that Dr. Kleinman had whispered into his ear. The digits were still floating across his field of view, gliding past Gupta's brown face and the computer screen behind him. And on that screen, quite coincidentally, David saw another sequence of numbers arranged in a neat column at the left side of the documents folder. They were the names of the telephone directories that Gupta had downloaded for his grandson: 322, 512, 845, 641, 870, and 733.

David stepped forward and pointed at the screen. "Are these file names supposed to be area codes? One for each of the phone directories?"

The professor looked annoyed. David had broken his train of thought. "Yes, yes. But I told you, those files have no equations in them."

David moved a bit closer to the screen and tapped his finger on the file name at the top of the column, the number 322. "This can't be an area code," he said. Then he tapped 733. "And neither can this."

Gupta turned around in his chair. "What are you talking about?"

"My son asked me the other day how many area codes there were. I did a little research and found out that there couldn't be more than 720. An area code can't start with a zero or a one, and the last two digits can't be the same. The telephone companies reserve those numbers for special uses. Like 911, 411, that kind of thing."

Gupta squinted at the numbers on the screen. He seemed un-impressed. "I probably mistyped them."

"But Dr. Kleinman could have also changed the file names. That would explain why the numbers don't make sense. He could've changed all six file names in just a few seconds."

"But why would he do that? You think that Hans boiled down the unified field theory to half a dozen three-digit numbers?"

"No, it's another key. Just like the one he gave me in the hospital."

Now Monique stepped forward. She leaned over Gupta and stared at the screen. "But there's a total of eighteen digits here, not sixteen."

"Let's concentrate on the first twelve," David replied. "Can you get on the Web site that maps latitude and longitude?"

Stepping around Gupta's chair, Monique grasped the mouse and clicked on Internet Explorer. She found the mapping Web site and bent over the keyboard. "Okay, read the numbers to me."

David didn't even have to look at the screen. He'd already memorized the sequence. "Three, two, two, five, one, two, eight, four, five, six, four, one."

Several seconds passed as the Web server retrieved the information from its database. Then a map of western Georgia appeared on the screen, with the Chattahoochee River on the left. "The address closest to the location is 3617 Victory Drive," Monique reported. "In Columbus, Georgia."

Professor Gupta jumped to his feet, elbowing David and Monique aside. He gazed angrily at the screen, as if the computer had just insulted his manhood. "That's Elizabeth's address!"

David didn't remember the name at first. "Elizabeth?"

"My daughter!" Gupta shouted. "That little—"

But before he could finish the sentence, the cabin's front door burst open.

LUCILLE WAS IN THE PASSENGER scat of one of the Bureau's SUVs, racing down Route 52 with the blue lights flashing. While Agent Crawford steered around the slower traffic, she spoke by satellite phone with Agents Brock and Santullo, who were crouched in the woods outside a cabin in Jolo. The connection was poor, probably due to the terrain where the agents were operating. Brock's gravelly voice rose and fell in volume, and occasional gusts of static obliterated it completely.

"Brock, this is Parker," Lucille shouted into the phone. "I didn't copy your last transmission. Say again. Over."

"Roger, we've sighted four suspects in the house. Gupta, Swift, Reynolds, and the unidentified teenage male. We're now moving to a new position so we can get a better view inside. There's a window on the other . . ." A surge of static buried his last words.

"Roger, I copied most of that. Just make sure you stay behind cover until the backup units get there. Don't confront the suspects unless they attempt to leave the house. You hear me, Brock?"

"Affirmative. We'll hold at the new position. Over and out."

Lucille felt a twinge of misgiving. It was unfortunate that Brock and Santullo were the first agents on the scene. Brock was her least favorite person on the task force—the guy was hotheaded and arrogant, almost to the point of insubordination. It would be just like him to start a firefight and kill one of the suspects. Or worse, get killed himself. That's why she'd ordered him to sit still. She wasn't going to lose any more agents.

Up ahead, a road sign emerged from the darkness: WELCH, 5 MILES. They were less than half an hour from Jolo, and three patrol cars from the West Virginia State Police were even closer. If everything worked as planned, they could all be off duty by midnight.

Then Brock's voice erupted from the satellite phone. "Mayday, Mayday! Request permission to move in immediately! Repeat, request permission to move in!"

Lucille pressed the phone to her ear. "What is it? Are they trying to leave?"

"We've sighted them again and they're crowded around the computer! Request permission to move in before they delete mission-critical information!"

She took a deep breath. It was a judgment call. Her primary task was to secure information that was vital to national security. And Brock could be right: the suspects might be trying to erase the data. But Lucille had great faith in the Bureau's computer experts. She'd seen them retrieve deleted data from a hundred hard drives. "Permission denied. Your backup is less than twenty minutes away. Hold your position until they get there."

"Roger, we're moving in!"

Lucille thought he'd misheard her amid the welter of static.

"No, I said hold your position! Do not move in! Repeat, do NOT move in!"

"Roger, we're going radio dark until we capture the suspects. Over and out."

A bolt of alarm ran through her. "GODDAMN IT, BROCK, I SAID HOLD YOUR POSITION! DO NOT—"

Then the phone went dead.

THERE WERE TWO OF THEM. Two muscle-bound assholes in dark blue jumpsuits with gold letters spelling out FBI. One was a tall blond bruiser and the other was a swarthy Mediterranean type with a handlebar mustache. Both held nine-millimeter Glocks that they leveled at Amil, David, and Monique.

Professor Gupta instinctively shielded his grandson. He stepped in front of Michael, who was kneeling on the floor next to the toy brontosaurus, oblivious to everything except his robotic pet. In response, the blond agent pointed his pistol at Gupta's forehead. "MOVE AGAIN AND I'LL BLOW YOUR BRAINS OUT!" he yelled. "GET YOUR HANDS IN THE AIR, YOU PIECE OF SHIT!"

The old man stared at the muzzle of the gun. His left cheek twitched and he let out a whimper. Slowly he raised his hands. Then he twisted around and looked down at his grandson. "Please . . . please stand up, Michael." His voice was low and shaky. "And hold up your hands like this."

The blond agent pivoted, pointing his gun at David now. The man's nose was misshapen, probably broken many times over, and his cheeks were webbed with fine, red lines. He seemed too dissolute to be an FBI man; he looked more like a bar brawler. "You, too, fuckface," he said. "Get your hands up."

As David raised his hands he glanced at Monique, who stood on the other side of Gupta and Michael. He knew there was a revolver tucked in the back of her shorts. He also knew that if she reached for it, they were as good as dead. He shook his head ever so slightly: Don't do it, don't do it. After an awful second of uncertainty, she raised her hands, too.

The blond agent turned to his partner. "Cover 'em, Santullo. I'll check for weapons."

The man went to David first and roughly patted him down. When he was done, he jammed his gun into David's ribs. "You're one stupid fuck," he said.

David stood absolutely still. No, he thought, the bastard won't shoot me. The government wants me alive. And yet he couldn't be sure. He pictured the bullet in its chamber, the hammer ready to strike.

But the agent didn't pull the trigger. Instead he leaned forward until his lips almost touched David's earlobe. "You should've stuck with your ex-wife," he whispered. "She's a lot better-looking than this nigger."

Then the man stepped away from him and moved on to Professor Gupta. David lowered his arms, dizzy with rage, but the agent named Santullo immediately pointed his Glock at him. "GET THOSE HANDS UP!" he shouted. "I'm not gonna warn you again!"

While David complied, the blond agent patted down Professor Gupta. The old man forced a smile and looked at his grandson. "Michael, this man is going to touch you in a minute. But don't worry, it won't hurt. See, he's doing it to me now and it doesn't hurt at all."

The agent leered. "What's wrong with the kid? He retarded?"

Gupta kept his eyes on Michael. "You don't have to scream, all right? He'll touch you for a few seconds and then it'll be over."

The professor's reassurances seemed to work: when the agent searched Michael, the teenager whined for a moment but didn't scream. Then the agent turned to Monique and quickly discovered her revolver. He pulled it out of her shorts and held it up for all to see. "Well, look at this," he crowed. "This girl's got some black power in her underpants."

Monique glared at him, obviously regretting her decision not to shoot it out. The agent holstered his own gun and opened the revolver's cylinder to see if it was loaded. "This is a lucky break for me," he said, "but very unlucky for you, Ms. Reynolds. I just found the murder weapon."

She shook her head. "I didn't kill anybody! What the hell are you talking about?"

He snapped the cylinder shut and returned to his partner's side. "I'm talking about this." He pointed the gun at Santullo's head and fired.

It happened so fast that Santullo's eyes were still focused on Amil, David, and Monique as the bullet sped through his skull. Blood and brains sprayed out of the exit wound. The impact knocked him sideways to the floor and his Glock fell out of his hand. The blond agent picked it up, and then he held Santullo's gun in one hand and Monique's in the other.

Michael started screaming as soon as he heard the gunshot. He dropped to the shag rug and clamped his hands over his ears. Professor Gupta bent over him, turning away from the dead man. But David was too stunned to look at anything else. Blood was fountaining from the entry wound just above the man's temple.

The blond agent stepped around the body, not even giving it a second glance. "All right, enough fucking around," he said. He flipped the safety on the Glock and tucked it into his pants, but kept the revolver trained on his captives. "We gotta get out of here before the troopers show up. We're gonna take a little walk through the woods and meet a friend of mine on the other side of the hill."

David looked hard at the agent's battered face. He realized with a chill that his initial suspicions had been correct: the man wasn't really with the FBI. He was working with the terrorists.

In three quick strides, the agent marched over to Professor Gupta and his screaming grandson. First he pushed Gupta aside, sending him sprawling. Then he grabbed Michael by the collar of his polo shirt and pressed the barrel of the revolver against the boy's head. "You're all gonna walk in a single file ahead of me. If anyone tries to run, the kid's dead. Got that?"

Monique was now on the agent's left side and David was on his right. She gave David an urgent look and he understood: the man was in a vulnerable position. He couldn't see both of them at once. If they were going to make a move, now was the time to do it.

Gupta slowly got to his feet. When he looked at the agent again, his face contorted into a fierce grimace. "Stop this right now, you imbecile!" he shouted. "Get your hands off my grandson!"

David gauged the distance between himself and the agent. He could spring on the bastard and maybe grab his shooting arm, but that wouldn't stop him from firing the revolver. They had to get him to point the gun at something besides Michael.

The agent grinned at the professor, amused. "What did you call me? An imbecile?"

Monique flashed David another look: What are you waiting for? And then he noticed that the robot brontosaurus was waving its segmented tail just a few feet away from her. His eyes fixed on the machine's spindly antenna.

"Yes, you're an imbecile!" Gupta shouted. "Don't you realize what you're doing?"

David mouthed the word *antenna* and pointed at the thing. At first Monique just looked confused. Then David clenched his right hand into a fist and twisted it. That did the trick. Monique bent over the machine and snapped off its antenna.

The alarm was even louder than David remembered. The agent automatically let go of Michael and pointed the revolver at the noise. Then David came at him from behind.

SIMON PARKED THE PICKUP TRUCK at the rendezvous point, a sharp bend in a dirt road about a kilometer south of the cabin. He'd chosen the spot with the help of a local map he'd found in the glove compartment. Rendezvousing at Carnegie's Retreat would've been unwise because the cabin was located at a dead end, and at least a dozen police vehicles were already converging there from the north. But the dirt road ran south through a tangled black forest, making it a perfect escape route into the neighboring state of Virginia.

He doused the headlights, then looked at the glowing hands of his watch: 9:21. Brock was due to arrive in nine minutes. Simon had promised him a substantial reward—$250,000—if he succeeded in delivering all four of the targets alive. The agent planned to make it look like the suspects had shot his partner and escaped into the woods. Simon suspected that the FBI might not believe this story, but that was Brock's problem, not his.

He rolled down the window and stuck his head outside, listening for the sound of five people stumbling through the leaf litter. But all he heard was the usual noise of the night forest: the whine of the cicadas, the croaking of the bullfrogs, the wind rustling through the treetops. After a few seconds he heard a muffled boom off to the west. A shotgun blast, most likely. And then he heard an odd, high-pitched shriek and four more gunshots in quick succession. These sounds came from the north, and they weren't shotgun blasts. He was quite adept at identifying the noises made by different types of firearms. This was a handgun, probably a revolver.

Not to worry, he told himself. It's just the sound of Agent Brock executing his partner. But why four shots? One bullet to the head was usually sufficient. No, no, don't jump to conclusions—maybe Brock was a poor marksman, maybe he'd fired three more times at his partner just to be sure he'd killed the man. But none of these possibilities eased Simon's anxiety. All his instincts were telling him that something had gone wrong.

Grabbing his Uzi, he opened the pickup's door and gingerly stepped to the ground. His right ankle was badly swollen, but he didn't have a choice.

DAVID RUSHED FORWARD AND SLAMMED his right shoulder into the agent's back. He hit him hard and fast and the man toppled forward, his legs flying out from under him and his chest smacking the floor. The revolver stayed in his hand, though, and he squeezed off a shot that exploded the robot dinosaur and silenced the alarm. David fell on top of him and pinned the agent's shooting arm. He fired again, wildly, and David pounded the man's head, smashing his knuckles against the bony knob at the base of his skull. He was following the hard lesson that his father had taught him: there's no such thing as a fair fight. There's only winning and losing, and if you want to win you have to keep on hitting the bastard until he stops moving. The agent's nose broke again as David mashed his face into the floor, and yet the man kept firing the revolver. Two more shots rang out, and David heard Monique scream. Enraged, he brought his knee down on the agent's forearm and the gun finally slipped out of his hand. But David didn't pause for a second. He heard his father's gin-soaked voice: For Christ's sake, don't give him a chance to get up! Smash him, pound him, fuck him over! And David followed his father's instructions, followed them to the letter, until the face of the man beneath him was just a bowl of bruised flesh, with the mouth gaping open and the eyes swollen shut. David screamed, "YOU FUCKER!" into the man's ear, but he wasn't even thinking of the agent anymore. He was screaming at his father, that drunken murderous bastard, as he rammed his fists into the man's purple face.

He would've kept on swinging until the man was dead, but he felt someone behind him, pulling his arms back. "Enough, enough! He's unconscious!"

He turned around and saw Monique. To his surprise, she didn't appear to be hurt. She looked at him with concern, then reached into the agent's shoulder holster and removed his semiautomatic. "Roll him over so I can get the other one," she ordered.

David lifted the inert body and Monique retrieved Santullo's gun from the waistband of the agent's pants. "Here, take this," she said, handing him the Glock. "Cover him in case he wakes up. I'll take care of Amil."

"Amil? What's wrong?"

He looked over his shoulder and saw Michael still crouched on the shag rug with his hands pressed to his ears. Beside him, Professor Gupta lay on his back in a spreading puddle of blood. It was gushing from an inch-wide hole in his left thigh. Propped on his elbows, he stared in horror at the wound. "It's coming out!" he screamed. "It's coming out, it's coming out, it's coming out!"

Monique pointed at David's shirt. "Quick, take it off," she said. Then she rushed over to Gupta and ripped off his left pant leg, which was already soggy. "Try to calm down, Professor," she told him. "Take deep breaths. You need to slow your heartbeat."

She took David's shirt—his softball-team shirt, with HITLESS HISTORIANS printed on the back—and folded it into a pad, which she placed over Gupta's wound. She wrapped the sleeves around his thigh, tied them in a knot, and pressed her palm against the dressing to stanch the bleeding. Then she moved her other hand to his groin and began probing the area just to the left of his fly. "Excuse me," she said. "I'm trying to find the femoral artery."

Gupta was busy taking deep breaths and probably didn't hear her. David watched with astonishment as she dug her fingers into the old man's crotch. After a few seconds she found the pressure point and jammed the heel of her hand against it, squeezing the artery against the pelvic bone. The professor yelped in pain.

Monique gave him a big smile. "There, that's much better," she said. "The bleeding will slow down now." But her face was grim when she turned to David. "We have to get him to a hospital."

Gupta heard her this time. Shaking his head violently, he tried to sit up. "No!" he cried. "You have to run! You have to get to Georgia!"

"Please, Professor, lie down," Monique urged.

"No, listen to me! The man said the state troopers were coming! If they catch you, they'll get the *Einheitliche Feldtheorie*!"

Monique struggled to keep the pressure on Gupta's femoral artery and her homemade bandage. "We can't leave you behind!" she shouted. "You'll bleed to death!"

"As soon as the authorities get here, they'll rush me to the hospital. Believe me, they won't let me die. I'm too important to them."

She shook her head. She didn't want to leave his side. David was impressed by her loyalty. He'd gotten the impression that Monique didn't even like the professor very much, and yet now she was willing to sacrifice everything for him.

Gupta stretched his hand toward her and touched her cheek. Then he pointed at his grandson, who was rocking back and forth on his heels. "Take Michael with you," he said. "If the police find him, they'll put him in an institution. Don't let that happen, Monique. Please, I'm begging you."

She kept her hand on the bandage, but she nodded. Then Gupta turned to David, pointing at the computer on the table. "Before you go, you need to destroy the hard drive. So the FBI doesn't see the code."

Without a word, David lifted the computer over his head and hurled it to the floor. The plastic case cracked open and David wrenched out the hard drive, which looked like a miniature turntable with a stack of silver disks. Holding the Glock by its barrel, he started pounding the glass platters with the handle of the gun. He kept at it until the disks were smashed into hundreds of tiny slivers.

Just as he finished, he heard a siren. It was the wail of a statetrooper car speeding up the gravel road, maybe a quarter mile away. He listened closely and heard two more sirens a little farther off. And then he heard an even more unwelcome noise, the rapid fire of a machine gun.

He jumped to his feet. Monique was still leaning over Professor Gupta, still pressing down on his bandage, but the old man was now whispering something in Michael's ear. "Come on!" David yelled. "We gotta go!"

"Go on," Gupta said, pushing both Michael and Monique away from him. He looked like he was getting weaker. "And don't forget . . . Michael's Game Boy."

Crying now, Monique stood up and headed for the door. David found the Game Boy and pressed it into the teenager's hands. Michael pushed a button and the screen came to life again. He resumed playing Warfighter at the point where he'd left off, as if nothing of significance had occurred in the interim, and he was distracted enough to allow David to grasp his elbow and guide him out of the cabin.

SIMON DEALT WITH THE STATE troopers first. Leaning against one of the trees next to the road, he strafed the windshield of the leading patrol car, killing both officers inside. The car slid off the gravel and smashed into a kudzu-covered boulder. The driver of the second vehicle didn't see the wreck until he came around the curve, which was much too late. He managed to stop the car in the middle of the road but Simon picked him off before he could throw it into reverse. The third driver wisely stayed out of range. In the distance Simon could hear the sound of officers dashing for cover and shouting into their radios. The task was done: now the troopers would stay on the roadside, cowering behind rocks and tree trunks for the next half hour or so, allowing Simon to focus his attention elsewhere.

He hobbled up the road to the cabin. The first sign of trouble was the open door. The second was the trio of bodies lying on the floor inside. Only one of them was dead—an FBI man with an absurd mustache, Brock's partner obviously. His brains were splattered on a nearby wall. A diminutive Indian man, the esteemed Professor Gupta, lay unconscious in a pool of blood. Someone had field-dressed his leg wound, but the bandage was already soaked. And last but not least, Agent Brock writhed on his belly, groaning in pain and spitting out pieces of his teeth.

Simon stood there a moment, deciding what to do. Swift and Reynolds, his primary targets, were probably not far away, running blindly through the woods with their teenage companion. Under ordinary circumstances, Simon would've pursued them, but his ankle was growing more and more inflamed and he knew it wouldn't support his weight much longer. For now, he'd have to be content with interrogating Dr. Gupta. Assuming that the old man didn't die of shock, chances were good that he could reveal where Swift and Reynolds were headed.

Brock staggered to his feet. His face was a bloody mess but he was otherwise serviceable. Working together, they could probably carry Gupta through the woods to the pickup. Simon grabbed the back of Brock's neck and shoved him toward the professor. "I have a new job for you, Mr. Brock," he said. "And if you want to stay alive, I suggest you take it."

Chapter Nine

LUCILLE KNELT BESIDE THE BODY OF TONY SANTULLO, A twenty-four-year-old agent who'd graduated from the academy just six months before, and forced herself to look at the gaping hole in his temple. Taking a deep breath, she pushed all distractions from her mind, all thoughts of guilt and anger and frustration, and concentrated on reconstructing what had transpired in the cabin. She examined the position of Santullo's corpse and the pattern of the blood splatter. She noted the presence of two more pools of blood at the other end of the room, suggesting additional casualties. And she surveyed the mechanical debris scattered across the floor, the broken computer case and the shattered hard drive and the plastic remnants of some kind of robot.

Agent Crawford stood behind her, holding a radio to his ear. "Brock, come in," he shouted. "Come in, come in. Respond at once, over."

Lucille shook her head. To be fair, there was a chance that Agent Brock had pursued the suspects into the woods and wasn't responding to radio contact now because he lay dead or wounded on the forest floor. But she doubted it very much. For the past twenty-four hours she'd suspected that there was a traitor on the task force, and now she knew who it was.

"Come in, Brock," Crawford repeated. "Come in, come—"

He abruptly lowered the radio and cocked his head, listening to some noise from outside. After a couple of seconds Lucille heard it, too: the beating of helicopter rotors. She rose to her feet and followed Crawford out of the cabin. They looked to the northeast and saw three Blackhawks skimming over the hills, their spotlights illuminating the treetops below. It was the advance guard of the Delta Force, arriving ahead of schedule.

✳ ✳ ✳

NAKED TO THE WAIST, DAVID ran headlong into the darkness. He couldn't see a thing but he charged forward anyway, trying to follow the sounds Monique made as she crashed through the undergrowth. With his left hand he groped at tree trunks and branches, and with his right he clutched Michael's elbow, dragging him along. The teenager screamed at first, but after running for half a mile or so he became too winded to protest. They tore through the black forest as if they were running on air, propelled by sheer terror.

They came to a clearing and Monique stopped short. David almost plowed into her. "What are you doing?" he hissed. "Let's go, let's go!"

"Where are we going? How do you know we're not running in circles?"

He looked up at the stars. The Little Dipper was to their right, which meant they were traveling west. He took Monique's hand and pointed it to the left. "We should go this way, start heading south. Then we—"

"Oh God, what's that?"

Three points of light rose above the treetops behind them and hung in the sky like bright new stars. As David stared in that direction, he heard the roar of helicopter rotors in the distance.

He grasped Michael's elbow and pushed Monique forward. "Go, go, go! Get under the trees!"

They dove into the woods again and scrambled up a rocky slope. The going was tougher here, more rugged. Monique tripped over something and landed with a cry. David rushed to her side, but as he bent over to ask if she was all right, he heard a slow deep voice say, "Stop right there." Then he heard the sound of two rifles being cocked into firing position.

David froze. For a moment he considered making a break for it, but when he turned around he saw that the Game Boy in Michael's hand was still turned on. The light from the screen was feeble, but it was enough to serve as a target.

A flashlight came on and the beam ran over them. Through the glare David tried to see the man who was holding the light, but all he could make out was a hefty silhouette. Probably not FBI, he thought. More likely a local sheriff or state trooper. Not that it made much difference at this point.

"What y'all doin' out here?" the hefty man asked. "This ain't no place for a picnic."

He sounded genuinely puzzled. David squinted into the flash-light beam and saw, to his relief, that the man wasn't wearing a uniform. He wore a pair of overalls and an extra-large flannel shirt, and the firearm he was pointing at them was a shotgun, not a rifle. To his left was another man with a shotgun, an old toothless fellow wearing a John Deere cap, and to his right was a short, stocky boy, maybe eight or nine years old. The boy carried a homemade sling-shot and had an oddly flattened face.

"You hear me?" the fat man said. He had a thick brown beard and a dirty bandage taped over his left eye. "I asked you a question."

David nodded. These were the backwoods hunters that Professor Gupta had mentioned. A grandfather, father, and son, no doubt. West Virginia mountain men, wary of outsiders. Probably not too inclined to sympathize with a black physicist and a bare-chested history professor. But they were probably not too fond of the government either. David wondered if he could use this fact to win them over. "We're in trouble," he admitted. "They're coming to arrest us."

The fat man fixed his good eye on him. "Who's coming?"

"The FBI. And the state troopers. They're working together."

The man snorted. "What'd you do, rob a bank?"

David realized, of course, that he couldn't tell the truth. He had to think of a story that the hunters would believe. "We didn't do anything wrong. It's an illegal government operation."

"What the hell do you mean by—"

He was interrupted by his son, who suddenly let out a high-pitched squawk, like the call of a tropical bird. The boy's face broke into a distorted smile and he swayed from side to side, as if buffeted by the wind. With a jolt, David realized what was wrong with him. The boy had Down syndrome.

The fat man paid no attention to his son. He kept his shotgun pointed at David. "Look, are you gonna tell me what's going on here?"

All right, David thought. They had something in common. That was a start, at least. He pointed at Michael, who was crouched on the ground and rocking back and forth. "They're after our son!" David shouted. "They're trying to take him away from us!"

Monique stared at him, aghast. But the lie, although far-fetched, wasn't completely absurd. In the dark, one might easily be persuaded that the dusky-skinned teenager was their son. And the hunters seemed to accept the possibility. The hefty one lowered his shotgun a few degrees, pointing it at their feet now. "Your boy, is he sick?"

David put on an indignant face. "The doctors want to put him in a mental hospital! We left Pittsburgh to get away from the bastards, but they followed us here!"

"We heard some shots a while back. Were they shooting at you?"

David nodded again. "And now they're bringing in reinforcements. You hear the helicopters?"

The rotor noise grew louder. The boy with Down syndrome gazed at the sky. The old fellow in the John Deere cap exchanged looks with the fat man. Then both of them lowered their weapons. The fat one turned off his flashlight. "Follow me," he ordered. "The trail's this way."

SIMON RECOGNIZED THE HELICOPTERS BY their silhouettes. Blackhawks flying low, just a few meters above the treetops. That was a Delta

Force tactic, flying nap-of-the-earth, below radar coverage. Simon's pulse raced—his enemies were near. The soldiers who flew into Chechnya, the ones who killed his wife and children, might even be among them. For a moment he considered firing his Uzi; a lucky shot could take out one of the pilots. But then the other Blackhawks would surround his position and the game would be over. No, Simon told himself, better stick to the original plan. You'll kill far more of them that way.

He and Brock soon reached the pickup truck and heaved Professor Gupta into the bench seat at the back of the cab. Then Brock collapsed in the passenger seat and Simon got behind the steering wheel. He knew he couldn't turn on the truck's headlights—the Blackhawk pilots would spot them immediately—so he put on his infrared goggles. On the device's screen the dirt road was cold and black, but the tree trunks and branches on the roadside glowed warmly, retaining some of the day's heat. The contrast was strong enough that he was able to drive quite fast, which was fortunate, because they didn't have much time. When Simon glanced over his shoulder, he noticed that Gupta's face was considerably cooler than Brock's. The professor was going into shock.

They were about twenty kilometers south of the cabin, across the Virginia state line, when Simon saw a house at a bend in the road. It was a fairly unremarkable two-story home with a front porch and an attached garage. What caught Simon's attention was the name on the mailbox. It was spelled in plastic letters that stood out clearly against the cold metal: DR. MILO JENKINS.

Simon skidded to a halt and turned into the doctor's driveway.

THE HUNTERS MOVED LIKE GHOSTS through the forest. Under the canopy of foliage, they followed a twisting trail that ran up the slope of a narrow mountain valley. Although they walked so fast that David, Monique, and Michael could barely keep up, the hunters didn't make a sound. David was able to follow them only because the light from a crescent moon glinted off the barrels of their shotguns.

For about half an hour they marched uphill, ascending a steep ridge studded with pine trees. Michael started to pant, but he didn't stop walking; keeping his eyes on his Game Boy, he allowed David to steer him by the elbow. When they reached the crest, David turned around and peered through a gap in the trees at the landscape to the east. He could see the spotlights of all three helicopters prowling the hills and hollows below, but they were now so far away that the noise of their rotors was just a dull rumble.

The hunters continued along the ridgeline for a mile or so, then began to descend into a neighboring valley. After several minutes David saw a light on the hillside. The hunters moved toward it, quickening their pace, and soon came upon an unpainted plywood shack resting on cinder blocks. It was long and narrow and slumped against a tree like a decrepit boxcar abandoned in the woods. A pair of mangy dogs circled the shack, yipping and yowling, but they quieted down as the men approached. One of the dogs ran over to the boy with Down syndrome and danced around his feet. His father, the fat man in overalls, turned to David. "This is our home," he said, offering his hand. "My name's Caleb. That's my pa and that's my boy, Joshua."

David shook his hand. He noticed that Caleb's ring finger was missing. "I'm David. This is my wife, Monique." The lie was effortless. Without any trouble at all, he'd created a new family. "And this is my son, Michael."

Caleb nodded. "Y'all should know that we ain't got any prejudices here. Black or white, it don't make no difference up here in the mountains. We're all brothers and sisters in God's eyes."

Monique forced a smile. "That's very kind of you to say."

Caleb stepped to the front end of the shack and opened the door, a rough-hewn board hanging askew in its frame. "Come in and set down. Y'all could use a rest, I bet."

Everyone filed into the shack, which contained just one long room. There were no windows at all and the only light came from a single naked bulb suspended from the ceiling. Some plastic bowls and a hot plate sat on a table at the front of the room; behind it were a couple of kitchen chairs with torn seat covers. A gray army blanket lay on the floor beyond the chairs, which was obviously the sleeping area. And in the darkness at the very back of the room was a sprawling pile of cardboard boxes and disheveled clothing.

Without saying a word, Caleb's father took off his John Deere cap and headed for the kitchen table. He turned on the hot plate and opened a can of Dinty Moore stew. Meanwhile, the boy raced to the back of the room and started playing tug-of-war with his dog. Caleb tousled his son's black hair, which looked like it hadn't been washed in some time. "Joshua's my special gift from the Lord," he said. "Mingo County Social Services has been trying to take him away from me ever since his ma died. That's why I built this place up here in the holler. We're a good two miles from the nearest road. Far enough that the sheriff's department usually leaves us alone."

Monique caught David's eye. She was probably thinking the same thing he was: it was a hell of a lucky coincidence that they found this guy. In that part of West Virginia, though, maybe it wasn't so unlikely for one group of fugitives to run into another. Anyone who lived in that godforsaken place had to be running away from something.

Caleb stepped toward Michael and tried to get the teenager's attention. "You're a gift from the Lord, too," he said. "Just like it says in the Bible, Book of Mark, chapter ten. 'Suffer the little children to come unto me, and forbid them not: for of such is the Kingdom of God.'"

Michael ignored him, his thumbs stabbing the controls of the Game Boy. After a while Caleb turned to the heap of old clothes draped willy-nilly over the cardboard boxes. He picked out a T-shirt and handed it to David. "Here, put this on," he said. "You folks are welcome to spend the night."

David glanced at the gray blanket spread across the floor. He was so tired he would've gladly slept on the thing, no matter how uncomfortable, but he was still worried about the helicopters he'd seen on the other side of the ridge. "Thanks for the offer, Caleb, but I think we should keep moving."

"Where are you headed, brother? If you don't mind my asking."

"Columbus, Georgia." David pointed at Monique. "My wife's got family down there. They can help us out."

"How you gonna get there?"

"We left our car behind when the cops started chasing us. But we'll get to Columbus somehow. We'll walk if we have to."

Caleb shook his head. "You don't have to. I think I can help y'all. There's a man in our church named Graddick? He's supposed to drive to Florida tomorrow. Maybe he can drop you off along the way."

"Does he live nearby?"

"No, but he's gonna come by here around midnight to pick up the serpents. I'm sure he'll give y'all a ride."

"Serpents?" David thought he'd misheard.

"I caught a few timber rattlers on the ridge last week and Graddick's gonna take 'em to a Holiness church in Tallahassee. It's a serpent-handling church, just like ours here in Rockridge." Caleb opened one of the cardboard boxes and removed a cedarwood crate about the size of a desk drawer. The crate had a Plexiglas lid with small circular holes. "We're trying to help our brothers in Florida, you see, but it ain't exactly legal. That's why we move the serpents at night."

David peered through the Plexiglas. A rust-colored snake, about as thick as a man's forearm, coiled inside the crate. It shook its rattle and the noise was a harsh, scolding "Shhhhhh!"

Caleb set the crate on the floor and removed another from the cardboard box. "The Bible commands us to do it. Book of Mark, chapter sixteen. 'These signs shall follow them that believe: They shall cast out devils, they shall speak with new tongues and they shall take up serpents.'" He pulled out a third crate and stacked it on top of the other two. Then he picked up the whole stack, holding it against his broad chest. "I'm gonna take these crates outside and clean 'em before Graddick gets here. You folks get some rest in the meantime. There's some beef jerky in the cupboard if you're hungry."

Joshua and his dog followed Caleb out of the shack. Caleb's father was still at the table, eating stew out of the can, and Michael was crouched on the army blanket. Monique sank to the floor next to him, her back against the plywood wall. Her face was grim, exhausted.

David sat beside her. "Hey, you all right?" he asked, keeping his voice low just in case the old man was listening.

She stared at Michael and shook her head. "Look at him," she whispered. "Now he has nobody. Not even his grandfather."

"Don't worry about Amil, okay? He'll be fine. The FBI will get him to a hospital."

"It's my fault. All I cared about was the theory. I didn't give a shit about anything else." She rested her elbows on her knees and clutched her forehead with both hands. "Mama was right. I'm a coldhearted bitch."

"Listen, it's not your fault. It's the—"

"And you're no better!" She raised her head and gave him a challenging look. "What are you gonna do once you find the unified theory? Have you even thought that far ahead yet?"

To be honest, David hadn't. All he had for guidance were the vague instructions Dr. Kleinman had given him: Keep the theory safe. Don't let them get it. "We'll have to entrust the theory to some neutral party, I guess. Maybe some kind of international organization."

Monique grimaced. "What? You're gonna hand it over to the United Nations for safekeeping?"

"Maybe that's not such a crazy idea. Einstein was a strong supporter of the UN."

"Oh, screw Einstein!"

She'd raised her voice enough to get the attention of Caleb's father. He stopped eating for a moment and looked over his shoulder. David smiled at him reassuringly, then turned back to Monique. "Calm down," he whispered. "The old man can hear you."

Monique leaned toward him, bringing her lips to his ear. "Einstein should've destroyed the theory as soon as he realized how dangerous it was. But the equations were too damn important to him. He was a coldhearted bastard, too."

She stared at him hard, itching for a fight. But David didn't respond, and after a while she seemed to lose interest. Yawning, she moved a few feet away and lay down on the gray blanket. "Ah, fuck it," she said. "Wake me up when the snake man gets here."

Within thirty seconds she was snoring. She lay curled on her side, her knees drawn to her chest. Her hands were clasped together under her chin as if she were praying. David grasped the edge of the blanket and folded it over her. Then he sat down beside Michael, the other member of his new family.

The teenager was still engrossed in Warfighter, so David contented himself with watching the action on the Game Boy's screen. An animated soldier in a khaki uniform was racing down a dark hallway. Another soldier appeared at the end of the hall but Michael immediately shot him down. His soldier leaped over the facedown corpse, then rushed into a small room where half a dozen figures were huddled. Michael jabbed a button and his soldier went into a crouch, spraying his M-16 at the enemy. Soon all six of the opposing soldiers lay on the floor, with simulated blood streaming from their wounds. Michael's soldier then opened a door at the other end of the room. The screen went black and a message appeared in flashing letters: CONGRATULATIONS! YOU'VE REACHED LEVEL SVIA/4! David guessed this must be an incredibly high expertise level in Warfighter, but Michael didn't show even a hint of satisfaction. His face remained as expressionless as ever.

David felt a sudden urge to make contact with the boy. He bent close to Michael and pointed at the screen. "What happens now?"

"It goes back to Level A1."

Michael's voice was monotone and his eyes stayed on the Game Boy, but it was an answer, an intelligible response. David smiled. "So you won the game, huh? That's great."

"No, I didn't win. It goes back to Level A1."

David nodded. Okay, whatever. He pointed again at the screen, which now showed the khaki soldier in an open field. "But it's a fun game anyway, right?"

Michael didn't reply this time. His full attention had returned to Warfighter. David sensed that the window of opportunity had closed, so instead of talking he simply sat next to the teenager and watched him play. He knew from his experience as a father that he didn't need words to communicate. During the afternoons he spent with Jonah, he always sat next to the boy while he was doing his homework. The proximity alone was comforting.

After ten minutes Michael had advanced to Level B3. Caleb's father finished his dinner and fell asleep in his chair. Then David heard voices outside, agitated voices. Alarmed, he rushed to the shack's door and opened it an inch. Through the crack he saw Caleb talking with another fat man. This one wore baggy jeans and a ratty gray sweatshirt. Like Caleb, he had a thick brown beard and carried a double-barreled shotgun. That must be Graddick, David thought with relief. He opened the door all the way and stepped outside.

Caleb spun around. "Go get your wife and your boy! You gotta leave right now!"

"What is it? What's wrong?"

Graddick stepped forward. His eyes, set in cavernous sockets, were an unearthly shade of blue. "Satan's army is on the move. There's a convoy of Humvees coming down Route 83. And the black helicopters are landing on the ridge."

"Armageddon's coming, brother!" Caleb shouted. "You better get going before they close the roads!"

✳ ✳ ✳

PROFESSOR GUPTA LAY ON A mahogany table in Dr. Milo Jenkins's dining room. Several cushions from the living-room sofa had been propped under Gupta's legs to elevate them, and Dr. Jenkins had jammed a surgical clamp into the thigh wound to stop the bleeding. Simon had been lucky indeed to find Jenkins; he was an old-fashioned country doctor who worked out of his home and had some experience treating the gunshot injuries of his hillbilly neighbors. Using the supplies from his medical cabinet, he'd cleverly fashioned an intravenous line that hung from the chandelier. But Jenkins shook his head as he leaned over the blood-slicked table, pressing his fingers into the side of Gupta's neck. Simon, who was pointing his Uzi at the doctor, sensed that something had gone awry.

Jenkins turned around to face him. The doctor wore a plaid nightshirt that was now streaked with dark red stains. "It's like I told you," he drawled. "If you want to save this man's life, you gotta get him to the hospital. I can't do anything more for him here."

Simon frowned. "And, as I told you, I don't care about saving his life. I just need him to regain consciousness for a few minutes. Just long enough for us to have a little talk."

"Well, that ain't gonna happen either. He's in the final stages of hypovolemic shock. If he don't get to a hospital soon, the only person he's gonna be talking to is his Maker."

"What exactly is the problem? You stopped the bleeding and you gave him fluids. He should be recovering by now."

"He's lost too much blood. He don't have enough red blood cells to deliver oxygen to his organs."

"So do a transfusion."

"You think I got a blood bank in my refrigerator? He's gonna need at least three pints!"

Keeping the Uzi trained on Jenkins, Simon rolled up the sleeve on his right arm. "My blood type is O negative. Universal donor."

"Are you nuts? If I take that much blood out of you, *you'll* go into shock!"

"I don't think so. I've done field transfusions before. Go get another IV kit."

But Jenkins didn't budge. He folded his arms across his chest. Curling his lip, the doctor gave him a look of pure hillbilly stubbornness. "No, I'm through with this. I ain't helping you no more. You can go ahead and shoot me if you want."

Simon let out an exasperated sigh. He was reminded of his stint with the Spetsnaz in Chechnya, and all the trouble he'd had with the reluctant soldiers under his command. The threat of execution was clearly not compelling enough to keep Dr. Jenkins in line. Simon needed to give him a stronger motivation. "Brock!" he called out. "Please bring Mrs. Jenkins in here."

AT 5 A.M., JUST AS THE sun was rising over Washington, D.C., the vice president stepped out of his limousine and headed for the side entrance to the West Wing. He wasn't an early riser by nature; given his druthers, he would've preferred sleeping until seven o'clock and getting into the office by eight. But the president was a fanatic about starting his workday at dawn, so the veep did likewise. He needed to be on hand at all times to prevent the commander in chief from doing anything stupid.

As soon as he walked into the building he saw the secretary of defense sitting in one of the wingback chairs in the lobby. The SecDef had a pen in his hand and a copy of the *New York Times* in his lap. He'd scribbled some notes in the newspaper's margins. The man never sleeps, the veep thought. He spends the whole night roaming the corridors of the White House.

The SecDef jumped to his feet once he spotted the vice president. He held up the front section of the *Times* and shook it angrily. "Did you see this?" he barked. "We got a problem. One of the New York cops spilled the beans."

"What do you—"

"Here, read it yourself." He shoved the paper into the veep's hands.

The story was in the upper left corner of the front page:

FBI ALLEGATIONS QUESTIONED
by Gloria Mitchell

A New York City police detective has challenged the Federal Bureau of Investigation's claim that a Columbia University professor was involved in the brutal slaying of six FBI agents on Thursday evening.

The FBI has launched a nationwide search for David Swift in the aftermath of the murders, which allegedly occurred during an undercover drug-buying operation in West Harlem. The Bureau claims that Swift, a history professor known for his biographies of Isaac Newton and Albert Einstein, was the leader of the cocaine-selling ring and ordered the killing of the undercover agents once their identities were revealed.

Yesterday, however, a detective in the Manhattan North Homicide Task Force stated that FBI agents took Swift into custody at about 8 P.M. on Thursday, three hours before the Bureau claims the killings took place.

The detective, speaking on condition of anonymity, said the agents arrested Swift at St. Luke's Hospital in Morningside Heights. At the time, Swift was visiting Dr. Hans Kleinman, a Nobel laureate physicist who was hospitalized for injuries suffered in an apparent burglary earlier that evening. Kleinman died from his injuries shortly after Swift arrived.

The vice president was too incensed to read any further. This was a fuckup of the first order. "How the hell did this happen?"

The SecDef swiveled his square head. "Typical cop stupidity. The detective was pissed at the feds for taking the Kleinman case away from him. So he gets his revenge by squealing to the *Times*."

"Can we shut him up?"

"Oh, we took care of that already. We figured out who he was—Spanish fellow named Rodriguez—and brought him in for questioning. But the bigger problem is Swift's ex-wife. She's the one who prodded the *Times* into doing the story."

"Well, can't we shut her up, too?"

"We're trying. I just got off the phone with her boyfriend, Amory Van Cleve, the lawyer who raised twenty million for your last campaign. Apparently, their affair has cooled off in the past twenty-four hours. Now he says he won't object if we bring her in."

"So go ahead and do it."

"The agents tailing her say she and her son spent the night with the reporter who wrote the *Times* article. Swift's ex is a clever girl. She knows we can't detain her while she's with the reporter. We have enough trouble with the *Times* as it is."

"One of their reporters is sheltering her? And they call themselves unbiased!"

"I know, I know. But we'll get her soon enough. We have half a dozen agents staking out the apartment. As soon as the reporter leaves for work, we'll move in."

The vice president nodded. "And what about West Virginia? How's that progressing?"

"No worries there. One squadron of the Delta Force is in place and two more are en route." He began edging toward the Situation Room. "I'm going to check with the commanders right now. They may have captured the fugitives already."

The veep gave him a stern look. The SecDef had the unfortunate habit of declaring victory too soon. "Keep me informed, please."

"Yes, yes, of course. I'll call you later today from Georgia. I'm going to Fort Benning this morning to give a speech to the infantrymen."

✳ ✳ ✳

DAVID AWOKE IN THE BACK of Graddick's station wagon and found
Monique sleeping in his arms. He was a bit startled; when they'd
dozed off several hours earlier, they'd carefully positioned themselves at opposite ends of the cargo area. (Luckily, the car was a
huge Ford Country Squire that had survived at least twenty West
Virginia winters.) But Monique had evidently squirmed toward David in her sleep and now her back was against his chest and her head
under his chin. Perhaps she'd snuggled against him for warmth. Or
perhaps she'd instinctively backed away from the rattlesnake crates,
which were concealed under a tarp below the rear window. Whatever the reason, she lay there in his arms, her ribs gently rising and
falling with each breath, and David was struck by an almost painful
feeling of tenderness for her. He remembered the last time he'd held
her like this, on the sofa in her tiny grad school apartment nearly
two decades before.

Trying his best not to wake her, David raised his head and
looked out the window. It was early morning and they were traveling down a highway bordered on both sides by southern pines.
Graddick was in the driver's seat, whistling to a gospel tune on the
car radio, and Michael was stretched out on the backseat, fast asleep
but still clutching his dormant Game Boy. After a while David saw
a sign: I-185 SOUTH, COLUMBUS. They were in Georgia, probably not
too far from their destination.

Monique began to stir. She twisted around and opened her
eyes. Surprisingly, she didn't pull away from his embrace. Instead
she simply yawned and stretched her arms. "What time is it?"

David looked at his watch. "Almost seven." He found it remarkable how nonchalant she was, lying beside him as if they really
were a married couple. "You sleep all right?" he asked. He kept his
voice low, although he doubted that Graddick could hear anything
over the sound of the radio.

"Yeah, I'm better now." She rolled onto her back and clasped her hands under her head. "Sorry about last night. I got a little testy, I guess."

"Don't mention it. Being chased by the U.S. Army could make anyone irritable."

She smiled. "So you're not upset about all the nasty things I said about Einstein?"

He shook his head, smiling back at her. This is nice, he thought. He hadn't had this kind of conversation with a woman in a long time. "No, not at all. In fact, you were right in some ways."

"You mean Einstein really was a coldhearted bastard?"

"I wouldn't go that far. But sometimes he could be pretty callous."

"Oh yeah? What did the bastard do?"

"Well, for one thing, he deserted his children after his first marriage fell apart. He left Mileva and their two sons in Switzerland while he went to Berlin to work on relativity. And he never acknowledged the daughter he and Mileva had before they were married."

"Whoa, hold the phone. Einstein had an illegitimate daughter?"

"Yeah, her name was Lieserl. She was born in 1902, when Einstein was still a penniless tutor in Bern. Because it was a scandal, their families hushed it up. Mileva went back to her home in Serbia to have the baby. And then Lieserl either died or was put up for adoption. No one knows for sure."

"What? How come nobody knows?"

"Einstein stopped mentioning her in his letters. Then Mileva came back to Switzerland and they got married. And neither of them ever talked about Lieserl again."

Monique abruptly turned away from him. Frowning, she stared at the shabby gray fabric that lined the floor of the cargo area. David was confused by the sudden change in her mood. "Hey, what's wrong?"

She shook her head. "Nothing. I'm fine."

Emboldened by their closeness, he cupped her chin in his palm and turned her face toward him. "Come on. No secrets between colleagues."

She hesitated. For a moment David thought she would get angry, but instead she turned away again and looked out the window. "When I was seven, my mother got pregnant. The father was probably one of the guys she bought heroin from. The day after she gave birth, she gave the baby away. She never told me anything about it except that the baby was a girl."

David slid his hand along the soft underside of Monique's jaw until his fingers touched her ear. "Did you ever find out what happened to her?"

Without looking at him, she nodded. "Yeah. She's a crack whore now."

A tear pooled in the corner of her eye, then trickled down her cheek. Unable to stop himself, David leaned over and kissed it. He felt the moisture on his lips, tasted the salt. Then Monique closed her eyes and he kissed her mouth.

For at least a minute they kissed silently on the floor of the cargo area, like a couple of teenagers hiding from the adults in the front seat. Monique wrapped her arms around his waist and pulled him closer. The station wagon began to slow, obviously approaching the Columbus exit, but David didn't lift his head, didn't look out the window. He kept on kissing her as the car cruised down the exit ramp, going into a long swooping curve that made him think of seagulls wheeling over the ocean and got mixed up in his head with the slippery feel of Monique's lips. Finally he pulled back and looked at her. They gazed at each other for several seconds, neither saying a word. Then the station wagon made a sharp right turn and came to a stop.

They quickly disentangled themselves and looked out the window. The car was parked in front of a run-down strip mall facing an avenue that was already busy with traffic. David could tell they were near the entrance to Fort Benning because the names of all the stores shared a military theme. The largest was Ranger Rags, an army-navy surplus store with a window display of mannequins in camouflage. Next door was a take-out place called Combat Zone Chicken and a tattoo parlor called Ike's Inks. A few yards farther down was a windowless cinder-block building with a big neon sign on its roof. The sign's orange tubing was twisted in the shape of a buxom woman reclining over the words THE NIGHT MANEUVERS LOUNGE. Contrary to its name, the lounge appeared to be a twenty-four-hour-a-day operation; at least two dozen cars were parked in front of the bar and a seedy-looking bouncer guarded the entrance.

Graddick heaved himself out of the driver's seat and lumbered around the station wagon. He opened the rear door but David was reluctant to leave the car. Kneeling beside the rattlesnake crates, he scanned both sides of the street, on the lookout for anyone in a uniform. Given their circumstances, this was a particularly risky place to be. "Where are we?" he asked.

Staring at them with his crazed, unearthly blue eyes, Graddick pointed at the Night Maneuvers Lounge. "See the number over the door? That's the address you gave me—3617 Victory Drive."

"No, this can't be right." David was bewildered. This was supposed to be Elizabeth Gupta's address.

"I know this place," Graddick drawled. "Before I was saved, I was a soldier in Satan's army. I was stationed here at Benning and we used to go to Victory Drive every time we got a weekend pass." With a fierce scowl, he spat on the asphalt. "VD Drive, we called it. It's a cesspool of harlotry."

David nodded. Now he was beginning to understand. He remembered what Professor Gupta had said about his drug-addict daughter. Making contact with her was going to be harder than he'd expected. "The woman we need to see, I think she works in that bar."

Graddick narrowed his eyes. "You said this woman is kin to your wife?"

Nodding again, David gestured toward Monique. "That's right, they're cousins."

"Harlotry and fornication," Graddick muttered, frowning at the cinder-block building. "Thou hast polluted the land with thy whoredom." He spat again as he stared at the lascivious neon sign. It looked like he wanted to tear the thing down with his bare hands.

It occurred to David that this hefty West Virginia mountain man might prove useful. At the very least they could use his station wagon. "Yeah, we're heartbroken about what's happened to Elizabeth," David said. "We've got to try to help her somehow."

As David had hoped, the idea seemed to appeal to Graddick. He cocked his head. "You mean you want to save her?"

"Absolutely. We've got to convince her to accept Jesus Christ as her personal savior. Otherwise she's going straight to hell."

Graddick thought it over, stroking his beard and glancing at the tarp-covered rattlesnake crates. "Well, I don't have to be in Tallahassee till five o'clock. That leaves me some time to kill." After a few seconds he smiled and threw his arm around David's shoulders. "All right, brother, let's do the Lord's work! Let's go into that den of iniquity and sing His praises! Hallelujah!"

"No, no, I'll go into the bar alone, okay? You drive around to the back and wait there until we come out the back door. If she starts making a fuss, you can help me carry her to the car."

"Good idea, brother!" Graddick cheerfully slapped him between the shoulder blades.

Before sliding out of the station wagon, David squeezed Monique's arm. "Keep an eye on Michael, all right?" he said. Then he headed for the Night Maneuvers Lounge.

He smelled spilled beer before he even reached the door. The old feeling of disgust clogged his throat, just as it had when he'd entered the bar in Penn Station two nights ago. But he took a deep breath and managed to smile as he handed the ten-dollar cover charge to the bouncer.

Inside, the room was blue with cigarette smoke. The old ZZ Top song "She's Got Legs" blared from the speakers. On a semi-circular stage, two topless dancers stood in front of an audience of hopelessly drunk GIs. One of the women slowly twined around a silver pole. The other turned her back to the audience and bent over until her head hung upside down between her knees. A soldier staggered forward and dangled a five-dollar bill near her mouth. She licked her lips, then clamped the bill between her teeth.

At first, the sight of all the uniforms made David nervous, but he quickly realized that these particular soldiers posed no danger. Most of them had probably been drinking for twelve hours straight, trying to enjoy every minute of their forty-eight-hour weekend passes. He edged closer to the stage and focused his attention on the dancers. Unfortunately, neither one looked like she could be related to Professor Gupta. The pole dancer was a freckled redhead and the woman with her head between her legs was a lily-white blonde.

David wandered over to the bar and ordered a Budweiser. Keeping the bottle at arm's length, he surveyed the three women doing lap dances for the soldiers on the bar stools. Two more blondes and another redhead. All of them were quite attractive, with firm, round breasts and taut behinds that they moved in slow circles for the soldiers' amusement, but David was looking for someone else. He began to worry that Elizabeth had gone home already; it was seven in the morning, after all, and the strippers most likely worked in shifts. Or maybe she'd started dancing at a different club. Or moved out of Columbus altogether.

Just as he was about to give up hope, he noticed someone in an olive-green army jacket slumped over a table in the far corner of the room. At first David thought it was a GI who'd passed out in his chair, but as he moved closer he saw a lustrous fan of black hair radiating from the figure's motionless head. It was a woman sleeping with her face pressed to the tabletop and her long, slender legs splayed underneath. She wasn't wearing a shirt under the army jacket, or any pants either; just a bright red bikini bottom and a pair of knee-high white boots.

David approached the table, trying to get a better look at her, but the corner was dimly lit and the woman's hair veiled her face.

There was no getting around it: he had to wake her. He sat in the chair opposite hers and gently rapped his knuckles on the table. "Uh, excuse me?"

No response. David rapped a little harder. "Excuse me? Can I talk to you for a second?"

The woman slowly lifted her head, pawing at the curtain of hair in front of her eyes. She pulled a few black strands out of her mouth, then squinted at David. "What the hell do you want?" she croaked.

Her face was a mess. A smear of crimson lipstick ran from the corner of her mouth to the center of her left cheek. The pouches under her eyes were puffy and gray, and one of her false eyelashes had partially detached from the lid, so that it flapped like a bat's wing every time she blinked. But her skin was caramel brown, the exact same shade as Michael's, and her tiny, doll-like nose looked just like Professor Gupta's. She looked about the right age, too: mid to late thirties, noticeably older than the other dancers in the club. Breathing fast, David leaned across the table. "Elizabeth?"

She grimaced. "Who told you that name?"

"Well, it's a long—"

"Don't call me that again! My name's Beth, you hear? Just Beth."

She curled her upper lip and David got a look at her teeth. Each one had a brown stain near the gum line. Meth mouth, the addicts called it. As they smoked the drug, the vapors corroded their enamel. Now David was certain that this woman was Elizabeth Gupta. "Okay, Beth. Listen, I was wondering—"

"What do you want, a blow job or a fuck?" The left side of her face twitched.

"I was hoping we could just talk for a minute."

"I don't have time for this shit!" She suddenly stood up and her army jacket flapped open, giving David a glimpse of a gold locket swinging on a chain between her breasts. "It's twenty for a blow job in the parking lot, fifty for a fuck at the motel."

Her face twitched again and she started scratching her chin

with scarlet fingernails. She must be in withdrawal, David thought. Her whole body was yearning for another hit of methamphetamine. He rose to his feet. "All right, let's go to the parking lot."

He tried to steer her toward the back door but she slapped his hand away. "You gotta pay first, dickhead!"

David took a twenty-dollar bill out of his wallet and handed it over. She slipped the bill into the inside pocket of her jacket and headed for the emergency exit. Walking behind her, David noticed she had a limp, which was the final confirmation of her identity. Elizabeth Gupta had been hit by a car as a young girl, breaking her left leg in three places.

Once she was outside she strode toward a grimy alcove between the club's cinder-block wall and a pair of Dumpsters. "Drop your drawers," she ordered. "We're gonna do this fast."

He looked over his shoulder and spotted the station wagon. Graddick had already stepped out of the car. Now David had some backup, just in case things turned ugly. "Actually, I don't want a blow job. I'm a friend of your father, Beth. I want to help you."

Her mouth opened and she gazed at him blankly for a moment. Then she clenched her rotting teeth. "My father? What the fuck are you talking about?"

"My name's David Swift, okay? Professor Gupta told me where I could find you. We're trying to—"

"That fuck!" She screamed the words across the parking lot. "Where is he?"

David held out both hands like a traffic cop. "Hey, hey, calm down! Your father's not here. It's just me and—"

"FUCKER!" She rushed toward him, aiming her long nails at his eyes. "COCKSUCKING MOTHERFUCKER!"

He braced himself, hoping to catch her by the wrists, but before she could get close enough, Graddick grabbed her from behind. Moving much more quickly than David would've thought possible, the mountain man immobilized Elizabeth by twisting her arms behind her back. "Mother of abominations!" Graddick shouted.

"Raise your eyes to your Lord Jesus Christ! Repent before judgment falls!"

After a moment of surprise, Elizabeth lifted her right knee and smashed her boot heel down on Graddick's toes. He let go of her, howling in pain, and she instantly sprang on David.

He managed to deflect her right hand, but the nails of her left raked the side of his neck. Jesus, he thought, this woman is fast! He shoved her backward but she came at him again, firing a kick that barely missed his crotch. It was like battling a wild animal, a fight to the death, and David was beginning to think he'd have to knock her out cold to get her into the station wagon. But then, before she could lunge at him again, Elizabeth saw something out of the corner of her eye. She stopped in her tracks and pivoted to the right, balancing on one of her lethal boot heels. Then she raced across the parking lot toward Monique and Michael, who stood in front of Graddick's car.

"Michael!" she cried, flinging her arms around her son.

THE DELTA FORCE HAD SET up its field headquarters in a Pentecostal church in Jolo. Lucille stared at the simple, wood-frame building— the Church of the Living Lord Jesus—and shook her head. This was a spectacular piece of military stupidity. If you want coopera- tion from the locals, you don't occupy their houses of worship. But the special forces had come straight from Iraq, where they'd obvi- ously lost some of their patience for local sensitivities.

Lucille and Agent Crawford stepped into the church and started looking for Colonel Tarkington, the squadron commander. His men had organized a command post beside the pulpit. Two soldiers worked the radio, another pair bent over a map of West Virginia, and two more pointed their M-16s at a group of blind- folded detainees sitting in the pews. Lucille shook her head again. The prisoners were sullen, mulish hillbillies who feared God but little else. Even if they knew the whereabouts of the fugitives, they certainly weren't going to reveal anything to the commandos.

She finally spotted Colonel Tarkington at the back of the

church. He was champing on the wet stub of a cigar and shouting orders into a field radio. Lucille waited until he ended the transmission before approaching him. "Colonel, I'm Special Agent Lucille Parker, your FBI liaison. I want to talk about the evidence your troops seized at Carnegie's Retreat last night."

The colonel eyed her and Agent Crawford for several seconds, using his lips and teeth to maneuver the cigar to the corner of his mouth. "What about it?"

"You need to send the damaged computer to the Bureau's lab in Quantico. We may be able to extract some of the data from the shattered disks in the hard drive."

Tarkington managed to grin around his cigar. "Don't worry about it, darling. We sent all that stuff to the DIA."

Lucille bristled at the "darling" but kept her voice steady. "With all due respect, sir, our equipment at Quantico is far superior to anything the Defense Intelligence Agency has."

"I'm sure our boys can handle it. Besides, we ain't gonna need that information anyway. We've shut down all traffic in this part of the state. We're gonna find those fugitives before lunchtime."

She doubted this very much. Over the past thirty-six hours she'd learned not to underestimate David Swift's talent for evasion. "Just the same, sir, the Bureau wants that hard drive."

The colonel stopped grinning. "I told you, the DIA's got it. Go talk to them. I got an operation to run here." Then he marched over to the pulpit to confer with his men.

Lucille stood there for a moment, fuming. To hell with him, she thought. If he doesn't want my help, what was the point in offering it? She was too old for this bullshit anyway. She should just go back to her office in Washington and sit on her ass like all the other goddamn bureaucrats.

She stormed out of the church and back to her SUV. Agent Crawford hurried to keep up. "Where are we going now?" he asked.

She was about to say, "D.C.," but then an idea occurred to her. It was such a simple, obvious thing, she was surprised she hadn't thought of it earlier. "That computer in Carnegie's Retreat, it had a connection to the Internet, right?"

Crawford nodded. "Yes, a cable connection, I think."

"Get on the phone with their Internet service provider. Find out if there was any activity last night."

ELIZABETH GUPTA LAY ON A bed in room 201 of the Army Mule Motel, across the street from the Night Maneuvers Lounge. This was the room where Elizabeth usually serviced the johns she picked up at the strip club, but now she was alone in the queen-size bed, lying under the covers in a terrycloth bathrobe. Monique sat on the edge of the bed, stroking Elizabeth's hair and murmuring softly, ministering to the girl as if she were a five-year-old with the flu. Michael sat in one of the chairs, playing with his Game Boy again, while David peeked through the window curtains, checking for any unusual activity on Victory Drive. They'd sent Graddick outside to get some coffee; his exhortations about redemption and divine forgiveness had turned out to be counterproductive.

Monique unwrapped a Nutri-Grain bar she'd bought from the motel's vending machine and offered it to Elizabeth. "Here, have some of this."

"Nah, ain't hungry," she rasped. Since her screaming fit in the parking lot, she hadn't spoken more than a dozen words.

Monique held the Nutri-Grain bar right under her nose. "Come on, take a bite. You need to eat something."

Her voice was gentle but firm. Surrendering, Elizabeth nibbled at a corner of the bar. David was impressed at how deftly Monique was handling the situation. It was clear that she had some experience dealing with addicts.

Elizabeth took another bite of the granola bar, then sat up in bed so she could sip some water from a Styrofoam cup that Monique pressed to her lips. Within seconds she was eating ravenously, jamming the bar into her mouth and picking up the crumbs that fell on the bedsheets. And the whole time she kept her eyes on Michael, staring fixedly at the teenager as her jaw moved up and down. When she finished eating, she wiped her mouth with the back of her hand and pointed at her son. "I can't believe it. He's grown so much."

Monique nodded. "He's a handsome young man."

"The last time I saw him, he was only thirteen. He barely came up to my shoulders."

"So your father never brought him down here for visits?"

The fierce scowl reappeared on Elizabeth's face. "That cocksucker never even sent me pictures. I used to call him collect once a year, on Michael's birthday, but the fucking asshole wouldn't accept my calls."

"I'm so sorry." Monique bit her lip. She seemed genuinely saddened. "I didn't—"

"So is the bastard dead? He told me I'd never see Michael again while he was still alive."

Monique glanced at David, uncertain how to answer. He stepped away from the window and approached the bed. "Your father's not dead, but he's in the hospital. He told us to bring Michael here because he didn't want the boy to go to an institution."

Elizabeth gave him a suspicious look. "That doesn't sound like my father. And why is he in the hospital?"

"Let's start from the beginning, okay? I used to be a student of your father's friend, Hans Kleinman. You remember him, don't you?"

The name struck a chord. Her face relaxed a bit. "Sure, I know Hans. He's my godfather. He's also the only person in the world that my father hates more than me."

"What?" David was thrown off balance. "Your father didn't hate Dr. Kleinman. They were close colleagues. They worked together for many years."

Elizabeth shook her head. "My father hates him because Hans is smarter than he is. And because Hans was in love with my mother."

David studied her face, trying to figure out if she was putting him on. "I knew Dr. Kleinman very well, and I find it hard to believe that—"

"I don't give a shit if you believe me or not. All I know is that I saw Hans at my mother's funeral and he was bawling like a baby. There were little wet blots all over the front of his shirt."

He tried to picture it, his old teacher weeping at Hannah Gupta's grave. It seemed so unlikely. Then David dispelled the image from his mind. No time for this now. Get to the point already. "Your father told us that Hans came down to Columbus a few years ago. He tried to help you get straight, right?"

A sheepish look came over her. She looked down at the bedsheets. "Yeah, he got me a job at Benning, answering the phone for some general. And he found an apartment for me, too. I even got Michael back for a few months. But I fucked it up."

"Well, that's why we're here, Beth. You see, Dr. Kleinman died a couple of days ago, but he left—"

"Hans is dead?" She sat bolt upright on the bed, her mouth wide open. "What happened?"

"I can't go into all the details right now, but he left a message saying he'd—"

"Jesus Christ," she muttered, raising her hand to her forehead. "Jesus fucking Christ!"

She grabbed a fistful of her own hair and tugged at it. Monique leaned closer to her and patted the back of her bathrobe. David was a bit surprised by Elizabeth's reaction; he'd assumed that a meth-addict hooker would be too hardened to feel any grief. But Dr. Kleinman was the only person in her life who'd ever tried to help her. There had obviously been a strong connection between the old physicist and his goddaughter. Maybe that was why he'd hid the Theory of Everything in Columbus.

David sat on the bed beside Elizabeth and Monique. The three of them were in a tight huddle now, their heads almost touching. "Listen, Beth, I'm going to be honest with you. We're in a lot of trouble. Dr. Kleinman had a secret, a scientific secret that plenty of people would love to get their hands on. Did Hans leave any papers with you when he came down here?"

Elizabeth scrunched her face, uncomprehending. "No, he didn't leave anything with me. Except some money. Enough to cover the rent on my apartment for a few months."

"What about a computer? Did he buy one for you?"

"Nah, but he got me a television set. And a nice radio, too." She smiled at the memory, but it faded an instant later. "I had to pawn that stuff after I lost my job at the base. All I got now is that box of clothes."

She pointed at a cardboard box beside the window, overflowing with panties, bras, and nylons. David doubted very much that the unified field theory was in there. "So this is where you live now? In this room?"

"Sometimes this room, sometimes the one next door. Harlan takes cares of all the motel bills."

"Harlan?"

"Yeah, he's the manager at Night Maneuvers."

In other words, her pimp, David thought. "Dr. Kleinman's message gave us the address of the bar. So Hans must've known what happened to you."

Elizabeth winced. She hunched on the bed, folding her arms across her stomach. "Hans called me after I got fired. He said he was gonna come down here again and get me into a treatment program."

Now David pictured Dr. Kleinman at the Night Maneuvers Lounge, another unlikely image. He started to wonder if the strip club had a computer in its office. "So did Hans see you at the club? And did he go into the club's office, by any chance?"

She squeezed her eyes shut and shook her head. "No, Hans never came. I was high when he called, so I told him to fuck off. And that was the last time we ever talked."

She bent forward until her forehead was just a few inches above the bedcovers. She didn't make a sound but her body began to shake with sobs, rocking the mattress.

Monique patted her back again, but this time it had no effect. So she went over to Michael and gently grasped his elbow, bringing the teenager to his mother's bedside. Elizabeth automatically embraced him. Michael would've screamed his head off if anyone else had tried this, but he seemed to have a natural tolerance for his mother's touch. He didn't return her affection, though, or even look at her. As she folded her arms around his waist, he turned a bit to the side so he could go on playing Warfighter.

After a while Elizabeth pulled back and held her son at arm's length. She wiped the tears from her eyes as she gazed at him. "Still playing that damn war game," she sighed, glancing at the Game Boy's screen. "I would've thought you'd be sick of it by now."

Michael didn't respond, of course, so Elizabeth turned to David and Monique. "Michael started playing that game when I was working at Benning. Hans fixed one of the computers in my office so Michael could play the game there." She ran her hand through the boy's hair, making a part on the left side. "On the days when the school for autistic kids was closed, I'd take him to work and he'd just sit in front of that computer for hours and hours."

Elizabeth lowered her hand a bit and caressed Michael's cheek. It was a touching sight, and ordinarily David wouldn't have interrupted. But his mind was racing. "Wait a second. Dr. Kleinman came to your office at Benning?"

She nodded. "Yeah, on my first day there. He wanted to introduce me to General Garner, my new boss. Hans knew the guy from way back. They worked together on some army project a hundred years ago."

"And while Hans was in your office, he worked on one of the computers there?"

"Yeah, that place was full of computers. It was called the VCS office, Virtual Combat Simulation. They had all kinds of crazy shit—treadmills, goggles, plastic rifles. The army didn't even use most of that crap, so they let Michael play with it."

"How long was Hans working on the computer?"

"Hell, I don't know. A few hours, at least. He and the general were old friends, so Hans had free run of the place."

David's heart was pumping fast now. He exchanged a look with Monique, then focused on the Game Boy in Michael's hands. By coincidence, the screen showed the same dark hallway that David had seen on the Game Boy when he'd looked over Michael's shoulder the night before. Once again, an animated soldier in a khaki uniform burst into a small room and fired his M-16 at half a dozen enemies. Once again, the opposing soldiers fell to the floor, bleeding simulated blood. And once again a flashing message appeared: "CONGRATULATIONS! YOU'VE REACHED LEVEL SVIA/4!"

"What the hell is that?" Monique asked, pointing at the screen. "SVIA/4?"

David had no idea, but he knew whom to ask. He bent over until his face was right in front of Michael's. The teenager had talked to him the night before. Maybe he'd do it again. "Listen to me, Michael. What's on Level SVIA/4?"

The boy tucked in his chin, avoiding David's stare. "I can't get to that level," he said in his toneless voice. "It goes back to Level A1."

"I know, you told me that already." David tilted his head, keeping his face in front of the boy's. "But why can't you go to Level SVIA/4?"

"The Game Boy doesn't have that level. It's only on the program that runs on the server. That's how Hans set it up."

"And why did he set it up that way?"

Michael opened his mouth wide, as if he were about to start screaming. But instead, for the first time, he looked David in the eye. "He told me it would be safe! It was a safe place!"

David nodded. Dr. Kleinman had apparently altered the War-fighter software. Because the Game Boy could fall into anyone's hands, it held a shortened version of the program. The complete version, containing all the information that Kleinman had added, was in a more secure location. "Where's the server?"

Before Michael could answer, the Game Boy let out a *ping* to announce that it had bounced back to Level A1. The teenager quickly turned away from David and left his mother's bedside. He retreated to the other side of the room, faced the wall, and resumed playing Warfighter.

Elizabeth glared at David. "Hey, stop asking him questions! You're upsetting him!"

"Okay, okay." He backed away from her bed. The truth was, he didn't need to ask Michael any more questions. He knew where the server was. Dr. Kleinman had chosen the most audacious hiding place imaginable. He'd put Einstein's unified field theory on a computer at Fort Benning.

DR. MILO JENKINS AND HIS wife lay facedown on their living-room carpet. If not for the bullet holes in their heads, Simon might've thought they were taking a nap. He'd finished them off at 9 A.M., shortly after the hillbilly doctor announced that Professor Gupta was out of danger and sleeping peacefully on the dining-room table. The shots woke up Agent Brock, who was sprawled on the doctor's living-room sofa, but after a few seconds he rolled over and went back to sleep.

Simon would've loved some sleep himself. He'd gotten precious little of it over the past thirty-six hours, and the blood transfusion had weakened him more than he'd expected. But his client, the enigmatic Henry Cobb, was due to make his daily phone call at nine-thirty to check on the progress of the mission, and Simon felt a professional obligation to give him some favorable news. So, with a weary grunt, he stepped into the dining room and approached the gore-encrusted table where Professor Gupta lay.

The intravenous line hanging from the chandelier was still attached to Gupta's arm, but the IV bag was empty. The tiny professor slept fitfully on his back, with his wounded leg propped on a sofa cushion. Whatever painkillers Dr. Jenkins had given him had surely worn off by now, so Gupta would be in agony as soon as he regained consciousness. Which was exactly what Simon wanted.

He started the process by pounding his fist on the sutured hole in Gupta's thigh. The professor's body convulsed: the back of his head banged against the mahogany tabletop and his uninjured leg kicked the sofa cushion to the floor. He emitted a long, ragged moan and his eyelids quivered.

Simon bent over the table. "Wake up, Professor. Time for class to begin." Then he smacked Gupta's thigh wound again, hard enough to strain the stitches that Dr. Jenkins had so carefully woven.

This time Gupta opened his eyes and let out a high-pitched scream. He tried to sit up, but Simon pinned his shoulders to the table. "You're a lucky man, you know that? You almost didn't make it."

Gupta looked up at him, blinking rapidly. The old man was obviously a bit confused. Simon gave his shoulders a squeeze. "It's all right, Professor. You're going to be all right. You just need to answer one question. Just one little question and we'll be done."

The professor opened and closed his mouth, but no words came out. It took him several seconds to find his voice. "What? Who are you?"

"That's not important right now. The important thing is finding your friends. David Swift and Monique Reynolds, remember? You were with them last night in the cabin. And then they left you behind, bleeding on the floor. That wasn't very considerate of them, was it?"

Gupta furrowed his brow. This was a good sign—his memory was coming back. Simon tightened his grip on the old man's shoulder. "Yes, you remember. And I think you also remember where they were headed. You would've gone with them if you hadn't been shot, correct?"

After a few seconds the old man narrowed his eyes and frowned. This wasn't such a good sign. Now that he had his memory back, Gupta was turning defiant. "Who are you?" he repeated.

"I told you, that's not important. I need to know where Swift and Reynolds have gone. Tell me now, or things will get very unpleasant for you, Professor."

Gupta's eyes darted to the left and for the first time he took in his surroundings: the mahogany table, the chandelier, the red-and-yellow wallpaper of the Jenkins dining room. He took a labored breath. "You're not FBI," he whispered.

Simon kept one hand on Gupta's shoulder and moved the other toward his injured thigh. "No, I have more leeway, fortunately. The Americans have a few tricks, of course—the water boarding, the sleep deprivation, the German shepherds. But I don't waste time with half measures." When his hand reached the bullet wound he grasped the gauze dressing and tore it off.

Gupta arched his back and let out another scream. But when Simon studied the man's face he didn't see the frozen look of terror that usually accompanied the frenzied contortions. The professor bared his teeth instead. "Imbecile!" he hissed. "You're just as stupid as that agent!"

Irritated, Simon dug two fingers into the wound, using his nails to wriggle between the sutures. Blood flowed again from the loose flaps of skin. "Enough of this. Where are Swift and Reynolds?"

"Imbecile! Idiot!" Gupta shouted, slamming his fist against the table.

Simon dug deeper into the wound. The blood pooled around his fingers and trickled down Gupta's thigh. "If you don't tell me where they are, I'll rip out these sutures. Then I'll peel the skin off your leg, strip by strip."

The professor lurched forward and glared at him with maniacal eyes. "You brainless Russian pig! I'm Henry Cobb!"

Chapter Ten

MONIQUE GAVE HIM A DISGUSTED LOOK. "THIS IS CRAZY. We're wasting our time."

They were in the station wagon again, but now they were arguing instead of kissing. The car was parked at a gas station on Victory Drive, about a quarter mile south of the Night Maneuvers Lounge, and Elizabeth Gupta was making a call at the station's pay phone. Graddick stood guard nearby, holding a cup of Dunkin' Donuts coffee, while David, Monique, and Michael waited in the car.

"It's not crazy," David insisted. "It makes perfect sense."

Monique shook her head. "If Kleinman wanted to keep the theory away from the government, why would he put it on a computer belonging to the U.S. Army?"

"Military computers are the most secure systems in the world. And he hid the equations in a piece of war-gaming software that no one uses anymore."

"But the army still has access to it! What if some captain or colonel in the Virtual Combat office gets bored one day and decides to play Warfighter?"

"First of all, you can't get to the theory unless you reach the highest expertise level. That's probably not so easy, unless you play the game all the time like Michael." David pointed at the teenager, who was crouched over his Game Boy in the backseat. "And second, even if you mastered the game and found the equations, you wouldn't understand what they meant unless you were a physicist. You'd just assume it was nonsense and ignore it."

She didn't look convinced. "I don't know, David. You have to admit, it's a pretty wild guess. Are you sure you—"

Before she could finish the thought, Elizabeth stepped away

from the pay phone and came striding back to the station wagon. She wore spandex tights and a T-shirt now, but she still looked very much like a hooker. "There's no answer," she told David through the car window. "Sheila probably went away for the weekend."

David frowned. He'd hoped that Sheila—a friend of Elizabeth's who still worked as a secretary in the Virtual Combat Simulation office—could help them get into Fort Benning. "Do you know anyone else who still works there?"

"Nah, nobody," Elizabeth replied. "Most of the guys in that office were computer geeks. The whole time I was there, they never once said hello."

Shit, David thought. There was no way they could get through Benning's security gate, much less into the VCS office, without a little help from someone who worked at the base.

"It's funny," Elizabeth continued, "I've never seen any of those geeks at the club either. They must get off on Internet porn."

An idea occurred to him. "Beth, do you have any steady customers who work at the base? Guys you see on a regular basis?"

"Fuck yes." Her voice turned defensive, as if he'd just challenged her. "I got some once-a-week guys. Plenty of 'em."

"Are any of them military police?"

She thought it over for a few seconds. "Yeah, I know a sergeant in the MPs, Sergeant Mannheimer. I've known him for years, ever since I started working at the club."

"Do you know his phone number?"

Instead of answering, she reached into the car and snapped her fingers in front of Michael's nose. The teenager's head shot up from his Game Boy. Elizabeth looked at him sternly. "Columbus directory," she said. "Mannheimer, Richard."

"706-555-1329," Michael recited. Then he lowered his head and returned to his game.

Elizabeth smiled. "Ain't that something? He memorized the Columbus phone book when he lived with me. The Macon phone book, too."

David wrote the number on a scrap of paper. He wasn't particularly surprised by Michael's memory feat; he knew that many autistic children had amazing powers of recall, and he remembered the telephone directories that were stored in the computer at Carnegie's Retreat. What unsettled him was how Elizabeth used her son's skill. She'd obviously done the finger-snapping trick before. It must've been a convenient way to keep track of her johns.

He handed her the scrap of paper. "Call the sergeant and ask him for a favor. Tell him you've got some friends in town who need passes to get on the base. Tell him we want to go to the barracks to visit our little brother, but we left our IDs at home by mistake."

She squinted at the phone number, then shook her head. "Mannheimer ain't gonna do this for nothing, you know. He's gonna want me to give him a freebie. Maybe two."

David had expected this. He took his wallet out of his pocket and removed five twenties from the billfold. "Don't worry, I'll cover it. A hundred now, two hundred when we're done. Deal?"

Elizabeth stared at the twenty-dollar bills. She opened her mouth and licked her lips, probably tasting the crystal meth already. Then she snatched the money out of David's hand and headed back to the pay phone.

David looked at Monique, but she turned away from him. She was pissed, no question about it, but she didn't say a word, and that was worse than any amount of yelling. They watched in silence as Elizabeth placed the call at the pay phone and started talking. Finally, David stretched his arm across the seat and touched Monique's shoulder. "Hey, what's wrong?"

She shrugged his hand off. "You know what's wrong. You're pimping her."

"No, I'm not! I'm just—"

"What do you think she's gonna do with that money? She's gonna spend it all on meth and go on a binge. And then it's back to the strip club, back to the motel room."

"Look, we need her help to find the theory. If you have a better idea, why don't you—"

Monique suddenly clutched David's arm. "Something's wrong," she said, pointing at the pay phone. Graddick stood beside Elizabeth, shouting at her. She ignored him and kept talking into the receiver. A moment later Graddick grabbed her by the waist and started dragging her toward the station wagon. David was confused until he looked down Victory Drive and saw half a dozen black SUVs parked in front of the Night Maneuvers Lounge. A swarm of men in gray suits were leaping out of the vehicles and surrounding the strip club.

Graddick opened the wagon's rear door and pushed Elizabeth inside. "Start the engine, brother! Satan's on our tail!"

KAREN STOOD IN THE LIVING ROOM of Gloria Mitchell's apartment, peering through the window blinds at the traffic on East Twenty-seventh Street. Two burly men in sweatshirts loitered on the sidewalk next to a delivery truck that hadn't moved in the past twelve hours. Every few minutes or so, one of the men cupped his hand over his mouth and pretended to cough. He was speaking into a microphone that ran down his sleeve.

Jonah sat on the couch, leafing through an astronomy book he'd found in Gloria's bookcase. Gloria herself was at the other end of the room, talking on her cell phone with her editor at the *New York Times*. She was a tiny, raven-haired spitfire of a woman, with skinny legs and a pointy chin and dark eyes in constant motion. When she finished the call, she snapped the phone shut and quick-stepped toward Karen. "I have to go," she reported. "Double homicide in Brooklyn. Just stay here till I get back."

Karen's stomach twisted. She pointed at the window. "Those agents are still outside." She kept her voice low so Jonah wouldn't overhear. "As soon as they see you leave the building, they're gonna come up here and grab us."

Gloria shook her head. "An illegal break-in at a reporter's apartment? They wouldn't dare."

"They'll break down the door and fix it before you get back. It'll look like Jonah and I just decided to leave. That's what the FBI will tell you when you ask them what happened to us."

"You really think—"

"Can't you ask your editor to assign someone else?"

She let out a loud *Ha*. "Forget it. The guy's a ballbuster."

Karen glanced at her son, who was poring over a picture of the asteroid belt. No way in hell was she going to let those bastards touch him. "Then we'll come with you. They won't arrest us if you're there to see it."

Gloria shrugged. "All right, suit yourself."

IF THIS HAD BEEN AN ordinary job, Simon would've shot his client by now. Professor Amil Gupta, aka Henry Cobb, was the most arrogant, infuriating man he'd ever worked for. As soon as the professor revealed his identity he started excoriating Simon in the most unpleasant terms. Although Gupta had some legitimate reasons for being displeased, the fault was really his own: the mix-up wouldn't have occurred if he hadn't insisted on that absurd alias. Simon tried to explain this as he rebandaged the man's bullet wound, but Gupta continued to insult him. Then, once the professor was able to walk, he began shouting orders. He outlined a new plan: he and Simon would take the pickup truck down to Georgia to follow the targets, while Agent Brock drove Dr. Jenkins's Dodge van to New York. When Simon asked why Brock was going back to New York, Gupta curtly told him to shut up and find the keys to the van. Simon's hand automatically reached for his Uzi, but he stopped himself from spraying Gupta's brains across the room. Be patient, he reminded himself. Focus on the goal.

Because Jenkins's house was a few kilometers outside the cordon that the American forces had set up, Simon encountered no resistance on the back roads of southwestern Virginia. By 11 A.M., they reached the town of Meadowview, where Brock headed north on I-81 and Simon and Gupta went south. The professor reclined in the passenger seat with his injured leg propped on the dashboard, but unfortunately he didn't doze off. Instead he checked his watch every five minutes and fulminated about the depths of human stupidity. After they crossed the state line into Tennessee, he abruptly leaned toward Simon and pointed at a sign saying EXIT 69 BLOUNT-VILLE. "Get off the highway," he ordered.

"Why? The road's clear. No military or police."

Gupta scowled. "We don't have enough time to get to Georgia. Because of your incompetence, Swift and Reynolds have a ten-hour head start on us. They've probably made contact with my daughter already."

"All the more reason for taking the interstate. The back roads will be slower."

"There's another alternative. I've done some work with a company in Blountville, a defense contractor called Mid-South Robotics. I built a few prototype machines for them, so they're hooked into my surveillance network."

"Surveillance?"

"Yes. If I'm right about where Swift and Reynolds are going, we may able to observe them."

Simon left the interstate and traveled about two kilometers down Route 394. Mid-South Robotics was located in a sprawling one-story building that covered a fair amount of the Tennessee countryside. Because it was Saturday morning, there was only one car in the parking lot. Simon pulled up next to it and then he and Professor Gupta headed for the security guard's booth. A gaunt, white-haired man in a blue uniform sat inside, reading the local newspaper. Gupta tapped on the booth's window to get the man's attention. "Hello there!" he called. "I'm Dr. Amil Gupta of the Robotics Institute. Do you remember me? I was here for a visit in April."

The guard put down the newspaper and stared at them for a moment. Then he grinned. "Oh yeah, Dr. Gupta! From Pittsburgh! I was here when you came for your tour of the plant!" He stood up and opened the door to the booth so he could shake the professor's hand. "It's mighty nice to see you again!"

Gupta forced a smile. "Yes, it's good to see you, too. Tell me, is Mr. Compton in the office yet? He asked me to stop by and take a look at one of his prototypes."

"Oh, I sure am sorry, but Mr. Compton ain't here. He didn't say nothing about you coming over today."

"He'll probably arrive later, I suppose. In the meantime, could you let me and my assistant into the testing lab? I can only stay for a couple of hours, so I need to get to work right away."

The guard glanced at Simon, then turned back to Gupta. He was starting to have second thoughts. "I guess I should call Mr. Compton first. Just to let him know you're here."

"Please, there's no need. I don't want to interrupt his weekend."

"Just the same, I think I'll call him."

He was retreating into his booth when the professor gave the nod. Simon stepped forward with his Uzi and shot the guard between the eyes. The man was dead before his body hit the floor. Simon bent over him and searched his pockets.

Gupta looked down at the corpse. "Fascinating. I lived for seventy-six years without witnessing a murder, and now I've seen two in the past twelve hours."

"You'll get used to it." After removing the keys from the guard's pocket, Simon began disconnecting the building's alarm system.

The professor shook his head. "It's like the collapse of a small universe. An infinite array of probabilities reduced to a single dead certainty."

"If it's such a tragedy, why did you tell me to kill him?"

"I never said it was a tragedy. Some universes must die so that others can be born." Gupta lifted his gaze to the sky, bringing his hand to his forehead to shield his eyes from the sun. "Humanity will take a great leap forward once we present the *Einheitliche Feldtheorie* to the world. We'll be the midwives to a new era, a golden age of enlightenment."

Simon frowned. He was a soldier, not a midwife. His mission was death, not birth.

IT WAS EASY TO SEE why Sergeant Mannheimer was one of Elizabeth's regular customers. Gawky, balding, beak-nosed, and loudmouthed, he probably couldn't get a date with anyone but a hooker. He sat in the backseat of the station wagon with his arm around Elizabeth, squeezing her waist and peeking at her cleavage, but he was also casting lascivious glances at Monique, who sat with Michael in the cargo area. Graddick grumbled as he steered the car toward Fort Benning's entrance; he obviously disliked the sergeant and wasn't happy about visiting the army base either. But David had insisted that it was necessary for Elizabeth's salvation, and that was enough to keep Graddick quiet, at least for the time being.

As they approached the security gate, David noticed a long line of cars ahead. It seemed like a lot of traffic for a Saturday morning. Pointing at the gate, he turned to Mannheimer. "What's going on?"

The sergeant was toying with the gold chain around Elizabeth's neck, trying to pull up the locket that hung between her breasts. "Everyone's coming to see Darth Vader. He's giving a speech at the base today."

"Darth Vader?"

"Yeah, the secretary of defense. The man who runs the Benning-to-Baghdad Express."

David looked again at the security gate and saw half a dozen MPs inspecting the cars at the front of the line. The soldiers were opening the trunks and kneeling beside the fenders to see if any bombs were under the chassis. "Shit. They've beefed up security."

"Chill out, dude." Mannheimer had successfully fished the locket out of Elizabeth's shirt and was now dangling it in front of her eyes. "Those are my boys. They won't hassle us."

Elizabeth giggled as the sergeant pretended to hypnotize her. She was in a good mood now that she had a hundred dollars in her pocket. Meanwhile, David grew ever more nervous as the car inched to the front of the line. After five minutes they reached the gate and a strapping young corporal with an M-9 pistol in his holster approached the station wagon. He bent over and stuck his face in the driver's-side window. "License and registration," he ordered. "And I'm gonna need ID for all the passengers."

Before Graddick could respond, Mannheimer leaned forward to get the corporal's attention. "Hey, Murph," he called cheerily. "We're just going to the PX to do a little shopping."

Murph saluted halfheartedly. From the expression on his face, David could see that he didn't think much of the sergeant. "We got new orders from the post commander, sir. All visitors have to show ID."

"Don't sweat it, buddy. These guys are with me."

"No exceptions, sir. That's what the commander said."

A second MP approached the car's passenger side. This one wore a helmet and carried an M-16. David reached for the door handle, but he knew it was all over. In three minutes they would all be in handcuffs.

Sergeant Mannheimer slid to the edge of his seat, moving closer to the suspicious corporal. He lowered his voice. "Okay, Murph, here's the deal. You see Beth over here?" He pointed his thumb at Elizabeth. "Well, she and the black girl are scheduled to give a little performance today. A private performance for the SecDef after he finishes his speech."

The corporal stared at Elizabeth, who licked her lips and stuck out her chest. His mouth fell open. "You got strippers for the SecDef?"

Mannheimer nodded. "Hey, the man works hard. He needs a break every now and then."

"Holy shit." Murph looked at his superior with newfound respect. "Does the commander know about this?"

"No, these orders came straight from the Pentagon."

The corporal grinned. "Damn, this is too much. The SecDef is getting his freak on." Then he stepped back from the car and waved them through the gate.

AS SOON AS LUCILLE SAW the records of Gupta's Internet activity—in particular, the Web page showing the location of 3617 Victory Drive—she issued new orders for the Bureau's Learjet. Two hours later she and Agent Crawford strode into the Night Maneuvers Lounge, which had already been secured by a team of agents from the Atlanta office. About thirty customers—mostly drunk soldiers with weekend passes—milled about the club's tables, while the employees—five dancers, a bartender, and a bouncer—sat at the bar. The bouncer and bartender had recognized David Swift when the agents showed them his photograph, and the bartender said he'd seen the suspect leave the club with another dancer who'd just finished her shift. This dancer, as it turned out, was Beth Gupta, the professor's daughter. Unfortunately, the Atlanta agents failed to find the woman when they searched her temporary residence at a motel across the street. The bartender, a skeevy character named Harlan Woods who was also the club's manager, said he had no idea where Beth could be, but Lucille suspected otherwise.

She spotted Harlan right away, a short, fat, bearded man wearing a T-shirt that said I GIVE MUSTACHE RIDES. Lucille went to the bar and folded her arms across her chest. "So you're the man in charge of this lovely establishment?"

He nodded rapidly. Perched on his chair by the bar, he looked like a dissolute gnome on a toadstool. "I want to help you, okay? But like I said before, I don't know where Beth is. She just works here, that's all. Where she goes during her spare time, I have no fucking idea."

Harlan was obviously on speed. He was talking a mile a minute and stank like a locker room. Lucille frowned. She detested addicts. "Slow down, Bubba. Does Beth have any friends here in town?"

He pointed at the dancers lined up at the bar, shivering in their G-strings. "Sure, the girls are all friends. Talk to Amber or Britney. Maybe they know where Beth is."

"Any other friends? Besides the girls you're pimping, I mean?"

"Fuck, I ain't a pimp! I'm just—"

"Don't bullshit me, Harlan. You better think fast, or else—"

"Okay, okay!" New beads of sweat leaked from the creases in his forehead. Like all addicts, he folded quickly. "There's a girl named Sheila, a real stuck-up bitch. She came in here once to give me hell. She and Beth used to work together on the base."

This was news to Lucille. The only information the Atlanta agents had given her was Elizabeth Gupta's arrest record. "Beth had a civilian job at Fort Benning?"

"Yeah, before she came here. Working with computers, she said. Some relative got her the job, but it didn't work out."

Lucille thought of the wrecked computer she saw in the cabin in West Virginia. The suspects were following a digital trail and she could make a good guess as to their next destination.

She turned to Agent Crawford, who was standing behind her as always. "Get me the commander at Benning," she ordered. "And that dumb-ass Colonel Tarkington."

THE FIRST THINGS DAVID SAW were the jump towers, three tall spires looming over the barracks and administrative buildings of Fort Benning. They looked like the famous Coney Island parachute jump, the amusement-park ride that shut down decades ago, but these towers were still very much in use. Paratroopers were leaping from the arms of the spires and floating to the ground like seedpods from an enormous steel flower.

Sergeant Mannheimer instructed Graddick to park the station wagon behind a sprawling yellow building called Infantry Hall. The Virtual Combat Simulation office was in the building's western wing. David had concocted a story explaining why they needed to go there—Monique had a younger brother in basic training who was suffering anxiety attacks and needed to talk to someone in private, and so on and so forth. It was clear that Mannheimer didn't believe a word of it, but fortunately the sergeant didn't seem to care.

Eager for his freebie, he only cared about finding an empty room where he could hump Elizabeth. He pulled her out of the car and led her toward the building's rear entrance.

Monique, David, and Michael also stepped out of the car. Graddick, who remained in the driver's seat, looked at them with concern. "What's going on, brother?"

David gave his shoulder a reassuring squeeze. "Just stay here till we get out. It'll only be a few minutes. Then we'll get to work on Elizabeth's soul, all right?"

Graddick nodded. Monique and David flanked Michael, each gripping one of the teenager's elbows, and hurried to catch up to Elizabeth and Mannheimer. David wished they could leave the boy in the car; it was appalling how his mother plied her trade right in front of him. But Michael was the only one who knew how to play Warfighter.

They rushed through the entrance and up the stairs to the third floor. Elizabeth and the sergeant stopped at an unmarked door at the end of a deserted hallway. Mannheimer began to rummage through the pockets of his fatigues. "So you're sure there's a couch?" he asked.

"Yeah, there's one in the director's office," Elizabeth answered. "I remember it, a big brown couch."

"But that was four years ago. Maybe they moved it since then."

"Jesus, just open the door!"

The sergeant finally found the skeleton key, but before he could slip it into the lock David heard something coming down the hall. It was a mechanical noise, oddly familiar. He turned around and saw a Dragon Runner, the boxy, silver surveillance robot that Professor Gupta had developed for the army. Riding on caterpillar treads like a miniature tank, the machine pointed its bulblike sensor at them. David froze. "Shit! They found us!"

Mannheimer chuckled. "At ease, soldier. Those things ain't operational yet."

"What?" David's heart thumped as the robot rolled past.

"They're still working out the bugs. It's like everything else the army does. They'll test the system for ten years and then decide it costs too much." Chuckling again, Mannheimer opened the door and nudged Elizabeth inside. "Okay, baby, where's the director's office?"

David followed them into the room. It was a big space, maybe forty feet long. At one end were several racks of servers that hummed and blinked on their steel shelves. Opposite them was a desktop PC with an extra-large flat-panel screen, and in the center of the room were two huge, hollow, transparent spheres, each at least nine feet high and resting on a platform studded with metal rollers.

Monique stood in the doorway and stared at the spheres, just as befuddled as David. But Michael bounded into the room, heading straight for a cabinet at the far end. While his mother and the sergeant disappeared into an adjoining office, he opened the cabinet and removed a bulky black device that looked like a stereoscopic viewer. David recognized the thing: it was a pair of virtual-reality goggles. Once you strapped them on, they displayed a simulated landscape; if you turned your head to the left or right, you'd see different parts of the virtual world. Michael beamed with joy as he adjusted the VR goggles, then dashed to the computer and began tapping its keyboard.

David and Monique went to the terminal and looked over Michael's shoulder. In a few seconds the screen showed an image of a soldier standing in the middle of a wide green field. The soldier wore a khaki uniform and a helmet emblazoned with a number, a big red 1.

"That's Warfighter," David whispered. "He's loading the program."

After a few more seconds the words READY TO START? appeared on the screen. Michael returned to the cabinet and pulled out a plastic rifle, a mock-up of an M-16. Then he approached one of the giant spheres, opened a hatch in its side, and wriggled into the transparent ball.

"Damn," Monique cried. "What's he doing in there?"

Michael closed the hatch from the inside and donned the VR goggles. Holding the plastic rifle like a real infantryman, he started walking forward, but of course he didn't get anywhere—the sphere just spun around him, rotating in place like a monstrous trackball. After a while Michael quickened his pace and the sphere rotated faster. Pretty soon the teenager was galloping like a hamster in an exercise wheel. When David looked at the computer screen he saw the khaki-clad soldier running across the field.

"Shit, this is fantastic." He put his hand on Monique's back and pointed at the platform below the sphere. "You see those rollers under the ball? They measure how fast the sphere is turning and the direction of its rotation. Then they send the data to the computer, which makes the soldier move just as fast as Michael is moving. And Michael can see the whole simulation on his goggles. He's running inside a virtual world."

"That's great, but where is he going?"

"It looks like he's just having fun. I guess he'll go up through the expertise levels like he always does."

"And what's going to happen when he reaches Level SVIA/4?"

"I don't know. There may be a way to download the theory from the server. But I bet you have to use the VR interface to access it."

David studied the icons at the bottom of the computer screen until he found the one he wanted: TWO-PLAYER GAME. He clicked on it and the words READY TO START? flashed on the screen again. While Monique gaped at him, he went to the cabinet and found another pair of VR goggles and another plastic rifle.

"I'm going in," he said. Then he stepped toward the second sphere and opened the hatch.

SIMON STOOD GUARD IN THE testing lab at Mid-South Robotics while Professor Gupta studied surveillance videos on the lab's computer.

The screen was divided into a dozen squares, each showing a live feed from one of the Dragon Runners deployed at Fort Benning. Just before noon, the computer let out a *ping*—the face-recognition program had found a match in one of the videos. Gupta identified the robot's location and expanded its surveillance feed so that it filled the screen. Simon moved a bit closer to the terminal and saw a tall, ugly soldier with his arm around the waist of a chesty slattern. Then he saw the targets: Swift, Reynolds, and Gupta's grandson.

"Interesting," the professor muttered. "They're at the VCS office."

"VCS?"

"Virtual Combat Simulation. I did some work for them, developing the VR interface for Warfighter." He paused, deep in thought. "And that's where Elizabeth worked. The job Hans found for her."

On the screen, the targets entered a room and closed the door behind them, cutting off the surveillance. Gupta quickly exited the program, stabbing at the keyboard. "Kleinman!" he shouted. "That old fool!"

"What is it?"

The professor shook his head. "He thought he was being clever! Hiding the thing right under my nose!"

"You mean the *Einheitliche Feldtheorie?*"

A new window popped up on the screen and Gupta typed in a user name and a password. He was trying to log on to some kind of network. "Luckily, it's not too late. All the VCS programs are designed for remote access. The army wanted soldiers at different bases to compete against one another in the virtual battles."

There was a delay of several seconds. Then the screen showed a long list of military servers and their activity reports. "Just as I thought," Gupta said. "They're running Warfighter."

Gazing over the professor's shoulder, Simon felt a tinge of anxiety. "Can they download the theory? Can they delete it?"

Gupta clicked on one of the servers. While the network established the connection, he turned around and glared at Simon. "Go into the supply room! There's no VR equipment here, but there might be a joystick."

DAVID STOOD IN A WIDE FIELD bordered by southern pines. Turning to the right, he saw a landscape of forested hills stretching to the horizon. When he turned left, the VR display showed a break in the trees and a cluster of low buildings. The graphics were amazingly realistic. He even heard birdcalls through the headset, which included miniature speakers and a microphone for communicating with other players. There was something strangely familiar about the simulated landscape, and after a couple of seconds he realized that the virtual world had been designed to look like the wooded training grounds of Fort Benning. Above the tops of the trees he could see the jump towers, which seemed to be several miles away.

"What are you waiting for?"

David raised his rifle when he heard the voice through the headphones. He could see the barrel of his M-16 on the display, but there were no other figures in the field or the woods. "Hey!" he called. "Who's there?"

"It's me, dummy." Monique's voice. "I'm at the terminal, watching you on the computer screen. You look just like Michael's soldier, but you got a big red 2 on your helmet."

"How did you . . . ?"

"You seemed a little lost, so I found a microphone at the terminal to tell you which way to go. Michael's in the village."

"The village?" He pointed his rifle at the cluster of buildings. "You mean over there?"

"Yeah, and he's already reached Level B2, so you better move your ass. From what I can tell, you have to get closer to Michael before he reaches SVIA/4. Otherwise you won't be able to enter the final level and download the theory."

Very gingerly, David took a step forward. The sphere turned effortlessly under his feet. He stepped to the left and the sphere turned sideways. He began to walk toward the break in the trees, slowly at first, then with greater confidence. "This isn't so bad. After a while it feels almost normal."

"Try running. You got a long way to go."

He broke into a trot. The VR display showed the landscape advancing: as David charged across the field, the buildings ahead loomed larger and he started to see dark figures lying facedown in the grass. They were the computer-generated enemy soldiers—dressed like terrorists, in black jackets and bandannas—that David had seen before on the Game Boy. "It looks like Michael took care of these guys."

"Keep your eyes open," Monique warned. "He didn't get all of them."

"What happens if they shoot me? How many lives do you get in this game?"

"Let me check the instruction file." There was a pause. "Okay, if you get shot in the body, you can't move anymore but you can still fire your gun. If you get shot in the head, you automatically go back to the start."

"And that's not good, right?"

"Not if you want to catch up with Michael. He just made it to Level B3."

David picked up the pace, zigzagging around the dead soldiers. After a few seconds he reached the edge of the village, which looked drab and desolate. On one side of the main street was a row of two-story buildings with sloping roofs; on the other was a simple white church with a bell tower. The street was empty except for the fallen soldiers, which clearly marked the path Michael had taken. David ran down the middle of the street until he came to a blocky yellow ware-house. Half a dozen simulated corpses lay just outside the building's entrance. Struggling to keep his balance inside the spinning sphere, he slowed and peered through the doorway. It was dark but he could make out shapes on the floor, more prostrate bodies.

He was just about to take a step inside when he heard gunshots. They seemed to be coming from behind, so he wheeled around. An enemy soldier was racing down the street, firing an AK-47. For a moment David forgot that he was watching a simulation; in a panic he crouched and pulled the trigger of the plastic rifle, aiming at the figure in the black jacket. The shots boomed in his headphones and David tumbled backward. He landed on his butt at the bottom of the sphere, which rocked back and forth. His VR display showed nothing but blue sky and the warehouse's yellow wall. But when he scrambled to his feet he saw the enemy soldier on his hands and knees, grimacing in pain but still clutching his rifle.

"Shoot him in the head!" Monique yelled in his headphones. "Quick, in the head!"

David fired at the soldier's skull and the figure sank to the ground. "Jesus!" he cried, sweeping his M-16 in a wide angle, scanning for any other enemies on the street. He was breathing fast. He heard more gunfire but couldn't tell where it was coming from.

"Go inside the building! Michael's on the second floor!"

He turned back to the doorway and stepped over the bodies inside. The display darkened as he went down a long, narrow corridor. His legs were wobbly now and he began to feel queasy. Sweat trickled down his forehead and collected at the rims of his goggles. "Shit, I can't see a thing!"

"Go left, LEFT! There's a stairway!"

He turned left, stumbling like a drunk. Gunshots echoed down the corridor but he saw only white flashes. The simulation was overwhelming his brain, making him nauseous. He felt like tearing off the headset. "Hold on, I gotta stop! Something's behind me!"

"No, keep going! Michael's at Level C3. He's almost finished!"

David finally found the stairway. The display brightened as he ascended, showing another corridor at the top of the steps. He started down the hall, passing several bare rooms with bloody corpses on the floor.

"Turn right when you get to the end of the hall," Monique instructed. "Then you—"

A soldier bolted out of one of the rooms, just a few feet ahead. David was so startled he dropped his M-16. He stepped backward, instinctively raising his hands, bracing himself for virtual death. But the soldier merely turned around and continued down the hall. David belatedly noticed that this figure wasn't in a black jacket; he wore a khaki uniform and had a bright red 1 on his helmet. It was Michael.

Elated, David picked up his rifle and followed him. At the end of the corridor Michael's soldier veered to the right and David heard a barrage of gunfire. By the time he caught up to the boy, all six of the remaining computer-generated enemies lay facedown on the floor.

"That's it!" Monique cried. "You're at the final level!"

Michael's soldier approached a doorway at the other end of the room. David held his breath, expecting to see *Herr Doktor*'s equations at last. But instead they entered what appeared to be a locker room. All four walls were lined with gray metal lockers, dozens and dozens of them. Michael's soldier headed for the nearest locker and touched it with his M-16. A new weapon materialized in his hands, a rifle equipped with a fat cylinder on the underside of the barrel. A grenade launcher.

David's heart sank. This wasn't the final level. It appeared to be an intermediate staging area, a place to acquire new weapons for another round of battle. "Damn it! How much longer does this go on?"

"Wait a second," Monique answered. "Look at the letters on the lockers."

Each locker had a set of initials stenciled on its door. The initials clearly stood for military ranks: The first locker was marked PVT for private, the second CPL for corporal, the third LT for lieutenant, and so on. David recognized the first dozen ranks, but as he went down the line the abbreviations became increasingly obscure: WO/1, CWO/5, CMSAF, MGYSGT.

"Check out the row on the far wall," Monique said. "The second-to-last locker."

David spotted the initials: SVIA/4. "Holy shit! The letters on the Game Boy!"

He rushed to the locker and tapped it with his M-16. On the VR display David saw the virtual grenade launcher materialize on his rifle. At the same time the initials on the locker door abruptly rearranged themselves. The S moved a bit farther to the left, the A/4 to the right. Then the VI rotated ninety degrees clockwise. The result was an equation:

$$S \le A/4$$

David didn't recognize it. But he wasn't the physicist. "Monique, do you see that?" he called into the microphone. "Do you—"

"LOOK OUT!"

He heard gunfire again. He turned around just in time to see Michael's soldier fall to the floor. Then the VR display turned red, as if splashed with blood.

IT WAS A POOR SUBSTITUTE for war, Simon thought as he looked over Gupta's shoulder at the computer screen. Even for a training exercise, the program was absurdly unrealistic. When the soldiers were shot they didn't writhe on the ground or scream for their mothers. They simply collapsed. It was a child's game, a toy. Gupta didn't need Simon's help; all he had to do was shoot a couple of cartoon soldiers in the back.

After Gupta dispatched his opponents, he advanced toward the locker with the odd symbols on its door. Toggling the joystick, he extended his soldier's rifle so that it touched the locker. First a grenade launcher appeared on the rifle and then, after a few seconds, a message flashed on the screen: READY TO DOWNLOAD? YES OR NO?

Gupta clicked on YES. The message changed to DOWNLOAD COMPLETE IN 0:46 SECONDS. The professor gazed intently at the screen as the numbers ticked down. He seemed entranced, as if he were viewing something that lurked deep inside the computer. "I'm sorry, *Herr Doktor*," he whispered. "But you shouldn't have kept me waiting."

"DAVID? WHERE ARE YOU? My screen's going haywire!"

He could hear Monique's voice but couldn't see anything. The VR display showed nothing but a thick red mist, like a bloody fog obscuring everything from view. The last thing he remembered was the sight of Michael's soldier falling, and as he pictured this image in his mind's eye he recalled something else he'd glimpsed in the background. Another soldier had stood behind Michael's. Not a computer-generated figure in a black jacket, but a soldier in a khaki uniform, with the number 3 on his helmet.

David tore off the useless goggles. Outside the transparent sphere, Monique was bent over the terminal, frantically working the keyboard. "Shit!" she yelled. "Someone else is accessing the server! There's a download in progress!"

To his left, in the other sphere, Michael was readjusting his goggles. He seemed neither surprised nor disappointed by their defeat. After a few seconds he raised his rifle and began running inside his sphere again. He was starting another game.

"We have to go back to the start," David said. "We'll just—"

"You don't have time!" Monique tugged at her hair. "There's only twenty seconds left!"

Unable to think of another option, David strapped on his goggles. The red mist was fading now, and he expected to find himself back in the wide field outside the village. But once the last red wisps vanished, he saw a row of lockers with stenciled initials on their doors. He was on his hands and knees, still in the locker room. He'd been shot in the body, not the head.

He couldn't move forward but he could point his weapon. The soldier with the 3 on his helmet stood in front of the locker, which now showed a countdown on its door instead of the equation. As the readout reached 0:09, David pulled the trigger.

❋   ❋   ❋

SIMON NOTICED SOME MOVEMENT ON the computer screen. Something small and round bounced against the row of lockers and passed out of sight.

"What was that?" he asked, pointing at the computer.

Gupta didn't answer. He was still entranced by the count-down.

"Something moved across the screen! It went to the left!"

Frowning, the professor flicked his joystick to the left, bring-ing the whole locker room into view. A green egg-shaped object lay on the floor. Simon recognized it at once. It was a U.S. Army M406 grenade.

DAVID'S LEGS NEARLY BUCKLED WHEN he stepped out of the sphere. He'd been inside the virtual world for less than fifteen minutes, but he felt as if he'd just stormed Iwo Jima. Tossing aside the VR goggles and the plastic rifle, he staggered toward Monique. "What happened?" he asked. "Did we stop it?"

She didn't look up. She stayed bent over the terminal, her eyes focused on the screen. "Why did you use the grenade? All you had to do was shoot the bastard to break his connection."

"But we stopped the download, right? He didn't get the theory, did he?"

"Oh yeah, you stopped the download. You also crashed War-fighter and deleted all the program files."

He gripped the edge of the desk. "What about the file contain-ing the theory?"

"It's gone. Wiped clean. Because the file was incorporated into the game software, crashing the program permanently corrupted it. Even if someone tried to recover the data on the server, they'd just get nonsense."

His stomach lurched. It was like stepping into the sphere again, but now the whole universe was spinning around him. The blueprints of the cosmos, the hidden design of reality—all gone in an instant because of his error.

Monique finally lifted her gaze from the computer screen. To David's surprise, she was smiling. "Luckily, Dr. Kleinman took some precautions. He built an escape hatch for the file. Just before the program was deleted, it saved the data on a flash drive."

"What?"

In her palm she held a small silver cylinder, about three inches long and an inch wide. "The theory's in here. Or at least I hope it is. I better grab a laptop to make sure."

David went limp. He took a couple of deep breaths as he stared at the flash drive. Until that moment he hadn't realized how important the theory was to him.

While Monique searched the office for a laptop, Michael emerged from his sphere. He put his VR goggles and rifle back in the cabinet, then picked up his Game Boy. It must've been a tremendous comedown, leaving the virtual-reality battlefield and returning to a device with thumb controls and a three-inch-wide screen, but Michael's face was as expressionless as ever.

A moment later his mother came out of the adjoining office. With a disgusted sigh Elizabeth smoothed a wrinkle in her tights and adjusted the ankle strap on one of her pumps. Then she headed straight for David. "Okay, where's the rest of my money?"

"Where's Mannheimer?"

"Asleep on the couch. He's a one-shot man. But you owe me two hundred just the same."

"All right, all right." David took out his wallet and removed the bills. "Listen, we have to leave the base before anyone gets suspicious. You better come with us."

She grabbed the roll of twenties and slipped them into the waistband of her tights. "That's fine. Just drop me off at the motel."

By this point Monique had found a laptop, a sleek silver MacBook. Before she could turn it on, though, David went to the window and noticed two disturbing developments. First, Graddick's station wagon was no longer parked by the rear entrance of Infantry Hall. And second, a squadron of MPs was running toward the building. From a distance they looked a lot like the virtual soldiers in Warfighter, but the M-16s in their hands were definitely not made of plastic.

LUCILLE STOOD ON A PARADE ground at Fort Benning, arguing with one of the SecDef's flunkies. The secretary was giving a speech from a podium in front of Infantry Hall. A crowd of at least three thousand soldiers and civilians stretched across the parade ground, and several hundred more people loitered behind the podium, blocking the building's main entrance. It was a security nightmare—with all these folks milling about, it was impossible to conduct a proper search for the suspects, who had apparently conned their way onto the base less than an hour before. Lucille wanted the SecDef to cut his speech short, but his Pentagon aide balked at the idea. He was a stocky kid in his twenties, dumb as a post.

"We've been planning this event for months," he said. "The troops have really been looking forward to it."

"Look, this is a matter of national security. You've heard of that, right? National security? That means it's more important than your goddamn event!"

The aide looked puzzled. "Security? I thought the MPs were handling security."

"Christ on a crutch!" In exasperation, she reached under her jacket and pulled her Glock out of its holster. "Do I have to shoot you to get your attention?"

But even the sight of the gun failed to pierce his thick skull. "Please, ma'am, calm down. The secretary is finishing up. He's getting ready to tell his joke about the three-legged chicken."

THE MPs RUSHED IN THROUGH the rear entrance of Infantry Hall and began climbing the stairs. David turned away from the window. "Let's go, let's go!" he shouted at the others. "This way!"

He pulled Michael down the corridor while Monique and Elizabeth clattered behind. He instinctively headed for the front of the building, away from the pursuing soldiers, although he knew that another squadron would most likely come from that direction as well. When David reached the stairway above the front entrance, he heard voices below, and at first he assumed these were the shouts of gung ho MPs racing up the steps. But after a moment he heard laughter and a great burst of cheering. It sounded more like a party than a manhunt.

They barreled downstairs and emerged in an entry hall crowded with soldiers and their families. Men and women in civilian clothes were lined up at a long table stocked with bowls of potato chips and six-packs of Coke. Some kind of reception was in progress. People were shaking hands and telling jokes and stuffing their faces. David threaded through the crowd, terrified that someone would raise the alarm, but no one paid any attention to him or Michael. A few of the soldiers leered at Elizabeth and Monique, but that was it. In half a minute they stepped outside and joined the stream of people who were heading for the parking lots. As they walked away from the building, David saw an old man with a familiar face shaking hands with several generals. Jesus, he thought, that's the secretary of defense. David tightened his grip on Michael's arm and walked a little faster.

They moved with the crowd for half a mile or so, going west past a series of parking lots where groups of spectators peeled off to find their cars. After about ten minutes the crowd had thinned out but the four of them continued walking in the same direction, following signs that said WEST GATE, EDDY BRIDGE. They passed a tennis court and a field where a dozen soldiers were playing football. David saw no MPs, nor any other signs of pursuit.

After another ten minutes they saw a river up ahead, a sinuous strip of muddy water with wooded banks on both sides. It was the Chattahoochie River, the western boundary of Fort Benning. A two-lane bridge spanned the water and on the near side was a security gate. The barrier was down and several cars were backed up behind it, waiting to leave the base. The drivers were pounding on their horns but the two MPs at the gate stood there like statues. Shit, David thought, they've locked the place down. He considered doing an about-face, but the MPs had probably spotted them already. Their only hope was to bullshit their way through.

They strolled up to the gate like an eccentric family on a hike. David waved to the MPs. "Hey, soldiers!" he called. "Is this the way to the campground?"

"You mean the Uchee Creek Campground, sir?" one of them replied.

"Yeah, yeah, that's the one."

"You cross the bridge and go two miles south. But you can't cross now, sir."

"Why not?"

"Security alert. We're awaiting further orders."

"Well, I'm sure the alert is only for cars. Pedestrians can go through, right?"

The MP thought about it for a moment, then shook his head. "Just wait here, sir. Hopefully it won't take too long."

While David and Monique exchanged nervous looks, a Humvee sped up to the gate. The driver jumped out of the vehicle and ran to the MPs. He held a couple of flyers in his hand; David couldn't see what was printed on them, but he was willing to bet that his own photograph was somewhere on the page. The MPs had turned their backs to them, so David quietly led Michael, Monique, and Elizabeth around the barrier. They headed for the bridge, which was about a hundred feet away.

"Halt!" One of the MPs had turned around. "Where the hell do you think you're going?"

David looked over his shoulder but didn't stop. "Sorry, we're in a rush!"

The other MP, who'd already scanned the flyers, pointed his pistol at him. "STOP RIGHT THERE, ASSHOLE!"

Within seconds, all three soldiers had drawn their M-9s. The drivers of the cars behind the barrier had ceased their honking; they were too busy watching the confrontation. But because all eyes were on either the soldiers or the fugitives, no one saw the rattlesnake until it landed at the feet of the MPs. It bounced on the asphalt, a thick, rust-colored serpent writhing in pain, and sank its fangs into the first moving thing it saw, which happened to be the calf of an MP's leg. The soldier screamed, and then a second snake came flying through the air. David looked ahead and saw Graddick crouched behind his station wagon, which was parked by the riverbank, not far from the bridge. With a great heave, Graddick tossed his third rattler at the MPs, who were now running for the woods. Then he waved at David. "Come on, you sinners!" he shouted. "Get in the car!"

KAREN AND JONAH WERE IN Brownsville, one of the poorest neighborhoods in Brooklyn, following Gloria Mitchell across the glass-strewn grounds of a public housing project. Gloria was an indefatigable reporter; she'd spent the entire day gathering details about the double homicide, first talking to the cops at the local precinct station and then interviewing the friends and relatives of the victims. She was still on the job at 9 P.M., trying to track down a witness to the shooting. Under ordinary circumstances Karen would've never dared to venture into Brownsville at night, but oddly enough she had no fear of the place now. The gangs of teenagers on the street corners didn't scare her one bit. What she did fear were the slow-moving SUVs that seemed to trail them wherever they went.

As they hurried through a deserted playground, a tall, thick-necked man stepped out of the shadows. The light was so dim Karen saw only a silhouette. She couldn't make out his face, but she could tell he was wearing a suit, and she noticed a coiled wire snaking behind his left ear.

Karen stopped in her tracks and squeezed Jonah's hand. But Gloria, afraid of nothing, marched right up to the agent. "Hey, buddy, are you lost?" she asked.

"No," he answered.

"The Bureau's office is in Federal Plaza, in case you were wondering. That way." She pointed west, toward Manhattan.

"What makes you think I'm with the Bureau?"

"Your cheap suit, for one thing. And the fact that your pals have been following me all day long."

"I'm not interested in you. Just your friend."

"Well, forget about it. If you arrest her, it's gonna be all over the front page of the *New York Times* tomorrow morning."

The agent reached into his jacket and pulled out a gun. "Fuck the *Times*. I read the *Post*." Then he aimed at Gloria's head and fired.

Karen grabbed Jonah and pressed his face into her belly so he wouldn't see. Her legs trembled as the agent stepped forward and a stray wedge of streetlight illuminated his face. His nose was swollen and bruises mottled his forehead, but she recognized him nonetheless. It was Agent Brock.

Chapter Eleven

SIMON KNOCKED BACK ANOTHER GLASS OF STOLI. HE SAT in the living room of a modest house in Knoxville belonging to Richard Chan and Scott Krinsky, two of Professor Gupta's former students. While Gupta used the telephone in their kitchen, Richard anxiously poured vodka into Simon's glass and Scott offered him a revolting tuna fish sandwich. At first Simon had assumed that the men were lovers, but after his second drink he realized that something more unusual was at work here. Richard and Scott were physicists at Oak Ridge National Laboratory, where they built equipment for generating high-intensity proton beams. They were pale, gangly, boyish, and bespectacled, and they treated Professor Gupta with a reverence bordering on the fanatical. What's more, they weren't at all surprised when Simon and Gupta showed up at their doorstep. The two young physicists were clearly co-conspirators, recruited by Gupta long ago. Although they didn't look very intimidating, Simon saw in them the essential quality of good soldiers: they would do whatever their leader ordered. Their devotion to the cause was as strong as any jihadi's.

As soon as Simon set his empty glass on the coffee table, Richard jumped up from the couch and filled it again. Not bad, Simon thought as he leaned back in his chair. He could get used to this sort of thing. "So you gentlemen work with beam lines, correct? Guiding the protons as they go 'round and 'round in the accelerator?"

Both of them nodded, but neither said a word. They obviously weren't too comfortable chatting with a Russian mercenary. "It must be a complicated job," Simon continued. "Making sure all the particles are targeted properly. Determining the ideal conditions for impact. Some strange things can happen when the protons smash together, eh?"

Richard and Scott stopped nodding and exchanged glances. There was some surprise in their faces, and a bit of confusion, too. They were probably wondering how this hired killer had learned about particle physics. "Yes, very strange," Simon went on. "And maybe very useful. If you had a unified theory that specified exactly how to set up the particle collisions, you could produce some interesting effects, no?"

Their eyes showed alarm now. Richard nearly dropped the bottle of Stolichnaya. "I'm . . . I'm sorry," he stammered. "I don't know what you're talking—"

"Don't worry." Simon chuckled. "Your professor has taken me into his confidence. At the very start of the mission he told me all about the possible applications of the *Einheitliche Feldtheorie*. Otherwise, I wouldn't have known what information I needed to extract from *Herr Doktor*'s colleagues."

This reassurance failed to put the physicists at ease. Richard tightened his grip on the Stoli bottle and Scott rubbed his palms together. Perhaps they didn't want to know too much about the methods used by their esteemed leader.

At that moment Gupta finished his phone call and stepped into the living room. Richard and Scott turned their heads simultaneously, like a pair of loyal Irish setters fixing their eyes on their master. The professor rewarded them with a kindly smile, then pointed at Simon. "Come with me. We have something to discuss."

Simon waited a few moments to make it clear that he was nobody's lapdog. Then he rose from his chair and followed Gupta into the kitchen. It was an ugly, cramped alcove with sagging cabinets. "Was that Brock on the phone?" Simon asked.

The professor nodded. "He's got Swift's wife and son. Now he's driving south as fast as he can. This could prove to be a useful bargaining chip."

"That's assuming Swift has the unified theory. We don't know that for certain."

"Of course he has the theory. Don't be stupid."

Once again Simon felt the urge to decapitate the old man. "Swift did more than simply stop our download. He deleted everything from the server. Maybe that was his intention all along, to erase the theory. Maybe that's what Kleinman told him to do."

Gupta shook his head. "No, impossible. That's the last thing Kleinman would've wanted. I'm sure he instructed Swift to preserve the theory."

"Well, maybe Swift will think twice about following those orders once he sees the equations."

The professor kept shaking his head. He seemed completely unconcerned. "Trust me, he has the theory. And he couldn't delete it even if he wanted to. The next step in humanity's ascent is inevitable. Nothing can stop us from staging our demonstration."

Simon let out a snort. He was growing tired of Gupta's messianic pronouncements. "All right, let's assume Swift has the theory. We still have to find him before the American soldiers do."

Gupta waved his hand in a dismissive way, brushing aside all difficulties. "That's also inevitable. Within a few hours we'll know where Swift and his companions are."

"And how exactly will that happen?"

The old man grinned. "My daughter is with them. She's a methamphetamine addict. And by now I'm sure she's getting a little desperate."

IN A REMOTE CLEARING IN the Cherokee National Forest, Graddick gathered dead leaves and branches for a campfire. This mountain man, as it turned out, was the perfect guide for the fugitives; all those years of smuggling serpents across the Appalachian states had made him an expert in dodging the law. After the escape from Fort Benning, David had wanted to head for Mexico or Canada, but Graddick argued that too many of Satan's minions stood between them and the border. Instead he drove into northern Alabama, steering his station wagon up the sinuous roads of Sand Mountain.

By nightfall they'd crossed into Tennessee and reached the Great Smokies.

Graddick seemed to know every hill and hollow in the area. At a crossroads called Coker Creek he went down a dirt path and parked the station wagon behind a thicket choked with kudzu. Then he started to build the campfire, whistling "Amazing Grace" as he collected the kindling. David couldn't help but marvel at the man's generosity. They'd met him just the night before, and now he was risking his life for them. Although David hadn't told him a word about Einstein or the unified field theory, Graddick clearly understood that something enormous was at stake. He viewed their situation in a religious context: they were engaged in an apocalyptic struggle, a battle against a demonic army that was trying to overthrow the Kingdom of God. And this view, David thought, wasn't too far from the truth.

The crescent moon, a bit thicker now than it was the night before, gave a pale glow to the pleated hills around them. David sat in the clearing with Michael, who'd propped his Game Boy on a tree stump. His mother was asleep in the station wagon; she'd grown increasingly agitated during the long drive into the mountains, cursing and shivering and demanding that they let her out of the car, but eventually she quieted down and dozed off. Monique had spent half her time comforting Elizabeth and the other half studying the laptop she'd purloined from the VCS lab.

The good news was that the flash drive did indeed hold a scientific paper written by Albert Einstein more than fifty years ago. The bad news was that the paper was in German. The title was *"Neue Untersuchung über die Einheitliche Feldtheorie,"* which David could sort of translate—a new understanding of the unified field theory, most likely. But that was as far as he could go. The paper contained dozens of pages of equations, but the symbols and numbers and subscripts were just as bewildering to David as the German words surrounding them. These equations didn't look anything at all like the ones he'd seen in Einstein's other papers. *Herr Doktor* had obviously ventured in an entirely new direction, employing a very different kind of mathematics. It was insanely frustrating: they had the answer in their hands, but they couldn't interpret it.

Monique now sat alone on a grassy patch in the clearing, still staring at the laptop's screen. David had looked over her shoulder for a while, but she complained that he was disturbing her concentration, so he'd retreated to the other side of the clearing. Shit, he thought, if only he knew German! But even if he were a native speaker, he'd still have trouble with the math. No, Monique was the better person for this. She was adept in many branches of mathematics, and she'd already told David that several of the equations looked familiar.

After stuffing a few wads of newspaper into the woodpile, Graddick set it alight with a match. He went to the station wagon and returned with five cans of Dinty Moore beef stew, which he opened and placed near the fire. Then he sat down on the grass next to David and Michael. "We're in luck," he said, pointing at the starry sky. "Ain't gonna rain tonight."

David nodded. Michael kept playing Warfighter. Graddick pointed at the moon, which was just above the eastern horizon. "We're gonna head in that direction tomorrow," he said. "Over to Haw Knob. We'll drive along the Smithfield Road until it ends and then we'll hike up the mountain."

"Why there?" David asked.

"It's a good place to hide. They got limestone caverns up there, and a mountain spring not too far way. And you can see for miles around, which gives you some warning if someone's coming after you."

"But what will we eat? I mean, after we run out of Dinty Moore?"

"Don't worry, I'll keep you supplied. Satan's men ain't looking for me, so I can come and go. You can hole up at Haw Knob till the end of the summer. By then the heathens will give up the hunt and you'll have an easier time getting to Canada or Mexico or wherever you want to go."

David tried to picture it, spending the summer in a limestone cavern with Monique, Michael, and Elizabeth. The plan was worse than impractical—it was hopeless. No matter how long they hid in the mountains, the army and the FBI wouldn't stop looking for them. And even if, by some miracle, they managed to elude their pursuers and make it across the border, they still wouldn't be safe. Sooner or later the Pentagon would track them down, whether they were in Canada or Mexico or the Antarctic Peninsula.

After a few minutes Graddick stood up and went to the fire, which was burning well now. Wrapping his hand in a gray handkerchief, he retrieved the heated Dinty Moore cans and distributed them to David, Michael, and Monique. He also handed out some plastic spoons he'd found in the glove compartment of his car. The stew was barely warm but David started to eat anyway, hoping to forget his troubles for a little while as he shoveled the viscid beef out of the can. Before he could take a second bite, though, he looked up and saw Monique looming over him, not more than three feet away, with the laptop and attached flash drive tucked under her arm. Even in the darkness he could tell she was agitated. Her mouth was open and she was breathing fast.

"I got something," she said. "But you're not going to like it."

David set the can aside and rose to his feet. He led Monique to a withered pine tree at the edge of the clearing, about twenty feet away from Michael and Graddick. He'd assumed he would feel exultant at this moment, but instead he was full of foreboding. The flickering firelight illuminated the left side of Monique's face, but the right side was in shadow. "Is it there?" he asked. "The unified theory?"

"I didn't think so at first. The equations looked like gibberish, to tell you the truth. But then I remembered what we talked about last night. The geon theory."

"You mean there's something to it?"

"It took me a while to see the connection. But the more I looked at the equations, the more they reminded me of the formulas you see in topology. You know, the mathematics of surfaces and shapes and knots. And that made me think of geons, the knots in spacetime. Here, let me show you."

Monique opened the laptop and stood next to David so he could view the screen. Squinting, he saw a page with a dozen equations, each a long string of Greek letters and odd symbols: pitchforks, pound signs, circles with embedded crosses. It certainly did look like gibberish. "What the hell is this?"

She pointed at the top of the page. "This is the unified field equation, expressed in the language of differential topology. It's similar to the classical equations of relativity, but it encompasses particle physics, too. Einstein found that all particles are geons. Each particle is a different kind of twist in spacetime, and the forces are ripples in the fabric!"

Her voice rose and she clutched David's sleeve. She pulled him closer so he could inspect the equations, but he still couldn't make heads or tails of them. "Hold on, hold on. Are you sure this is real?"

"Look, look here!" She moved her finger down to the bottom of the page. "This is one of the solutions to the field equation, describing a fundamental particle with a negative charge. It's a geon, a minuscule wormhole with closed timelike curves. The solution even specifies the mass of the particle. Do you recognize the number?"

Just beneath Monique's fingernail was this:

$$M = 0.511 \, MeV/c^2$$

"Jesus Christ," David whispered. "The mass of an electron." Although the mathematics was way beyond him, he knew that one of the hallmarks of the Theory of Everything was that it would predict the masses of all the fundamental particles.

"And that's just the start. He's got at least twenty more solutions for particles with different charges and spins. Most of these particles weren't discovered until long after Einstein died. He predicted the existence of quarks and the tau lepton. And he's got solutions for particles that haven't even been found yet. But you can bet your life that they exist."

Monique scrolled through the file, revealing page after page of topological equations. As David stared at the laptop's screen a burgeoning joy filled his chest and began to spread throughout his body. The only thing he could compare it with was the elation he'd felt when Jonah was born. It was the ultimate triumph of physics, a classical theory that incorporated quantum mechanics, a single set of equations that could describe everything from the inner workings of a proton to the structure of the galaxy. He turned away from the screen and smiled at Monique. "You know what? This isn't too different from what the string theorists are trying to do. Except the particles are loops of spacetime instead of strings of energy."

"There's another similarity. Take a look at this." She scrolled down a few more pages and tapped her finger on an equation that stood out from the others:

$$S \leq A/4$$

"That's the equation I saw in Warfighter!"

Monique nodded. "It's called the holographic principle. The S stands for the maximum amount of information that can be jammed into a region of space and the A stands for the surface area of that region. Basically, the principle says that all the information in any three-dimensional space—the position of every particle, the strength of every force—can be contained in the two-dimensional surface of the space. So you can think of the whole universe as a hologram, like the ones you see on your credit cards."

"Wait a second, I think I've heard of this."

"String theorists have been talking about the principle for years, because it offers a way to simplify the physics. But it turns out that Einstein came up with the idea half a century ago. His unified theory is built around it. He used the holographic principle to map out the whole damn history of the universe. It's in the second section of the paper, right here."

She pointed at another odd-looking equation. Beside it was a sequence of computer graphics; Dr. Kleinman had apparently reproduced three sketches that Einstein had drawn by hand long ago. The first image showed a pair of flat sheets moving toward each other. In the second image the sheets bent and rippled as they collided, and in the third they pulled away from each other, now pockmarked with newly born galaxies:

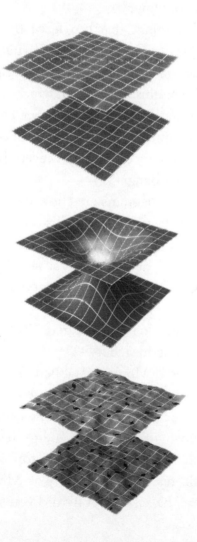

"What are those things?" David asked. "They look like sheets of tinfoil."

"In string theory, they're called branes. They look two-dimensional in the diagrams, but each actually represents a three-dimensional universe. Every galaxy and star and planet in our universe is contained in one of those branes. It's more like flypaper than tinfoil, because nearly all the subatomic particles stick to it. The other brane is a completely separate universe, and they're both moving through a larger space called the bulk, which has ten dimensions in all."

"Why are they colliding?"

"One of the few things that can leave the brane and travel through the bulk is gravity. One brane can gravitationally attract another, and when they collide they get twisted and generate shitloads of energy. I've worked on this idea myself, which is why I recognized the diagrams right away, but nothing I've done comes even close to this. Einstein worked out the exact equations for our brane and how it evolved. His unified theory explains how everything got started."

"You mean the Big Bang?"

"That's what these diagrams are showing. Two empty branes collide and the energy from the crash fills our universe, eventually turning into atoms and stars and galaxies, all of them hurtling outward in a gigantic wave." She grabbed his sleeve again and looked him in the eye. "This is it, David. The answer to the mystery of Creation."

He studied the drawings, bewildered. "But where's the proof? I mean, it's an interesting idea, but—"

"The proof is here!" Monique stabbed at the formulas below the diagrams. "Einstein predicted all the observations that astronomers have made for the past fifty years. The expansion rate of the universe, the breakdown of matter and energy, it's all right here!"

Overwhelmed, David gazed at the topological equations. He wished he could read them as easily as Monique could. "So what's the problem?" he asked. "Why did you say I wasn't going to like it?"

She took a deep breath and scrolled down to yet another page of esoteric symbols. "There's something else that can travel out of the brane and into the extra dimensions of the bulk. You remember what a neutrino is, right?"

"Sure. It's like the electron's kid brother. A particle with no charge and very little mass."

"Well, some physicists have speculated that there may be a particle called a sterile neutrino. They call it sterile because it usually doesn't interact with any other particles in our universe. The sterile neutrinos fly through the extra dimensions and pass right through our brane like water molecules through a sieve."

"Let me guess. The unified theory has the equation for this particle, too."

She nodded. "Yeah, it's in the paper. And the equation predicts that twisting the spacetime of our brane can generate bursts of the particles. If the brane is twisted enough, the sterile neutrinos can shoot out of one part of our universe and travel to another part by taking a shortcut through the bulk. Take a look at this."

She pointed at a reproduction of another diagram drawn by Einstein:

David recognized the picture. "That's a wormhole, right? A bridge that connects distant regions of spacetime?"

"Yeah, but only sterile neutrinos can take this kind of shortcut. And according to the unified theory, the particles can gain energy as they move through the extra dimensions. A hell of a lot of energy if the beam of neutrinos is oriented in the right way."

David shook his head. This was starting to look bad. "What happens when the energized particles come back to our universe? Does the theory say anything about that?"

Monique closed the laptop and turned off its power. She wasn't going to let David see the final equations in the paper. "The returning particles can trigger a violent warping of the local space-time. The amount of energy released depends on how you set up the experiment. Under the right conditions, you could use this process to generate heat or electricity. But you could also use it as a weapon."

A breeze rustled the needles of the pine tree beside them. Though the air was still warm, David felt a chill. "So you can choose the point where the particles reenter our universe? Launch the beam of sterile neutrinos from Washington and ricochet it through the extra dimensions so that it hits a bunker in Tehran?"

She nodded again. "You'd have fine-tune control over the coordinates of the target and the size of the blast. A single burst of sterile particles could take out a nuclear lab in Iran or North Korea, even if it's buried a mile underground."

Now David knew why the FBI had chased them halfway across the country. A weapon like this would be perfect for the war on terror. The Pentagon could eliminate its enemies without deploying commandos or cruise missiles. Because the particle beam would travel through the extra dimensions, it would evade radar, antiaircraft fire, and all other defenses. "How much energy can the beam deliver? What's the upper limit?"

"That's the problem. There's no limit. You could use this technology to blow up an entire continent." She held the laptop at arm's length, as if it might explode at any moment. "But here's the worst part: it's a lot easier to build this kind of weapon than to manufacture a nuke. You don't need to enrich any uranium for a warhead, or launch a ballistic missile to deliver the thing. All you need are the equations and a team of engineers. The Iranians and North Koreans could do it without much trouble. Not to mention Al-Qaeda."

David turned away from her and stared at the campfire. "Shit," he muttered. "No wonder Einstein didn't want to publish it."

"Yeah, it's pretty clear he understood the implications. In the last part of the paper he included the formulas for generating the extra-dimensional beams. You'd have to warp a tiny piece of space-time in a perfectly spherical pattern. You could probably set it up by smashing protons together in a collider."

David's heart started pounding. "You mean someone could build this weapon using a particle accelerator?"

The campfire shifted in the breeze and for a second Monique's face seemed to disappear. "The accelerators at the national laboratories are already designed to maximize the number of particle collisions. You know the Tevatron, the collider at Fermilab? The physicists there can cram trillions of protons into a particle beam that's narrower than a human hair. Of course you'd have to adjust the collider in exactly the right way to warp the spacetime and generate the sterile neutrinos. But Einstein's equations would allow you to calculate the necessary adjustments."

Her last words rang across the dark clearing. David nervously looked over his shoulder and saw Graddick toss an empty Dinty Moore can into the fire. Then the mountain man picked up another can, a full one, and headed for the thicket where he'd parked his station wagon. He was going to wake up Elizabeth to see if she wanted any supper.

David turned back to Monique. "Okay, we have two choices. We can smuggle the flash drive across the border and make contact with the UN or the World Court, some organization that can be trusted to safeguard the theory. Or we can hide the thing ourselves. Maybe we can find a better place than—"

"No, we can't hide it." Monique removed the flash drive from the USB port of the laptop. The small silver cylinder glinted in her palm. "We have to destroy it."

David's muscles tensed. He felt an urge to grab the flash drive out of Monique's hand. "Are you nuts! This is the Theory of Everything!"

She frowned. "I know what it is. I've spent the past twenty years working on this problem."

"Then you know we can't throw it away! We have to save it, not destroy it!"

Monique wrapped her fingers around the cylinder. "It's too risky, David. If Einstein couldn't keep the theory hidden, what makes you think you can?"

He shook his head, bursting with frustration. "Dr. Kleinman told me to keep it safe! Those were his last words, 'Keep it safe.'"

"Believe me, I don't want to do this. But we have to think of everyone's safety. The terrorists want this theory just as much as the government does, and they've already come close to getting it. Remember the soldier in the Warfighter program, the one with the number 3 on his helmet?"

She tightened her grip on the flash drive. As David watched her, a visual memory of Einstein's equations flashed through his mind. It was still gibberish to him, but he remembered several of the formulas. "It's too late," he said. "We've seen the theory. It's in our heads now."

"I didn't show you all the equations. And my memory isn't as good as yours. After we destroy the flash drive, we should turn ourselves in to the FBI. They'll interrogate us, but they can't force us to say anything. I'd rather deal with them than the terrorists."

David grimaced, recalling his interrogation in the FBI's complex on Liberty Street. "It won't be so easy. Look, why don't we—"

A distant shout interrupted him. It was Graddick's voice. He came running back to the clearing, sweaty and wild-eyed. "She's not in the car!" he yelled. "Elizabeth's gone!"

JESUS FUCKING CHRIST, BETH THOUGHT, there's nothing but trees here! Barefoot, she stumbled down the dirt road, trying to find a way back to the state highway. The woods were so thick she couldn't see a damn thing, and she kept stubbing her toes on the roots and rocks. She'd left her pumps behind in the fat fucker's station wagon and now the soles of her feet were cut all to hell, but she didn't care. What she needed right now was a long hit of meth, and even though she had $300 stashed in her pants, she sure as fuck wasn't going to find any dealers in the goddamn forest.

She finally saw a light up ahead, blinking through the leaves. She sprinted toward it and came to Route 68, a one-lane road glowing faintly in the moonlight. All right, she thought, we're back in business. Sooner or later, some horny good ol' boy would drive by. She slapped the dirt off her feet and brushed the hair out of her eyes and tucked her T-shirt into her pants to make her tits stand out. But the highway was empty. Not a single fucking car. After ten minutes she began walking down the road, hoping to find a gas station. It wasn't very cold but her teeth started chattering. "Shit!" she screamed at the trees. "I need a fucking hit!" But all she heard in reply was the crazed whine of the cicadas.

Beth was just about to collapse when she rounded a bend and saw a long, low building. It was a small strip of stores—a gift shop, a post office, a propane supplier. Hallelujah, she thought, civilization at last! Now all she needed was a truck driver who could give her a lift to the nearest city. But as she ran toward the building she noticed to her dismay that all the stores were closed and the parking lot was empty. She clutched her stomach, suddenly nauseous. And then she saw it, in front of the post office: a BellSouth pay phone.

At first she just stood there, paralyzed. She knew a number she could call, but she didn't make a move. Of all the people in the world, this was the last bastard she wanted to speak to. But he'd told her long ago that she could always call him in an emergency, and she'd memorized his cell-phone number just in case.

Beth went to the phone. With trembling fingers she dialed the operator and placed a collect call. After a brief wait, the bastard came on the line.

"Hello, Elizabeth dear. What a pleasant surprise."

＊ ＊ ＊

JONAH, THANK GOD, HAD FINALLY fallen asleep. For the past three hours Karen had watched him struggle against the cords binding his ankles and wrists. That monster Brock had also tied a gag over Jonah's mouth to muffle the boy's screams, and of course this only made him more terrified. Karen was bound and gagged, too, but she could feel her son shivering as he lay next to her on the floor of Brock's van. Her worst agony was that she couldn't comfort him—couldn't put her arms around him, couldn't whisper, "It's all right, everything's going to be all right." All she could do was touch her forehead to his and try to make a soothing noise through the damp rag over her mouth.

Sometime around midnight, after they'd traveled at least two hundred miles, Jonah stopped screaming. His exhaustion overcame his terror and he drifted off with his wet face pressed into his mother's neck. Once he was asleep, Karen squirmed onto her side so she could get a glimpse through the van's windshield. She spotted a sign: EXIT 315, WINCHESTER. They were in Virginia already, heading south on I-81. She had no idea where the hell they were going, but she was willing to bet a lot of money that it wasn't the FBI headquarters.

Brock was in the driver's seat, eating potato chips from a family-size bag and listening to a rebroadcast of the *Rush Limbaugh Show*. Even the back of his head was ugly, with pink splotches below his hairline and behind his ears. She closed her eyes for a moment, remembering the cold smile on the agent's face after he shot Gloria Mitchell and pointed his gun at Jonah and Karen. Then she opened her eyes and squinted hard, aiming all her silent fury at the ugly son of a bitch. You're dead, she whispered into her gag. Before this is over, I'm going to kill you.

IN DISGUST LUCILLE SLAMMED HER fist on one of the huge transparent spheres in the Virtual Combat Simulation lab. After spending sixteen hours dissecting the lab's servers and terminals, a team of Defense Department computer experts had just concluded that the data stored in the war-gaming software had been irretrievably lost. Now it was eight o'clock in the morning and Lucille was madder than a boar in a peach orchard. The army had thoroughly botched the search for the suspects; after letting them slip off the base, the post commander had waited two hours before alerting the state police in Georgia and Alabama. The Delta Force had set up checkpoints on some of the major highways leading out of Columbus, but at least half the roads in the area were left unguarded. The plain truth was that they didn't have enough troops. The army had sent so many soldiers to Iraq that they couldn't even defend their own backyard.

Lucille turned away from the spheres and slumped into a chair. While the Pentagon's computer geeks packed up their equipment, she dug into her pants pocket and found a pack of Marlboros. Luckily, there were two cigarettes left. She removed one of them and began searching for her Zippo, but she couldn't find it in either her pants or her jacket. Jesus, she thought, what the hell happened to that thing? It was her favorite lighter, the one with the Lone Star on it. "Goddamn it!" she shouted, startling the computer geeks.

She was just about to apologize when Agent Crawford came into the lab, looking as cocky as ever. He marched up to her chair and leaned over so he could whisper in her ear. "I'm sorry to interrupt, ma'am, but I have something from Washington."

Lucille frowned. "What now? Does the SecDef want to reassign the case to the Marine Corps?"

Crawford held up a palm-size digital recorder. "Someone left a message on your voice-mail at headquarters. One of the administrative assistants forwarded it to me."

She sat up straight. "Is it another sighting? Did someone recognize one of the suspects?"

"No, it's better than that." Grinning, he pointed at a private office adjoining the lab. "Let's go in that room so I can play it for you."

Lucille jumped out of her chair and followed Crawford into

the office. A burst of new energy filled her tired limbs, as it always did when she got a lucky break. Crawford closed the office door.

"I think you'll recognize the voice," he said. He pressed a button on the digital recorder and after a few seconds it began to play:

> Hello, Lucy. This is David Swift. I see from the newspapers that you're looking for me. I suppose you want to continue the conversation we started back in New York. I've been a little busy the past couple of days, but I think I can make some time for you this morning. I've turned on my cell phone so you can find me. I have just one request: Don't bring any soldiers with you. If I see even one helicopter or Humvee, I'm gonna pulverize the package I picked up at Fort Benning. I'm willing to cooperate, but I don't want any trigger-happy commandos pointing their guns at me. Are we clear?

THEY CALLED THIS MOUNTAIN RANGE the Great Smokies because of all the water vapor rising from its tree-covered slopes. Mixing with the hydrocarbons exuded by the pine forest, the vapor usually thickens into a smoky blue haze that shrouds the rugged landscape. But this morning a stiff breeze had dispelled the mist and David could see mile after mile of sunlit hills and valleys, stretching to the horizon like a great, rumpled blanket.

He stood at the top of Haw Knob, looking down at a one-lane highway that twisted along the steep eastern slope, some six hundred feet below. No black SUVs had come down the road yet, but it was still early. The FBI needed some time to retrieve his cell phone's GPS coordinates, which had been transmitted to the nearest tower when he'd turned the thing on. And then of course the agents had to formulate their assault plan and assemble their strike teams. From the summit David had an excellent view of the trail that the agents were most likely to use, a path that started at the highway about half a mile to the south. He would see the men coming long before they arrived.

Graddick had left his station wagon on a dirt road a few miles to the west. He'd led them to Haw Knob and planned to retreat to his car before the agents pounced, but now that the time was near he seemed reluctant to leave. He stood in front of Michael with his big hands covering the boy's head and murmured some unintelligible words, a blessing probably. The batteries in Michael's Game Boy had finally died a few hours before, but the teenager had accepted this event with equanimity and now seemed the better for it: he appeared more alert than usual, turning this way and that, completely unbothered by the fact that his mother was no longer with them. Meanwhile, Monique glanced anxiously at David, waiting for him to give the word. Although they'd already discarded the laptop, throwing its shattered remains into the Tellico River, she still held the flash drive in her fist.

David had agonized over the choice for much of the previous night. The *Einheitliche Feldtheorie* was one of science's greatest achievements, and erasing its equations seemed like a wanton act, a crime against humanity. But Elizabeth's disappearance had made it clear that they couldn't hide forever. Sooner or later something else would go wrong and the soldiers would find them. Then the Pentagon would have the unified theory and nothing in the world would stop them from using it. Within a few years the army would build devices that could launch sterile particles into the extra dimensions and destroy every terrorist hideout in the Middle East. The generals might be able to keep the theory to themselves for a while, their new secret weapon in the war on terror. But no weapon can remain secret for long. Eventually the knowledge would spread to Beijing and Moscow and Islamabad, and the seeds of the world's annihilation would be planted. No, David couldn't let that happen. He had to break his promise to Dr. Kleinman and eliminate the last traces of the theory. Until now he'd resisted that irrevocable step, but he couldn't put it off any longer.

He stepped toward a jagged, gray, semicircular outcrop that jutted from the summit like a giant tiara. Reaching across the rock shelf, he picked up a loose chunk of quartzite with a tapering edge that would fit in his hand. A stone tool, he thought, like something a prehistoric caveman might've used. He turned to Monique. "All right, I'm ready."

She came to his side and without saying a word placed the flash drive on the shelf, which was nearly flat. Her face was tense, almost rigid. She pressed her lips so firmly together that David imagined she was trying not to scream. It must've been excruciating, to sacrifice the very thing she'd spent her whole life searching for. And yet that was her decision. If Einstein himself could've looked fifty years ahead and seen the awful start of the twenty-first century, he would've done exactly the same.

David raised the heavy rock. As he held it above the flash drive, he gazed again at the dazzling green mountains all around them, folded and bent in myriad shapes like the wrinkles of spacetime. Then he swung his arm down and smashed the rock as hard as he could against the silver cylinder.

The plastic case shattered and the circuit board inside cracked into a dozen pieces. David aimed his second blow directly at the memory chip and the silicon disintegrated into hundreds of black shards, each as small as a pencil point. He kept pounding the thing until the chip was reduced to dust and the surrounding pins, circuits, and switches were a hash of metallic flecks. Then he scooped the debris into his palm and threw it over the lip of Haw Knob's eastern slope. The strong wind caught the dust and scattered it across the pine forest.

Monique forced a smile. "Well, that's that. Back to the drawing board."

David hurled the rock down the slope, then grasped her hand. All at once he was overcome with a strange mix of emotions, a blend of sadness and sympathy and gratitude and relief. He wanted to thank Monique for everything she'd done, for journeying more than a thousand miles by his side, for saving his ass a hundred times over. But instead of saying the words out loud, he impulsively raised her hand to his lips and kissed the brown skin between her knuckles. She gave him a curious look, surprised but not displeased. Then she spotted something over David's shoulder and her face tensed again. He turned around and saw a convoy of black SUVs snaking down the highway from the southeast.

He stepped back from the cliff and pulled Monique behind the outcrop. "Get over here!" he yelled at Graddick, who immediately dragged Michael into the shadow of the rock shelf. Kneeling in the dirt, Graddick peered over the shelf and scowled. "The scarlet beast!" he hissed. "Full of abominations!"

The cars slowed as they approached the trailhead. The agents had obviously studied the topographic maps and figured out the fastest way to the top of the mountain. David's plan was to stay hidden as the assault team climbed the trail so the FBI men wouldn't be tempted to take any potshots at them; once the agents came within earshot, he would give a yell to reveal where they were hiding. Then, presumably, the leader of the team would order them to come out slowly, with their hands up. It seemed the safest way to surrender. Of course the agents wouldn't be too happy once they discovered the fate of the unified theory. But that couldn't be helped.

As the SUVs parked on the shoulder of the road, David turned to Graddick. He belatedly realized that he'd never learned the man's first name. "Uh, brother? It's time for you to go."

With his fists clenched, Graddick stared at the SUVs. One by one the car doors opened and the men in gray suits came pouring out. "Yea, they are as numerous as the sand of the sea," he recited. "But the fire shall come down from heaven and devour them!"

David grew worried. There was no good reason for Graddick to stick around. The FBI didn't know his name. If he left now, he could get away scot-free. "Listen, brother. We must render unto Caesar what is Caesar's. But your place is in the wilderness, understand? You have to go."

The man grimaced. He probably wished he had a few more

rattlesnakes to throw at the agents. But after a moment he clapped his hand on David's shoulder. "I'll go, but not far. If there's any trouble, I'll come back."

Before leaving, he raised his hand to David's forehead and offered another unintelligible blessing. Then he spun around and scuttled down Haw Knob's western slope, disappearing into the dense shadows under the pine boughs.

The federal agents were now marching single file up the trail. The path was steep and rocky, forcing some of the men to scramble on all fours. David guessed they were about ten minutes away. He ducked behind the outcrop and checked on Michael, who was calmly studying the parallel fractures in the rock shelf, oblivious to the approaching danger. To be honest, though, David was more concerned about Monique. Because she was the expert on theoretical physics, the agents would interrogate her the hardest. He took her hand again and squeezed it. "They're going to split us up for the interrogations. I may not see you for a while."

She smiled, giving him a sly look. "Oh, I don't know about that. Maybe we'll run into each other at Guantánamo. I hear the beaches down there are nice."

"Don't be afraid of them, Monique. They're just following orders. They don't—"

She leaned against him and pressed her index finger to his lips. "Shhh, stop worrying, all right? They can't hurt me, because I have nothing to say. I've already forgotten the equations."

He didn't believe it. "Come on."

"It's the truth. I've always been good at forgetting things." Her face turned serious. "I grew up in one of the shittiest places in America, a place that usually scars you for life. But I forgot all that and now I'm a professor at Princeton. Forgetting can be a very useful skill."

"But last night you—"

"I don't even remember the title of the paper. Untersoochick-something? I remember it was German but that's it."

Michael stopped examining the rock shelf and turned to Monique. "'*Neue Untersuchung über die Einheitliche Feldtheorie,*'" he said in flawless German.

David stared at the boy. How did he know the title of Einstein's paper? "What did you say?"

"'*Neue Untersuchung über die Einheitliche Feldtheorie,*'" he repeated. Then he turned back to the rock shelf and resumed his inspection of the fracture patterns.

Monique raised her hand to her mouth and looked at David. They were both thinking the same thing. Michael hadn't looked at the laptop the night before, so he must've seen the title somewhere else.

David grasped the boy's shoulders. He tried to be gentle but his hands were shaking. "Michael, where did you see those words?"

The boy heard the fear in David's voice. His eyes strained to the left, avoiding contact. David recalled the teenager's mental feats, how he'd committed entire telephone directories to memory. Jesus, he thought, how much did the kid know? "Please, Michael, this is important. Did you read the file while you were playing Warfighter?"

Michael's cheeks turned pink but he didn't answer. David tightened his grip on the boy's shoulders. "Listen to me! Did you ever download the file from the server? Maybe a long time ago, when you still lived with your mother?"

He shook his head in quick jerks, as if he were shivering. "It was a safe place! Hans told me it was a safe place!"

"How much of it did you read? How much, Michael?"

"I didn't read it!" he screamed. "I wrote it! I wrote it all down and put it on the server! Hans told me it was a safe place!"

"What? I thought Kleinman put the theory there."

"No, he made me memorize it! Now let go of me!"

The boy tried to wriggle out of his grasp, but David held on tight. "What do you mean? You memorized the whole theory?"

"Leave me alone! I don't have to tell you anything unless you have the key!" Then, with a terrific wrench, he freed his arm from David's grasp and punched him in the stomach.

It was a good, solid punch, strong enough to knock the wind

out of him. David lost his balance and landed on his back. The broad blue sky seemed to spin around him. And as he lay there in the dirt, struggling for breath, a string of numbers slowly passed before his eyes. They were the sixteen digits Dr. Kleinman had whispered on his deathbed, the sequence he'd called "the key." The first twelve were the coordinates of the Robotics Institute at Carnegie Mellon; the last four were the phone extension of Professor Gupta's office. But David recalled now that the extension wasn't Gupta's direct phone line—it was the number for the reception area, the desk where Michael had sat. The truth hit David at the same moment that the air rushed back into his lungs.

Kleinman's sequence didn't point to Amil Gupta.

It pointed to Michael.

David lay there motionless for several seconds. Monique bent over him and shook his arm. "Hey? Are you all right?"

He nodded. Fighting off dizziness, he crawled back to the rock shelf and peeked over the top. The agents were only a few hundred yards away, charging up the final stretch of the trail. They'd probably heard Michael's scream and were now rushing to investigate.

The teenager was hunched against the outcrop, staring at the ground. David didn't touch him. Instead, he employed the same technique Elizabeth had used to retrieve phone numbers from the boy: he snapped his fingers under Michael's nose. Then David recited the numbers Dr. Kleinman had given him: "Four, zero . . . two, six . . . three, six . . . seven, nine . . . five, six . . . four, four . . . seven, eight, zero, zero."

Michael looked up. His cheeks were still pink but his eyes were calm. "*Neue Untersuchung über die Einheitliche Feldtheorie,*'" he started. *"Die allgemeine Relativitätstheorie war bisher in erster Linie eine rationelle Theorie der Gravitation und der metrischen Eigenschaften des Raumes . . ."*

It was the text of Einstein's paper, spoken with a German accent that was exactly like Dr. Kleinman's. The old physicist had found a marvelously clever hiding place. Michael could easily memorize the entire theory, but unlike a scientist, he'd never be tempted to work on the formulas or share them with his colleagues, because he didn't understand a single word or symbol. And under normal circumstances, no one would dream of looking for the equations inside the mind of an autistic teenager. But the circumstances now were anything but normal.

David grabbed Monique's arm. "Do you hear this? He knows the whole fucking theory! If the FBI gets us, they're gonna interrogate the kid, and sure as fuck they're gonna find out he's hiding something!"

While Michael continued to reel off the theory, David heard a familiar noise. He peeked over the rock shelf again and saw a pair of Blackhawk helicopters hovering over the highway. Panicking, he removed his cell phone from his pocket and tossed it to the ground. Then he pulled Monique and Michael to their feet.

"Come on!" he shouted. "Let's get the hell out of here!"

GOD DAMN THAT COLONEL TARKINGTON, Lucille thought as she raced up the trail. The Delta Force commander had promised to keep his soldiers in reserve, but now two of his helicopters had popped over the horizon, in plain sight of anyone within a five-mile radius, and her team had to dash to the summit of Haw Knob before the suspects got spooked. The last stretch of the trail was a steep, slippery chute, but Lucille bounded up the path without breaking her ankles and came to a big, gray outcrop standing in the middle of a grassy clearing. A dozen of her agents fanned out to the left and right, pointing their Glocks in all directions. Holding her own semiautomatic with both hands, Lucille sidled to the edge of the rock shelf. No one was hiding behind it. Then she scanned the western slope of the mountain and caught a glimpse of three figures running under the pine trees.

"Stop right there!" she bellowed, but of course they didn't stop. She turned to her agents and pointed toward the woods. "Go, go, go! They're straight ahead!"

The young men hurtled down the slope, moving twice as fast

as Lucille could. She felt a sense of impending relief: one way or another, this assignment would soon be over. But as the assault team reached the edge of the forest, Agent Jaworsky suddenly let out a cry and tumbled to the ground. The other men stopped in their tracks, bewildered. A moment later, Lucille saw a fist-size rock fly out of the branches and strike Agent Keller in the forehead.

"Look out!" she yelled. "Someone's in the trees!"

The agents crouched in the grass and started firing wildly. There was no order, no targeting. The gunshots echoed against the mountainside and clusters of pine needles fell from the boughs, but Lucille saw nothing else moving in the woods. Shit, she thought, this is ridiculous! The whole team was pinned down because someone had thrown a couple of rocks! She yelled, "Hold your fire!" but nobody could hear her over the din, so she ran across the clearing. Before she could reach her men, though, the Delta Force's helicopters came over the hill.

The Blackhawks flew low, only twenty feet over the clearing. Both choppers moved into position above the crouching agents and turned parallel to the line of trees. Then the door gunners opened up with their M-240 machine guns.

The barrage went on for almost a minute, slicing branches from the pines and chipping bark off their trunks. The agents in the clearing threw themselves on their stomachs and covered their ears. Lucille groped for her radio but she knew it was hopeless: the dumb beasts couldn't be stopped. Finally she saw a large object fall from one of the trees. It bounced against a lower limb and landed with a thud on the forest floor. The machine guns fell silent and the agents rushed toward a heavy, bearded man whose chest had been ripped apart by the eight-millimeter rounds.

Lucille shook her head. She had no idea who the dead man was.

MONIQUE LOST SIGHT OF DAVID and Michael soon after the gunfire started. As the Glocks boomed behind her and the bullets whizzed overhead, she ran blindly down the tree-covered slope, leaping over roots and rock piles and hummocks, forgetting everything except the need to put as much distance as possible between herself and the squadron of FBI agents. She ducked under the pine branches and skidded through heaps of dead needles. When she came to a shallow stream at the bottom of the slope she splashed right across and charged up the opposite bank. She kept on running as long as she could hear the guns, propelled by an instinct she thought she'd forgotten, a lesson her mother had taught her when she was a girl in Anacostia: If you hear shots, honey, you better haul ass.

After what seemed like an eternity the gunfire stopped. That was when Monique noticed she was alone. The forest was empty on all sides. She jogged up the next ridge, moving in the direction where she thought she'd find David and Michael, but when she finally reached the crest all she saw was a dirt road up ahead and the two helicopters hovering over the woods behind her. They were almost a mile away but the rapid beat of their rotor blades was still quite loud. She quickly headed for thicker cover, and as she stumbled downhill again she heard another noise off to her right, a distant but familiar shrieking. It was Michael.

Monique sprinted toward his echoing screams, hoping to hell that he wasn't hurt. It was impossible to tell how far away he was, but given the amount of time that had passed, she calculated that it had to be less than half a mile. She jumped over another streambed and tore through a thicket shrouded with kudzu.

Then, without any warning, she felt a sharp blow to the back of her head. Her vision blurred and she dropped to the ground.

Just before she blacked out she saw two men looming over her. One was a big bald man wearing camouflage pants and carrying an Uzi.

The other was Professor Gupta.

SIMON HAD ALWAYS BELIEVED IN making his own luck. When Gupta had gotten the phone call from his daughter the night before, Simon and the professor immediately drove to the Great Smokies

and picked up Elizabeth. In return for a small vial of methamphetamine, she showed them where Swift and Reynolds had stopped
for the night. Unfortunately, the fugitives had already abandoned
their camp, correctly anticipating that Elizabeth would sell them
out. But Simon suspected they were still nearby. In the morning
he rendezvoused with Agent Brock and ordered him to monitor
the emergency frequency on his FBI radio. When they heard the
transmissions about the planned assault on Haw Knob, they headed
straight for the mountain. They parked their vehicles on a dirt road
and were racing toward the summit when Gupta heard his grandson screaming. The professor declared that fate was on their side,
but Simon knew better. He'd made his own luck every step of the
way, and his reward was coming.

After he knocked out Reynolds, he dragged her inert body
toward the dirt road. Gupta limped alongside, still blathering about
fate. Brock was several hundred yards to the north, pursuing Swift
and the shrieking teenager. When Simon got to the pickup truck
he swiftly bound Reynolds's wrists and ankles with electrical cord.
Elizabeth already lay on the backseat, bound and gagged and stu-
porous. She started to struggle when Simon dumped Reynolds beside her, and her thrashing woke up the dazed physicist. Reynolds
opened her eyes and then she began thrashing, too.

"Fuck!" she yelled. "Get me out of here!"

Simon frowned. There was no time to tie a gag on her; he had
to drive north as quickly as possible so he could help Brock intercept the others. He climbed into the driver's seat and put the keys
in the ignition.

Gupta was in the passenger seat. As Simon started the engine,
the professor looked over his shoulder at the two squirming women.
"I'm sorry about the cramped quarters, Dr. Reynolds, but until we
can transfer you to the van, you'll have to share the backseat with
my daughter."

Reynolds stopped struggling and gaped at him. "Jesus, what
are you doing here? I thought the agents got you!"

"No, they were too slow. My associate reached me first." He pointed at Simon.

"But he's one of the terrorists! He's the bald motherfucker who drove the yellow Ferrari!"

Gupta shook his head. "That was a misunderstanding. Simon isn't a terrorist, he's my employee. He's assigned to do the same thing you were doing, Dr. Reynolds—helping me find the *Einheitliche Feldtheorie*."

Reynolds didn't respond at first. The truck was silent as Simon drove down the dirt road, which was so twisting and rutted he could barely go ten miles an hour. When she spoke again her voice quavered. "Why are you doing this, Professor? Do you know what can happen if—"

"Yes, yes, I've known for years. What I didn't know were the exact terms of the equations, which are crucial to the process. But now that we have the theory, we can take the next step. We can finally unwrap *Herr Doktor*'s gift and let it transform the world."

"But we don't have the theory anymore! We destroyed the flash drive and that was the only copy."

"No, we have it. We've had it all along, but I was too foolish to see. Michael memorized the equations, didn't he?"

Reynolds kept her mouth shut but her face gave her away. Gupta smiled. "Several years ago I asked Hans what he would do with the theory when he died. He didn't want to tell me, of course, but after I badgered him a bit, he said, 'Don't worry, Amil, it'll stay in the family.' I assumed at the time that he meant the family of physicists, the scientific community. I didn't realize the truth until yesterday, when I saw that a copy of the theory was in War-fighter." He leaned back in his seat and propped his injured leg on the dashboard. "I knew Hans couldn't have put it there. He was a pacifist. Putting *Herr Doktor*'s theory in a war game would've been anathema to him. But Michael loves Warfighter, and he loves to make copies of everything he memorizes. That's why he transcribed all those telephone directories on the computer, remember? And what's more, he's a member of the family. Both my family and *Herr Doktor's*."

Reynolds said nothing. Too lost in despair, most likely. But Simon turned away from the treacherous road for a moment and stared at the professor. "What are you saying? Was the old Jew your father?"

Gupta chuckled again. "Please, don't be ridiculous. Do I look like *Herr Doktor*? No, the relation was on my wife's side."

Simon had no time to inquire further. In the next instant he rounded a bend in the road and saw Brock's vehicle up ahead, the old Dodge van that had formerly belonged to Dr. Milo Jenkins. Simon pulled up alongside and saw that the driver's seat was empty; Brock had obviously gotten out of the van here to pursue Swift and the teenager on foot. When Simon rolled down his window he could hear the teenager's shrieks quite clearly, coming from a ravine just east of the road.

DAVID COULDN'T STOP MICHAEL FROM SCREAMING. He'd started when the FBI agents had opened fire, and he'd continued wailing in long, agonized gusts as he and David ran through the forest. The boy took a frantic gulp of air after every shriek and tore through the undergrowth in a path as straight as a bullet's. David struggled to catch up, his lungs burning. After a few minutes the sound of gunfire ceased and Michael slackened his pace, but the screams kept erupting from the teenager's throat, each just as long and powerful as the last.

Judging from the position of the sun, David guessed they were moving northwest. He'd lost sight of Monique but he couldn't stop to look for her. He was worried that Michael's screams would make it easy for the FBI to find them; although the agents had evidently halted at the edge of the woods, sooner or later they were sure to advance. In a desperate burst of speed, David caught up to the boy and grasped his elbow.

"Michael," he panted. "You have to . . . stop screaming. Everyone . . . can hear you."

The teenager shook his arm free and let out another shriek. David clapped his hand over Michael's mouth, but the boy pushed him away and dashed over a ridge. He descended into a narrow ravine with rocky cliffs on both sides and a clear brook trickling down the middle. The cliffs echoed Michael's screams, making them even louder. Although David was at the limits of his endurance, he flung himself down the slope and grabbed Michael from behind. He covered the boy's mouth, trying to muzzle him, but the kid jammed an elbow into his ribs. David stumbled backward, landing in the mud at the edge of the brook. Christ, he thought, what the hell am I going to do? And as he shook his head in exasperation he looked downstream and saw a man in a gray suit.

David's skin went cold. This wasn't one of the agents from the assault team. Although the man stood a hundred yards to the south, David recognized him right away because his face was still mottled with big purple bruises. It was the renegade agent, the man who'd tried to abduct them two days ago in West Virginia. Except now he carried an Uzi instead of a Glock.

David snatched Michael's hand and began running in the opposite direction. At first Michael resisted, but when they heard a burst from the Uzi the teenager sprinted ahead. They charged through a thicket that gave them some cover, but after a while David realized he'd made a mistake. As they moved north the cliffs on either side grew higher, and after a few hundred yards the ravine dead-ended. They were in a hollow, a box canyon, closed on three sides; ahead of them was another fractured cliff, too steep to climb.

In a frenzy David scanned the wall of rock. Just above the base he saw a horizontal crevice that looked like a giant mouth. The opening was about the size of car's windshield, but the fissure was dark and seemed to go deep into the cliff. A limestone cavern, he thought. Graddick had said there were plenty in the area. David clambered to the crevice as fast as he could, then pulled Michael up. While the boy scurried back to the deepest part of the fissure, David lay on his stomach and looked out the opening. He reached into the back of his pants and removed his pistol, the one he'd taken from the agent who was hunting them now.

Michael was still screaming, and although the cavern muffled the noise, some of it leaked outside. After a minute or so David saw the agent approach the cliff, trying to figure out where the screams were coming from. He was about twenty feet below, so he couldn't see into the fissure yet, but he was getting closer. David steadied the Glock on the lip of the crevice, aiming at the ground in front of the agent. Then he fired.

The man whirled around and ran back to the thicket. In a few seconds he started firing his Uzi at the cliff, but the bullets whanged harmlessly against the rock. David was inside a natural bunker, an ideal defensive position. He could hold off this bastard for hours. The real FBI agents would eventually flood the area, along with several regiments of soldiers; when they came near, David would fire again to get their attention. Then he and Michael would surrender to the government men. It was a grim prospect, but a hundred times better than surrendering to the terrorists.

After a while Michael's screams began to ebb. David peered over the lip of the crevice and saw the agent still crouching in the thicket. And then he spotted another man, a bald man, standing by the brook in the middle of the ravine. He wore camouflage pants and a black T-shirt. With his right hand he wielded a Bowie knife and with his left he clutched a squirming boy by the scruff of his neck. The tableau was so strange that it took David several seconds to recognize the youngster. When he did, the pain in his chest was so sharp he dropped his pistol and clawed at his heart.

"Dr. Swift?" the bald man shouted. "Your son wants to see you."

Chapter Twelve

THE ODDEST THING ABOUT THE VICE PRESIDENT, LUCILLE thought, was that he looked like a goddamn Communist. He had the barrel chest and balding pate and ill-fitting blue suit of a Soviet commissar. She'd never noticed this similarity when she'd seen the man on television, but it was hard to miss now that she sat in his office in the West Wing. His mouth was set in an asymmetrical sneer as he surveyed the papers on his desk. "So, Agent Parker," he started, "I heard you had a little trouble this morning."

Lucille nodded. By this point she was past caring. She'd already written her letter of resignation. "I take full responsibility, sir. In the rush to apprehend the suspects, we failed to properly coordinate with the Defense Department."

"What went wrong, exactly? How did they get away?"

"They probably escaped on one of the dirt roads heading west. The army was supposed to secure the perimeter but they didn't deploy fast enough."

"And where does this leave us?"

"Back at square one, unfortunately. We need more resources, sir, more boots on the ground. We have to catch these sons of bitches before they share their information with anyone else."

The vice president frowned, pulling back his bloodless lips. "The Delta Force will take care of it. The defense secretary and I have decided that the mission no longer requires the FBI's assistance. The operation will be strictly military from now on."

Although she fully expected it, the dismissal still hurt. "And is that why I'm here? So you could kick me off the case?"

He tried to smile but it didn't quite work. His grin went askew, sliding to the right side of his face. "No, not at all. I have a new assignment for you." He picked up a copy of the *New York Times* and pointed to a headline on the front page: REPORTER SHOT TO DEATH IN BROOKLYN. "We have a containment problem. The *Times* is accusing the FBI of killing one of their reporters, the one who was sheltering Swift's wife. Apparently they found some witnesses who said the shooter looked like an agent. It's an absurd claim but it's getting some attention."

"I'm afraid there might be some truth to it. One of our agents is missing, and there's evidence that he's working for the other side. He may have shot the reporter to get to Swift's wife."

Lucille had assumed the vice president would have a fit when he heard this news, but he brushed it aside. "That's irrelevant. I've already scheduled a press conference. I want you to deny this story in the strongest terms. Stick with the drug angle. Say that your team is investigating the possibility that Swift's partners in the drug business kidnapped his wife and killed the reporter."

Lucille shook her head. She was sick to death of this bullshit. "I'm sorry, sir, but I can't do that."

The veep leaned across his desk. His face had reverted to its characteristic sneer. "This is just as important as finding the suspects, Parker. We need tools to fight the terrorists. And Congress is already trying to take those tools away. The last thing we need is a disclosure of this magnitude."

She sighed and got to her feet. It was time to head back to Texas. "I better get going. I gotta clean out my desk."

The vice president stood up, too. "Well, I have to admit, this is a disappointment. The director of the Bureau assured me that you were a woman with balls."

Lucille glared at him. "Believe me, the disappointment is mutual."

THE VAN CAME TO A STOP. Because Karen's hands were tied behind her back, she couldn't look at her watch, but she guessed that it had been about six hours since they'd left the pine forest. Shivering, she squirmed closer to Jonah. Jesus, please Jesus, she whispered, don't let the bastards take him away again. The last time they took her son, Karen had nearly gone out of her mind, and although Brock had brought Jonah back to the van only twenty minutes later, the boy cried for hours afterward.

Brock stepped out of the driver's seat and walked around the van. When he opened the rear doors Karen got a whiff of dank air and saw a large dark garage with broken windows and crumbling walls. They were in some kind of decrepit warehouse, some old building that had been abandoned years ago. Three white delivery trucks were parked nearby and a dozen young men stood next to the vehicles. They had the unmistakable look of graduate students: skinny, pale, and poorly dressed. Their eyes widened as they stared at Jonah and Karen and the two other women prisoners, all of them bound and gagged and lying on the van's floor. Then Brock yelled, "What the hell are you waiting for?" and the students leaped forward.

Jonah contorted wildly as a pair of them climbed into the van and picked him up. Karen screamed "No!" behind her gag and then another pair of students came for her. She jackknifed her body but they held on tight, carrying her out of the van and across the garage.

They approached one of the delivery trucks. The words FERMI NATIONAL ACCELERATOR LABORATORY had been stenciled on the side panel. A lanky student who seemed particularly disheveled— he wore a ratty T-shirt displaying the periodic table—rolled up the door to the truck's cargo hold. The pair of students holding Jonah put the boy in the truck, and then the pair holding Karen did the same. She sobbed in relief as they set her down beside her son. For the moment, at least, they were still together.

From the floor of the cargo hold she saw their two fellow prisoners, the calm black woman and her jittery companion, being transferred to another truck. This place must be a rendezvous point, Karen guessed, where the bastards could pick up new vehicles and supplies. She scanned the room for identifying signs, any clues that could reveal where on earth they were, but she saw none. And then she noticed a commotion at the other end of the garage. Two more students stood beside a pickup truck, struggling to carry yet another bound prisoner. Karen's throat tightened—it was David. He was bucking and twisting so violently that the students lost their grip and he dropped to the floor. Karen screamed behind her gag again. Then a third student joined the others and together they lifted David and bore him toward the last delivery truck.

IT WAS LATE, WELL PAST MIDNIGHT. The trucks were moving slowly down a winding road. Although Monique couldn't see outside, she could hear the rumble of the wheels and feel the turns in her stomach. They were probably taking the back roads to avoid any checkpoints on the interstate.

To her left, Professor Gupta and his students stood around a computer that had been set up in the far corner of the cargo hold. Just a few feet away Michael sat on the floor, playing Warfighter on his Game Boy again. (Someone had recharged the batteries for him.) Gupta had been huddled with his grandson for the past several hours, asking whispered questions about the *Einheitliche Feldtheorie* while his students entered Michael's answers into the computer, but now the professor had apparently gotten everything he needed. He grinned in triumph at the computer screen, then broke away from the group and came over to where Monique lay. Her first instinct was to reach for the bastard's throat, but unfortunately she was still bound and gagged.

"I want you to see this, Dr. Reynolds," he said. "For a physicist, this is a dream come true." He turned to a pair of pale, gangly students with thick glasses. "Scott, Richard, would you please escort Dr. Reynolds to the terminal?"

Grabbing her by the shoulders and ankles, the students carried her across the cargo hold and deposited her on a folding chair in front of the computer screen. Gupta leaned over her shoulder.

"We've developed a program that simulates the creation of the extra-dimensional neutrino beam. Thanks to the information we gleaned from Jacques Bouchet and Alastair MacDonald, we already knew we could use the Tevatron to generate the beam. And once Michael told us the field equations, we were able to calculate the necessary adjustments to the collider. Now we can do trial runs on the computer, so we'll know how to proceed once we get to Fermilab." He reached for the keyboard, tapped the enter key, and pointed at the screen. "Watch carefully. The first thing you'll see is a simulation of the particle collisions inside the Tevatron."

She had no choice but to look. The screen displayed a three-dimensional lattice, a rectilinear grid drawn with faint white lines that wavered ever so slightly. This was obviously a representation of a vacuum, a region of empty spacetime with small quantum fluctuations. But it didn't stay empty for long. After a few seconds she saw swarms of particles streaming from the left and right sides of the screen.

"Those are simulations of the proton and antiproton beams that travel through the Tevatron," Gupta noted. "We're going to pulse them in convex waves so the particles will collide in a perfectly spherical pattern. Watch!"

As Monique squinted at the particles she saw that they were actually tiny folded clusters, each sliding through the spacetime lattice like a slipknot on a string. At the moment of impact, the collisions lit up the center of the screen and all the knots simultaneously unraveled, violently twisting the surrounding lattice. Then the grid of white lines ruptured and a barrage of new particles shot through the breach. The sterile neutrinos.

Gupta pointed excitedly at the particles. "See how they escape? The collisions will warp the spacetime enough to propel a beam of sterile neutrinos out of our brane and into the extra dimensions. Here, let me switch to a wider view."

He tapped the keyboard again and the screen showed a wrinkled, undulating sheet of spacetime against a black background. It was the brane of our universe embedded within the ten-dimensional bulk. The swarm of neutrinos erupted from a sharp twist in the sheet. "We'll have to configure the experiment very precisely," he said. "The beam has to be aimed so that it returns to our brane, preferably at a point about five thousand kilometers above North America. That way everyone on the continent will be able to see the burst."

The particles traced a straight path through the bulk, brightening and accelerating as they plowed through the extra dimensions. The beam crossed the empty space between two folds in the brane and then reentered the spacetime sheet, which writhed and shook and glowed white-hot at the point of impact. This was obviously the burst that Gupta had referred to. He tapped one of his long fingernails against the computer screen. "If we do everything right, the reentry should release several thousand terajoules of energy into our brane. That's roughly the equivalent of a one-megaton nuclear blast. Because the beam will be targeted so far above the atmosphere, it won't cause any damage on the ground. But it'll make a spectacular sight. For several minutes it'll blaze like a new sun!"

Monique stared at the glowing section of the brane, which gradually dimmed as the energy dissipated across spacetime. Jesus, she thought, why the hell is Gupta doing this? Unable to pose the question aloud, she turned to the professor and narrowed her eyes.

He read her look and nodded. "We need to make a public demonstration, Dr. Reynolds. If we simply tried to publish the unified theory, the authorities would suppress the information. The government wants the theory for itself, so it can build its weapons in secret. But the *Einheitliche Feldtheorie* doesn't belong to any government. And it's much more than just a blueprint for making new weapons."

Gupta bent over the keyboard and with a few strokes he switched the computer screen to an architectural drawing of a power plant. "By exploiting the extra-dimensional phenomena, we could produce limitless amounts of electricity. No more need for coal-burning generators or nuclear reactors. But that's just the beginning. We could apply the technology to medicine, precisely targeting the neutrino beams to kill cancer cells. We could use the beams to launch rockets and propel them across the solar system. We could even accelerate a spacecraft to nearly the speed of light!" He turned away from the screen and gazed at Monique. There were tears in his eyes. "Don't you understand, Dr. Reynolds? When humankind wakes up tomorrow morning, they'll see the full splendor of the unified theory. No one will be able to hide it anymore!"

Monique had heard enough. She didn't doubt the truth of what Gupta was saying. The unified theory was so all-encompassing, it could certainly lead to many wonderful inventions. But there was a price, a terrible price. She couldn't stop thinking of the white-hot burst at the center of the computer screen. The professor had said it would be a demonstration, a grand announcement written across the sky, but Monique wondered exactly what the people below would take away from it. Hiroshima had been a demonstration, too.

Of course she couldn't express all this with a gag over her mouth. Instead she stared at Gupta and shook her head.

The professor raised an eyebrow. "What is it? Are you afraid?"

She nodded vigorously.

Gupta moved a step closer and rested his hand on her shoulder. "Fear can be a very debilitating emotion, my dear. *Herr Doktor* was afraid, too, and look what happened. Kleinman and the others kept the *Einheitliche Feldtheorie* hidden for half a century. And did their timidity help anyone? No, it was a waste, a shameful waste. We need to overcome our fears before we can step into the new age. And that's what I've done, Dr. Reynolds. I'm not afraid of anything anymore."

The old man squeezed her shoulder and Monique was suddenly filled with revulsion. She howled behind her gag and tried to hurl herself at Gupta's computer. But the professor caught her before she fell out of the chair. He smiled again, evidently amused.

"I sense you have some doubts, but soon you'll see that I'm right. The world will hail us as saviors once we unveil the theory. They'll forgive us for everything once they see—"

Gupta was interrupted by a crackle of static. Unhooking a radio from his belt, he muttered, "Excuse me," and went to the other end of the cargo hold. After about twenty seconds he returned to his students and raised his hands in a benedictory gesture. "Gentlemen, we're making another stop before we reach Fermilab. We need to pick up some equipment for modifying the Tevatron."

DAVID SAT WITH HIS BACK against the wall of the cargo hold. The truck had stopped fifteen minutes ago and the students had loaded a dozen wooden crates inside. Because the crates took up nearly all the space in the hold, the students had moved to a different truck in the convoy, and now David was alone with the bald maniac in the camouflage pants, who was alternately cleaning his Uzi and swigging from a bottle of Stolichnaya.

For the thousandth time, David tried to loosen the cord that bound his hands behind his back. His fingers were numb but he kept trying anyway, twisting his arms until he could feel the tendons strain and scrape. Sweat dripped down his cheeks and soaked into his gag. As he struggled against the cord he fixed his gaze on the bald mercenary, the son of a bitch who'd held a knife to Jonah's throat. David's fury put new strength into his sinews, but after a minute or so he closed his eyes. It was his own damn fault. He should've surrendered to the FBI agents when he'd had the chance.

When he opened his eyes he saw the bald man standing over him. The mercenary held out the bottle of vodka. "Relax, comrade. Take a break from your valiant efforts."

Repelled, David tried to back away, but the bald man crouched beside him and waved the Stoli bottle under his nose. "Come on, have a drink. You look like you need one."

David shook his head. The smell of the vodka was sickening.

"Fuck you!" he shouted through the gag, but it came out as a desperate gurgle.

The mercenary shrugged. "All right, then. But it seems a shame. We have a whole case of Stolichnaya and not much time left to drink it." Grinning, he tilted the bottle and took a long pull. Then he wiped his mouth with the back of his hand. "My name's Simon, by the way. I want to offer my compliments, Dr. Swift. The book you wrote about Einstein's assistants was very helpful. I've consulted it quite often since taking this job."

David fought to control his rage. Taking a deep breath through the fetid gag, he focused all his attention on the killer's voice. Although he had a thick Russian accent, his command of English was excellent. Contrary to appearances, this was no brainless hit man.

Simon took another swig of vodka, then reached into his pocket. "The past few hours have been a little dull for me. Before the last stop I was in the professor's truck, the one ahead of us, but he was busy interrogating his grandson and giving orders to his students. To pass the time, I had a chat with Gupta's daughter, and I found something that might be of interest to you."

He pulled a circular object out of his pants and cupped it in his palm. David recognized it at once: it was the gold locket that Elizabeth Gupta wore around her neck. Simon opened it and stared at the picture inside. "In your line of work, I suppose you'd consider this a piece of evidence. A late addition to your historical research, eh? It certainly explains a few things."

He turned the locket around so David could see the picture. It was an antique photograph, a sepia-toned portrait of a mother and daughter. The mother was a beauty with long dark hair; the girl was about six years old. Both stared blankly at the camera, unsmiling. "This photo was taken in Belgrade before the war," Simon noted. "The late thirties, most likely. Elizabeth was unsure of the date." He pointed first to the daughter. "This is Hannah, Elizabeth's mother. She came to America after the war and married Gupta. An unfortunate choice." His finger shifted to the dark-haired mother.

"And this is Elizabeth's grandmother. She died in the concentration camps. She was half Jewish, you see. Here, I'll show you."

He pried the picture out of the locket and turned it over. On the reverse side of the photograph, someone had scribbled *Hannah and Lieserl.*

Simon grinned again. "You recognize that name, don't you? I can assure you it's not a coincidence. Elizabeth told me the whole story. Her grandmother was *Herr Doktor*'s bastard daughter."

Under any other circumstances, David would've been bowled over. For an Einstein historian, this was the equivalent of discovering a new planet. Like most researchers, David had assumed that Lieserl died in infancy; now he knew she'd not only survived, she had living descendants. But in his present state he felt no joy in the revelation. It was just another reminder of how blind he'd been.

Simon put the photograph back into the locket. "After the war, *Herr Doktor* learned what had happened to his daughter. He sent for his granddaughter, Hannah, who'd been hiding with a Serbian family, but he never acknowledged his relationship with the girl. As you know, the old Jew wasn't much of a family man." He closed the locket and slipped it back into his pants. "Hannah told Gupta about it, though. And Kleinman, too. That's why they fought over her. Both of them wanted to marry *Herr Doktor*'s granddaughter."

He took another gulp of vodka, tilting the bottle straight up. He'd drunk more than half of it. "You're probably wondering why I'm telling you all this. It's because you're a historian. You should know the history behind this operation. After Gupta married Hannah, he became *Herr Doktor*'s protégé, his closest assistant. And when *Herr Doktor* confided that he'd discovered the *Einheitliche Feldtheorie*, Gupta assumed the old Jew would share the secret with him. But *Herr Doktor* must've sensed there was something wrong with Gupta, even back then. So the old Jew passed the theory to Kleinman and the others instead. And that's what drove Gupta mad. He thought the theory should be his."

Simon was starting to slur his words. David leaned forward

and studied the man carefully, looking for other signs of vulnerability. Maybe an opportunity would present itself. Maybe the son a bitch would do something stupid.

The mercenary turned toward the front of the truck. He was quiet for half a minute or so, staring at the walls of the cargo hold. Then he turned back to David. "Gupta's been planning this demonstration for years. He put millions of dollars into building up his little army of students. He's convinced them that they're going to save the world, that people will start dancing in the streets once they see the flash in the sky from the neutrino beam." He made a disgusted face and spat on the floor. "Can you believe anyone would fall for such nonsense? But Gupta believes it, and now his students do, too. He's a madman, you see. And madmen can be very persuasive."

Simon took one more swallow of Stoli, then thrust the bottle at David again. "Look, you have to drink. I won't take no for an answer. We're going to make a toast. To tomorrow's demonstration. To Gupta's new age of enlightenment."

He began to fumble at the knot that tied the gag over David's mouth. The vodka had made his fingers clumsy, but after a while he managed to loosen the cloth. David felt a surge of adrenaline. This was the opportunity he'd been waiting for. Once the gag was off, he could scream for help. But what good would that do? In all likelihood they were driving through deserted countryside, the woods and fields of Kentucky or Indiana. Screaming would accomplish nothing. He had to talk to Simon. He had to convince the mercenary to set him free. It was their only chance.

David's jaw ached as the gag came off. He took a gulp of fresh air and looked Simon in the eye. "And how much is Gupta paying for your services?"

Simon frowned. For a second David feared that the mercenary would change his mind and retie the gag. "That's an impolite question, Dr. Swift. I didn't ask how much money you earned from your book, did I?"

"This is different. You know what's going to happen after everyone sees the burst. The Pentagon will start doing its own research and—"

"Yes, yes, I know. Every army in the world will try to develop this weapon. But no one's going to be doing any research in the Pentagon. Or anywhere else near Washington, D.C."

Thrown off track, David stared at the mercenary. "What? What do you mean?"

Simon was still frowning, but his eyes held a glint of satisfaction. "Professor Gupta's demonstration will be even more impressive than he expects. I'm going to change the orientation of the neutrino beam so that it reenters our universe inside the Jefferson Memorial." He pointed the Stoli bottle at the back of the truck and closed one eye as if he were aiming down the bottle's neck. "Not that I bear any ill will toward Thomas Jefferson. I've chosen the target because its location is conveniently central. Equidistant from the Pentagon, the White House, and Congress. All three will be completely incinerated in the blast. Along with everything else in a ten-kilometer-wide circle."

At first David thought the mercenary must be joking. He did have a strange sense of humor. But Simon's face seemed to harden as he peered down the neck of the vodka bottle. His upper lip pulled back from his teeth, and as David stared at the man's vicious frown, his own mouth went dry. "Who's paying you to do this? Al-Qaeda?"

Simon shook his head. "No, this is for myself. For my family, actually."

"Your family?"

Very slowly, Simon put down the bottle of vodka and reached into his pocket again. This time he took out a cell phone. "Yes, I had a family. Not so different from yours, Dr. Swift." He turned on the phone and held it so that David could look at the screen. In a couple of seconds a picture appeared: a young boy and girl smiling at the camera. "Those are my children. Sergei and Larissa. They died five years ago in the Argun Gorge, in the southern part of Chechnya. You've heard of the place, I assume?"

"Yes, but—"

"Shut up! Shut up and look!" He leaned forward, shoving the phone into David's face. "My boy Sergei, he was six years old. He looks a bit like your boy, doesn't he? And Larissa, she was just four. They were killed with their mother in a rocket attack. A Hellfire rocket launched from a Delta Force helicopter that was operating near the Chechen border."

"An American helicopter? What was it doing there?"

"Nothing useful, I can assure you of that. It was another botched counterterrorism operation that killed more women and children than terrorists." He spat on the floor again. "But I don't really care about their reasons. I'm going to eliminate everyone involved in commanding and deploying that unit. That's why I've targeted the Pentagon and the civilian leaders as well. The president, the vice president, the secretary of defense." He snapped the phone shut. "I have only one opportunity to strike, so I need a wide blast zone."

David felt sick. This was the very thing Einstein had feared. And it was going to happen in a few hours. "But it sounds like what happened to your family was an accident. How can you—"

"I told you, I don't care!" He picked up the bottle of Stoli by its neck and waved it like a club. "It's intolerable! It's unforgivable!"

"But you're going to kill millions of—"

Something hard smashed into David's cheek. Simon had struck him in the face with the bottle. David fell sideways and his forehead slammed against the truck bed. He would've passed out, but Simon grabbed his collar and pulled him up. "Yes, they're going to die!" he screamed. "Why should they live when my children are dead? They're all going to die! I'm going to kill them all!"

David's ears were ringing. Blood streamed from the gash on his cheekbone and swarms of greenish dots clouded his vision. All he could see now was the enraged face of the mercenary and even that image was blurring in his mind, melting in red, pink, and black rivulets. Hoisting David with one hand, Simon raised the bottle of Stoli with the other. Remarkably, it was unbroken and still held a

few ounces of vodka. He lifted it to David's lips and poured the alcohol into his mouth. "Here's to the end of everything!" he shouted.
"The rest is silence!"

The vodka stung the back of David's throat and pooled in his
stomach. When the bottle was empty, Simon tossed it aside and
let go of his collar. Then David sank to the floor and let darkness
overtake him.

LUCILLE ARRIVED AT THE FBI headquarters very early Monday morning so she wouldn't run into any of her colleagues, but when she
got to her office she discovered that the goons from the Defense
Intelligence Agency had already cleaned out her desk. Her files on
Kleinman, Swift, Reynolds, and Gupta were gone. So was her copy
of *On the Shoulders of Giants*. The only things left were her personal
effects: her payroll stubs, her certificates of commendation, a glass
paperweight in the shape of a Texas six-shooter, and a framed photograph of her shaking hands with Ronald Reagan.

Well, she thought, they did me a favor. Now it won't take so
long to pack.

She found a cardboard box and in half a minute loaded everything inside. It was amazing—the whole kit and caboodle weighed
less than five pounds. For thirty-four years she'd poured her heart
and soul into the Bureau, but now there seemed precious little to
show for it. She gazed with resentment at the antiquated computer
on her desk, the cheap plastic tray of her in-box. It was depressing
as hell.

And then she saw the folder lying on the tray. One of the
agents on the overnight shift must've delivered it after the DIA
goons came through. For several seconds Lucille just stared at the
thing, telling herself to leave it alone. But in the end her curiosity
got the better of her. She picked it up.

It was a list of Professor Gupta's recent telephone calls. Lucille
had requested the information from his cellular carrier three days
ago, but the idiots at the phone company had taken their sweet

time. The records were pretty sparse—Gupta didn't use his cell phone much, only two or three calls a day. As she leafed through the pages, though, she noticed something unusual. Every day for the past two weeks he'd placed a call to the same number. It wasn't Swift's number or Reynolds's or Kleinman's. What made it suspicious was that Gupta had always made the call at precisely 9:30 A.M. Never a minute earlier or later.

Lucille reminded herself that she was no longer assigned to the case. In fact, she'd already filled out her retirement forms.

But she hadn't submitted them yet.

SIMON WAS DRIVING THE TRUCK at the head of the convoy as they sped toward the lab's East Gate. It was five o'clock in the morning, just a few minutes after dawn, and most of the houses along Batavia Road were still dark. A lone woman in red shorts and a white T-shirt jogged past the driveways and lawns. Simon stared at her for a moment, admiring her long mane of auburn hair. Then he pinched the bridge of his nose and yawned. He was still a bit wobbly from last night's binge. To wake himself up, he reached into his windbreaker and clasped the stock of his Uzi. The day of retribution was here. Very soon it would all be over.

Just past the intersection with Continental Drive the truck jounced over a railroad crossing and the landscape opened up on both sides of the road. Instead of suburban homes and lawns, Simon saw a vista of wide green fields, a stretch of virgin Illinois prairie. They were on federal property now, the eastern edge of the laboratory's grounds. Up ahead was a small guardhouse and sitting inside it was an enormously fat woman in a blue uniform. Simon shook his head. It was hard to believe that the laboratory would hire such an obese person to do security work. Clearly, no one at this installation was expecting any trouble.

As Simon slowed his truck to a halt, the woman heaved herself out of the guardhouse. He smiled at her and handed over the paperwork that Professor Gupta had prepared, a thick sheaf of forged invoices and requisition letters. "Here you go, sweetheart," he said, trying to sound like an American truck driver. "We're making an early delivery today."

The woman didn't smile back. She carefully examined the papers, comparing them with a list on her clipboard. "It's not on the schedule."

"No, but we have all the approvals."

She continued studying the paperwork. Either she was a very slow reader or she enjoyed making him wait. Finally she lifted her massive head. "All right, step out of the truck and open the back doors. And tell the drivers behind you to do the same."

Simon frowned. "I told you, it's been approved. Didn't you see the letters?"

"Yeah, but I gotta inspect everything that comes in. Just turn off the engine and—"

He cut her off by pumping two bullets into her skull. Then he went to the back of the truck and knocked three times on the rear door. "Open up, Professor," he shouted. "We need to take on another load."

One of the students pulled up the door and helped Gupta out of the truck. The professor seemed alarmed when he saw the security guard on the ground. "What happened? Didn't I tell you to avoid any more casualties?"

Simon ignored him and turned to the students. "Come on, get the body in the truck!"

Within half a minute they'd stowed the corpse in the cargo hold and mopped up the blood from the asphalt. If anyone should pass by, it would look like the woman had simply abandoned her post. Simon returned to the driver's seat and Gupta got into the truck's cab on the passenger side. The professor shot him a stern look. "No more killing, please," he said. "I used to work with some of the physicists here, back in the eighties when they were building the Tevatron."

Simon shifted the truck into gear. He was in no mood to talk, so he said nothing. The convoy began moving again.

"In fact, I was the one who suggested the name for the particle collider," Gupta continued. "*Teva* is short for a trillion electron volts. That's the top energy that the protons in the accelerator can achieve. At that energy they're moving at 99.9999 percent of the speed of light." The professor whirled one of his fists in a circle, then smacked it into his other fist to simulate a particle collision. He was so keyed up he couldn't keep his hands still. "Of course the Large Hadron Collider in Switzerland can reach higher energies now. But the Tevatron does an excellent job of packing the protons into a tight beam. That's what makes it suited for our purpose."

Simon gritted his teeth. He couldn't take this nervous chatter much longer. "I don't care about all that," he growled. "Just tell me about the control room. How many people will be there?"

"Don't worry, there won't be more than a skeleton crew. Five or six operators at the most." He waved his hand dismissively. "It's because of all the budget cuts. The government doesn't want to pay for physics anymore. The national laboratories need private donations just to keep their accelerators running." The old man shook his head again. "Last year my Robotics Institute donated twenty-five million dollars to Fermilab. You see, I wanted to make sure they didn't shut down the Tevatron. I had a feeling it might prove useful."

The road veered to the left and Simon saw a strangely shaped building on the horizon. It looked like a pair of giant mattresses leaning against each other. Near the building he spotted a low embankment that swept across the grassland in a great circle.

Gupta pointed at the unusual building first. "That's Wilson Hall, the lab headquarters. I used to have an office on the sixteenth floor. Wonderful views." He lowered his arm slightly and pointed at the embankment. "Under that ridge is the Tevatron's beam tunnel. The particle raceway, we used to call it. A four-mile ring with a thousand superconducting magnets to guide the beams. Protons go clockwise, antiprotons counterclockwise. Either beam is powerful enough to burn a hole through a brick wall." Then he pointed at another building closer to the road. It was a nondescript windowless structure, very much like a warehouse, sitting directly above a section of the beam tunnel. "And that's Collision Hall. Where the protons and antiprotons smash into each other. Where we'll launch the neutrinos into the extra dimensions."

The professor fell silent, gazing at the facility through the truck's windshield. Grateful for the interlude, Simon drove past a row of cylindrical tanks, each bearing the words DANGER COMPRESSED HELIUM. Then he came to a long reflecting pool that lay in front of Wilson Hall and mirrored its odd silhouette.

"Turn here and go behind the building," Gupta instructed. "The control room is next to the Proton Booster."

The convoy coasted down a driveway that bypassed Wilson Hall, then came to a parking lot in front of a low, U-shaped structure. Gupta's estimate of the number of personnel in the facility appeared to be correct: there were fewer than half a dozen cars in the lot. That number was sure to increase in three hours or so, when the regular workday began, but with any luck they'd finish the job before then.

Simon parked the truck and began issuing orders. One team of students unloaded the crates of electronic equipment while another transferred the hostages to the truck Agent Brock was driving. Simon had decided it would be best to keep Brock away from the control room so he wouldn't figure out what was going on. The former FBI man had been told that their mission was to steal radioactive materials from the lab. Simon strode to Brock's truck and got his attention. "Take the hostages to a secure location," he ordered. "I don't want them getting in the way. There are some unoccupied structures about a kilometer west of here. Find one and sit tight for a couple of hours."

Brock gave him a belligerent look. "We need to talk when this is over. You're not paying me enough for all the shitwork I'm doing."

"Don't worry, you'll be suitably compensated."

"Why are we keeping the hostages alive, anyway? We're gonna

have to shoot them sooner or later. All of them except the professor's daughter, I mean."

Simon leaned a bit closer and lowered his voice. "It amuses the professor to keep them alive, but I don't care. Once you're out of sight, you can do whatever you want with them."

THE STUDENTS HAD DUMPED DAVID next to Monique and Elizabeth in the cargo hold, but as soon as the vehicle started moving again he squirmed toward Karen and Jonah. As he struggled across the floor of the truck, his son's eyes widened and his ex-wife began to cry. Someone had retied the gag over David's mouth, so he couldn't say a word; instead he simply huddled close to his family. He was still sick from the vodka and the beating Simon had given him, but for a moment his chest swelled with relief.

After a couple of minutes the truck stopped once more. David listened carefully and heard a harsh grinding noise, the sound of metal being twisted. Then Brock opened the truck's rear door and David saw a dome-shaped, grass-covered mound. It was about twenty feet high and a hundred feet across, a man-made hillock that sat atop an underground structure, some kind of large cellar or bunker. The truck was parked in front of an entrance dug into the side of the mound. Over a roll-up door that Brock had already wrenched open, a sign said FERMI NATIONAL ACCELERATOR LABO-RATORY, BOOSTER NEUTRINO EXPERIMENT.

As Brock climbed into the cargo hold he reached into his jacket and pulled out a Bowie knife, identical to the one that Simon had held to Jonah's throat. Grinning, the agent approached the Swift family. David screamed, "No!" behind his gag and tried to shield his son, but with his arms and legs tied he could barely sit up, much less fend off an attack. Brock stood there for a few seconds, turning the knife so it caught the light. Then he bent over and cut the cord that bound David's ankles. "You're gonna do exactly as I say," he whispered. "Or else I'll butcher your kid. Understand?"

Brock cut the cords binding Jonah's ankles, then did the same for Karen and Monique. He ignored Elizabeth, who'd passed out in the corner. Keeping one hand on his Uzi, which hung from a shoulder strap, he hoisted the others to their feet. "Get off the truck," he ordered. "We're going into that shed."

Their hands were still bound behind their backs, but they managed to descend from the cargo hold and march single file toward the roll-up door. David's heart thumped as they neared the entrance; the agent was obviously leading them to a hidden spot where he could kill all four of them at his leisure. Shit, David thought, we have to do something fast! But Brock was right behind Jonah, pointing his Uzi at the boy's head, and David didn't even dare to step out of line.

They entered a dark room lit only by flickering LEDs. Brock closed the door and told them to keep moving. At the back of the room was a spiral stairway leading down. David counted thirty steps as they descended into the blackness. Then Brock flipped a light switch and they found themselves on a platform overlooking an enormous spherical tank. It rested in a concrete pit like a golf ball in a cup, except in this case the ball was nearly forty feet wide. The platform was level with the flattened top of the steel sphere, which was crowned with a circular panel, like a giant manhole cover. As David stared at the tank, he realized that he'd read about it in *Scientific American*. It was part of an experiment for studying neutrinos, which were so elusive that researchers needed a huge apparatus to detect them. The tank was filled with a quarter-million gallons of mineral oil.

"Sit down!" Brock yelled. "Against the wall!"

This is it, David thought as they cowered on the floor. This is when the bastard starts shooting. Brock came closer, carefully aiming his machine gun. Monique leaned against David while Karen closed her eyes and bent over Jonah, who buried his face in his mother's belly. But instead of firing, Brock tore off David's gag and threw it across the room. "All right, now we can get started," he said. "We got some unfinished business."

Brock grinned again, clearly savoring the moment. He wasn't going to kill them quick. He was going to stretch this out as long as possible. "Go ahead, Swift, start screaming," he said. "Scream as loud as you want. No one outside can hear you. We're way underground."

David opened and closed his mouth to put some life back into his jaw muscles. Brock probably wouldn't let him talk for long, so he had to do this quick. He took a couple of deep breaths, then looked the agent in the eye. "Do you know what's going on at the Tevatron? Do you have any idea what they're doing over there?"

"To tell you the truth, I don't really give a shit."

"You should, especially if you have any friends or relatives in Washington, D.C. Your Russian partner is getting ready to blow up the city."

Brock laughed. "Really? Like in the movies? With a big mushroom cloud?"

"No, he's got some newer physics. He's gonna change the targeting of Gupta's neutrino beam. But the effect will be the same. No more White House, no more Pentagon. No more FBI headquarters."

Monique gave a start and stared wide-eyed at David, but Brock just kept laughing. "Wait, let me guess. I have to let you go, right? Because you're the only one who can stop him? Is that what you're trying to say?"

"I'm saying you won't live very long if your partner succeeds. If the government gets wiped out, the army will probably take over the country, and their first order of business will be finding the bastards who blasted Washington. If your plan was to slip across the border and disappear, forget about it. They're gonna hunt you down and string you up."

David spoke as earnestly as he could, but the agent wasn't buying it. He seemed thoroughly amused. "And all this gets started with a . . . what did you call it? A neutral beam?"

"A neutrino beam. Look, if you don't believe me, go talk to Professor Gupta. Ask him what—"

"Yeah, yeah, I'll be sure to do that." Chuckling, Brock turned away and gazed at the giant spherical tank. He strolled to the tank's cover and stomped his foot on the steel panel. The clang echoed against the walls. "What's in here? More neutrinos?"

David shook his head. It was useless. Brock was too thickheaded to understand. "It's mineral oil. For detecting the particles."

"Mineral oil, huh? Why the hell do they use that stuff?"

"The detector requires a transparent liquid with carbon in it. When the neutrinos hit the carbon atoms, they emit flashes of light. But like you said, who gives a shit?"

"Mineral oil can be good for other things, too. It's a lubricant, you know."

Brock began fiddling with the clamps around the panel. After a few seconds he figured out how to release them. Then he pressed a red button with his foot and an electric motor began to hum. The panel opened like a clamshell, revealing a pool of clear liquid about the size of a Jacuzzi. "Well, look at that. There's enough here to last a long, long time."

Kneeling at the side of the pool, Brock dipped one of his hands into the mineral oil. Then he stood up and held the glistening hand in the air. He stared at David as he rubbed the fingers together. "We got a score to settle, Swift. You got the jump on me in that cabin in West Virginia. Fucked up my face pretty good. So now I'm gonna fuck with you."

David's throat closed. For a moment he couldn't breathe. He swallowed hard. "Go ahead," he managed to say. "Just don't hurt the others."

Brock stared at Karen for several seconds, then at Monique. The mineral oil dripped from his fingertips. "No, I'm gonna hurt them, too."

THE TAKEOVER OF THE TEVATRON'S control room was effortless. As soon as Simon stepped through the door with his Uzi, all the gaunt-faced operators sitting at their consoles turned away from the banks of computer screens and raised their hands above their heads. While Professor Gupta's students took their places, Simon escorted the Fermilab employees to a nearby storage closet and locked them inside. He assigned four students to sentry duty, handing each a radio and an Uzi. Two of them took up positions in the parking lot while the other pair patrolled the entrances to the collider's beam tunnel. If any other employees showed up, Simon planned to waylay the new arrivals and add them to the group in the closet. The authorities would have no clue that anything was amiss for at least two or three hours, giving Gupta and his students more than enough time to prepare the Tevatron for their experiment.

The professor stood in the center of the room and directed his students like an orchestra conductor. His eyes swept across the jumble of switches and cables and screens, surveying all the readings. Whenever something in particular caught his attention, he'd swoop toward the student who was manning that console and demand a status report. Gupta's intensity was so extreme that it tightened the skin around his eyes and forehead, erasing all signs of age and fatigue. Simon had to admit, it was an impressive performance. So far everything was proceeding according to plan.

After a while one of the students called out, "Initiating proton injection." The professor replied, "Excellent!" and seemed to relax a bit. He looked over his shoulder and smiled at his idiot grandson, who sat in the corner of the control room, playing with his Game Boy. Then, still smiling, Gupta tilted his head back and gazed at the ceiling.

Simon approached him. "Are we getting close?"

Gupta nodded. "Yes, very close. Our timing was lucky. The operators were already preparing a new store of particles when we arrived." He returned to surveying the computer screens. "Now we've made the necessary adjustments and we're beginning to transfer the protons from the Main Injector to the Tevatron ring. We have to move thirty-six bunches, each containing two hundred billion protons."

"How long will that take?"

"About ten minutes or so. Ordinarily the operators insert the bunches evenly around the ring, but we need to alter the arrangement to produce the spherical collision pattern. We've also modified some of the magnets on the ring to create the proper geometry for the proton swarms. That was the purpose of the equipment we brought here in the crates."

"So in ten minutes you can start the collisions?"

"No, after we finish transferring the protons, we have to inject the antiprotons. That's the trickiest part of the process, so it may take a little longer, maybe twenty minutes. We have to be careful that we don't cause a quench."

"A quench? What's that?"

"Something to be avoided at all costs. The magnets that steer the particles are superconducting, which means they work only if they're cooled to four hundred and fifty degrees below zero. The Tevatron's cryogenic system keeps the magnets cold by pumping liquid helium around the coils."

Simon began to feel uneasy. He remembered the tanks of compressed helium he'd seen while driving past the beam tunnel. "So what can go wrong?"

"Each particle beam carries ten million joules of energy. If we aim it the wrong way, it'll tear right through the beam pipe. Even if we make a very small error, the particles can spray one of the magnets and heat the liquid helium inside. If it heats too much, the helium becomes a gas and bursts out. Then the magnet ceases to be superconducting and electrical resistance melts the coils."

Simon frowned. "Could you fix it?"

"Possibly. But it would take a few hours. And a few more hours to recalibrate the beam line."

Fucking hell, Simon thought. He should've realized there were more risks to this operation than the professor had let on. "You should've told me this earlier. If the government finds out we're here, they'll send in an assault team. I can hold them off for a while, but not several hours!"

Some of the students turned around and looked at him nervously. But Gupta put a reassuring hand on Simon's shoulder. "I told you, we're going to be careful. All my students have experience operating particle accelerators, and we've run dozens of simulations on the computer."

"And what about the targeting of the neutrinos? When will you input the coordinates for the burst?"

"We'll do that when we inject the antiproton bunches. The trajectory of the neutrinos will depend on the exact timing of the—" He stopped in midsentence and stared blankly into space. His mouth opened and for a moment Simon feared that the old man was having a stroke. But soon he smiled again. "Do you hear that?" he whispered. "Do you hear?"

Simon listened. He heard a low, quick beeping.

"That means the protons are circulating in the beam pipe!" Gupta shouted. "The signal starts out low and rises in pitch as the beam grows more intense!" Tears leaked from the corners of the professor's eyes. "What a glorious sound! Isn't it wonderful?"

Simon nodded. It sounded like an unusually rapid heartbeat. A slab of muscle pounding frantically just before the end.

THE ELECTRICAL CORD SLICED INTO David's wrists. He made a final, crazed attempt to yank his hands free, feverishly twisting his arms behind his back as Brock stepped toward Karen and Jonah. All the hours of struggling and straining in the truck's cargo hold the night before had loosened the cord a few millimeters, but it wasn't enough. He screamed in frustration as the agent approached Karen, who was hunched in a tight ball, folding her body around Jonah's. Bending over, Brock gripped the back of Karen's neck. He was about to wrench her away from the boy when David stood up and hurtled toward them.

His only hope was momentum. He lowered his right shoulder and charged toward the agent like a battering ram, his torso parallel with the floor. But Brock saw him coming. At the last moment he stepped to the side and extended his foot into David's path to trip him. For an instant David hung in the air, weightless. And then, because he couldn't break his fall with his hands, he landed on his face. His forehead cracked against the concrete. Blood streamed from his nostrils into his mouth.

Brock laughed. "Nice move, shit-for-brains."

The room darkened and wheeled around him. David blacked out for a few seconds, and when he opened his eyes he saw Monique running toward the agent. Her attempt proved equally futile. As soon as she came close, Brock slammed his fist into her chest. She tumbled backward and the agent laughed again. His face had flushed bright pink around the bruises and his eyes were exultant. Looming over Monique, he transferred the Uzi to his left hand and slipped his right hand into his pants pocket. It looked like he was going to pull out another weapon, a switchblade or a garrote or a set of brass knuckles, but Brock kept his hand in his pocket and moved it slowly up and down. The bastard was rubbing himself.

Brock suddenly turned around and went back to the tank of mineral oil. This time he let the Uzi hang from its shoulder strap and dipped both hands into the pool. "Come on, Swift!" he yelled. "Don't you have any fight left in you? Or are you just gonna sit there and watch?"

David clenched his teeth. Get up, he told himself, get up! He clambered to his feet and lurched forward, but now he seemed to be moving in slow motion. Brock sidestepped again and grabbed the cord binding David's wrists, then spun him around and forced him to his knees. The agent's hands were greasy and cold. "The nigger will be fun," he whispered. "But not as much fun as your wife. I'm gonna take off her gag so you can hear her scream."

Brock threw him to the floor. David's head hit the concrete a second time and the pain knifed into his skull. But he didn't black out. He dug his fingernails into his palms and bit his lower lip until it bled, putting all his will into remaining conscious.

Woozy, nauseated, and terrified, he saw Brock pull Karen away from Jonah and drag her toward the steel tank. He watched the agent tear the gag off Karen's mouth and he heard her make a barely audible whimper, which was more heartrending than any scream. The sound drove David into a frenzy. He thrashed on the floor, trying to rise to his feet again. And as he struggled, his right hand slipped out of the loop of electrical cord that Brock had inadvertently moistened with mineral oil.

David was so surprised that he stayed there on the floor for a few seconds, keeping both hands behind his back. All at once his wooziness dissipated and he could think clearly again. He knew he was too weak to fight. If he tried to wrest the Uzi from Brock, the agent would simply push him away and start firing. He needed to incapacitate the bastard, and in his sudden clarity of mind he saw exactly how to do it. He reached into his back pocket and gripped the cigarette lighter he'd taken from Agent Parker, the Zippo embossed with the Lone Star of Texas.

Pretending his hands were still tied, David stumbled to his feet. Brock smiled and let go of Karen. "That's more like it!" he crowed, stepping over her and squaring off. "Bring it on, big guy! Let's see what you can do!"

He didn't run this time. He staggered forward until he stood right in front of the agent. Brock shook his head, disappointed. "You don't look so good, you know that? You look like—"

David spun the Zippo's flint wheel and thrust the lighter into Brock's face. The agent raised his arms, reflexively warding off the blow, and both of his oily hands caught fire.

With all his remaining strength, David grabbed Brock by the waist and started pushing him backward. The agent madly flapped his hands, but this only fanned the flames. David counted two steps, three steps, four. Then he shoved Brock into the tank of mineral oil.

The flames spread across the pool as soon as Brock's hands hit the surface. But even if it weren't for the fire, the agent would have been doomed. He sank into the liquid like a stone, disappearing immediately. In addition to being highly flammable, mineral oil is less dense than water. And because the human body is mostly water, it's impossible to swim in any fluid that's much lighter. David had forgotten a good deal of the physics he'd learned in school, but fortunately not that part.

THE SIGNAL IN THE CONTROL room no longer sounded like a heartbeat. The pitch had steadily risen until each beep was a shrill inhuman cry. It sounded like an alarm, an automated warning of some mechanical breakdown, but Professor Gupta didn't seem concerned. He looked up at the ceiling again, and when he turned back to Simon there was an openmouthed smile of ecstasy on his face. "The beam is strong," he declared. "I can tell just by listening to the signal. All the protons are in the ring."

Wonderful, Simon thought. Now let's finish the job. "So are we ready to input the target coordinates?"

"Yes, that's the next step. Then we'll load the antiprotons into the collider."

The professor moved toward the console manned by Richard Chan and Scott Krinsky, the pale, bespectacled physicists from Oak Ridge National Laboratory. But before Gupta could issue any instructions to the men, Simon grasped the professor's arm and aimed the Uzi at his forehead. "Wait a moment. We need to make a small adjustment. I have a new set of coordinates for the burst."

Gupta gaped at him, uncomprehending. "What are you doing? Get your hands off me!"

Richard, Scott, and all the other students turned their heads. Several rose from their seats when they saw what has happening, but Simon wasn't worried. No one else in the control room was armed. "If you value your professor's life, I suggest that you sit down," he said calmly. To underline his point, he dug the muzzle of the Uzi into Gupta's temple.

The students obediently sank to their chairs.

❋ ❋ ❋

"WHY ARE YOU CALLING ME? You don't work for me anymore."

Lucille hardly recognized the Bureau director's voice. It snarled out of the earpiece of her telephone. "Sir," she started again, "I have some new—"

"No, I don't want to hear it! You're retired now. Hand in your gun and badge and get out of the building."

"Please, sir, listen! I've identified a cell-phone number that may belong to one of the—"

"No, *you* listen! I just lost my job because of you, Parker! The vice president has already chosen my replacement and leaked his name to Fox News!"

She took a deep breath. The only way to make him listen was to get it out fast. "This suspect could be working with Amil Gupta. His phone number is registered to an alias, a Mr. George Osmond. Fake identity, fake address. According to the cellular company's records, for the past two weeks he's turned on his phone once a day, to receive a call from Gupta, and then immediately turned it off. But I think Mr. Osmond just made a mistake. At one o'clock this morning he turned on the phone and left it on, and it's been tracking his position ever since."

"You know what, Lucy? It's not my problem anymore. By this afternoon I'm gonna be back in the private sector."

"I got the tracking data from the cellular carrier. It looks like the suspect traveled along secondary roads to Batavia, Illinois. That's where he is right now, at the Fermi National—"

"Look, why are you telling me all this? You should be talking to Defense. They're in charge now."

"I tried, sir, but they won't listen! Those idiots at DIA keep saying they don't need any assistance!"

"Well, let them hang, then! Let them all go to hell!"

"Sir, if you could just—"

"No, I'm through. Fuck the Pentagon, fuck the White House, fuck the whole administration!"

"But all you need to do is—"

She heard a click. The FBI director had just hung up on her.

DAVID LED KAREN, JONAH, AND Monique out of the underground lab and back to the truck. Although the lab's sprinkler system had already extinguished the fire in the mineral oil tank, they were still eager to get the hell out of there. Once they were outside, David untied the cords on their wrists. Karen and Jonah fell into his arms, weeping, but Monique ran back into the lab.

"Wait a second!" David called. "Where are you going?"

"We gotta find a phone! They took our cell phones!"

Gently disentangling himself from his ex-wife and son, David returned to the lab's doorway. Monique was pacing across the room, searching for a telephone amid the long banks of computers. "Jesus!" she cried. "Where's the phone in this place? They got a million dollars' worth of equipment here, but not a single damn phone!"

David remained in the doorway, reluctant to step inside. "Let's go," he urged. "That Russian bastard might send reinforcements any minute."

Monique shook her head. "We gotta call for help first. Gupta's made all the preparations for the spacetime rupture. If they're targeting Washington now, they're gonna—whoa, what's this?" She pointed at a metal panel on the wall, not too far from the doorway. "Is it an intercom?"

Against his better judgment, David stepped into the room to take a closer look. It did indeed look like an intercom, with a row of colored buttons below the grille of a loudspeaker. The buttons were labeled CONTROL ROOM, BOOSTER, MAIN INJECTOR, TEVATRON, and COLLISION HALL. "Don't press Control Room," David warned. "That's probably where Gupta is."

"Maybe we can reach an office they haven't taken over yet. If we can find one of the Tevatron's engineers, maybe we can convince him to turn off the power for the collider." She studied the row of buttons for a moment, then pressed the one labeled TEVATRON. "Hello? Hello?"

No one answered. But when David cocked his ear toward the panel he heard a rapid, high-pitched beeping.

"Shit," Monique whispered. "I know that signal." She grasped his arm to steady herself. "The beams are almost ready."

"What? What do—"

"No time, no time!" She headed for the doorway, pulling him along. "We got ten minutes, fifteen minutes at the most!"

She raced to the truck and grasped the handle of the driver's-side door. Unfortunately, it was locked. The keys were probably still in Brock's trousers, at the bottom of the tank of mineral oil. "Damn!" she yelled. "We're gonna have to run!"

"Where? Where are we going?"

"The beam tunnel! It's this way!"

While Monique dashed ahead, running south toward the Te-vatron ring, David rushed over to Karen, who was kneeling on the ground beside Jonah. Leaving them alone scared the shit out of David, but what was happening in the collider was even more frightening. "We have to split up," he said. "You and Jonah should get away from here as fast as you can." He pointed at a strip of pavement about two hundred yards to the north. "Go to that road and make a left. If you see any security guards or police, tell them there's a fire in the beam tunnel and they need to shut off the power. Got that?"

Karen nodded. David was amazed at how calm she was. She took his hand and squeezed it, then pushed him in the direction of the beam tunnel. "Go, David," she said. "Before it's too late."

SIMON WAS IN A QUANDARY. He'd just tried calling Brock on the radio, but there was no response. He tried three more times and heard nothing but static. It was hard to imagine that a man armed with an Uzi could've been overcome by a handful of bound-and-gagged hostages. But there it was.

Simon was still holding Professor Gupta at gunpoint, and the students in the control room were still monitoring the Tevatron, obediently adjusting the proton and antiproton beams so that they conformed to the new target coordinates. In about ten minutes the particle beams would be ready, and after another two minutes of acceleration the collisions would begin. But if Swift and Reynolds had indeed escaped from Brock, there was a good chance that they'd head for the beam tunnel and try to disrupt the experiment. Now Simon had to choose between going after them and staying in the control room.

After several seconds of thought, he jammed his Uzi against Gupta's skull and shoved him forward. The old man was so terrified, he could barely stand up. Holding him by the scruff of his neck, Simon addressed the students. "Professor Gupta and I are going to observe the experiment at another location, not very far away. I expect all of you to follow the orders I've given. If the demonstration fails, I plan to kill your professor in the most painful way imaginable. And then I'll come back here and kill each one of you."

The students nodded and turned back to their screens. They were weak and frightened and easily cowed, and Simon had no doubt that they would comply. He went to the back of the control room and opened the cabinet that held the keys to the beam tunnel's access points. The professor's idiot grandson stared at them for a moment, uncomprehending. Then he lowered his head and returned his attention to the Game Boy as Simon dragged the professor out the door.

IT WAS HALF A MILE to the Tevatron. David and Monique ran down a paved road for several hundred yards, then dashed across a muddy field. Soon they could see the grass-covered ridge that ran above the beam tunnel and a low cinder-block structure with a chain-link gate instead of a door at its entrance. There were no vehicles parked nearby and not a person in sight.

Monique pointed at the structure. "That's one of the tunnel entrances. The F-Two access point."

"Shit," David panted. "The gate's probably locked. How the hell are we gonna get inside?"

"Fire axes," she replied. "They're at every access point, in case there's an emergency in the tunnel. I remember seeing them the last time I worked on an experiment here."

"What about the control panels for shutting down the beams? Do you remember where they are?"

"There are manual shutdown switches inside the tunnel, but Gupta probably disabled them. I bet that was one of the first things he did."

With a final sprint they arrived at the cinder-block building and quickly located the fire-safety cabinet, which was mounted on an exterior wall. Monique removed the ax and rushed to the building's entrance. Through the chain-link gate, David saw a stairway going down to the tunnel. He gripped Monique's elbow. "Wait a second! How are you going to shut down the accelerator if the switches are disabled?"

Monique hefted the ax. "With this thing. One clean cut through the beam pipe should do the trick."

"But if the beam's running, the protons are gonna spray everywhere! You're gonna get showered with radiation!"

She nodded grimly. "That's why you're gonna stay up here and guard the entrance. There's no sense in both of us getting fried."

David tightened his grip on her elbow. "Let me do it. I'll go down instead."

Her brow creased. She looked at him as if he'd just said something asinine. "That's ridiculous. You have a kid, a family. I don't have anyone. It's a simple calculation." She jerked her arm out of his grasp and positioned herself in front of the gate.

"No, wait! Maybe we can—"

She raised the ax over her head and was just about to bring it down on the gate's lock when the bullet tore through her. David heard the shot and saw the blood spurt out of her side, just above the waistline of her shorts. She let out a surprised "Uhhh" and dropped the ax. He grabbed her shoulders as she collapsed and swiftly pulled her around the corner of the building. "Jesus!" he screamed. "Monique!"

Her face contorted in pain. She clutched David's biceps as he laid her on the ground and pulled up her shirt. There was an entry wound on the left side of her abdomen and an exit wound on the right. Blood flowed freely from both. "Fuck!" she gasped. "What happened?"

He peered around the corner. About fifty yards away he spotted a pair of Gupta's students hugging the wall of another cinderblock building. Although both of them carried Uzis, the students just stood there, frozen in place, evidently shell-shocked by their first taste of gunplay. One of them was speaking into a radio.

David turned back to Monique. "There's two, but more are coming," he reported. Kneeling beside her, he slipped one arm under her back and the other under her knees. "I'm getting you out of here." But she screamed as he tried to lift her, and blood gushed from her exit wound, soaking his pants.

"Put me down, put me down!" she groaned. "You'll have to do it yourself. There's another access point a half mile south of here."

"I can't—"

"There's no time to argue! Just take the ax and go!"

SIMON LOCKED PROFESSOR GUPTA INSIDE a storage closet in Collision Hall. Once they were out of earshot of the control room, he could've easily killed the old man without anyone knowing, but he decided it would be more fitting if the professor lived to see the results of his experiment.

Just as Simon was leaving Collision Hall, he received a radio transmission from the pair of students he'd assigned to patrol the beam tunnel. Three minutes later Simon arrived at the F-Two tunnel entrance. The students stood about ten meters away from Reynolds, both nervously training their submachine guns at her even though she was obviously in no condition to return fire. She lay on her back in a pool of blood, still alive but just barely.

"Was she alone?" Simon asked them. "Did you see anyone else?"

The fat student shook his head, but the skinny one looked uncertain. He wiped the sweat from his brow and pushed his glasses up the bridge of his nose. "After Gary shot her, I'm pretty sure that someone pulled her around the corner. But I didn't get a good look at him."

Simon stepped toward the myopic dunce. "Which way did he go?"

"I don't know, I didn't see him again. I was busy calling you on the radio, and by the time we—"

With a pull of the trigger Simon silenced the fool. Then he turned on his heel and executed the fat one, too. These students were useless. Now Swift was on the loose, probably running to another tunnel entrance, and Simon had no idea which point on the four-mile ring he was aiming for. Infuriated, he stomped on the face of the first student he'd shot, breaking the corpse's glasses.

Then the wounded woman let out a moan, a throaty, broken "Daaaaaavid." Her eyes were closed but she was still conscious. Perhaps, Simon thought, she knew where Swift was.

Simon removed his combat knife from its sheath. To inflict the maximum amount of pain, it was best to start with the fingers.

KAREN COULDN'T BELIEVE HER GOOD LUCK. As she ran with Jonah down the road that David had pointed out, she saw three fire trucks and a red-and-white Jeep heading their way. She waved her arms wildly to flag them down. The trucks sped by her, their sirens blaring, but the Jeep, which had the words FERMILAB FIRE CHIEF written on the driver's-side door, came to a stop. A balding man with a jolly round face leaned out the window. "Can I help you, ma'am?"

She paused for a second to catch her breath. "There's a fire! In the beam tunnel! You have to shut off the power!"

The fire chief smiled, unruffled. "Now, now, slow down. We got a report that the sprinkler system activated in the Neutrino Detector. That's where the trucks are going."

"No, no, that fire's already out! You have to go to the beam tunnel instead! You have to shut off the power before they blow it up!"

The chief's smile faded a bit. He gave Karen a once-over and glanced at Jonah, who was still crying. "Excuse me, ma'am, do you have a Fermilab visitor's pass?"

"No! They brought us here in a truck!"

"I'm afraid you can't enter the laboratory grounds without a pass. You have to—"

"Jesus Christ! There's a bunch of terrorists taking over the place and you're worried about a goddamn visitor's pass?"

The smile disappeared altogether. The chief shifted his Jeep into park and opened his door. "You're breaking the law, ma'am. I think you better come with—"

Karen grabbed Jonah's hand and bolted down the road.

DAVID RAN THROUGH A STAND of oak trees, which gave him some cover as he followed the curving ridge above the beam tunnel. He didn't look back to where he'd left Monique. He'd already gone half a mile, far enough that he probably couldn't have seen her anyway, but still he refused to look back. He had to push everything out of his mind except the beam line.

Carrying the fire ax, he sprinted toward the E-Zero entrance, a cinder-block structure that was identical to the one he'd just left. A bulky yellow electric cart was parked next to the building; it was probably used to ferry maintenance workers or tow equipment from one access point to another, but no one was on the job yet this morning. All he heard was the twittering of the songbirds and a low hum that came from the stairway leading down to the beam tunnel.

He quickly examined the gate at the head of the stairs. It was secured with a chain and a Master Lock, but the chain was cheap and thin. David grasped the handle of his ax as if it were a baseball bat and took a couple of practice swings. Then he pulled it all the way back and smashed the blade against the chain's spindly links.

The impact jarred his hands and he almost lost his grip, but when he looked at the chain again it was cut in two.

He opened the gate and dashed down the stairway. At the bottom of the steps, though, he had to stop—there was another locked gate blocking the entryway to the tunnel. Through the gate's bars he could see the beam pipe, long and curving and silver gray, running about a foot above the tunnel's floor. This was another thing he'd read about in *Scientific American*. The superconducting magnets sandwiched most of the pipe; they were strung along its length like beads on a giant necklace, except that each magnet was about twenty feet long and shaped like a coffin. The magnets kept the protons and antiprotons in line, kept them traveling in tight beams inside the steel pipe. And with the flip of a switch, the same magnets would draw the beams together and ignite the apocalypse.

David lifted his ax again, but the second gate was a tougher obstacle than the first. It was locked with two dead bolts that extended from the jamb. When he took a swing at them, the ax blade didn't even make a dent. He tried aiming at the center of the gate instead, but the bars just rattled. Part of the problem was that the corridor was too narrow—he didn't have enough room to take a full swing. In frustration he chopped at the dead bolts again and this time the head of the ax broke right off. David shouted, "Fuck!" and clubbed the gate with the broken handle. He was within spitting distance of the beam pipe but he couldn't get any closer.

Lacking a better idea, David ran back up the stairway. Although he could probably find another fire ax somewhere on the premises, he knew it wouldn't do much good. He might be able to breach the gate if he could hammer away at it for half an hour or so, but he only had a few minutes at best. As he stepped outside he looked around wildly for some kind of deliverance—a key, a hacksaw, a stick of dynamite. And then his eyes fixed on the electric cart.

Luckily, the cart's motor started with the push of a button. David got into the driver's seat and steered the vehicle toward the tunnel entrance, which looked like it would be just wide enough.

Flooring the pedal, he accelerated the cart to about 20 mph. Then he leaped out of the vehicle and watched it career down the flight of steps.

The crash was tremendously loud, raising David's hopes. He rushed down the stairway and saw the yellow cart balanced on a heap of crumpled fencing. The vehicle's front end was inside the tunnel while the rear end hung just outside the gate. The back wheels were spinning madly in the air—the cart's motor was still working and the accelerator pedal had evidently gotten stuck—but David managed to squeeze past the chassis and clamber through the breach.

He slid to the tunnel's concrete floor, which was littered with bits of glass from the cart's headlights. The beam pipe, though, appeared to be undamaged. A few feet away David found a control panel on the wall. Muttering a quick prayer, he opened the panel and threw the manual shutdown switch. But nothing happened. The long line of superconducting magnets kept on humming. Gupta had disabled the switches, just as Monique had predicted.

David picked up a piece of debris from the crash, a heavy steel bar that had been torn from the gate. He couldn't see any other option. It would be impossible to disable one of the superconducting magnets—the coils were encased in thick steel columns—and all the power lines for the collider ran along the arched ceiling of the tunnel, out of reach. No, the only way to shut down the Tevatron was to smash the beam pipe. He had to pummel it hard enough to disrupt the stream of particles, which would then spray into his body like a trillion tiny darts. David's eyes began to sting. Well, he thought, at least it'll be quick.

He rubbed his eyes and whispered, "Good-bye, Jonah." Then he raised the steel bar over his head. But as he stepped toward a section of the beam pipe that ran between two of the magnets, he noticed another pipe running just above, with HE printed on it in black letters. It was the pipe that delivered the ultracold liquid helium to the magnets. The helium was what made the magnets superconducting—it lowered the temperature of their titanium coils to the point where they could conduct electricity without any resistance. And as David stared at the thing, he realized there was another way to stop the particle beams.

Adjusting his grip on the steel bar, he took aim at the helium pipe. All he needed to do was make a puncture. Once exposed to the air, the liquid helium would turn into a gas and escape; then the magnets would overheat and the Tevatron would shut down automatically. Swinging the bar as hard as he could, David struck the pipe directly on the black HE. A sharp clang echoed up and down the tunnel. The blow had made an inch-wide dent—good, but not good enough. He struck the pipe again in the same spot, making the dent wider and deeper. One more time should bust it, he thought as he raised the steel bar again. Then someone grabbed the bar out of his hands and yanked him away from the beam line.

David's head hit the concrete wall of the tunnel. He didn't see his attacker, but as he crumpled to the floor he heard a familiar voice.

"Hello again, Dr. Swift. Your colleague Dr. Reynolds was kind enough to tell me where you were. And I only had to remove two of her fingers."

"NO, MA'AM, THERE'S NOTHING GOING ON. Just another beautiful day here at the lab. Seventy-five degrees and not a cloud in the sky."

Adam Ronca, the chief of security for Fermilab, had a cheery Chicago accent. As Lucille listened to him over the phone, she imagined what he looked like: chunky, ruddy, middle-aged. An easygoing guy who'd found a job that wasn't especially strenuous. "What about your incident reports?" she asked. "Any signs of unusual activity in the past few hours?"

"Well, let's see." He paused, rustling some papers. "At four-twelve A.M., the guard at the West Gate saw some movement in the woods. Turned out to be a fox. And at six twenty-eight the fire department responded to an alarm at the Neutrino Detector."

"An alarm?"

"It's probably nothing. They've been having trouble with the sprinkler system over there. The darn thing keeps—" A burst of static interrupted him. "Uh, excuse me, Agent Parker. The fire chief is calling on the radio."

Lucille shouted, "Wait!" but he'd already put her on hold. For nearly a minute she drummed her fingernails on her desk, staring at the tracking records for George Osmond's cell phone. Fermilab wasn't a likely terrorist target—there were no weapon designs at the lab and very little radioactive material. But maybe Mr. Osmond was interested in something else.

Ronca finally came back on the line. "Sorry about that, ma'am. The fire chief needed my help with something. Now what were you—"

"Why does he need your help?"

"Oh, he spotted a couple of trespassers. Some crazy woman and her kid. It happens more than you'd think."

Lucille squeezed the telephone receiver. She thought of Swift's ex-wife and their son, who'd disappeared two days before. "Is the woman in her midthirties, blond, about five foot eight? With a seven-year-old boy?"

"Hey, how did you know—"

"Listen carefully, Ronca. A terrorist attack may be in progress. You gotta lock down the lab."

"Whoa, hold on. I can't—"

"Look, I know the director of the Bureau's Chicago office. I'll tell him to send over some agents. Just make sure no one leaves the facility!"

PROFESSOR GUPTA KNEW EXACTLY WHERE he was. The closet he was locked inside wasn't very far from the Collider Detector, Fermilab's crown jewel. As he sat with his back against the wall he could hear the low hum of the device and feel the vibrations in the floor.

The detector was shaped like a giant wheel, more than ten meters high, with the beam pipe in the position where the axle would be. The protons and antiprotons would collide at the very center of the wheel, a point surrounded by concentric rings of instrumentation—drift chambers, calorimeters, particle counters. During the normal operation of the Tevatron, these instruments tracked the trajectories of the various quarks, mesons, and photons ejected from the high-energy collisions. But today there would be no particles flying outward from the center of the wheel. Instead the collisions would tear a hole in our universe, allowing the sterile neutrinos to escape into the extra dimensions beyond, and no instrument on the planet would detect their presence until they came screaming back to our spacetime. Gupta had overheard the new target coordinates that Simon had given to his students, so he could make a good guess at the reentry point. It was approximately a thousand kilometers to the east. Somewhere along the Eastern Seaboard.

The professor lowered his head and stared at the floor. It wasn't his fault. He'd never intended to hurt anyone. Of course he'd known from the start that the effort might require some sacrifices. He'd recognized that Simon would have to apply some pressure on Kleinman, Bouchet, and MacDonald to extract the *Einheitliche Feldtheorie* from them. But that was unavoidable. Once the equations were in Gupta's hands, he'd tried to avoid any violent acts that would mar his demonstration of the unified theory. He couldn't be blamed if his orders weren't properly carried out. The problem was simple human perversity. The Russian mercenary had been deceiving him all along.

As Gupta sat there in the darkness he heard a new noise, a distant thrumming. It was the sound of the RF system, which was now generating an oscillating radio-frequency field to accelerate the protons and antiprotons. Every time the particles went around the ring, fifty thousand times a second, the RF field gave them another boost. In less than two minutes the proton and antiproton swarms would reach their top energies and the superconducting magnets would point the beams at each other. The professor raised his head and listened carefully. He might not be able to hear the rupture in spacetime, but he would know soon enough whether the experiment had worked.

DAVID LAY FACEUP ON THE floor of the beam tunnel. Simon loomed over him, stepping on his chest, making it difficult to breathe and impossible to stand up. Dizzy and gasping, David grabbed the man's leather boot and tried to lift it off his rib cage, but the mercenary just pressed down harder and dug in his heel. For good measure, Simon also pointed his Uzi at David's forehead, but he didn't seem particularly inclined to fire. Maybe he was worried that a ricocheting bullet would hit the beam pipe. Or maybe he simply wanted to gloat. As he ground his boot heel into David's breastbone, the hum of the superconducting magnets grew louder and the floor of the tunnel began to vibrate.

"Hear that?" Simon asked, his sweaty face breaking into a grin. "That's the final acceleration. Only two minutes left."

David twisted and kicked and beat his fists against Simon's leg, but the bastard just stood there, impervious. He looked like a man in the throes of passion, staring openmouthed at the victim he'd pinned to the floor. After a while David's strength began to ebb. His head throbbed and blood seeped from the gashes on his face. He was crying now, crying in pain and despair. It was his own fault, the whole damn thing, from start to finish. He'd thought he could get a glimpse of the Theory of Everything without suffering any consequences, and now he was being punished for this sin of pride, this rash attempt to read the mind of God.

Simon nodded. "It hurts, doesn't it? And you've felt it for only a few seconds. Imagine what it's like to live with it for years."

Despite the pressure on his chest, David managed to suck some air into his lungs. Even if it was completely hopeless, he was going to keep fighting this bastard. "Fucker!" he gasped. "You fucking coward!"

The mercenary chuckled. "You can't spoil my mood, Dr. Swift.

I'm happy now, for the first time in five years. I've done what my children wanted me to do." He glanced over his shoulder at the beam pipe. "Yes, what they wanted."

David shook his head. "You're fucking crazy!"

"Maybe so, maybe so." His mouth hung open and his tongue lolled obscenely on his lower lip. "But I've done it anyway. Like Samson and the Philistines. I'm going to topple the pillars of their house and bring it down on their heads."

Simon clenched his free hand into a fist. He turned away from David for a moment and gazed at the wall of the tunnel. "No one's going to laugh over my grave," he muttered. "No laughter, no pity. Nothing but . . ." His voice trailed off. He blinked a few times and pinched the bridge of his nose. Then, regaining his train of thought, he glared at David and dug in his heel again. "Nothing but silence! The rest is silence!"

David felt a jolt in his chest, but it wasn't from Simon's boot. He stared intently at the mercenary's face. The bastard looked drowsy. His jaw was slack and his eyelids were drooping. Then David looked at the liquid-helium pipe he'd tried to puncture. The section near the HE was still intact, but the pipe was slightly bent at a junction several feet to the left. It looked like there might be a small leak in the fitting—not enough to overheat the magnets, but maybe enough to displace some of the oxygen in the tunnel. And because helium was the second-lightest element, it would expand more rapidly in the upper part of the tunnel than in the space near the floor.

Simon blinked a few more times. "What are you doing? What are you staring at?" He stretched his right arm, lowering the Uzi to within a foot of David's brow. "I should shoot you right now! I should send you to hell!"

The mercenary was breathing fast. That was one of the symptoms of oxygen deprivation. Another was loss of muscle coordination. David held up his hands as if surrendering. Maybe he still had a chance. "No, don't shoot!" he yelled. "Please, don't!"

Simon curled his lip. "You pitiful worm! You . . ."

David waited until Simon blinked again. Then he swung his right arm and batted the Uzi out of the bastard's hands. As the submachine gun skittered across the concrete floor, Simon shifted his weight off the foot that was crushing David's chest. Gripping the boot with both hands, David wrenched it like a corkscrew and Simon crashed to the floor.

The gun, David thought. I have to get the gun. There was less than a minute left. He rose to his feet but stayed low so he wouldn't breathe too much helium. It took him a couple of seconds to spot the Uzi, which had slid beneath the beam pipe, nearly twenty feet down the tunnel. He started running for it, but he'd waited too long. Before he could go three steps, Simon caught up to him and grabbed his waist. The mercenary threw him against the wall and sprinted toward the Uzi.

For a moment David just stared in horror. Then he turned around and raced the other way, back to the tunnel entrance. He was running on instinct, thinking only of escape, but there was no escape now unless he shut down the collider. While Simon knelt on the floor and reached for his Uzi, David looked frantically at the debris around the gate, searching for something heavy to fling at the beam pipe. Then he raised his eyes and saw the electric cart. It was halfway through the breach, its chassis balanced precariously on the crumpled gate and its motor still turning the rear wheels in midair.

As he reached for the cart he heard footsteps behind him. Simon was charging down the tunnel with his Uzi. He didn't pull the trigger, though; shooting from a distance was too risky because of the chance of a ricochet. The bastard held his fire, giving David a precious second to act. Clutching the front of the yellow cart, he pulled with all his might. But it didn't budge. The cart was heavy, at least four hundred pounds, and its undercarriage rested on a heap of twisted metal. David pulled again, but it was no good. The damn thing was stuck.

When Simon came within ten feet he raised his Uzi and took

aim. David let out an animal yell, a scream of defiance. The mercenary fired, but David crouched to make one last pull and the bullets whizzed over his head. And in the same instant the cart finally yielded to his will and slid into the tunnel.

The vehicle bucked like a bull as soon as its rear wheels touched the floor. Simon abruptly lowered his Uzi and hurtled forward. He dove toward the cart, reaching for its steering wheel, but at the last moment one of his boots slipped on a piece of broken glass. He fell into the path of the vehicle just as it barreled toward the beam pipe.

David leaped over the broken gate and rolled to the side, behind a concrete wall. Then there was a flash of white light and a deafening bang.

PROFESSOR GUPTA HEARD A DISTANT POP. A moment later the hum of the superconducting magnets subsided. Within a few seconds Collision Hall was silent. The Tevatron had shut down.

Crouched in the corner of the storage closet, Gupta could hear his heart thumping. He closed his eyes and saw a wrinkled, undulating sheet, the same sheet that had appeared in the computer simulation he'd created. He saw a swarm of sterile neutrons break free of the sheet and run between its folds like a trillion white-hot cinders. And then he collapsed and saw nothing but blackness.

He was awakened by the shrill cries of his students. They were fairly close, shouting "Professor! Professor!" in anguished voices. Forcing himself up, Gupta crawled to the front of the closet and pounded his fist on the door.

The voices came closer. "Professor? Is that you?"

Someone found the key and opened the door. The first ones Gupta saw were Richard Chan and Scott Krinsky, who rushed into the closet and knelt beside him. The others followed right behind, crowding into the small space. Gupta's mouth was so dry, he could hardly speak. "Richard," he rasped. "What happened?"

Richard's cheeks were wet with tears. "Professor!" he sobbed.

"We thought you were dead!" With childlike abandon, he flung his arms around Gupta.

The professor pulled away. "What happened?" he repeated, louder this time.

Scott came forward, his glasses askew. An Uzi hung from a strap over his shoulder. "We were following Simon's instructions, but a few seconds before impact there was an explosion in the E-Zero sector of the beam tunnel."

"So the collisions never started? There was no spacetime rupture?"

"No, the explosion disrupted the beam line and the Tevatron went down."

Gupta felt a warm rush of relief. Thank heaven.

"We started looking for you after the shutdown," Scott added. "We were afraid Simon would kill you like he said." He bit his lower lip. "He killed Gary and Jeremy. We found their bodies outside the F-Two tunnel entrance. I took one of their Uzis."

Gupta stared at the ugly black gun. "Where's Michael?" He looked past Scott and Richard, searching for his grandson's face. "Didn't he come with you?"

They looked at each other nervously. "Uh, no," Scott answered. "I haven't seen him since we left the control room."

The professor shook his head. His students stood around him like a band of helpless children. They'd failed him miserably and now they were waiting for forgiveness and their next instructions. Gupta's anger at them put new strength in his limbs. He stretched his hand toward Scott. "Help me up," he ordered. "And give me that gun."

Without hesitation Scott helped him to his feet and handed over the Uzi. Gupta cradled it at his hip as he stepped out of the closet. "All right, we're heading back to the control room," he announced. "We're going to find Michael and restart the experiment."

Richard stared at him in dismay. "But there's major damage to the beam line! The readings showed that half a dozen of the magnets are down!"

Gupta waved his hand dismissively. "We can repair the damage. We have all the necessary equipment."

He marched through Collision Hall toward one of the exits, his students anxiously straggling in his wake. It wasn't too late to make another attempt. It might take several hours to fix the beam line, but with a little luck they could accumulate another particle store by the end of the day. This time they would target the neutrinos at the original coordinates, five thousand kilometers above North America. The burst would spread its gorgeous rays across the sky just as night fell.

As they stepped outside Scott caught up to him and gently gripped his elbow. "There's another problem, Professor," he said. "The lab's security guards know we're here. We saw three of them heading for the control room right after we left."

Gupta kept going, striding across a parking lot toward the ridge that ran above the beam tunnel. "It doesn't matter. We're going to fulfill our destiny. We're going to remake the world."

"But the guards have guns! And more of them are coming!"

"I told you, it doesn't matter. Humanity has been waiting for more than half a century. The *Einheitliche Feldtheorie* can't stay hidden any longer."

Scott tightened his grip on Gupta's elbow. "Professor, please listen! We have to get out of here before they arrest us!"

The professor shook off Scott's hand and raised the Uzi, pointing the barrel at the fool's chest. The other students stopped in their tracks, bewildered. Imbeciles! Couldn't they see what had to be done? "I'll shoot anyone who tries to stop me!" he yelled. "Nothing in the world can stop me now!"

Scott raised his hands but he didn't back away. Instead the fool took a step forward. "Please be reasonable, Professor. Maybe we can try again sometime, but right now we have to—"

Gupta shut him up by firing into his heart. Then he shot

Richard, who tipped backward to the asphalt. The others just stood there, wide-eyed. They didn't even have the sense to run away. Enraged by their stupidity, the professor continued shooting, sweeping the Uzi across their stunned faces. They jerked like marionettes as they died. Gupta fired several extra rounds to make sure they were all dead. They were worthless anyway, a waste of breath. He would go back alone and fulfill his destiny.

He headed for Wilson Hall, marching beside the ridge, but now a black SUV pulled off the road and three men in gray suits jumped out of the car. They crouched behind the vehicle, pointing their pistols at him and shouting indecipherable nonsense. More stupidity, the professor thought. There was an endless supply of it today.

Annoyed, Gupta pivoted toward the men and raised his Uzi, but before he could pull the trigger he saw a yellow muzzle flash from one of their pistols. A nine-millimeter bullet sped through the air, moving as straight as a high-energy proton although not nearly as fast. The collision splintered Gupta's skull, ejecting particles of skin and blood and bone. And then the professor's mind broke free of our universe and melted into the cloudless sky.

AN AMBULANCE AND A FIRE truck idled beside the F-Two tunnel entrance. David quickened his pace, hobbling as fast as he could toward the cinder-block building. He'd blacked out after the explosion in the beam tunnel, so he had no idea how much time had passed since he'd left Monique. Twenty minutes? Thirty? He remembered the terrible wounds to her stomach, the blood spurting from both sides. He hoped to God that the paramedics had gotten to her in time.

When he was about twenty yards away he saw a body on the ground with a sheet covering it. Two firefighters in full gear stood nearby, looking down at the corpse. David stumbled to a halt, his legs quivering. His chest tightened as he spotted a second sheet-covered corpse a few feet to the left. And then, still farther to the left, he saw two paramedics in blue jumpsuits heaving a stretcher into the back of the ambulance. He caught a glimpse of a brown face with an oxygen mask over the mouth. "Monique!" he cried, bounding toward the stretcher. She was alive!

A third paramedic, a tall kid with a black mustache, intercepted him before he reached the ambulance. "Hey, slow down, buddy!" the kid said, grasping his arm and looking him over. "What happened to you?"

David pointed at the stretcher. A blanket of gauze was wrapped around Monique's midsection. One of her hands was also bandaged. "How is she? Is she going to be all right?"

"Don't worry, we stabilized her. She's lost a lot of blood, but she'll be okay. And the surgeons can reattach the severed fingers." He stared with evident concern at the gashes on David's forehead. "It looks like you could use some help, too."

Tensing, David stepped backward and pulled his arm out of the paramedic's grasp. He'd been so concerned about Monique, he'd forgotten what he'd just gone through himself. Although he'd rolled behind a concrete wall before the beam pipe shattered, he knew that high-energy protons could generate all sorts of nasty secondary particles. "Don't touch me," he warned. "I was in the beam tunnel, so I might be hot."

The kid's mustache twitched. He backed away and turned to one of the firefighters standing by the corpses. "Alex! I need a radiation reading, quick!"

Alex rushed over with a Geiger counter, a thick metal tube connected to a handheld monitor. If David had been exposed to the shower of particles from the beam pipe, the counter would detect some radioactive material on his clothes or skin. He held his breath as the firefighter waved the tube in front of him, tracing a convoluted pattern from his head to his feet.

The man finally looked up. "Nothing detectable," he reported. "You're clean."

David whistled in relief. He might have absorbed some radiation, but not enough to kill him. Thank God for concrete shielding. "You should send a unit to the E-Zero entrance," he told the firefighter. "That sector of the tunnel needs to be secured. There's another fatality down there. Not much left of him, actually."

Alex shook his head. "Jesus! What the hell's going on this morning? We got people shooting each other with Uzis, we got a wacko teenager going on a rampage, and now you're saying we got another dead body in the—"

"Hold on. A teenager?"

"Yeah, some nut job screaming in the parking lot by the control room and bashing all the equipment inside the trucks and . . . hey, where do you think you're going?"

David started running. While the firefighters yelled at him and reached for their radios, he dashed past the cinder-block building. This was the last leg of his journey, the last five hundred yards. He was alone now and exhausted to the point of collapse, but he had just enough strength left to scramble along the curving ridge, past the Main Injector and the Antiproton Source and the Booster and the Accumulator, until he reached the sprawling complex that housed the Tevatron's control room.

He charged full speed into the lot where Gupta's trucks were parked. First he noticed the black Suburbans positioned at both exits to prevent anyone from leaving. Then, to his delight, he saw Karen and Jonah, sitting on the hood of one of the SUVs. A couple of FBI agents stood nearby, offering Jonah a breakfast bar and handing Karen a cup of water. These agents seemed remarkably tame; neither pulled out his gun as David jogged toward them. One of them even smiled as Jonah slid off the hood and jumped into David's arms.

After waiting for father and son to finish hugging, the agents took David aside and patted him down. Then their commander, a cheery, gray-haired gentleman with a Notre Dame pin in his lapel, came over and shook his hand. "I'm Agent Cowley," he announced. "Are you all right, Dr. Swift?"

David eyed him warily. Why the hell was he being so nice? "Yeah, I'm fine."

"Your ex-wife's already told us about the ordeal you've been through. You're a very lucky man." Turning serious, the agent lowered his voice. "Nearly everyone else is dead, I'm afraid. Professor Gupta and all his students. It was a bloodbath."

"So you know about Gupta? And what he was trying to do?"

"Well, yes, in a general sense. I got a rundown from Agent Parker on the way over here. We still have a few questions, though. We'd greatly appreciate it if you could come back to our office and help us fill in the blanks. After we get you bandaged up, I mean."

The agent smiled in a grandfatherly way and squeezed David's shoulder. None of this fooled him, of course; the FBI was still after the same thing. This false politeness was just a change in tactics. Their previous attempts had failed, so now they were trying something new.

David smiled back at him. "All right, I can do that. But I'd like to see Michael first."

"Michael? You mean Professor Gupta's grandson?"

"Yeah, I want to see if he's okay. He's autistic, you know."

Agent Cowley thought it over for a second. "Sure, you can see him. The boy's not so talkative, though. He was screaming his head off when we found him, but now he won't say a word."

Placing his hand on David's back, the agent led him to one of Gupta's delivery trucks. As they came closer David saw a heap of broken computer equipment that looked like it had been tossed from the back of the truck. The FBI agents had roped off the area with yellow crime-scene tape, but it seemed unlikely that they'd be able to recover anything useful from the debris. All the computers Gupta had used to simulate the spacetime rupture had been pried open and the hard drives removed. Shiny splinters of the glass memory disks were scattered across the parking lot.

Michael stood just outside the crime-scene tape, flanked by two more agents. His hands were cuffed behind his back, but he didn't seem perturbed. He was grinning at the pile of shattered equipment as if it were a birthday present. David had never seen the boy so happy.

Cowley gave a signal to the agents guarding Michael and they stepped back a couple of feet. "Here he is, Dr. Swift. He made quite a mess of things, but now he's settled down."

David gazed in wonder at the damaged circuits, chips, and disks that had held, at least for a brief time, the unified field theory. He realized now that he'd seriously underestimated Michael. Although the boy had fallen prey to his grandfather's wiles, David felt certain that Michael would never reveal the theory to the FBI, no matter how much they interrogated him. He was, after all, Einstein's great-great-grandson. Just as Hans Kleinman had kept the vow he'd made to *Herr Doktor,* Michael would keep the promise he'd made to Hans.

David smiled at the boy and pointed at the heap of debris. "Michael, did you do this?"

The teenager leaned forward, bringing his lips close to David's ear. "I had to," he whispered. "It wasn't a safe place."

Epilogue

ON A WARM SATURDAY AFTERNOON IN OCTOBER IT WAS hard to imagine a better place to be than the school yard on West Seventy-seventh Street. Within a rectangle of asphalt fifty yards long, about two dozen kids tossed footballs, dribbled basketballs, waved lacrosse sticks, and swung baseball bats. Their parents mostly sat on the park benches along the perimeter, reading newspapers or eating barbecue chicken from the take-out place across the street. But David stood in the center of the yard, right in the middle of all the action, and played catch with Jonah and Michael.

Rearing back, David hurled the baseball way up in the air, at least fifty feet high. Jonah snagged the ball in the webbing of his glove, then threw a grounder to Michael, who scooped it up and fired it back to David. The ball made a satisfying thwack in his mitt. Not bad, he thought. The boys had been playing baseball every weekend since August and the practice showed. If you play any game long enough, he thought, you're bound to get good at it. The same was true for chess and piano and physics.

Karen sat on one of the park benches with Ricardo, her new boyfriend. Ricardo was a bassist in a jazz combo that performed in several small clubs around Manhattan. The guy had long Jesus hair, never wore socks, and was practically penniless, but Karen was crazy about him. And to tell the truth, David liked Ricardo a lot more than her old boyfriend, the geriatric lawyer, Amory Something-or-other. David couldn't even remember the old fart's name now.

Monique sat on a neighboring bench, reading the *New York Times*. She and Michael had been coming into the city pretty regularly ever since she gained custody of the teenager. Monique had bonded with the boy during the two weeks she was at the University of Chicago Medical Center, recovering from her gunshot wounds and the mutilation of her hand. The FBI had let David and Michael visit her every day; at that point, the agents were still playing nice, still hoping to wheedle some information out of them. When the Bureau finally gave up, the agents tried to release Michael to his mother, but Beth Gupta wouldn't take him. After two weeks in detention, she was itching to get back to Victory Drive. So the head of the FBI task force—Lucille Parker, the same woman who'd interrogated David—surprised everybody by recommending that the boy live with Monique in Princeton.

David tossed another high pop to Jonah. The more he thought about it, the more he realized how lucky they were. Agent Parker could've kept them in detention for months, wearing them down with daily interrogations, but instead she went easy on them. David got the sense that she regretted the whole affair and just wanted to get it over with. But she may have also seen the risks of digging too deeply. From the evidence at Fermilab she'd probably surmised that Einstein's theory had fallen into the hands of a madman who nearly did something catastrophic. The fact that neither David nor Monique would say a word about the theory clearly indicated how dangerous it was. And maybe Agent Parker came to the same conclusion that Einstein had reached a half century earlier: the Theory of Everything had to stay hidden. Even the government couldn't be trusted with it.

As the baseball went around again, David glanced at the benches and saw that Karen and Ricardo were leaving. They were going to one of Ricardo's gigs downtown; Jonah would spend the night at David's apartment. Karen waved good-bye, blowing kisses at Jonah and reminding him to brush his teeth. And then, just before departing, she bent over to kiss Monique. For David, the most surprising thing of all was that his ex-wife and his new girlfriend had become close friends. The horrible episode at Fermilab had drawn the two women together, and now Karen was advising Monique on how to handle David's various neuroses. The universe was indeed a strange and wondrous place.

"Hey, Dad!" Jonah yelled. "Throw the ball already!"

David had been absentmindedly fingering the stitches on the baseball. He lobbed it to Jonah and took off his mitt. "Play with Michael for a while, okay? I gotta take a break."

He went to Monique's bench. She was reading something in the newspaper's international section, her eyebrows curled in concentration. David sat down next to her and glanced at the front page. SECRETARY OF DEFENSE RESIGNS was the lead headline. And just below it, in smaller type: VICE PRESIDENT PRAISES HIS RECORD.

"You reading about the secretary of defense?" David asked. "We caught the tail end of his speech at Fort Benning, remember?"

Monique shook her head. She spread the paper and pointed at a story near the bottom of page 14. The headline was PHYSICISTS DISCOVER NEW PARTICLE. "I know these researchers," she explained. "They're at the Large Hadron Collider in Geneva. They found a boson with a rest mass of two hundred and thirty-six billion electron volts."

"And what does that mean, exactly?"

"According to the standard theories, this new particle shouldn't exist. But the unified field theory predicts it. Einstein predicted it."

"I still don't—"

"It's a clue, David. And when physicists see clues, they start theorizing." She folded the newspaper and tossed it aside. Her forehead was creased with worry. "After a few more discoveries like this, they'll start to piece it together. It's only a matter of time before someone figures it out."

"You mean the unified theory? Someone's going to rediscover it?"

She nodded. "They're already pretty close. For all we know, some grad student at Princeton or Harvard could be working on the equations right now."

David took her hand. There was nothing else he could do. For the moment *Herr Doktor*'s secret was safe in Michael's head, but all their precautions would be for naught if another physicist discovered the theory and published it. On that day they'd have nothing left but hope. David shivered as he sat next to Monique, staring at the school yard full of frenetic children. It's all so fragile, he thought. It could be gone in an instant.

Then he moved his hand to Monique's belly, splaying his fingers over the soft cotton of her blouse. She turned to him and smiled. "It's too early to feel anything yet. She won't start kicking till the fourth or fifth month."

David smiled back. "How come you keep saying 'she'? You're sure it's gonna be a girl?"

Monique shrugged. "I just have a feeling. I had a dream the other night that we were taking her home from the hospital. I was putting her in the car, strapping her into the infant seat, and all of a sudden she started talking. She actually introduced herself to me. She said her name was Lieserl."

"Whoa. Pretty strange." He rubbed her belly just above the navel. "So is that what you want to call her? Lieserl? Or maybe Albert if it's a boy?"

She made a face. "Are you crazy? The last thing the world needs is another Einstein."

David laughed, and although he knew it was strictly impossible, he could've sworn he felt something move under his palm.

Author's Note

I WAS HALFWAY THROUGH WRITING *FINAL THEORY* BEFORE I realized how perfect this novel was for me. My job at *Scientific American* is to simplify bewildering ideas such as string theory, extra dimensions, and parallel universes. In 2004, while I was editing a story for a special issue on Albert Einstein, I became interested in his long search for a unified theory—a single set of equations that would incorporate both relativity and quantum mechanics, combining the physics of stars and galaxies with the laws of the subatomic realm. Einstein struggled with this quest from the 1920s until his death in 1955, but all his efforts to formulate a unified theory met with failure. As I read about this part of Einstein's life, I began to wonder: What would've happened if he'd succeeded? The discovery of a unified theory would be one of the greatest achievements in the history of science, but it could also have unintended consequences. Einstein knew all too well that his theory of relativity had laid the groundwork for the atomic bomb. Would he have published the unified theory if he knew it would've paved the way for weapons that were even more terrible? Or would he have kept it secret?

My fascination with Einstein began in college. I was an astrophysics major at Princeton University and my adviser was the renowned theorist J. Richard Gott III (author of *Time Travel in Einstein's Universe*). For my undergraduate thesis, Professor Gott suggested that I work on a problem in relativity: How would Einstein's field equation work in Flatland, a model universe with only two spatial dimensions, like a tremendously wide sheet of paper. After filling a notebook with scribbled equations, I showed the solution to Dr. Gott, who gave me the best compliment you can get from a theoretical physicist: "This solution is nontrivial!" We coauthored a research paper titled "General Relativity in a (2 + 1)-dimensional Spacetime," which was published in a scientific journal called *General Relativity and Gravitation* in 1984.

By the time the paper appeared, however, I'd decided that I wanted be a poet rather than a physicist, so I entered the MFA writing program at Columbia. Two years later, when I realized that poetry would never pay the bills, I became a journalist. I worked for newspapers in Pennsylvania, New Hampshire, and Alabama before returning to New York and writing for *Fortune, Popular Mechanics,* and CNN. I came full circle in 1998 when I started working at *Scientific American.* I was amazed at how much had changed in astronomy and physics since I'd left the field. And I soon discovered, to my great surprise, that the obscure article I cowrote with Professor Gott had become an important paper for physicists who were continuing Einstein's search for a Theory of Everything. Over the past two decades the article has been cited more than one hundred times in various physics journals. As it turns out, theorists are very interested in testing their hypotheses in two-dimensional models because the mathematics is simpler.

This article became the inspiration for *Final Theory.* The research paper that my hero, David Swift, coauthors with his own adviser, Professor Kleinman, is about relativity in two dimensions. Like me, David is a former physics student who now writes about science for a general audience. Except David is a professor instead of a magazine editor. And he's a lot braver and better looking than me.

I've tried to make sure that the scientific principles presented in the novel, and the high-tech gadgets as well, are authentic. For example, the Highlander robotic car is a real vehicle built by the Robotics Institute at Carnegie Mellon University. The Dragon Runner surveillance device, also developed by the Robotics Institute, has been tested by the U.S. Marines in Iraq. The Virtual Combat Simulator that appears in Chapter Ten is similar to the VirtuSphere, a system I tried myself during a visit to the U.S. Naval Research Lab. And the idea that sterile neutrinos may take shortcuts through extra dimensions is a real hypothesis that has been proposed to explain some anomalous experimental results that were reported at the Fermi National Accelerator Laboratory in 2007.

I knew early on that I wanted the climax of the novel to take place at Fermilab, so I arranged a visit to the facility and got a tour of the Tevatron, the four-mile-long circular tunnel where protons and antiprotons are accelerated to nearly the speed of light and then smashed together. The best part of the tour was the requisite safety briefing, during which the lab personnel explained the various hazards we might encounter in the tunnel, such as radioactivity left over from stray proton collisions or the possibility of asphyxiation from helium evaporating from the superconducting magnets. As I took notes, I thought, This is fantastic material! The book is going to write itself!

In the end, though, I had a lot of help. My colleagues at *Scientific American* have been wonderfully supportive. The members of my writing group—Rick Eisenberg, Johanna Fiedler, Steve Goldstone, Dave King, Melissa Knox, and Eva Mekler—gave me invaluable criticism and encouragement (especially Rick, who read every page of the first draft and filled the margins with sound advice). I'm very lucky to have a superb agent, Dan Lazar of Writers House, and a marvelous editor, Sulay Hernandez of Touchstone/Fireside. But I owe the greatest debt to my family. My parents nurtured my love for science, and my wife, Lisa, supported my dream of becoming a novelist long after the point at which any reasonable person would've given up hope. This book is for her.